TANNER

THE BILLIONAIRES OF WHISPERS
BOOK 1

SAMANTHA SKYE

ISBN 978-0-6486083-4-9 (ebook)

ISBN 978-0-6486083-5-6 (Paperback)

ISBN 978-1-923258-03-7 (Alternative Paperback)

Cover Design: Angela Haddon

Editor: Nice Girl Naughty Edits

Proofreading: Kimberly Dawn

Model Photography: Wander Aguiar

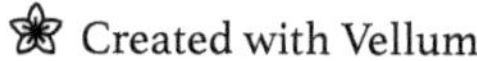 Created with Vellum

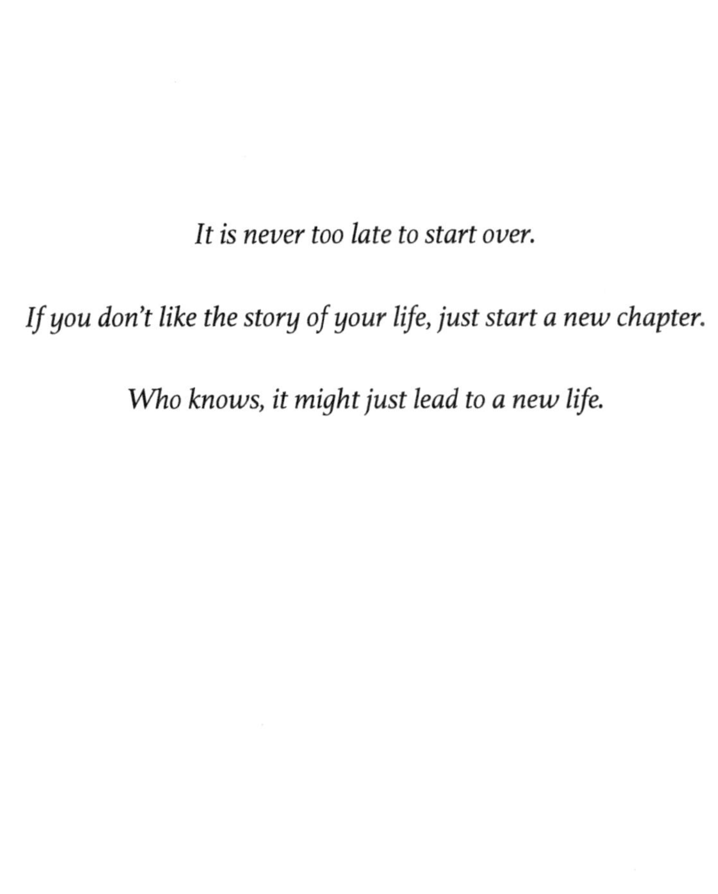

It is never too late to start over.

If you don't like the story of your life, just start a new chapter.

Who knows, it might just lead to a new life.

1

VICTORIA MCARTHUR

I should feel defeated. Sad, a little deflated. But I don't. I feel like I can breathe again for the first time all day.

"It's just not the one. These things take time," my friend, Fiona, says from next to me, seeming to think my quiet reflection is related to disappointment about not picking a wedding dress. *God, if she only knew.*

"I know," I say, trying to hide my relief. My feelings toward marrying Josh haven't progressed to joy yet... I don't think they ever will. Every dress within my budget that I tried on looked utterly ridiculous. Even Fiona agreed. It's the universe telling me to stop the wedding, I know it. Something just doesn't feel right about it anymore. Not that it ever did. I shake my head as I put my key in the door of my apartment, glad to finally be home.

"You know what. Let's just have a glass of wine. My feet are killing me," she says dramatically with an eye roll that makes me smile for the first time today.

"Deal. You get the glasses, and I'll grab the wine. Plus,

you still need to fill me in on the guy you hooked up with last night. Tyler Grant? Did you know he is one of the city's richest men?"

As much as I want the juicy details, I feel bereft for a moment, realizing that even though I am engaged, I have never had that kind of feeling. The *sweep me off my feet* feeling. That heart-pounding feeling. The *I love you more than I can breathe* feeling. I just feel suffocated. Permanently.

I throw my new bag onto the counter as I walk in, the bright-pink tote causing the pile of mail I have been ignoring to spread. "Shit," I mumble, collecting it all and sifting through it quickly as Fiona heads straight to grab the wineglasses. Bill after bill filters past my vision until a letter catches my eye. It looks formal, with a stamp of a law firm in the corner. I throw it in my handbag to look over later and smile at my friend.

"What's that music?" Fiona asks, coming to stand next to me as I listen to the loud dance beats thumping my walls from down the hall. My fiancé Josh stayed home today while we went dress shopping. After popping the question a few months ago, he has been pushing me out the door every weekend to plan a wedding that he is happy to play no part in organizing. If I were to be honest, neither am I.

"It's too loud. Let me go let Josh know we are back, and I will turn it down." Pushing off the counter, I walk down the small hall.

My apartment is my sanctuary and has been for years. A small two-bedroom on the Upper East Side that is high enough to catch the morning sun. My landlady is a lovely older woman who is currently enjoying retirement in Florida. I have decorated the place in subtle tones of coffee and crisp white. With a fascination for interiors, I spend every waking hour either shopping for the latest decoration or furnishing to adorn my home or too many hours sifting through magazines and Pinterest, designing my dream homes. While my day job selling advertising pays my bills, it does very little to quench my creative desires.

I open my bedroom door and stop short, my breath catching in my throat at the sight in front of me.

"Hey, where is your bottle open—" Fiona doesn't finish the question as she pulls to a sharp stop next to me, and we both stand in the doorway, our mouths agape. "Oh... My... God," she whispers at seeing my fiancé grinding into—

"Natalie?" I shriek when the realization hits me that my fiancé and his colleague are in my bed together. *Naked.*

They don't hear me above the loud music, with Natalie currently whimpering as Josh slams into her from behind. Neither of them see us, as her face is buried in my silk pillow that I scoured the globe for and finally found in the Philippines. The silk is so fine that I already know it is ruined just from her ridiculous fake moans. My heart races, but I can't move. I am rooted to the spot, frozen in shock. I look at my fiancé, the man who told me only a few hours ago that I was the most important person in the world to him, and see his eyes closed as his hips continue to thrust forward.

I should shout or yell, but I can't. I can only grimace.

My body remains rigid, my heart thundering to the point of feeling lightheaded. All I see is his pasty, skinny ass flex with every paltry thrust. But as I tilt my head, really taking this in, my body oddly starts to calm and my breath leaves my lungs in an exhale that feels like it lifts a thousand pounds off my shoulders.

"What the hell is going on here!" Fiona yells for me, jolting me from my realization, and the two jump apart like they have been burned. Natalie grabs my bedsheets and pulls them to her naked chest—the ones I saved up for months to buy from Saks, the ones that are Egyptian cotton with the highest thread count available. The sheets I had on my wish list for over a year, that cost more than my monthly salary, and I itch to rip them from her grasp.

"It's not what it looks like..." Josh says, out of breath, and my eyes flick to him as the poor excuse falls from his mouth. We all know exactly how stupid that statement is, considering I just saw his dick in her vagina.

"You have five minutes to get dressed and get out of *my* apartment," I say, looking between them. My teeth grit out of anger, yes, but more so disbelief. How did I not see this? How did I not know this was going on? I am such an idiot. I could have ended this shambles of an engagement months ago, but the trepidation of his assumed heartbreak, coupled with the fear of failure that sprinkles across all my relationships, held me back. I mean, dating in New York is hard. Hell, dating anywhere is hard. It is hard to find your person, and I guess I just settled, thinking he truly loved me.

"Victoria, I can explain..." Natalie starts to say, then

trails off as I stare at her with a glare that probably tells her she should keep her mouth shut. I'm reining in my wrath that threatens at their disrespect, at the fact they had the audacity to do this in *my* space. And I don't know her well enough to want an explanation, anyway.

"Just leave," I repeat without a hint of emotion, swallowing it all down.

"Baby, let's talk. It's nothing. She... she means nothing to me," Josh rushes to explain as he takes a step toward me, and Fiona snorts. Natalie bolts upright, her body now mostly clothed, her heels in her hands.

"Nothing?" she spits out, staring at my fiancé in disbelief. I am not sure, but I think that makes it even worse. That he was so willing to throw me away over someone who "means nothing."

"Two minutes," I tell them, not giving either of them more of my time. They can have their lovers' tiff somewhere else.

"Victoria, I..." Natalie tries again, stepping toward me like I am an injured animal and she isn't sure if I will strike. I cut her off.

"Get. Out. Of. My. Home." I look her dead in the eye, unflinching. I watch her swallow roughly, nodding, her expression riddled with guilt. Then she walks right past me and straight out the door, her heels in hand and makeup smeared.

While I am still in shock and comically relieved, I hate being played the fool, and anger swirls inside my chest that I let this happen to me. My mother raised me to be strong and independent. Deep down, I know Josh and I are not soulmates, but seeing them in my bed together makes me vomit a little in my mouth.

I look back at Josh who stands in front of me, his jeans now on, his pale chest doing nothing to entice me. "Vic, baby," he says smoothly, swaggering closer, his arms wide open. Like he thinks we're about to kiss and make up.

"You too." My jaw clenches so I don't scream or shout. I don't want to give him the satisfaction, even though I feel disgusted, betrayed, and like I can barely breathe. I don't want to be the cliché scorned woman. I want my dignity intact. I wonder briefly if this is how my mother handled it when my womanizing father finally got caught. I will have to ask her. *Men, they're all the same.*

"What?" he asks, his head rearing back with a frown.

"Get your things and get out of *my* apartment," I emphasize steadily, but I'm losing the last of my patience. And he has the nerve to look at me like I'm crazy.

"But... I just moved in. I have nowhere else to go."

It's true. He gave up his apartment to move in with me. My apartment and location are much better than his was, and given we were going to be married in mere months, we both thought it was a logical step. Obviously, it was a step I shouldn't have taken. I shimmy the rock off my finger—the thing is too gaudy for me anyway—and I throw it at his chest. It's another weight lifted.

"No longer my problem. We are *done*," I bite out the last word, and his eyebrows hit his hairline as he catches the ring.

"You go, girl," I hear Fiona whisper from down the hall, where she had retreated to give us privacy.

"Baby, come on... It was a little slipup," he croons once more, like he is apologizing for being home late after drinks with the boys, rather than cheating on me. *In my own bed. On the day I was wedding dress shopping.* It is then I realize that this man, somewhat attractive and with a good corporate job on Wall Street, is nothing but a self-absorbed, cheating asshole who has probably never had a woman say no to him before.

"We are over. It's as simple as that." I cross my arms over my chest and roll my shoulders back. What can I say, I am a Scorpio. There are no second chances with me.

"Vic, honey, we can work through this," Josh says, nearly begging, and now it is my turn to frown. Is he fucking serious right now? I knew I shouldn't have said yes to his proposal. I knew then, when he was down on bended knee on New Year's Eve, in front of his boss and work colleagues. I knew then he wasn't the one, but I said yes anyway. Hoping that I was just nervous, a little caught off guard. Besides, who can say no to a proposal on New Year's Eve. In New York City, of all places. In front of an audience.

"Get. Out. Right Now." This time, my voice rises. Whether it is the look in my eyes or the finality of the words, Josh finally picks up his clothes.

"We will talk once you have calmed down. You're clearly too emotional right now," he says, trying to make me feel like I'm overreacting.

I grit my teeth and remain tight-lipped as he walks past me and out the door. Still in my bedroom, I stand unmoving as I survey the damage. Pillows, sheets, blankets strewn all over the space, a condom wrapper on my bedside table, and design magazines I had been book-marking tossed to the floor. Not to mention, the take-out containers piled on the floor, since they must've enjoyed lunch together before their afternoon delight. He may not have been the love of my life, but I have quite a mess to clean up.

My eyes burn as the music suddenly stops, my head whipping to the side to see Fiona walking in with two glasses of wine.

"I just opened a second bottle of red to air. Figured we might need it," she says, looking at me with concern as I take a glass and bring it to my lips.

"You figured right."

Her arm wraps around me, and I break down, the fight leaving me fully as my emotions take over.

2

———

TANNER WHITEMAN

Looking over the land, I hum in approval.

"The plans I have drawn up encompass the entire space. We will have to demolish the entire structure, and the amenities will run along the border here at the east so we can position the new building from east to west," Griffin says as he holds the plans in his hands, the paper blowing a little in the breeze.

"We would start from here." He continues, giving me the plans as he runs across the yard and bends over to hammer a steel peg into the ground to indicate the start of the building. "And end over here." Running almost the length of the property, he hammers in another peg, so we can gauge the size of the construction.

It's big. Just how I want it.

"That's good. The side deck will get the morning sun, with the distillery in view, and then the sun setting in the west will coat the main deck, with the rolling hills as its scenery," I say, already visualizing it.

Whiteman's Whiskey is growing. The small whiskey distillery I started decades ago has grown to be a billion-dollar business. Now, I'm planning a new boutique accommodation development here in Whispers that will house weekend visitors, allowing them to sample our whiskey, eat in our restaurant, and spend money in the small town I have called home all my life. Call it my community service, even though the six-star stay will be financially out of reach for most people who live around here.

"You know we haven't acquired the land yet, right?" Sawyer asks, watching me from where he stands next to the truck. He looks out of place in his shiny shoes and three-piece suit pressed to perfection, as Marie's goat walks nearby, chewing the grass. I spot her milking cow out in the field, doing the same.

Sawyer is a good lawyer, but not a country boy. He can talk his way out of most things—like all city folk, he has the gift of the gab—so while he doesn't have a connection to the land, he is the best person to secure this plot of land for me. That is why I have flown him out from New York. He needs to see the vision.

"It is just a matter of time. Marie had no family. No friends, apart from a few locals. Even that dwindled down these past few years as she got older. We just need Jerry to show up with the papers and I will buy it and get this plan in motion. I want to start building as soon as the papers are signed," I tell them, gazing out over the run-down house and land my elderly neighbor called home for years.

Marie was a tough old woman. Lived alone. Didn't

have any family that visited. Kept to herself mainly, but as she aged, the community and I helped her where we could. That's what a good neighbor does. Her farm is small, and although the milking cow and a few goats were never going to make her any money, they kept her company.

"He's here now. Let's see what he says," Sawyer says as he pushes off the car, not sounding convinced. The familiar red truck of our local town lawyer pulls up in the driveway. Technically, we are trespassing. This land is not mine yet.

"Morning," Jerry greets us, looking a little frazzled in his dress slacks and shirt. Not as crisp as Sawyer, but at seventy, he still does a good job of keeping this town together.

"Morning, Jerry. Got the papers? I've got a meeting with Connor I need to get to," I say, keen to get this done. My son and I need to discuss distribution of our latest release in an hour, and any time I get with him these days is precious.

"Unfortunately, there is a hiccup," Jerry says, and my shoulders stiffen. Eyes narrowing, they flick to Sawyer, who appears just as surprised. This should be a simple transaction. Single old lady dies, has no one claiming her legacy, and so it is put up for sale as a deceased estate.

"What hiccup?" Sawyer asks as Griffin steps closer, the three of us all looking at Jerry for answers.

"I formally reviewed Marie's will..." he starts tentatively, and my hands find my hips.

"And?" I push him, already knowing I'm about to be frustrated.

"And... she has a niece. She has named her as the sole beneficiary of her possessions, including her house, land, and money."

"A niece?" Griffin asks. He is a tough guy who has been my contractor for years. He is the man who helped me build the entire distillery here in Whispers. As we have expanded over the years, so has he. His company now builds new ranches and luxury homes all around the country. Makes good money from it all too.

"She never said anything about any niece," I grumble, my jaw tight. This is less than ideal.

"Her will is old; she wrote it over a decade ago. There is no mention of any siblings or anyone else," Jerry confirms.

"So does the niece want to sell?" Sawyer asks, and my attention moves back to Jerry, hoping he says yes. If not, I will up my price and just pay her out. This place is so run-down, only a fool would be interested in taking it on. As I glance over the land again, I only see one goat. I swore there were two of them this morning.

"The will stipulates that the niece be notified in writing, and then she has thirty days to claim. If she doesn't come forward within thirty days, the property will be sold, with the proceeds donated to local charities," Jerry explains, and I huff a laugh.

"Marie did know how to play games," I murmur, thinking of my old neighbor. She was feisty, especially in her younger days. I never knew her to have a partner. Her family was raised here, and she stayed even after her parents passed. She liked the quiet of the country and could be a little quirky at times.

"I sent the letter already, so the clock is ticking. I will let you know if I hear from her," Jerry says.

"Tell her I want to buy and will pay top dollar," I call out to Jerry as he walks back to his truck, and he just nods and waves because he already knows. And he's just one of many. I have already submitted the plans to the town planner for early approval, and it was raised at the last town meeting. Everyone in Whispers knows how much I want this land and that I will do anything to get it.

"That throws a wrench in the works," Griffin says, looking out at the vibrant green expanse, which is now starting to overgrow due to lack of maintenance. The view has me steeling my spine. This is a mere bump in the road; I know this land will be mine.

"Let's hope the niece stays where she is." I hate waiting, but my mom always said good things come to those who wait.

And good things are coming, I can feel it.

3

VICTORIA

I trudge into my apartment, feeling like half the woman I am. Throwing my bag on my sofa, I barely register the contents spilling out as I slump down next to it.

"Worst year ever," I say out loud to no one as I rest my head back on my plush sofa. My eyes coast around my space. Even though it is spotless and decorated just how I like it, it feels empty. I look to my side and pick up my handbag to find my cell, and as I do, a letter falls out. Grabbing it, I realize it is the legal letter from the kitchen counter, which I forgot all about after catching Josh and Natalie. I flip it over and again see the details of a law firm from out of town.

"Whispers?" I say to myself as I carefully open it. My heart rate increases as I try to make sense of what I am reading.

An aunt who died? An estate? Whispers? I rub my eyes before I grab the envelope again to ensure it is, in fact, addressed to me. Hearing my cell vibrate, I pull it out with a groan. Josh has been calling me nonstop, and I swear if it is him, I am throwing my phone against the wall. But thankfully, it's my mom.

"Hey, Mom," I say in a sigh.

"Hi, sweetie, how are you doing today?" She asks the same question she has every day since I threw out my fiancé. She didn't like him either, so we are both moving quickly through the grieving process. Although the logistics of canceling a wedding venue and all the additional plans has hit me harder than I was expecting.

"Well, I have officially decided that this year Mercury must be permanently stuck in retrograde," I tell her, unsure what I've done to inflict such bad karma on my life.

"What happened now? Josh didn't come back to the apartment, did he?" she asks, because when he came back a few days ago to gather his things, I had to call the super to get him out. He was adamant that he was staying, that we could make it work, that sleeping with his colleague was just a one-time thing. It seems Josh doesn't like being told no, and the whole thing left me feeling a little unsettled.

"I wish that was it," I say, tears threatening, but I sniff them back. *This is not going to break me.*

"What is it?" I hear what sounds like her cooking. She loves to cook, especially in her beautiful and spacious kitchen—the kind you don't typically find in New York City, at least with a reasonable budget. Her desire to leave the city finally took over in her older years, and she now has a nice, safe community and a good number of friends in Connecticut.

"Well, my fiancé cheated on me, I lost my job today, and oh, and I just got a letter from a law firm in a small country town that says my aunt Marie died. I think that is what people call a trifecta." I scoff and rub my eyes, hoping I don't get a headache.

"What happened to your job? And wait! Oh my God, what happened to Marie?" she asks, her voice rising as her words topple over each other.

"So I do have an aunt Marie?" I ask, confused. I thought surely the letter was incorrectly addressed or something since I have never heard of her before.

"I need wine," she says under her breath, and I huff a laugh as I hear her open the bottle. "Okay, let's start with work. Tell me."

I imagine her leaving whatever deliciousness she was making out on the counter as she heads to her living space, sitting on her sofa, her legs curled underneath her as she gives me all her attention. I miss her. My father left us when I was only little, and since then, it's always been just Mom and me. I was devastated when she said she wanted to leave the city. Years of working two jobs just to get me through college, the cold, dark winters, and the masses of people all burned her out, which is why the quiet of the suburbs called to her.

"Basically, they are restructuring. The advertising sales are now being run from corporate, and my entire team and I were let go today," I say, blowing out a breath. I didn't love my job, as selling advertising space in magazines was never a career dream of mine. But it paid the bills, and I was good at it.

"Are you okay for money?" she asks, and I sigh.

"I haven't had any leave in years, and I got a nice commission the last two quarters, which I was saving for the wedding. It's not much, but I can afford to take my time and find the right next step." My fingers play with the paper from the letter that sits on my legs. "So I have an aunt Marie?" I ask, moving on to the other topic that has spiked my interest.

"You do. She was your father's older sister. I met her a few times when you were younger. She had a small farm a few states over handed down to her from your grandparents. Even though she was a cranky woman, when we visited, she was totally enamored with you," Mom says, and my eyebrows rise.

"Really? I can't remember it." Frowning, I try to think back.

"You wouldn't. You would have only been five or six. She was much older than your father, she had some animals, and she spent all day taking you outside, showing you how to milk a cow and grow vegetables. Of course, you just ended up muddy, but she enjoyed it. It was a highlight for her since she didn't have any kids of her own," my mom explains, and I find myself smiling.

"So what happened to her?"

"When your father left us, I lost contact with his family. When your grandparents passed, no one else ever reached out except once, and it was Marie. I got a letter about a decade ago from her, asking about you, and I sent her a long letter back, with photos. We exchanged Christmas cards for a little while, but that was about it. It's sad to know she has gone."

"She left me her house," I tell her as my eyes flick through the letter again.

"What?" My mom shrieks so loudly that I need to pull my phone from my ear.

"Her house and... farm?" I say as I quickly read through the letter again. "And a small amount of money. She left me everything..." I say in surprise and awe.

"Oh my God. In Whispers?" Mom asks, and I look at the address in the letter.

"Yes. Do you think that is where Dad is?" I ask, more scared than hopeful. He wasn't a nice man, and all I know of him is that he ran off with a mistress and never looked back.

"No, I doubt it. He hated anything to do with the outdoors. He grew up there but couldn't wait to get out of the place and never went back after college until we went with you. Being a city girl, I never pushed it either. He also never got along with Marie. They didn't see eye to eye, and I would be surprised if she ever saw him after our last visit when you were a child. Maybe that is why she left you everything instead of him. You are the only grandchild on that side of the family, her only niece. There was no one else."

I sigh a heavy breath. The family dynamics sound too dramatic for me to even comprehend.

"What should I do?" I ask, knowing she will tell me exactly what she thinks.

"What do you mean? You need to go!" she says, and my brow crumples.

"What?" I sit up straight, my heart picking up pace at the thought.

"You thought the universe was delivering you bad karma with Josh and now your job, but what if the universe was pushing you to go to the exact place you need to be?" While she has always been a little woo-woo, I like her optimism.

"But I can't leave, I've got—" I start to say, and she cuts me off.

"A loving fiancé and a wedding to plan? A fantastic job that is offering you a promotion? Victoria, can't you feel the opportunity in this?" She's almost pleading with me.

"Mom! It is a farm, in a town I have never been, far away from the city. I have no idea what I am meant to do with it," I tell her with a shake of my head she can't see. She has clearly had too much wine. This is crazy. I can't live on a farm. I have never even been out of the city much before.

"Well, you could sell it, take the money, and then sit in the city and figure out your next steps. Probably get back into advertising, find another Wall Street guy..." she starts.

"Or?" I prod. None of that sounds appealing at all, and her lack of enthusiasm matches mine at those options.

"Or you could take yourself on a wonderful adventure and flip your life upside down," she says, and I know she is smiling just from the tone of her voice. She has always been adventurous.

"I'm not sure..." Looking back over the letter, I notice there is a deadline, and it's only a few days away.

"You loved that farm when you were little, and for Marie to leave it to you tells me that you had an impact on her as well. She obviously didn't leave it to your father, wherever he is now."

"Will you come with me?" I ask. Could I really just pack up my life as she is suggesting?

"Oh no. I had my adventure out here already. Besides, I think this might be good for you and exactly what you need. You just turned thirty. There is no better time to really spread your wings." As she sighs longingly, I can tell she's getting serious.

"The city isn't going anywhere, sweetie. If it doesn't work out, you can always sell, return to the city, and get back to the life you had."

Maybe she is right. Maybe this is the universe telling me to take a chance and do something new.

"Who knows, maybe you can renovate the old place. Turn it into one of those beautiful interior countryside bed-and-breakfast farm stay thingies. You are so good at decorating and designing," she says, and I bite my bottom lip. That is a secret dream of mine. To renovate a home and make new from old. At the mere mention of that possibility, my stomach flutters in equal parts fear and excitement. And suddenly, I know what I want.

"I'm going to do it," I say, determination filling me. Mom is right, I need an adventure. What else have I got? Sure, there is Fiona, and my beautiful apartment, but I can keep it here, leave it waiting for me for a few months until I work out if I am coming back or not.

"Great! I'm so excited for you, sweetie! Let's book your plane ticket," she says quickly, and we chat for the next forty-five minutes, making arrangements. She tells me everything she knows about Marie and Whispers, and before long, I have already started a new Pinterest board.

4

———

VICTORIA

"So, you're from the city?" the old man who is driving my taxi asks. He has been trying to make small talk the entire ride from the airport.

"Yes, that's right," I tell him, not sure how much personal information to give him. In the city, I don't talk much about myself, but out here, it appears people love to know things.

"The bright-pink scarf gave it away. Not too many people around here wear colors like that. So, you are going to Marie's place?" he asks, and my head turns swiftly to look at him in the rearview mirror. I decide not to ask about the pink reference, not having the energy.

"Did you know her?" My eyes thin in question. We drove through the town of Whispers about five minutes ago. It was beautiful, very quaint. But now we are driving through some forests, and I don't want to panic, but the only thing telling me that I am fine with this strange man in this strange town is the map app on my cell phone that is tracking me to my final destination.

"Oh, everyone knew Marie. She lived here for years. Kept to herself a lot, but everyone knew her," he says, and I nod.

"I'm her niece. Victoria," I tell him. I wonder for a moment whether that is a smart thing to do, but he smiles, and it seems genuine.

"Well, good to know she had someone. I'm Peter, the local taxi. The only one. If you ever need a ride anywhere, you just call me," he says as we pull down Distillery Drive, the road to my new adventure. There are signs everywhere for the Whiteman's Distillery, and in my research on the town, I now know that it's home to the country's finest whiskey. I prefer champagne or cocktails over the hard stuff, but each to their own.

"You can find anything you need in town. The Delish Diner is great for breakfast or coffee. Rochelle runs that. Then Jasmine at the local florist is about your age, I think. You should pop in and make yourself known to her. The supermarket is open every day; tourists fill the town on the weekends, and there are a lot of people living here who appreciate their privacy, but many others you will see out and about. Well... here we are."

I try to remember all that he is telling me and bank it away for later. I look out the cab window as we pull up to the home that looked a lot newer in the photos I found online.

"Wow." I'm almost lost for words as I step out of the car. The house needs work. *A lot of work.* As I take it all in, I start to become overwhelmed.

"I'll bring your bags to the front door," Peter says as he heads around to the trunk, and I take a few steps toward the property. I look for miles and see nothing but beautiful thick green grass surrounding the house. Over the small hill toward the back, I spot the top of what I assume is part of the distillery, with Marie's place and the distillery being the only two properties on this road.

"There you go, Victoria. I assume you are meeting Jerry?" the man says, nodding over to the red truck that is parked down the driveway a little. "That's him."

"Oh, okay. What do I owe you?" I ask, grabbing my handbag.

"Nothing at all. First ride is on the house. Welcome to Whispers. I am sure I will see you around." He smiles and I do the same, watching him reverse out and drive away.

"Miss McArthur?" an older man in a suit calls out, walking up the driveway as I start walking toward him. "I'm Jerry Walker, your aunt's lawyer and Whisper's only legal counsel. Welcome. I hope your flight was alright?"

Meeting halfway down the driveway, from here, I get a better look at the backyard. It seems to stretch for miles and overgrown doesn't even come close to describing it. I swallow hard.

"Hi, Mr. Walker. Nice to meet you," I say, shaking his hand. He seems nice. Much like Peter, he appears friendly enough, and I feel immediately at home, even though I should still be on guard. I don't know any of these people. They could all be axe murderers or part of a cult, for all I know.

"We have some paperwork to sign off, and I can give you a tour and leave you all the keys," he says, and I nod.

"I would like that."

"I must say, before your call this morning, and with

less than twenty-four hours to spare, we didn't think you were coming," he says with a chuckle.

"We?" I ask and look at him.

"Ahh, well... me." He clears his throat, and I let it go. Maybe he has staff or something. I am sure in a small town like this, I would be a talking point. Especially since Marie probably never mentioned me.

I look around some more as we walk. "What's that?" I spot the large building in the distance again.

"That is Whiteman's Distillery. They own most of the land out here. Quite keen on this property too, if you were considering selling?" he asks, looking at me, seemingly hopeful.

"I'm not," I say quickly and firmly, shaking my head. After the discussion with my mom and the acute understanding that I have nothing left for me in the city, I am giving myself at least three months. If I don't make it work after that, then I can think about potential next steps. A decision I don't feel so good about right now as I step onto the mess of a lawn and immediately feel the dampness of the grass seeping into my bright-pink flats I wore today to match my new scarf. I make a mental note to order some boots.

"Alright, good to know." He nods, a small smile on his face. "So Marie couldn't keep up with it much in her later years, but the house itself is solid. Maybe some minor renovations are needed, but structurally, it is sound. The farm here is small, but again, it was a handful for her. There is one milking cow, and Kevin, the young boy from down the road, has been cycling up here daily to milk it, then takes the milk home with him. He is keen to keep doing that if you will allow him, but I told him to talk to you about it when he is here next."

"That sounds fine." I have no idea how to milk a cow and can't remember the last time I drank dairy milk.

"There were two goats, but one seems to have gone missing. So now this one goat has free range of the yard in this fenced area, but it needs to be locked up at night. You know, bobcats and such." As he continues, I want to tell him that *no*, in fact, I don't know, but instead, I add that to my very long list of research topics.

"There is this shed, which has all the tools and materials you will need for the time being. I understand there is a lot of work to do here. Bob runs Whispers Hardware in town, and they will have everything you need and can help you out with anything to do with the maintenance, renovations, or farm. Likewise with the truck," he says, and my eyebrows rise.

"Truck?" I ask.

"Marie's truck. I assume that will be your transportation while here. I mean, we have Peter, but that's all. We don't have any fancy Ubers like in the city," he says with a chuckle. Transportation is not something I thought about, so I am glad I have access to a vehicle. He nods in the direction of the shed, so I look around the large door and spot a run-down truck that is a bit rusted.

"She looks old but runs fine. It was recently serviced," Jerry says, like he knows what I'm thinking.

"Right," I say with a nervous laugh and an awkward smile, looking back up at the house.

"Have you ever been on a farm before, Miss

McArthur?" he asks, glancing at me with concern, and I swallow harshly.

"No, I haven't." My response has him grimacing, but he turns it into a smile just as quickly. How hard can it be? There is a fat goat chewing the grass; the cow looks bored with life, and a scattering of chickens run around at their feet. But then I look at the fencing that needs repair, the screen door on the house that's rusted and barely hanging on, the chipped paint on just about everything, and my breathing quickens as understanding washes over me that I am severely underprepared for this. I haven't even stepped inside yet.

"Everyone in town is nice and helpful. If you run into any major concerns, you can call me. Here are the keys. The electricity and water are still connected. I have left the paperwork for all that inside on the counter. I just need you to sign the contract of ownership, and I can leave you to it." He rocks back on his heels.

"Okay," I say on a breath. I can do this. "Thank you, Mr. Walker. Let's head inside." I turn toward the house, and as I do, I get a vision. It is run-down now, needs some maintenance, but I can see it. Big, beautiful, and white. A porch that runs all the way around. Beautiful flowers scattered in the garden. I envision the potential of the new I can make of the old, and my excitement comes barreling back.

5

TANNER

It is day twenty-nine. I have called Jerry every day for the past month to see if he has heard anything because I am keen to get started on my plans. But as of yesterday, no long-lost niece has come to take ownership, so I am excited to get things in motion.

"I love this jet," Sawyer says as we step off my private aircraft after a week in New York. A twelve-seater with white leather seats and dark wood paneling, the bar stocked with my whiskey. There is a lot to love.

"Do I get to take the cost of transporting you off your retainer?" I smirk at him as we jump into the truck already sitting on the tarmac for me. I don't like having a driver when at home. My team knows to just deliver my truck and let me drive.

"Nah, I might increase your rates and buy my own," he quips. *Smart-ass.* I turn out of the small airport and hit the road, looking out the window at the green pastures, and take a breath, relieved to be home. I hate the city. But with business booming and Connor managing the office there at the moment, I need to travel frequently.

"Is everything organized?" I ask Sawyer again, probably for the hundredth time.

"Yes. Paperwork is ready to sign; funds are also ready to go. Griffin and his team are just waiting for the go-ahead. The only thing we need is for the deadline to end officially and for Jerry to answer my call." Nodding to me, I know he has it all under control.

"I have Griffin flying in tomorrow," I tell him, feeling everything finally coming together. If it all goes to plan, I should have my new building operational before the end of the year and just in time for the holidays.

"We can sign the papers first thing tomorrow and transfer the funds. I will put a rush through for final building permits, and Griffin and his team should be able to start demolition almost immediately," Sawyer confirms, and I nod, eager about this new venture.

The distillery was something I started in my youth. The art of making whiskey was handed down to me from my father, and the one thing that I was good at. Becoming a dad as a teenager wasn't part of my plan, and so instead of moving away for college, I stayed home and delved into the whiskey business, working from my dad's shed while being a devoted dad to my son. I had to make the whiskey business work, for both our sakes. I kept my head down and built Whiteman's up to where it is today. The country's most premium brand of whiskey—the only whiskey to be in the White House with President Rothschild and it has turned our small family of two into billionaires.

"I still haven't heard from Jerry today," Sawyer says, rolling his cell in his hand.

"I spoke to him yesterday, told him we will see him when we land. He knows I want this place immediately." Jerry being quiet today is unusual, but I'm not worried. With only twenty-four hours left, I know the land is mine.

"What do you plan to do with the animals?" Sawyer asks, looking at me.

"I will rehome them. Shit, might even keep that stupid goat that bleats all night. It could be a good security alarm to have around the back of the distillery." We both chuckle at that.

"Why do you want it so much?" Sawyer asks me, looking at me seriously for a moment. "I mean, you have a lot of land surrounding the distillery. You could build your accommodation in any number of places. Why this one?"

"It's special, that area. Grass is always green, the natural springs are on that parcel of land, and the soil is nourished so you can grow anything. The wind blows from the west across the springs, so the air is fresh, no matter what time of the day. Plus, the outlook onto the distillery is photo worthy. It's quiet, picturesque. There is just something magical about that place," I tell him.

Seeing the look on Sawyer's face I know he doesn't quite get it, so I turn it into business speak. "People will pay top dollar for a weekend here, and adding accommodation to the site will just further push the destination of Whispers."

"You love this town, don't you?" he asks, and I swear I

see some admiration in his expression as we drive through the small place I have called home my entire life.

"It's in my blood. Whispers and whiskey. You can't have one without the other."

"You missed a *W*," Sawyer says, and I frown, wondering what he is talking about.

"Women. You need whiskey, Whispers, and women."

I haven't taken another woman permanently into my life since Connor's mom skipped town over thirty years ago. Heard she came back once. By the time I went to her parents' place to see her and ask why she ran out on her only child, she had already gone. She stayed an hour to pick up some paperwork and fled. So it was clear that the life I had and the son we shared was not what she wanted. Her parents helped out a little in the beginning, but their support eventually waned as well, before they both passed about a decade ago.

That's not to say I have been a saint. I meet women, mostly in the city when I visit. There is something city women seem to like about me. I'm not sure if it is my slight country accent, my ruggedness, my money, or just that I am from out of town, but either way, I am never short of female attention. I just never commit.

When Connor's mom left, I had to focus on him. He was and still is my number one priority. I tried to be the best dad I could and to be there for every milestone. I cooked his birthday cakes, coached his baseball team, nursed him when he was sick, helped with homework. The town talked, of course. I was young, just a kid myself. So I had to prove to them and myself that I could do it. There wasn't time to look at girls or go on dates, regardless of how many tried. Connor already had a mother figure leave him, and I wasn't going to be responsible for that to potentially happen again. The fear of being left is something that festers inside of me and has for years.

When Connor went away to college, it coincided with the distillery business booming. So when he left, I filled the void with work, kept my head down, developed new batches, new labels, turned my millions into billions, and the distillery became my new baby. I nurtured it, and I worked hard to build something for Connor to come back to. Women have always been a distant second to all that. I thought someone would cross my path along the way, pique my interest, but as the years roll on, I am more settled being on my own with Connor and the business.

I don't need any complications. Besides, I am fifty-one, too old and too grumpy to even think about it.

"Whiskey and Whispers are fine," I growl, gripping on to the steering wheel tight. Connor and the boys are always on my case about finding someone. He is scared that I am going to end up alone. But that is exactly how I like my life.

"I think you just came up with your new slogan. *Whiskey and Whispers, you can't have one without the other.* Better let the marketing team know. I think it would work well with your new accommodation offering," Sawyer says, and I smile.

"What, so now you want a bonus?" I smirk, knowing he doesn't need a bonus. His law firm is one of the biggest in the country. At the helm of it, he's just as wealthy as the rest of us.

"Nah, just my own jet will be fine, thanks," he says in

jest. I chuckle as I turn down Distillery Drive, the road that houses exactly two properties, my distillery and Marie's place.

"Is that Jerry's truck?" Sawyer sits forward, looking out the window.

"I'll pull up," I say, coming to stop in the middle of the road and Jerry's truck does the same. I open the window to chat.

"Jerry, we can meet you at Marie's and sign the papers today if you want?" I tell him, keen to get this sorted.

"She turned up," Jerry says in disbelief. *Well, shit.*

"She turned up?"

"Yes, she is here," Jerry says, nodding back to where Marie's place is located.

"Shit," Sawyer mutters, looking at me.

"What do you mean, she turned up? Who even is she?" I ask, my tone growing angry and desperate.

"Pretty little thing. Looks like she was plucked straight out of a movie set. I sure as hell know she has never set foot on a farm before. Hell, she probably hasn't ever left New York. Fancy clothes, hair nice and neat, friendly and polite," Jerry says, and I frown, not liking this at all.

"I don't understand. Why would she leave New York for here?" Sawyer asks, astounded. He catches my eye, and his face changes. "I mean, Whispers is lovely. Of course, she would want to be here." He rolls his eyes, and I send him a scowl.

"Is she planning to stay?" I bark, my body feeling tighter by the second.

"She didn't elaborate on her plans. I told her that you were keen to buy, but she didn't seem interested."

My jaw pops in irritation. "So if she doesn't want to sell, what is she thinking?"

"There is only one thing she must be doing," Jerry tells me, and I impatiently wait for him to continue. "She is going to stay and live on Marie's farm."

I almost laugh at how ridiculous that idea sounds. The farm is so run-down and is not a money earner, so she will need another income.

"What the hell? That farm needs a lot of work." Sawyer's seemingly just as confused and startled as I am.

Jerry chuckles. "I don't think she will last the day. She wasn't even wearing boots."

"I'm going to see her," I state, not interested in waiting another day. Jerry looks at me like I am crazy.

"I don't think—" he starts to advise, but I cut him off.

"I'll present her an offer she can't refuse. I want to get started on the demolition, get the wheels in motion. Sawyer, get the check ready. I am sure a few zeros will be all it takes. See you, Jerry."

Then I take off down the road, leaving Jerry in a cloud of dust as his mouth moves open and closed like a goldfish in surprise. Forcing someone's hand is not my usual way of doing business, but I am sure money will talk. It usually does. A small smile comes to my face. I should have ownership by the end of the day. Then I can get to work on the expansion.

Little Miss City Slicker will be putty in my hands.

6

VICTORIA

I have just managed to get my bags into the bedroom upstairs and change into jeans when I hear a vehicle approaching. Looking out the dusty window, it isn't Jerry, but the vehicle has driven right up to the house, so clearly they are familiar with the place. The truck is luxurious, shiny and black, with a gold logo on the side doors that says Whiteman's Whiskey. I know my only neighbor out here is the distillery, so maybe they came to say hello. It makes sense since everyone else has been super friendly so far. A big change from the city, and I already like it.

With a small smile on my face, I run my fingers through my hair to try to tame it as I walk down the beautiful hardwood staircase. These stairs are old but in great condition. Just a light sand will make a world of difference. I open the front door just as I hear two truck doors slam closed.

Barefooted, in just my jeans and a half-buttoned white shirt, I step out on the porch, watching two men approach. Well, one man and one... *very large man.* The first guy is dressed in a suit and looks like he belongs on Wall Street, and with that thought, my shoulders tense and my smile falters. I then look at the other man, although I am not sure I can describe him as just a man with how ridiculously big he is. Tall, broad, in dark denim jeans and a black button-down shirt that fits tight across his shoulders, showing me that he must work out. *A lot.* I take in a short breath as he looks right at me, his face striking, in a ruggedly good-looking kind of way, and I notice the black shirt has the same gold emblem on his chest pocket that matches the truck.

"Can I help you?" I ask, clearing my throat, trying to dismiss his handsome features. I know by the looks on their faces that they aren't the welcoming committee I first thought they were. They seem serious, their eyes assessing me, and I am slightly intimidated as they come closer, but I push my shoulders back.

"Miss McArthur, I would like to intro—" the guy in the suit starts to say, but the other man cuts him off.

"I'm Tanner Whiteman, owner of Whiteman's Whiskey and your neighbor." The large man walks forward purposefully, putting out his hand. They clearly know exactly who I am. The small-town gossip grapevine in full effect. My eyes flick to his hand, and I spot a Rolex on his wrist before I look back at his face. Deep-brown eyes stare back at me, and like his branding, they have flecks of gold. His skin is tanned and lined from too much time in the sun, thick, dark hair sprinkled with hints of gray and a little ruffled. Once my gaze drifts down to his sharp jaw, then broad chest, I force myself to meet his eyes again, blinking as the sun beats down on us.

"Victoria McArthur, nice to meet you," I say, shaking his hand, trying to sound professional, even though my guard is up. My hand gets completely lost in his, so much so, I gasp and look at where we join. His hands are roughened, hardworking, and huge, just like every other part of him. There is a lot to look at. I swallow quickly, and he clears his throat, which has my eyes snapping back to his. When I let go of his hand, his lingers a little longer than my own.

"Look, I am not going to waste your time. I would like to buy your aunt's property from you," he states as his hands find his hips. This guy clearly is wealthy. It isn't just his expensive truck or the shiny watch. He has that well-put-together monied look about him. But I am not sure if this man is a businessman or a cowboy, as either would suit him right about now. I bring my mind back to the conversation, and it is then I understand he must be the "we" that Jerry mentioned earlier.

"Thank you for the offer, but I am not selling," I say politely, trying to remain courteous. I don't want to get off on the wrong foot, since we are neighbors and all, but I am also not going to be a pushover.

"I will make it worth your while." With a small smirk, he puts one foot up on the first step to my porch, seemingly relaxed, like this is a done deal in his mind. My back straightens a little more. I don't like being played a fool, and since I have already had one man completely take me for an idiot this year, I don't need another, regardless of how good-looking he is. *They sure don't make men like this in the city.*

"I'm sorry, I am not interested," I reiterate, stepping forward and crossing my arms over my chest, meeting him in defense. His eyes flick to my chest and back up to my eyes as I paste a small smile on my face, biting back my annoyance of having to tell him twice.

"Miss McArthur, we would be looking to offer you a sum of one million dollars, which as I am sure you know is well above market rate in this area," the suited man chimes in, grabbing my attention. I turn my head and look at him, frowning. He clearly sees me as a dumb city girl who doesn't know a thing about real estate. A few days ago, he would've been right, but too bad this city girl has had nothing better to do than research this town, this house, and the opportunities that could become available if I manage to renovate and turn it into a bed-and-breakfast. There is no other accommodation this close to both the town and the distillery. There is also no other accommodation that is so secluded and private, aside from large ranches, and they are farther out of town. I can make this something great, even with a small budget, and I at least want to try.

"Sorry, you are?" I ask, tilting my head with thinned eyes. I am not usually confrontational. Sassy is not a personality trait of mine. But ever since I found my fiancé balls deep in another woman, I seem to have grown a stronger backbone and now have an excellent bullshit radar. And these two are pinging off the charts. Again, more men turning up in my life who don't like taking no for an answer.

"Sawyer Silvers, lawyer for Whiteman's Whiskey," he says with a large movie-star smile on his face, showcasing his pearly whites that tell me he is from the city. Tanner stands watching me closely, like he is trying to figure me out. I see his eyes roam down and back up my body. *Is he checking me out?* The thud in my chest tells me that my heart didn't dry up and shrivel after Josh's act of betrayal. Small creases form around his eyes in his assessment. I am not sure how old he is, but he is older than me by at least a decade, maybe two.

"Well, *Sawyer* the *Lawyer*, as I have said, I have no plans to sell, so you can throw all the money in the world my way, but my answer will remain the same," I tell him, looking at Tanner. His lips thin, clearly frustrated.

"This is a large property. Too much for one person," Tanner says. *Arrogant much?*

"I can handle it," I throw back at him, moving my arms to my hips in defiance and watching his jaw tic. I truly have no idea what I am in for, but he is still not getting my property.

Tanner huffs a laugh. "I'll give you a few days, a week tops. Then you will be begging me to buy it," he says, his smirk making him even more attractive. *I bet this man gets everything he wants.*

"Is this how you greet all new residents of Whispers or just the single females? Do you make a habit of barging onto their property, demanding they sell, and when they decline, make fun of them?" I ask, pissed off now at his inability to actually hear what I am saying. His eyebrow quirks, like he is surprised that I'm calling him out on his bullshit welcome. "As I am sure you know, my aunt's family built this property. She spent her entire life here in this town, and in her passing, she has given it to me to look after. So that's my plan," I tell him, strong in my stance.

"One million is a lot of money, Victoria. How 'bout you sleep on it?" His low rumble of a voice with a slight drawl of a country accent has my pussy pulsing, even though he is absolutely infuriating.

"Seems you are like every other man I have come across lately and don't like to hear the word *no*, Mr. Whiteman, so let me just spell it out for you. *N.O*," I say, stepping back from him and his sidekick, both sporting furrowed brows. "But, of course, I appreciate your offer. If you will excuse me, I have some cleaning to do."

Sawyer steps back to the truck, while Tanner takes a small step toward me. We are at eye level with him standing on the bottom step and me a few steps up on the porch. As he bends his head closer to mine, I don't move. Holding my breath, his head dips to my ear, and his voice is deeper as he says, "I am not like any other man you have come across before, I can assure you that."

My heart thuds dangerously loud as he pulls back, giving me a smirk before he says, "Welcome to Whispers, Victoria." The sound of my name rolling off his tongue vibrates down my breasts, my traitorous nipples now peaking to attention like I am in an icebox. *What is going on with me?* Giving me a wink, he walks to his truck as I watch him go.

"Thanks, neighbor," I say, not able to help the slight sarcasm. If they think they can come here and flash money around, trying to get my property, they are sorely mistaken. Not even if the man trying looks like he was God's favorite. Renovating and designing a home like this has been a dream of mine for so long, and the universe put it straight in my lap. I am not going to give it up.

They were willing to pay me a million dollars, which is simply confirmation this property is worth keeping. Renewed enthusiasm fills my bones. It's time to get to work.

7

___

TANNER

I push through the door and into the boardroom back at the distillery, Sawyer hot on my heels. My strides are long, my adrenaline high, my ears ringing as my blood feels like it's coursing around my body at a speed that has me antsy.

"That was interesting..." Sawyer says, taking a seat at the large oak table I built over a decade ago. Woodworking is a hobby of mine, this desk one of my biggest projects. It is not the shiny polished timber you would find in the city. This is all recycled, damaged, dented, and from the old barrels. Stained in places, it's sanded back to reveal the inner workings of the wood. It is unique, just how I like things.

"I can't believe she turned down a million dollars," I say in awe, unsure of my next move. She surprised me when we barreled up to her place, offering money she has probably never seen and yet still rejected. She wasn't what I was expecting.

"We could up our price? Perhaps offer her another

few hundred thousand, pay for her flight home and any incidentals so she isn't out of pocket for coming here," Sawyer suggests, and what he offers makes sense. I want that property, and I will do anything to get it.

Scrubbing a hand over my face, I sigh, and even though it is early, I walk over to my whiskey bar and pour myself one finger. My new neighbor has me feeling off-kilter. She is feisty and stubborn. Assertive and clearly knowledgeable. *I like her.*

Jerry said she was pretty, but she was fucking stunning. The image of her standing there barefoot, her toes polished a soft shade of pink, her hair blowing in the small breeze. She is naturally beautiful. I shake my head. Not only do I already know she is going to be a massive pain in my ass, but she's also way too young for me to be having these kinds of thoughts.

"Something tells me she still won't take it," I murmur, throwing my drink back, not even feeling the burn I desperately need right now.

"I want you to put through the paperwork with the town planner," I tell him abruptly.

"But you can't. You don't own the land," Sawyer says.

"Adverse possession. That property is as good as mine." I'm confident that I will get it.

"I don't think that will work." Sawyer shakes his head at me, frowning.

"I did everything for Marie. I have spent more time on that land than that niece of hers ever has. I've been in the field and managing the land more than even Marie in her later years. Plus, I know the town planner... Maybe I can make him some sort of offer..."

"If you are talking about bribery, then I don't want to know. But let me put in the paperwork to attain via adverse possession, and we'll see what happens. It's a long shot, but I might as well try. She is crazy to turn down that money," he murmurs, rubbing his chin in thought.

"Or smart," I throw back at him with a smirk. She was confident but polite, and I can't help but wonder how far I can push her. The fire I saw in her eyes sure makes me want to.

"What do you mean?" He looks at me in question.

"Well, *Sawyer* the *Lawyer*..." I say, teasing him with what will no doubt become his new nickname around here. He gives me a dirty look, which I ignore. "She clearly knows the worth of the place, so she has done her research. Now we have shown her our hand; she knows that I want it and will pay top dollar for it. If we put in the paperwork, that can be our backup plan—because that will take a while to process—but in the meantime, maybe we can play it out?" I take a seat in the large brown leather chair at the end of the table, still thinking about the woman who has breezed into town, seemingly without a care in the world, and is turning her hand to living in the country. It is a brave move. Very brave.

"So we leave her to it and wait for her to fail?" he asks, and I ponder his words. I love this town and everyone in it. It is not in my nature to just let people fail. I help a lot of people, donate to the local charities, help fund the local school. I have the means to, and this town has been good to me.

Leaning back in my chair, I run a hand through my

hair. I had my heart set on that place for our expansion. I am used to getting what I want, when I want it. But... I don't mind a little bit of friendly competition.

"I'll get Connor to do some research on her, find out what he can, and I will chat with her some more this week and see what I can work out with her," I tell him, resting my body back into the soft leather, happy with my decision. Sawyer raises his eyebrow at me.

"So you plan to go visit her again?" Sawyer asks, a small smile dancing on his lips. I pay him too much money for his teasing, but I indulge him anyway.

"Spit it out."

"Well, she was fucking beautiful for a start," he says, and I growl. His eyes widen, and so does his smirk. "She is obviously single, because she is here on her own and there was no ring on her finger..." As he continues, my shoulders stiffen. He is right; there was no ring adorning her hand. I know because I was looking.

"Don't start, you're as bad as Connor." I know exactly where he is going with this. "She looks half my fucking age, not to mention now my new enemy number one. I want that land, Sawyer." I can't go there. She looks young enough to be my daughter. Hell, she is probably better suited to Connor. That thought alone gives me a pang in my stomach.

"Who knows? She'll need a neighborly hand at some point, no doubt. You always used to help her aunt. But maybe you should stay clear of her, as I said, let her fail, let her have a tough time so she doesn't want to be here anymore once she knows how hard this life is," Sawyer offers, and I nod to him, knowing that it makes sense. It is the right move. Leave her alone, wait for her to fail, and then pay her out and watch her scurry back to the city with her tail between her legs.

"I don't think she will last long," Sawyer says with a scoff.

"She might surprise us."

Sawyer gives a fake shiver. "I love it here, but to move here? Be out here permanently? No thanks."

"Take the jet, go back to the city, and I'll call Connor to see if he can start digging around and find out more about her. In the meantime, let's see how she fits in around Whispers. As you said, I'm sure a city girl like her will hate it."

"And you will leave her alone? No driving over there to help her out?" Sawyer asks, and I look at him with a scowl.

"I'm not promising anything." I stand up and walk back to the small bar positioned against the wall, pouring another glass of my latest batch and throwing it back, this time feeling the burn I am after.

8

VICTORIA

After spending a few days cleaning the house and gathering some basic supplies from town, I am now bleary-eyed and planning out the way I want the house to look. The truck worked a treat, although I have a feeling that at some point it will start to give me trouble. I don't think it is very reliable.

"There is a lot to be done," I tell Fiona and my mother on the three-way conversation we are having. My first few nights in my new home were terrible, but I am not going to tell them that. After the confrontation with my new neighbor, my senses have been heightened, and I have no idea what to expect from him next. But so far, my time included adding things to Pinterest, ordering way too many décor items and furnishings online, and jumping at each bleat I hear from the goat every night, all night long. Hence why sleep has not been something that has come easily.

"Put the camera on, I want to see," Fiona says excitedly. The overwhelm is building. I have walked around outside and back inside again numerous times, each time noticing something new that needs fixing. The list I have now is almost a page long.

"Here," I say, turning on the camera and giving them a tour.

"Oh, sweetie, it looks just how I remember it," my mother gushes, like she is seeing something beautiful and not the dark, run-down house that I am looking at.

"How so?" I ask, knowing my mom is the voice of reason in all this.

"I am pretty sure behind that board against the wall is a beautiful open fireplace. From what I can remember, the tiles around that were a brilliant vibrant blue."

I walk over to the area she is suggesting and pull back the board a little to see that she is right. The blue is striking and will look amazing against the stark white walls and the timber floorboards that I plan to sand and stain.

"Those drapes are thick and heavy-looking. You could get rid of those and let in more natural light. I am sure once you sand the floorboards, that will really lighten up the place," Fiona says, and that is something I have already thought about. Plantation shutters might work well, as would soft, floating drapes.

"I agree. I ordered a new sofa and armchair from Pottery Barn because they were on sale, and it will take a few weeks to come, so I have plenty of time to get the place ready for it." I'm happy with the progress I have made so far with all the online ordering. Me and my tape measure had lots of fun.

"Oh, and those high ceilings are amazing. We were

there around Christmas and Marie got an enormous tree and we decorated it together. It looked amazing in the corner by the staircase. Of course, your father wasn't happy the entire time, which just put a damper on it all." My mom scoffs as I walk around, visualizing my own tree sitting in the corner of this room between the open fire and the front windows.

"Why was Dad such an asshole?"

"I think it was probably because of this property, actually," she says, and my interest is piqued.

"How so?" Fiona asks.

"Oh, it was a generational place. I think his grandparents built it, but when they passed, they left it to Marie. Not sure why. I didn't get involved in all that. His family were always a little strange. Marie was the only one who seemed content and grateful in her life, even if she could be a grump at times," Mom remarks, and I sigh, never understanding family dynamics since I only remember just Mom and me.

I walk up the stairs to the top floor where all the bedrooms and the bathroom are.

"Oh my God, is that a claw-foot bath?" Fiona almost shrieks as I make my way down the hall, showing them the rooms.

"I do love that," I murmur, looking at it again. "I also ordered soft Egyptian towels from Saks that will match this color scheme. Apart from a new vanity and shower screen, there really isn't too much needed in here." I'm happy about that fact because bathrooms and kitchens are the most expensive to renovate and the kitchen needs a complete overhaul.

"Sweetie, I really think with your eye and passion for interiors, you can make this something special," my mom says, and I can tell by her voice that she is in love with the place.

"You should start a blog. You know, document your journey. Put it out on social media," Fiona suggests, and I stop short.

"That is a great idea," I tell her, kicking myself that I hadn't thought of that earlier.

"Make sure you take a heap of before photos, of the inside and outside, of each room," my mom says.

"I can see it now, city girl turns country. Hashtag Whisperwoman," Fiona says, making all three of us laugh.

"I love that idea." I already see it coming to life in my head as I take more notes.

"How's everything in the city, Fiona?" I ask her, even though I only flew out a few days ago.

"I saw Josh at the café down the street, if that is what you are asking. He was on his lunch break. Natalie was with him, although he didn't look pleased about that fact. He jumped up when he saw me and came straight over, asking why you won't take his calls."

"What an idiot. What did you say?" I ask, knowing she would have told it to him straight.

"I told him that you were traveling. That you were having the time of your life with the various men you are meeting and to stop calling you." She sounds so proud of herself, and I bark out a laugh.

"Good thing that he is in the past and this fantastic house is your future, darling. Josh is not worth the time thinking about," my mom says, and I agree. I have already spent too many weeks thinking about it all and have moved on. We were only together for a year, and if I am truthful with myself, I knew he wasn't the one. And since he so easily cheated on me with another woman, I didn't mean much to him either. That thought sparks another idea of how this house could be used in the future.

"Totally agree, Ms. McArthur," Fiona says as the two of them start talking about me like I am not even on the call.

"Alright, I need to go out and get Garry," I tell them, breaking up their chatter, wondering how I am going to get the goat back into its pen.

"Garry? Don't say you have met a man already?" my mom asks playfully. I instantly think of my neighbor. The tall, dark, brooding man who wants to buy my property. Tension builds in my shoulders, and my heart does a weird flip-flop at the thought of him. He makes me equal parts angry and intrigued.

"Well, if by man, you mean a four-legged goat that bleats at everything, so much that I barely sleep at night, then yes. Garry is my new boyfriend, and I need to get him back into his shed for the night."

"Oh look, she is already one with the animals," Fiona says, laughing.

"Garry and I are now friends. He followed me into the shed last night, no problem. Very obedient." My tone is full of sarcasm, but I smile to myself with pride that I actually figured it out myself. Even if it took me an hour last night to get him into the shed, and in the end, I had to coax him with food.

"Can goats be obedient, or do you think he just liked the smell of you or something?" Mom asks, and since neither of us have the answer, we just end up in fits of laughter at this weird and wonderful situation I have found myself in.

Ending the call, I sigh, looking around the place, then grab my laptop to make some notes about a new website and blog. Operation Hashtag Whisperwoman starts now.

AFTER GETTING the truck started and stalling it in the driveway three times, I am relieved to finally be in town and gathering all the things I need. I have no idea how I managed to start it, but I do hope that I can get home without any more issues. With another quick dash to the grocery store for more food, I am now walking around the hardware store, the cart I am pushing almost full when my cell vibrates with a text message from Josh.

Where are you?

Why won't you answer my calls?

You are being childish.

My screen fills with his rant, seemingly frustrated that I am not giving him the response he thinks he's entitled to.

"Can I help you there, miss?" a voice asks, and I startle as an older man walks up to me in a pair of over-alls and a small smile.

"Well, I think I'm taking most of the store home with me, so I hope that means I am doing okay," I say with a small chuckle at myself as I slide my still vibrating phone into my pocket. I push Josh and his persistence to the back of my mind and refocus on why I am here. I have no idea what the hell I am doing with the house. At this point, I am relying on the internet for my renovation education.

"I haven't seen you around here before; are you Marie's niece?" Boy, news does travel fast around here.

"Yes. I'm Victoria," I say, putting out my hand.

"I'm Bob. Jerry told me that you might be in this week. I was sad to hear of Marie's passing. She kept to herself a lot but was always a nice woman to me. I hear there is a fair bit to fix out on the property?"

"Thank you. There is, but it is mainly cosmetic," I say, trying to remain upbeat. "So I do need to get some paint." Looking around, I'm not able to see it.

"Sure thing. What are you looking for, inside or out?" he asks, already walking down the aisle, and I follow him.

"Both. Ideally, stark white for interior and Grey Goose for exterior," I tell him, already knowing the color scheme. Visualizing my new place has me giddy with excitement. My plan is to paint outside in the sunshine during the day and then start painting inside during the evenings. I hope within a week or two of painting day and night, I will have it done. It's going to make a massive difference.

"Sounds like a hell of a job. Are you sure you're okay with it all?" He turns to look at me with concern.

"I'll be fine," I say, trying not to be offended about

how the men in this town seem to think a woman can't cope with these types of tasks. Sure, I haven't painted a house before, but how hard can it be?

"You're neighbors with Tanner Whiteman out there. I am sure he will be happy to help you."

I bite my tongue. That is the one person I will *not* be asking for help. I am sure he will take too much enjoyment out of seeing me fail, and I am starting to feel like I need to prove everyone wrong in this town.

"Alright, well, how many gallons do you need?" he asks, and I balk. Shit. I have no idea.

"Oh, umm…"

"Outside, I'm guessing you will need a few tins of this one," he says, starting to put them in my cart. "If you need more, you can always come back in. For inside, let's start you with a few tins of this one. Plus, don't forget your undercoat…"

Ten minutes later, I am packing up the truck with all my supplies that will keep me busy for a few weeks. Bob is just as friendly as everyone else, and by the end of my trip, he ensured I had every tool and material known to man, along with another suggestion to lean on Tanner if I need to. *Over my dead body.*

Bob even had a floor sander to rent, so I grabbed that as well, thinking I might try that today when I get home. Everything so far is coming in on budget, and as I inhale a deep breath, I smile.

I scan the street, seeing people coming and going and stop for a moment to take it all in. Large trees line the street; flower beds are full of color now that spring is here; the sky is clear of any clouds. Everyone is smiling and friendly as they go about their days. No horns beeping, so yelling, no city smells from the subway grates. Only fresh air and friendly greetings. A small church sits at the end of the main street, almost welcoming people into town, and I spot Delish Diner and a few other stores I'll need to investigate next time I'm here. I even spot a small interiors shop down the street that's calling my name. Sometimes small towns have the best surprises.

Whispers is a pretty town, picturesque. And it's my new home. *I am doing this. I am really doing this.*

I am about to jump back in the truck to go home when Flourish catches my eye. I remember what Peter, the taxi man, said about meeting the owner of the florist. Deciding that there is no time like the present to start meeting more locals, I walk down the street and push open the door, a small bell announcing my arrival.

"Oh, hi! You must be Victoria?" A woman who looks close to my age walks toward me from the back of the store.

"Ahhh, I am, yes." I'm shocked she knows me before an introduction.

"Sorry, small town," she says, rolling her eyes. "I'm Jasmine. Welcome to Whispers. How are you finding Marie's place?" she asks, and she, like everyone else I have met, is overly friendly, so I just go with it.

"News travels fast," I comment with a smile. It is to be expected in a small town; I just need to remember that. "Marie's place is great." That has Jasmine looking at me as though I am crazy.

"We are talking about the same house, right? The old,

run-down white one near Whiteman's Distillery?" she asks, and I nod.

"That's the one," I say cheerily. I am in a good mood. I have survived a few nights, I have supplies, online orders are placed, and now I am ready to get to work.

"Have you met Tanner Whiteman yet? Owner of Whiteman's Whiskey? I heard a rumor that he wants to buy Marie's place. Or rather, your place now."

I try to remain impartial, but the fact that everyone keeps mentioning his name is starting to become maddening.

"Oh, I am not planning to sell. I am renovating."

"Renovating? Really? I thought Tanner would probably offer millions." She's dumbfounded if the expression on her face tells me anything.

"He did, but I am not taking it. The house needs a little work, but I love design and just stocked up on all the supplies to get started. I will be renovating and documenting the journey online. Besides, it is a family property; I can't just sell it," I tell her, chuckling, and she smiles.

"Huh... that sounds amazing." She clears her throat. "Well, you will need some immediate color in the place to brighten your day. I have this amazing bunch of red roses that will look fantastic," she says, grabbing a bunch of flowers.

"They are beautiful. Thank you. How much?" I ask as I follow her to the counter.

"First bunch is on the house," she says with a wink.

"Are you sure?" I tilt my head in question, hating taking something I am not paying for.

"Think of it as a welcome to Whispers." She starts to wrap them up in paper, then pauses to look back up at me. "If you're not doing anything tonight, I will be hanging out at Whiteman's Bar with my friend, Lacy. Feel free to join us. There aren't many young women in town these days, so we kinda have to stick together."

I look out the window and spot a black timber building with gold writing.

"Is that owned by Tanner Whiteman as well?" I know the answer is yes before she even responds. My grumpy older neighbor seems to be everywhere.

"Most of the town is," she admits, and while I don't really want to support the man who wants my land, I do need to make new friends. I find myself nodding.

"Thank you. I would like that. I can be there around seven," I tell her, trying to mentally calculate the work I need to do this afternoon and how long it will take me.

"Perfect. Oh, and here's my number. I am sure it is pretty quiet out at the house, so if you need anything, just call."

I take her card. It is a beautiful soft pink embossed business card. So cute and feminine and very much my style.

"Thank you. And thanks for the flowers. See you tonight!"

I feel lighter and happier than I have in weeks as I walk toward my truck. But the smile quickly fades as I spot a shiny black truck, with the now familiar gold logo on the doors, drive up the street and park right next to mine.

With flowers still in hand, I take a breath and get

ready for another onslaught as the man himself steps out. His thick thighs and strong body glide out onto the street, his forearms showing with his sleeves rolled up, eyes sparkling as he looks at me. Gripping my flowers tighter, I take a moment to drink him in. He can't be real. This is exactly how imaginary boyfriends look. Tall, dark, brooding, handsome. He looks how he did in my dream last night.

The one that made me come twice.

9

TANNER

I drive past my new neighbor's place and force my eyes to stay on the road ahead of me and not look in as I make my way into town.

"Dad, are you listening?" Connor asks from the speakerphone.

"Listening just fine. We are signing on for the new hotel in Tennessee with Van Cleef," I repeat to him. I listen to everything he says.

"It's a solid investment. The Rothschilds are in on it. You know Harrison, all about domestic growth now," he quips about his best friend since college who is now president, and I nod even though he can't see me.

"I need you to look into someone for me," I tell him as I hit the open road.

"Sawyer mentioned something about our new neighbor. A woman?"

"Victoria McArthur. She is from the city. Thought you could dig into her financial situation." I'm eager to get some history on this woman that I could use against her.

"Sawyer said she was nice. Why do you want to know so bad? Can we just offer her above market rate and grab the property?" Connor makes perfect sense.

"I did. She didn't take it. I don't think she is the kind of woman who is interested in that much money," I murmur as I think about my sexy blond neighbor and how her eyes were absent of dollar signs when I landed on her doorstep a few days ago. Most women I meet seem to hook on to the fact that I'm wealthy, and I can spot them from a mile away. I don't look like a typical billionaire, rarely in a suit, prefer to live in Whispers, but my new neighbor doesn't appear to know that much about me and also doesn't seem to care. It is refreshing and sexy as hell.

"Sawyer mentioned she was beautiful too." Connor is fishing for information, and my hand tightens on the steering wheel.

"Sawyer needs to mind his business," I grumble.

"So you do like her!" Connor says jubilantly, and I can tell he has a smart-ass smile on his face. The same one that I get from time to time.

"She is probably closer to your age." The thought of it makes me feel older than I am.

"So?" His comeback is quick.

"So, I'm probably old enough to be her father," I reiterate. "Besides, she will be gone by the end of the week. She won't last." They never do. Just like his mom, no women tend to stick around Whispers for long.

"Well, age shouldn't really come into it, Dad. Some of the women you meet in the city are young, and what difference does that make to you?" he challenges, and my nostrils flare as I pull in air. It's true, the women I meet when in the city tend to be younger. But that is a one-night thing. I have only met Victoria once, but that was enough to know she most certainly wouldn't be a one-night thing for me.

"Just see what you can find out about her. Sawyer will help," I tell him, getting this conversation back on track. As I drive down the main street, I spot Marie's truck outside Flourish. Good to see Victoria getting out and about, and at least she got the rust bucket started. The truck is road worthy, having organized the servicing on it myself, but it still looks like an accident waiting to happen. That fact doesn't sit well with me.

"I have to go. Call you later." I end the call quickly as I pull up next to her and see her stepping out from Jasmine's shop, a large bouquet of red roses in hand, completely contrasting the bright-pink scarf she has draped around her neck. Coupled with her long blond hair that flows in waves down her back, she is picture-perfect. Her pretty smile falls immediately as she spots me pulling in beside her, and a red blush comes to her cheeks. Most likely in anger as she isn't pleased to see me, that is for sure.

"You probably shouldn't be driving that," I tell her as soon as I step out of the truck and pace toward her on the sidewalk. Shit, I sound like a dick. Her eyebrows shoot up and her lips press together.

"Good morning to you too, Tanner," she says diplomatically before walking around me, not wanting to engage. She has me off-kilter. I didn't even say good morning.

I grab her arm firmly as she passes by, and she spins around to look at me, her hair whipping my shoulder. We are close, mere inches between us, and I can smell a floral scent—from her or from the flowers in her hand, I don't know. But it is nice. Feminine. Something that has been missing from my life for a very long time.

"I just mean that it isn't safe," I growl low to her, tilting my head down so she hears me. She looks up at me, sucking in a small breath, and I soften my hold on her but don't let go. I don't want to.

"Jerry said it was fine," she says, now looking at the truck with concern, sounding a little unsure.

"Jerry wouldn't know a thing about trucks if one hit him on the road. I had it serviced for Marie not long before she died. It should get you from point A to point B okay, but no long trips, alright? Town and back, and that's it. Marie never drove it out of town." My sudden concern for my new neighbor takes me by surprise.

"Are you trying to scare me or something?" Her eyes thin, and I let out a sigh. Frustration, at her and myself. We have clearly gotten off on the wrong foot, and it is obvious that she doesn't find me genuine. Sure, I want her land, but I am usually not so much of an asshole to the locals, even if they are prohibiting me from business expansion.

"Just offering some friendly advice, take it or leave it. This isn't the city. If the truck breaks down, you will need to walk," I tell her straight before letting go of her arm completely. She remains where she is, looking up at me, the sun hitting her hair and making it shine a warm honey color, like a whiskey aged just a few years. Up close like this, I can see her bright-blue eyes better, the way her lips pout a little in the middle. Fuck, I need to get a grip. I have never noticed this shit about women before. I'm not sure why it is happening now.

"Thank you for the advice," she says in a tone that lets me know I have put my foot in it again. All I can do is nod, because I don't trust my mouth to say anything remotely intelligent to her at the moment. As she steps away, my body hates the distance.

She opens the door to the truck, and I watch her pull herself up and in, the squeals from the door hinges almost deafening. She needs a better vehicle. Her eyes dart to me, almost daring me to say something, and I clench my jaw tight. Seeing she has a tray full of hardware, she has obviously been to see Bob this morning, which is not a great sign. The last thing I need is for her to get busy turning that house into a home. I stand rooted to the sidewalk, watching her back out and drive down the street, a large plume of black smoke trailing behind her.

"Shit," I say to myself, knowing the truck won't last much longer.

"Bit of an old rust bucket, isn't it?" Jasmine says, stepping out of her shop to stand next to me, the two of us watching our new resident drive away.

"It's a danger to the roads," I growl, and she huffs.

"It really is. She should take it to Dad's garage," Jasmine suggests.

"Dad's?" I ask her. She lives in the next town over, although she is always at the distillery, either dropping off new floral arrangements for the restaurant or having conversations with my team. With not many other young people in the town, I already know that she has Victoria in her sights to be her new BFF.

"My dad owns the garage in Williamstown. He can probably service it for her," she says, her eyes assessing me like they always do.

"I had it serviced a few months back, but it is old."

"Well, she will be at the bar tonight. I invited her for drinks. We will be there at seven, just in case you want to know," she says coyly, and my eyes narrow.

"Why would I want to know that?" I grumble, but even so, I pocket that little piece of information.

"Oh, I don't know. Perhaps because you jumped on her the minute she left my shop. Perhaps the way you grabbed her and pulled her close, or perhaps the way that you are still standing here on the sidewalk, looking down the road for any last trace of her. I never see you looking at any other woman like that."

She's fishing for information, and I need to stop being so obvious.

"I've got to get back to it," I say, stepping away from her, not entertaining her ideas. When I walk back to my truck and open the door, Jasmine's voice stops me.

"She really likes flowers. Just so you know," she hollers at me before I jump in my truck, wondering why I am now memorizing that little piece of information too. I slam the door, put the truck in gear, and drive straight back to the distillery, looking everywhere along the way for a rusted red truck and not happy until I see it exactly where it should be. Parked at Marie's place and in one piece.

10

VICTORIA

I push through the large wooden door of the bar and am pleasantly surprised. It's big, with high ceilings and people everywhere, giving a nice hum of conversation to the place, along with some country music playing in the background. It is new and polished, yet rustic. Lots of soft brown leathers, hardwood floors, and amazing antler chandeliers hanging from the exposed beams above. It is what I would class as *luxe country* and I love it.

"Oh, you're here!" I hear a squeal and look to my left, spotting Jasmine at the bar waving frantically. I huff a smile, which is hard to erase at the sight of her seemingly excited to see me. As I take another quick look around, I am thankful that I dressed appropriately. No little black dress required here. Instead, I opted for darker jeans and a black silk camisole top since it is pretty warm tonight. My hair's up in a ponytail, because after working all day, it was just a mess and no amount of blow-drying was going to help. And I finished off with a lick of bright-pink lipstick.

Walking over to her, I laugh at her excitement, but it's kind of nice to make a new friend. A few people turn and look, and I'm suddenly a little self-conscious. Since I am new in town, I am still hot gossip. I feel a bit like an animal in a zoo, with many eyes on me, so I keep my eyes forward and try to smile. I don't want to have resting bitch face as their first impression of me.

"Hey, you, glad you made it," she says as I pull up a barstool and sit next to her. I see Bob over at a table against the wall, and I give him a smile. He holds up his beer in a cheers as his greeting.

"This is Lacy. Lacy, this is Victoria." Jasmine introduces me to the woman behind the bar. She is beautiful, looks a little younger than me, and she gives me a wide smile.

"Great to finally meet you. I have heard a lot about you already," she says, leaning on the bar, clearly working tonight.

"Oh, I hope it was good?" I ask playfully.

"Of course. Even prettier in real life. What are you drinking?" She smiles as she wipes down the bar in front of us. She seems nice, and I try to pick up some energy, but I am exhausted.

"Please tell me you have a margarita?" I ask almost pleadingly.

"Not common around here, but I can put one together." With a smile, she gets to work in front of us.

"Big day?" Jasmine asks. From where she sits at my

side, she sips on what looks like cola, but I am sure has liquor in it.

"Renovations have officially started," I say, propping my hands on the bar.

"Oh my God, look at your hands!"

My eyes flick to my fingers that are red and dry.

"I spent the afternoon sanding the floors and then cleaning walls and taping up, ready to paint, before I hosed down the outside, so I'm ready to start the exterior painting tomorrow," I tell her. My bones in my body are so sore from all the physical work of being up and down ladders and ripping tape and soaking sponges in cleaning fluid to remove stains and buildup from the walls. "The floor sanding went great. Although I think I went through at least ten rolls of painter's tape just to tape up the windows and arches, but it will be worth it."

"You're painting the whole house? Today you mentioned renovating, but I didn't know you were doing so much!" Jasmine asks, surprised, or potentially looking at me like I am certifiably crazy. Could be either one at this point.

"What? Marie's place?" Lacy asks.

"That's the plan. Bob helped me out today with all the paint and supplies," I tell them, as Lacy slides over what looks to be one of the best margaritas I have ever had in my life and I haven't even had a sip yet.

"That is going to take a while. So you are planning on staying?" Jasmine asks.

"Well, I have nothing but time. My plan is to do the outside during the morning and then inside during the afternoon. A few coats, and hopefully I will have it done in a week or two, maybe?" I say with a shrug. This is what I signed up for, and even though I am excited about it all, now after a full day's work, the novelty has worn off a little.

"Have you renovated homes before?" Lacy asks, and I huff a laugh.

"No. It's my first time. But I have a passion for design. I always wanted to do something like this, and when I got the letter about Aunt Marie, it was like it was meant to be. Oh, and I started a blog," I say, pulling out my cell.

"That's so fun! Show us!" Jasmine says, her smile wide as she bounces a little in her seat. I open the social media and show the girls the images so far. All the before photos, a small video I put together, plus I spent some time last night taking progress photos and editing them so they look really good. My feed is already garnering followers.

"Oh, I'm going to follow," Lacy says, pulling her cell from her back pocket.

"Me too!" Jasmine squeals.

"Should we take a photo? I can put it up?" I ask, smiling at how supportive they're being.

"Yes!" The girls are immediately on board and the three of us squish our heads together. I quickly take the photo and upload it with #newfriends, tagging both the florist shop and the bar.

"So were you close to Marie?" Lacy asks as I sip the cocktail. It tastes so delicious, I'm regretting that this will be my one and only. Tanner's warning about driving Marie's truck is still fresh in my mind so I want to have my mind clear for the drive home.

"No, I didn't know she existed. I came here as a kid, apparently, but I don't remember. But like a fairy godmother, she left her estate to me just as my life was starting to crumble," I tell them, licking the salt off my lip.

"Really, what happened?" Jasmine sits forward, totally hooked on my story.

"My fiancé had a terrible accident." I look at both of them seriously and watch their eyes widen as they wait for more.

"What happened?" Lacy asks, holding on to the edge of the bartop.

"He fell into his colleague's vagina."

They both pause for a second as I take another sip of my cocktail, looking at me, wide-eyed, before I give them a smile and we all burst into laughter. It feels good to be able to laugh about it. The only sting remaining is from being so stupid that I didn't notice what was going on earlier.

"Oh my God, what an asshole," Jasmine says.

"What a shit colleague," Lacy states, and I nod.

"Oh, then a week later, I lost my job. So you could say Marie saved me when she passed her estate on to me. It was divine timing." They both look at me in admiration.

"Wow, that calls for the hard stuff," Lacy says, putting three shot glasses on the bar and grabbing a bottle of whiskey.

She pours the amber liquor perfectly, not spilling a drop.

"To new beginnings," Jasmine says, holding up the

shot glass as I grab mine hesitantly. I've never had straight whiskey before.

"To new beginnings," Lacy and I say together, and we throw back our glasses. My eyes burn instantly, my throat on fire.

"Wow, that's strong," I cough out, blinking as my eyes water. The other two look at me like they didn't just drink something akin to gasoline.

"It's Whiteman's," Lacy says, putting the bottle on the bar. The label's black with gold writing—at least his branding is on point. There is no mistaking it. In this town, I am surrounded by him.

"Of course it is. He is a bit of an asshole, isn't he?" I ask, looking at them both.

"Who, Tanner?" Jasmine clarifies, her head tilting in confusion.

"Yeah. He isn't overly friendly..." I say, not sure if I can be completely honest with them yet. They look at each other before looking back at me. I am not sure my radar for picking decent men is firing right after Josh, and I certainly don't need another man to make me feel less than.

"Are we talking about the same man? That one over there, who's been looking at you since you walked in." Jasmine points, and I follow the direction of her hand to a booth down the back. Familiar brown eyes burn my skin as Tanner looks right at me. He is with yet another good-looking man who seems a bit younger than him, someone more my age. But it is my older grumpy neighbor who has all my attention.

"Tanner is great. Gave me a job a few months ago

the minute I came back to Whispers. I don't know if he needed me or if it was a favor to my mom, but there was no interview, no reference checks. He hired me, and now I work the bar sometimes and work in his office during the week," Lacy says, shrugging like it is no big deal. I barely see her out of my peripheral vision as my eyes remain locked with my neighbor while she talks. He's wearing what seems to be his signature black button-down, open at the collar, his hair looking like he has run his hand through it a few times. Sitting back, one arm slung over the back of the booth, he nurses what looks like a glass of whiskey. He is watching me closely. *Probably wondering how to kill me and hide the body.*

"Tanner is with Hudson for dinner," Jasmine says, filling me in on the other guy.

"Hudson?" I am not sure what is in the water around here, but the men in this town are the most attractive I have ever come across.

"He is a doctor in LA. But he grew up here, comes back a lot. I think he might move back and take over the medical clinic, or at least Tanner is trying to talk him into it since our resident doctor will be retiring soon," Lacy says, and I see her blush a little talking about him. *Interesting.*

"Tanner wanted to buy Marie's," I murmur, taking another sip of my margarita, hoping to get the whiskey taste out of my mouth.

"I know. He isn't used to not getting what he wants around here," Lacy warns.

"Well, he isn't getting my place." I say it with a smile,

and we get back to the topic of renovations and the happenings around town.

After a couple of hours, I am trying to rehydrate with water and feeling sleepy, all the work I did today and the fact that my goat kept me up all night finally catching up to me.

"So, Victoria, I didn't think to mention this earlier, but I can't push it from my mind after hearing what you said about Tanner..." Jasmine says warily, and that makes me uneasy.

"What is it?" I ask, turning to face her.

"I heard he put in a request for adverse possession."

"I don't know what that is..." I can feel my brow pinching as I wait for her to explain.

"Essentially, he had his legal team put forward that given the time and energy he has spent over the years at the property and assisting Marie, he applied for owner-ship. I only know because I heard some guys talking about it when they came into the shop to grab flowers for their wives. I think most of the town knows."

My head swivels to Lacy, but she looks just as dumb-founded as I do. "I had no idea," she says, frowning. "It doesn't sound like something he would do..."

With my stomach suddenly in knots, I finish my glass of water, trying to wrap my mind around this.

"I could be mistaken. But I know Tanner, and he always goes after what he wants." Jasmine jumps off her stool. "Well, I have to run. I have to be up early to get to the flower markets in Williamstown tomorrow," she says, referring to one of the other larger towns nearby, acting like she didn't just drop a bomb on me.

"Thanks for tonight," I tell her, giving her a small hug, happy to have had a great night and met two amazing new friends. But now I'm also feeling a little off, knowing my neighbor is digging his heels in to get my property.

"I'll bring some wine around tomorrow night. I want to see what you are doing with the place," she says, and I smile.

"I would love that. You too, Lacy," I tell them both and they nod. I watch Jasmine go, and Lacy walks over to the booths to offer last drinks.

I should go. I need to organize myself for tomorrow so I can start bright and early, then get some sleep. If that's even possible. I now also need to do some more research and see if this legal paperwork Tanner has submitted has any legs.

"A nightcap for you, from Tanner," Lacy says, putting a glass in front of me and pouring another shot of whiskey. It is from a different bottle than the last one, but the branding is the same.

"Ahhh, thanks?" I say, unsure, and she just smiles and gets back to other customers. I sit staring at it for a moment. Turning the glass around in my hand, I look at the liquid in different lights. It kind of reminds me of the color of his eyes a little with those gold flecks. I lean down and smell it. The aroma almost burns my nose hairs. Again, it is strong, and honestly not my favorite.

"You gonna drink that or look at it?" His low grumble comes from beside me, and my heart picks up pace as I look at him.

"What's so special about it?" I ask, pulling my eyes from his handsome good looks and back to the glass in front of me, not understanding how Whiteman's can be any better or different than others. All liquor is the same, isn't it? I also debate throwing it in his face after what Jasmine just told me. But I need to be smart about this. It could just be small-town gossip and I don't want to make enemies in front of the entire town here tonight.

Even though I'm not looking at him, he is hard to miss. He stands close. I can smell him. A woodsy cologne, very masculine, just like the man himself. My body starts to betray me, but I take a deep breath and stare at the whiskey.

He pulls up a stool next to me and sits, one arm on the bar, his body facing me, and I look at him again. Swallowing hard, I take him in. His dark shirt is crisp, the kind you know is made of good quality and professionally pressed. With the collar open, I can see a sprinkle of chest hair, some gray, showing his age. Jaw tight, his eyes sparkle, and I take in another deep breath. It isn't the first time we have been this close. In fact, over the past few days, I have been physically closer to him than I have anyone else. I can see a few people looking at us with interest. Great, more small-town gossip.

"This whiskey is a single malt. Using barley from our farmlands. It is aged in oak casks that I individually select from our supplier in Southern California. This single malt is the same recipe my father used over thirty years ago to make the very first batch of Whiteman's. Although it wasn't a business then, more just his hobby. But our family blood still runs through both this whiskey and this town."

I appreciate the lesson in whiskey. *Is this the start of our truce?*

"I don't drink whiskey. I don't know anything about oak casks or barley. But I know family. Family is important to me," I tell him, nodding.

"Good. So are you gonna stop being a pain in my ass and sell me that property?" he asks, and at first I think he has to be joking, but then his eyes thin as they search mine. I sigh, chest burning with disappointment. He clearly just came to talk to me because he still wants my property, not for any other reason.

"Like you said, Tanner. It's about family. Aunt Marie was my family and she left me her place to look after. It is important that I do that. For her and for me," I say, slipping off the stool, grabbing my bag, and walking out the door, leaving him and the shot of whiskey at the bar.

Now I'm even more determined to get back to work... and get my mind off my annoying neighbor.

11

TANNER

I watch her walk away from me, and again regret is a bitter pill to swallow. Why can't I get it together around her and stop being a jerk? Yes, I want her property. I am a businessman, after all, and I need to try and go after what I want. But I don't need to be a total asshole. Instead of making nice conversation tonight, I railroaded her again. So much so, she couldn't wait to get away from me. Yet another thing about her that is different from every other woman I meet.

She left the glass on the bar. Full of our best release, the one that costs upward of fifty dollars per pour, and she didn't even do more than sniff it. She also left me sitting here. Alone. I should have known better than to approach her in such a public setting. The two of us will become hot gossip before the weekend is over if the looks I'm getting are any inclination.

I glance back at the door she just walked through and crack my neck. She is as maddening as she is fucking beautiful.

"Seems like she got under your skin, boss," Lacy says as she wipes down the bar and smirks. Lacy is a nice young girl I hired a few months ago. A local girl who went away for college and had to come home once she graduated because her mom is sick. She needed work to pay for medical bills, so I hired her, made up a job for her, and now she does whatever I need her to do. Tonight, it is tending bar. Next week, I'll probably have her help out at the distillery. I plan to put her marketing degree to good use once Connor gets back to town to manage her.

Grabbing the glass of whiskey, I throw it down, raising my eyebrows at Lacy before walking back to the table.

"So you managed to run a woman off. That is a first," Hudson says, smirking.

"She's my new neighbor." I maneuver my tired body into the booth, positive he has already worked it out.

"Marie's niece?" he confirms, and his smile gives him away. I already know he has been speaking to Connor. The two of them are as thick as thieves these days.

"Apparently." I'm being short because I'm pissed off. Pissed off I can't get this property and pissed off that I want to see her again even more.

"She doesn't look anything like Marie," Hudson remarks.

"That is because Marie was old and gray and knew more swear words than a damn dictionary." I huff, thinking about my old neighbor. She was a strong, capable, tough woman. Traits I think her niece has inherited.

"She looked pretty hot, actually... Not many women around here would wear bright-pink lipstick like that,"

Hudson says, and my narrowed eyes flick to him. He is here temporarily, and I don't need him looking at her lips. He and his brother Huxley grew up here, but like most kids, they left for college, and now Hudson is a single dad who resides in LA with his young son.

"Ohhhh, I get it." His smile widens.

"What?" I bite out.

"A pretty thing like that comes to town, who wouldn't want to have her. Even Mr. Cold Heart over here might defrost a little?" he pushes me, and my frown deepens.

I don't get involved with local women. For a man like me, who likes to be home here in Whispers rather than anywhere else, that has been challenging. Not only is there no one here who piques my interest, but I also don't like to be town gossip in that way. But Victoria... she's getting to me. She makes my heart race.

I watched her all night as she laughed with the girls. The way her hair swished around in a ponytail teased me to grab it. Her pink-coated lips had me swallowing harshly. She is fit, young, and full of spirit. The blond bombshell is the complete opposite of me. My eyes were glued to her, taking in every inch of her body from the moment she walked in, the jeans that fit her ass too well, and the smile that looked like she was having too much of a good time in my town.

"Tanner, are you even listening to a damn word I am saying?" Hudson asks, eyeing me suspiciously.

"Not interested," I tell him, my scowl firmly in place.

"You're never interested." Hudson sighs like I am a lost cause.

"They're only trouble," I grumble.

"That one looks like a whole lot of trouble. The kind of trouble that I would like to find."

I notice his eyes following Lacy's movements around the bar, and I clear my throat so he looks at me.

"When are you going to move past it all? Connor's mom left over three decades ago, and you still won't commit to anyone else. Please tell me it doesn't hurt for that long?" he asks, and I feel bad. Hudson was married to a nice city girl for before she fell ill with cancer and lost her life to it. Like me, he is now a single dad, although his son is young. I sure hope he finds someone.

"Enough about women. Let's talk about when you are moving back here. We need you to run the medical clinic and be lead doctor at the hospital." Hudson regularly visits, but it wasn't until his wife died that he began to spend more and more time here.

"What do you mean? I am working here for a few weeks already." It's true. He is staying for a month to get a feel for it. To see if it is what he wants before he commits. Our current doctor is nearing retirement, and Hudson is more than qualified for the job.

"You know me, always trying to bring good people to Whispers," I say with a small smile, happy to have him back home.

"I have a feeling that your neighbor is good people." Giving me a nod, he raises his eyebrow, almost challenging me to contest that statement.

"Time will tell."

I FLEW OUT of Whispers a few days ago, and my shoulders feel tight as I sit in our New York office boardroom, talking to Connor. The multimillion-dollar view from our office is of gray clouds today. From so high up, the rush and noise of people and cars don't infiltrate.

"That meeting went well," Connor says with a proud smile.

We both just met with Valerie Van Cleef and talked through her proposal to make Whiteman's the exclusive supplier to all her hospitality venues. The deal is good, one of our best ones to date, and Connor is to thank for that. While he has a good financial mind, my skill set lies in whiskey making and brand building. That is why I am still the president and he is my VP. But he knows Whiteman's will all be his one day.

"Are you coming home soon?" I ask him, because he has been out here for weeks securing this deal. We both like to be in Whispers as much as we can, and I know he is itching to get home. Our team here handles the day-to-day requirements, and Connor and I both take remote meetings from Whispers as much as possible. For him, he still needs to fly here monthly, but for me, a little less so.

"Yeah, the city is getting to be a bit much for me, and I miss the distillery," he says, sitting in the chair next to me.

I pull at my tie, feeling too constricted now that we're able to relax. I suit up whenever I come to the city, but I prefer my jeans and shirt.

"The distillery misses you too," I tell him, grabbing his shoulder. I am proud of my boy, but I do miss him when he is gone.

"Did you find that timber you were after?" Connor

asks me. I have been trying to find the perfect grain for a new project. But no matter what I find, I always come back to the used whiskey barrels. There is something about using recycled wood, giving it another life, and keeping the whiskey barrel alive longer that makes me take great pleasure in my hobby.

"Not yet. Might use the stack of old barrels out back," I tell him, thinking more about it.

"So... how's Victoria? Heard she was at the bar the other night," he says, a small grin coming to his face. Hudson must have spoken to him. Bastards are ganging up on me.

"Seems she is pals with Jasmine and Lacy already," I tell him with a shrug, acting like I don't really care.

"She fits right in, then. Have you asked her out yet?" He already knows the answer to that question, yet he likes to rile me up.

"Don't be stupid," I scoff, not giving him an inch.

"You should!"

"You haven't even met her. She is infuriating." That might be a lie. More like, she's not what I was expecting.

"Yeah, but you are thinking about her. She moved next door, and I would guess you have seen her nearly every day since."

I think about his words. It hasn't been every day... I've been here in the city for most of this week.

"That's because I want her property." Even though I have hardly thought about our expansion since she firmly rejected it at the bar.

"Keep telling yourself that, old man," he says slyly, and I ignore him. "So I've got some info on her."

"You waited this long to tell me?" I say, my voice a little raised as I look at him sharply.

"Calm down. I didn't realize it was that important. My financial background check picked up that she rents an apartment close to the Upper East Side," he starts, and I nod. It is a nice part of the city.

"She did work in advertising, until recently."

I assume she left that to move to Whispers. Brave of her.

"Boyfriend?" I ask too quickly, and Connor watches me closely.

"That kind of information doesn't come up in a finance search... but I did see some deposits for a wedding venue on her credit details." He eyes me suspiciously, and I frown. "I also looked up Marie as well. She had a brother, so that must be the connection."

"I had no idea. She never said anything about family, and I never met him over the years."

"He looks like he has a bit of a sketchy past, been bankrupt a few years ago... but didn't have the same address as Victoria for the past two decades, at least," he explains, and my eyebrows shoot to my hairline.

"What else?" I ask. This level of digging we don't normally do, but I am interested in what he found out.

"He doesn't sound like an upstanding guy. He has a criminal history too. Nothing too bad, but nothing light either. Armed robbery and shoplifting, mostly."

"So she is estranged from her father, raised by a single mother. Her father's family left her their property, and now..." I trail off, my thoughts once again becoming consumed with the blond beauty.

"Now, you need to ask her out," Connor says, and my eyes shoot to his with an exasperated sigh.

"*Now*, I need to get to the car; otherwise, I won't get home until late." I stand, ending this conversation, not needing any more of his input on the topic of my neighbor. "See you at home in a few days?"

"Hopefully earlier," he confirms, standing and giving me a hug. It's only ever been the two of us. We are close. I slap him on the shoulder as I walk away and straight to the lift to get to my waiting town car.

I hate people driving me, but here in the city, it makes more sense. Within the hour, I am in my jet with both my tie and my jacket off. I have my helicopter at the Whispers airport to fly me directly to the distillery today instead of driving. We have some VIPs coming in for the weekend. They usually have a private tour with me, a long lunch in our restaurant, and I like to have my chopper there for them for any day trips or quick getaways after they finish their tour, lunch, and tastings. *That* is why I need to build accommodations. People would love to stay for the weekend, and I just need to start building.

Looking at my watch, I should land midafternoon. I wonder what my new neighbor is up to.

12

VICTORIA

After a full afternoon with little Kevin from down the road, I feel a little more relaxed as I finish drying my hair. He is a good kid. He has been here every day after school to milk the large cow that seems content, and he takes the milk home with him.

I realize I have no idea where exactly he lives, but if he needs milk for his family, I am happy to continue providing it. We spent time together today and he showed me how to handle the milking process. I was one hundred percent awkward, but I got the hang of it eventually. He tells me I should also milk her twice a day, so I might give it a try once renovations have finished.

The house looks amazing. After Jasmine and Lacy came over on the weekend for wine night, they ended up coming back the next day to give me a hand. Plus, with a surprise visit from Bob from the hardware store, who dropped by with a delivery and ended up staying, the four of us got a solid two coats on the outside by the end of the weekend, and I finished off the inside myself after painting each night this week. I am exhausted, but the place is already brighter, and when the sun shines through, it looks even better.

Now, as I walk around freshly showered from our yard work and cleaning up, I throw on my robe over my underwear and tie it around my waist, then duck outside to look for fresh eggs to make a late afternoon snack.

I find three eggs in the chicken coop and smile as I place them in my basket, next to the herbs I picked earlier from the small vegetable patch Marie started, feeling like a lady of the land. Locking up the chicken enclosure, I sit on the porch steps of the house and bask in the late afternoon sunshine. I couldn't do this back in the city. It feels nice to have the sunlight on my bare legs, and I close my eyes, soaking up the warmth.

My cell ringing beside me interrupts my peaceful moment, and I grab it, already having a feeling who it is. And I'm right as I see Josh's name on the screen. This is the fourth time he's called just today. I should block him, but I answer instead.

"Josh, what do you want?" I ask through my irritation.

"At long last, you answer," he says smugly.

"What do you want?" I ask again, no warmth in my tone. I shiver a little, my choice of being outside with just a robe probably not as smart as I first thought.

"I want to talk to you. We left everything so... uncertain."

There was nothing uncertain about the way he had sex in my bed with another woman.

"We are over, Josh. You need to stop calling me. It is

getting ridiculous." My shoulders feel tense. I wish he would just let me get on with my life.

"We are not over, Victoria. I love you. We are getting married!"

Even though he can't see me, I roll my eyes in annoyance.

"The wedding is canceled. I am not marrying you. We are no longer together," I tell him like he doesn't already know, ready to end this pointless conversation.

"Fiona says you're traveling. Where are you?" He switches tack, and I almost get whiplash.

"I'm with family. Now stop calling and move on. Goodbye, Josh." I hang up immediately, not wanting to entertain him further. No sooner have I ended the call than he calls again. So I go back to ignoring him. Eventually, he will get the hint. *I hope.*

Pushing him out of my mind, I snap a shot of my garden and basket of eggs with my bare painted toes in the background for my socials, quickly posting it with the hashtag #ladyoftheland. I take a few moments to look through and see that my followers have grown rapidly since just the other night, my mother loving the photo instantaneously, which makes me smile. I scroll through, looking at my previous posts, before my phone shrieks in my hand, and Fiona's name lights up the screen.

"Hey," I say quickly. This call is already better than the last.

"That is such a cute photo. Are they fresh eggs?" she asks, and I giggle.

"Straight from the coop!" I tell her with a broad smile.

"It looks better there than this stupid cubicle," she

huffs out, and I imagine her typing away at her computer in the small office in the city, the iridescent lighting showering her from above. I am even more grateful for the fact that I am here, in the fresh air, in the sunlight, experiencing something new.

"The farm is great, and I have so many photos. I keep finding new things." The property provides fantastic content from the garden, the views, the plants. Even the shed, the equipment, and the truck. It all paints a picture of small-town, rural life. *My new life.* Looking back on everything now, I feel a sense of accomplishment at how I have been able to not only make the move, but also start to get the place in order and meet new friends.

"Any nice men there?" she teases, and I roll my lips.

"None. I have a very annoying neighbor, though, and he wants my property..." I've been meaning to share this with her.

"Oh, interesting! Tell me more."

This is probably the most exciting thing she's heard today from her eager tone. It makes me laugh.

"His name's Tanner, and he owns Whiteman's Whiskey. He is somewhat of a town hero, it seems. Everyone likes him and everyone knows him. His distillery is next door and he wants to buy this place. Obviously, I told him no. But Fiona, he is like... God's gift to women everywhere." Just thinking about him, my heart races. I can't remember a man who has gotten under my skin as much as he has. "But of course, he is arrogant and annoying and..."

"Hmm... you said that already," she teases me, and I huff.

"He is older, at least a decade or two older than me."

"So? Who cares about age?" She snorts at me like I am being ridiculous, and she is right, age is nothing but a number. It certainly hasn't stopped the visions I have been having of him at night. The very naughty images. Clearly, I am just having crazy thoughts. Who in their right mind would have sexy thoughts about their maddening neighbor? I should be thinking of ways to get rid of him, the same way he is thinking about me. I know all he wants is my property.

"You're right. What are you up to anyway?" I ask, changing the subject before she puts any more crazy thoughts in my head.

"Well, I wanted to ensure farm life was still treating you well and to also let you know that Josh has started calling me, continually asking where you are. Apparently, he has been banging on your apartment door and the super told him you have left for a few months," she says, and a groan rumbles from my chest.

"I just spoke to him and confirmed that we are no longer together. Hopefully he stops calling you now too. I have no idea why he even cares."

I might be exhausted with all the work I am doing here, but I am also happy. The happiest I have been in a long time. My mother was right; this change in my life has been so good, and with spring now in the air, I feel my season of change blooming as Whispers slowly becomes home. The last thing I need is my cheating ex to cause trouble.

"He is a cheating asshole. Probably thought his life was planned out. Work on Wall Street, marry a smart, beautiful woman, but keep some candy on the side. He is such a moron. What do you want me to tell him?" she asks, and I have no idea. I am a far cry from the city professional I was. It is like my life has done a complete one-eighty.

"God, if Josh could see me now." I laugh at myself. Bare legs out, sitting on my porch in a robe, surrounded by grass and plants and a goat.

"If you look so delightful, take a selfie and put it up on your channel. I can let him know your new social media details and it might work in scaring him away."

"I have a feeling nothing will scare him away," I tell her honestly. It isn't like he is just calling occasionally. His calls to me are increasing to numerous times a day. It's gotten disturbing.

"Maybe take a selfie with that hot neighbor of yours and post that instead. I just searched him up online, and he is pretty damn good-looking... and rich. Hell, did you know he is a billionaire?" She gasps.

"I didn't, but I'm not surprised. He came in here flashing his checkbook. Money or not, he is just another man who won't take no for an answer." I haven't seen him since the bar. Since he offered me a shot of whiskey and yet again asked about buying my property. He is persistent.

"At least you always have Garry," she quips, and I look over to see where my friendly goat is, and he is looking straight at me before he bleats. He is getting fat. I am sure he is bigger than he was when I first arrived. It must be all this long grass he is eating. At least I don't have to mow it with him around.

Hearing a weird thud in the distance, I stand up, looking around, trying to figure out what it is. A black dot in the sky comes closer before it is almost right on top of me. *A helicopter?* I squint into the sun as it flies over my property. Shiny black with gold writing on the side. It is so close it is blowing my trees and causes Garry to start running around berserk. *Shit, I left the gate open.*

"What is that noise?" I hear Fiona ask.

"My horrible neighbor! I gotta go. Call you later." Throwing my cell down near my basket of produce, I jump from the porch.

"Garry!" I scream over the loud noise, hoping to get his attention, but it's no use. Barefoot, I break into a run over to the far side of the yard to shut the gate before he runs through it. Just as the chopper passes by, I get there in time, puffing out a breath as I lock it. My feet are no longer nice and clean, but rather a little dirty and muddy from the run. As I look back at Garry, he's running in the other direction, then putting his head in my basket, eating some of the herbs I picked from the garden.

"Garry! No!" I scold him and take off running again, the grass and dirt underfoot making me cringe as it squishes through my toes, before I stumble a little. "Dammit." I should have just gotten changed and put shoes on like a normal person after my shower. Taking another a step, I stumble forward, feeling a sharp pain shoot through my ankle, enough to take my breath away before I start to fall.

"Ahhhh!" I yell out to no one as I face-plant onto the ground, my body landing with a thud.

"Oohhhhhh." I groan, seeing stars for a moment as

my nose throbs. Pushing off the muddy soil, I try to breathe through the pain in my ankle. I look down at my feet, seeing blood and a cut across my skin. It isn't too deep, but it stings badly. *Of course this would only happen to me.*

When I notice my robe, I curse. I might be good at interior design, but right now, I look like a zombie, my robe streaked with mud and probably Garry's shit. The new black lace underwear set I have on underneath is the only thing on my body that looks remotely clean, but clearly, it isn't farm appropriate. So much for romanticizing my life today. Who wears lace underwear when they're just walking around at home, alone?

I try to stand but hiss as the pressure on my ankle increases the sting. Between my throbbing face and ankle, I am sore from tip to toe. Walking is out of the question. I can't even hop because I feel a little dizzy. There is no fence nearby to pull myself up on, and I look around but can't find any stray sticks to use as a walking stick.

Feeling the sting in my ankle increasing, as is the blood flow, I look up at the house now fifty yards away, seeing my basket of eggs and herbs sitting on the porch near my cell phone. Garry stares at me like he is wondering what the hell I am doing, but I don't miss the green herbs dangling from his lips as he continues to chew.

"This can't be happening..." I moan, frustrated that I have hurt myself. I feel my nose and move it a little to ensure it isn't broken because it still throbs. It isn't, thank God, but my eyes water at the continual sting

pulsating through my cheekbones. I hope I don't get black eyes.

I have no idea what to do. I don't know exactly how bad it is, but I have a feeling walking isn't a good option. As I sit here, I pull my short robe down to try to cover my bare thighs, my eyes flicking around my property, hoping that some idea comes to me. I try to crab walk, but I can't even do that because that causes the blood to run a little more.

Lying back on the grass, I gaze at the blue sky above me to gather my thoughts, feeling helpless and stupid. If I can't make it to the house to at least get my phone, I will probably be here all night until Kevin comes back and finds me tomorrow.

I swallow the thought of being so alone out here, looking across the long grass at what hit my leg. And that's when I spot a steel stake sticking out of the ground, barely above the grass, almost completely hidden. I have no idea where that came from. It isn't mine, and I assume it must be old, but it looks new, still silver and shiny.

"Come on, Victoria, think!" I scold myself out loud, which causes a bleat from Garry. I give him the evil eye. We are no longer friends.

"I should have let you run out of the gate," I grumble to him.

I see and hear no one, and with no way to call anyone and no visitors expected, I do the only thing I can think of. I pull my arms into my torso tight and start to roll. Like a pencil, I roll slowly along the grass. I remember doing this at the park as a kid. Back then, it was fun, and I giggled nonstop. My mom took photos. But now, as mud and Garry's shit coat my bare legs and beautiful satin robe, and with my ankle throbbing and bleeding, joy is not the emotion I am experiencing.

I scrunch my nose as my face and hair get coated in mud as well. I hear Garry bleat again, and I stop mid-roll, looking at him, his eyes watching me like he is thoroughly confused now.

"Don't laugh! This is all your fault!" I chastise him before he goes back to eating the herbs from my basket and I focus on what I am doing. My roll is slow, my ankle painful, so I close my eyes, grit my teeth, and take a deep breath before continuing.

"I love this farm. I love this farm. I love this farm," I start to chant quietly to myself. At this rate, I should get to my phone before Garry eats it.

I hope.

13

TANNER

The chopper lands at the distillery, and I jump out quickly, the blades starting to slow, but the wind gusts still blow. I know she is home because I saw her out the window as we were coming in. The one woman I can't seem to stop fucking thinking about. It looked like she was wearing a pink robe, and her long legs looked fucking amazing, almost as good as her perfectly painted toes in the image she just posted to her socials.

I'm not on social media much, but when she tagged the bar with an image of her and the girls, I had a look at her page. I am now more addicted to social media than I ever have been before. Seeing the work she is doing on the house in her before-and-after photos, it is impressive, especially in such a short amount of time.

It's been almost a week since I saw her in the bar, and she looks even better than I remember. So does the house. She has painted the outside and the garden's a little tidier already. She must have gotten help, because there is no way one person could have accomplished all that in a week. I need to find out who is helping her and get them to stop. The more work she does, the less likely she is to sell, and I want that property.

The chopper obviously startled her. She was running after the goat. I feel bad for not warning her. I know the chopper scares the animals, and since she arrived, I haven't told her that choppers are in use around here at times.

"I need you to go over the stock. I have the new batch ready for tasting," Lacy says as I walk through the distillery door. She follows behind me quickly, notepad in hand, no doubt a list a mile long for me to start ticking off since I have been away for most of the working week. I usually hit the ground running when I get home. There are always things to do, paperwork to sign, staff issues to deal with.

"I'll be back in a minute. I just need to check on something," I tell her, walking straight past her, through the distillery, and out the front door to my waiting truck.

"But—" She looks at me, mouth agape. She is clearly surprised because I normally don't land and then leave again. But I won't be long. I'll just check if Victoria is okay with the animals and then come back and get straight into it.

"Five minutes!" I say, jumping into my truck and then driving down the road. In less than one, I am pulling up to my neighbor's house and start walking around the back to where I saw her last.

"Victoria?" I call out but hear nothing. I just saw her

out of the helicopter window and her truck is sitting in the drive, so I know she is here.

"Hello?" I shout as I turn the corner of the house, admiring the paint job. I only make it a few more steps before I stop short as I see her on the ground in the backyard. Her arms are tucked by her sides and she is rolling toward the house like a pencil or something. But it is the fact that she is wearing next to nothing, her long legs bare all the way up to what looks like black lace underwear, that has me swaying on my feet.

What the hell is she doing? I watch her, confused. Her eyes are closed, and she is talking to herself or the goat or something. Walking toward her, I stand, waiting for her approach, but she doesn't notice me and she rolls right into my feet. Her eyes flick open, and she screams.

"Ahhhhh!" Her voice is high-pitched as her body freezes across my feet.

"You alright down there?" I ask her with a frown, though I'm a bit amused. She is disheveled, grass tangled in her hair. I am not sure why she's only wearing a pink robe, considering it is the middle of the afternoon, but as it gapes a little at the chest, I swallow roughly. Her eyes are wide and my nostrils flare as I take a breath and immediately wish I hadn't.

She smells like shit. Literally.

"I fell and hurt my ankle. Don't you knock?" she says, looking at me accusingly but making no attempt to get up as she lies at my feet like a fucking offering that is becoming increasingly hard to deny. Her hair is splayed around her on the bright-green grass, her chest rising and falling in quick breaths, and I need to clear my throat to get my head back in the game.

"How did you fall?" I ask, looking around. There is nothing high around here for her to fall off. I can't see any ladders.

"I was trying to get Garry away from my herbs—"

"Garry?" I ask, totally confused.

"Garry the goat?" I look at her like she is crazy. *Why the hell is she calling a female goat Garry?* And I can't believe she has already hurt herself. She will kill herself out here if she isn't careful, and while I want her property, I don't need her death on my conscience.

"Yes, Garry and I still haven't become firm friends, but I am hopeful," she says on a breath, starting to calm down, but then I see her wince.

I spot the measuring tape and things on the back porch when I glance back at the house. There are boxes galore from various shops on the porch. Clearly, she has been ordering a lot online, the deliveries arriving today.

"You've started renovating, I see."

"Yep, it needs some more work, but it has good bones." She looks up at me suspiciously.

"So you're definitely staying, then?" I need to hear her say it.

"That's the plan."

I can't hold back my sigh.

"Can you walk?" I ask, shoving away my frustration. Looking down her body to her ankle, I see it is already purple and the size of a large potato, with blood also trickling. My jaw clenches, hating that she is hurt.

"Yes. I mean... I think. I don't really know. I tripped

over a stake that I didn't see in the long grass. Marie must have been planning on building something." Her words stumble over each other, and I immediately feel like shit. They must be the stakes that Griffin put into the ground months ago before we knew anything about her. I didn't bother removing them, because at the time, we thought the property was as good as mine. Since then, I totally forgot. *Probably because all I have been thinking about is her.*

"Better get you inside," I murmur before I lean over and put my arms underneath her knees and shoulders.

"Ahh, what are you doing!" She gasps, her hands gripping on to my neck.

"This alright?" I ask as I lift her, sealing her to my chest. She feels way too good in my arms. My voice seems to have lowered an octave on its own, and again, I clear my throat, trying to get a handle on myself. I am never flustered with women.

"Are you planning on taking me out back and putting me out of my misery or getting me medical attention?" She says it with a little humor, and my mouth quirks. Her hands wrap in my shirt, her head resting on my shoulder, making her lips too fucking close to mine. I grit my teeth.

"You need medical attention." I confirm the latter as I start walking with her in my arms back to the house.

"I am sure I will be fine. I just need ice."

"Do you have a first aid kit?" I ask, knowing if she doesn't, then she needs one.

"I think I saw one in the kitchen. But you don't have to carry me. I smell like shit!" It's like she just realized with the way her head pops up from my shoulder, eyes wide.

"Believe me, I know," I tell her as I open the back door

to her place and take a few steps forward, planting her on the kitchen counter. She has made the place nice. It is a vast improvement already to what it was. It has life. Character. I carefully help her adjust her leg on the stool so she is comfortable, and she closes her eyes, taking a breath like she is exhausted. Looking at the backyard and then back at her, I have a feeling she has been working all day and all night to get this place to how it looks today.

"You still are not taking no for an answer, are you?" she asks with a quirked eyebrow, resigned to the fact that I am looking after her leg whether she likes it or not. I lean across her to grab a small twig from her hair, our bodies close. We are merely inches apart, and I can feel her hot breath trace across my cheek as she looks at me. I have the urge to lean in more, but I blink a few times and come back to earth, grabbing the twig and throwing it across to the sink.

"I rarely do. Only one person has said no to me so far this year, and I am looking at her," I tell her honestly before I turn around and open the cupboard closest to the refrigerator, knowing that is where Marie always kept her first aid kit, grinning as I see it is still there.

As I walk back to her, a small smile on my face, I have a feeling this might be our ceasefire.

14

VICTORIA

Mortification doesn't really come close to what I am feeling at the moment. Completely immobile, lost most of my independence since I can't walk or even limp and currently smell like a disgusting sewer with goat shit all over me. Not to mention, I am still in my robe, so I am completely self-conscious that I am almost nude. And to top it off, the person coming to my rescue is the one man who is trying to take my land.

"I have ruined your shirt," I murmur as I look at him. He is dressed differently today in suit pants and a crisp white shirt—well, except for the mud that now coats it— like he has just come from a business meeting.

"It's just a shirt." His eyes stay on the first aid kit as he digs around for whatever he is looking for.

"It's a nice shirt." I like the way it fits over his broad shoulders.

"It's still just a shirt," he confirms, his eyes meeting mine before running down my body quickly, then going back to the first aid kit. He is wearing a different Rolex than the last time I saw him. This one is silver and glistens in the light every time he moves his wrist.

I catch my reflection in the kitchen window and almost die on the spot. I look like I was dragged through the forest backward. My hair is everywhere, twigs and grass sticking out from my strands. As suspected, I have dirt all over my cheeks, and my nose is swollen and a little red. I belong in a horror movie.

"You look fine," he mumbles next to me, my hands stopping midair as they brush through my hair.

"I look like I have been deserted in a forest for a century!" I didn't think he was that old, but can he not see me properly?

He looks over at me, those eyes drifting down my body once more, and my traitorous heart starts to thud at his inspection.

"You look good to me."

I almost forget to breathe. *Is he complimenting me?* As I stare at his side profile, I notice his jaw pop.

"I will pay for your dry cleaning," I tell him, wondering if there is a dry cleaner in Whispers or if I have to take it to a nearby town.

"No need." He's now a man of few words, it seems. The air feels a little thick between us with it being so quiet in my kitchen. This is the first time we have been together like this, in a small space for a longer period of time.

He concentrates on grabbing the bandages and antiseptic, and I observe the small creases in his face, showing history, dependability. The dark stubble on his jaw has a scattering of gray, making him look both distinguished and rugged. What is it like to kiss a man with stubble? Josh was always clean-shaven, and past boyfriends the same.

I pull my head away from him and look back out the window. I need to stop these thoughts. He is my neighbor. He is after my land, and I can't let my guard down. Even if his hard-set face seems to soften for me. I did that with Josh and look what happened. He completely swiped my legs out from under me. He made me feel stupid and unwanted. There is no way I want to ever feel like that again.

"What was with the chopper anyway?" I ask, curious since this debacle all stemmed from that.

"I just got back from a week in the city. We have private guests that come out to the distillery, and I have some booked for lunch this weekend. So, I leave the chopper at the distillery while they are there in case it is needed for a quick getaway or tour of the region. I should have told you about it earlier." His eyes flick to me. *Is that an apology from the grumpiest man I have ever met?*

"So Whispers really is a playground for the wealthy, then?"

"I'll never tell," he teases, and a small smile comes to my face at his attempt at humor. "So why are you barefoot and only wearing a robe out in the yard?" he asks, and I swallow, my mortification coming back to me full force. At least we are not biting each other's heads off, although I am still wary of him.

"I just showered and was running out quickly to grab some eggs. Obviously, it wasn't such a good idea."

"The robe or the eggs?" He lifts my ankle to get a better look at it.

"The robe," I confirm, wincing as he dabs it with a wet cotton ball.

"The robe looks good. In need of a wash, but it looks good." He swallows audibly, and his Adam's apple bobs. I forget to breathe.

We remain silent for a moment as he cleans my ankle, and I clear my throat. "Apparently, I loved gardening here with Marie when I was younger, so maybe that is why I enjoy running around barefoot so much," I say with a small smile, trying to inject a little humor before I completely suffocate around this man. His brow furrows as he looks at me.

"She never mentioned anything about you."

I am not sure if it is meant to be accusing or not, but I let it slide.

"I don't remember her, and my mom fell out of touch with her over a decade ago, but we visited, and her and my mom wrote to each other." I want him to know that there is a connection for me here. He can't just swoop in and take what isn't his.

"The property has good soil due to the natural springs a few hundred yards away on your property, so you should be able to grow anything," he says, and I whip my head around to look at him.

"Natural springs?" I ask, confused. I didn't see any of that mentioned in the plan or the paperwork I signed.

"Just over the backyard and down the hill. They are yours. On your property. I don't think they are listed on the plans, but the kids from town, from time to time, like to sneak in and take a dip. Otherwise, it is left alone."

"Is that why you want the place?" I ask, broaching the sore subject.

"One of," he confirms simply, and I leave it at that.

"I plan on going exploring some more once I get the house in a bit more order. Although now my plans might be delayed." I wince again as I attempt to move my leg slightly. His eyes shoot to me, deep concern etched in his brow before he realizes I am okay.

"What else have you got planned?" He seems genuinely interested as he opens a Band-Aid.

"I have new blinds getting installed on Monday. I also have someone coming to help replace the shower screen and bathroom vanity later in the week." He looks at me surprised but doesn't say anything. "I work fast when I am passionate about something." I shrug.

"There, as good as new. Maybe don't go walking around out there barefoot anymore. You're on a farm, so you need to wear boots; it's common sense."

I am not sure whether to thank him for his caring nature or be annoyed at him for telling me what to do.

"Are you trying to tell me what to do on my own property? Or are you saying I have no common sense?" I ask as I try to wiggle off the kitchen counter, feeling at a disadvantage.

He sighs. "You need proper boots is all I'm saying." His head shakes, and my teeth grind. "And a shower."

"You need to stop telling me what to do," I say sharply. "I am perfectly fine." My argument would hold more weight if I wasn't still struggling to get off this stupid kitchen counter without exposing my black lace under-wear to him.

"Let's go," he says as his hands wrap around my waist, and he lifts me completely off the counter like I weigh nothing.

"Ahh, where are *we* going?" I ask through a squeal, looking at him like he is crazy.

"Think you can get to the shower by yourself? Be my guest." Setting me on my feet gently, he makes an exaggerated sway of his arms, encouraging me to go and sort myself out while he stands firm, just looking at me.

"You are infuriating," I mumble as I hobble a little, trying to prove to him that I can walk just fine on my own but failing.

"I'm infuriating? You're a pain in my ass," he says honestly from beside me, sounding much too casual about it while looking ready to catch me when I fall.

"Pain in your ass? *You're* a pain in *my* ass." I make it to the base of the stairs, then look up, not knowing how I am going to do this on my own.

"I'll get you up there, don't you worry." Stepping forward, he swoops me back up into his arms. I quietly seethe in his warm embrace, scrunching my nose, acutely aware that we both now smell like a sewer.

"You are such an asshole," I murmur as I grip on to his shirt, his skin hot underneath.

"I'm helping you, aren't I," he grits out.

"It is because of you I am in this position," I say, exasperated at the entire situation. I hate feeling like a burden, as now as my devastatingly good-looking neighbor walks me up my stairs to the bathroom, I feel exactly that. A burden. "If it wasn't for your stupid helicopter. Who the hell has their own helicopter anyway?" I continue to push him as he places me at the dresser in my room so I can grab some fresh clothes, and I yank the drawer open with purpose.

"I do. I also have my own distillery, my own real estate portfolio, my own city office, my own jet, a penthouse in Manhattan, and a son." His voice rises, even though he's apparently keen to share his entire life with me. Slamming the drawer shut, I open the next one with even more force.

"Why are you so angry with me? This is all your fault!" I shout, throwing some sweats on the bed, along with a shirt, before I look up at him. He is breathing quickly, just as riled up as I am, and neither of us is backing down. As angry as I am at him, he is still the most handsome man I have ever met, and his eyes sparkle back at me, making my heart pound harder.

"You got injured. You were outside in a robe and bare feet, *rolling* in the backyard. Who knows what would have happened if I didn't turn up!" He steps closer, bringing us almost toe to toe.

"That doesn't matter. If it wasn't for your stupid helicopter, none of this would have happened!" I fist my hands tight as his arms cross over his chest. We are going around in circles; it's ridiculous.

"You shouldn't be here on your own. A farm is too much..." Shaking his head, he speaks more calmly this time, and I look at him like I want to gut him. Is he implying I can't handle it?

"I know you want my land. But listen to me, Tanner,

and listen good. I. Am. Not. Selling." I seethe as I point my finger at his very hard chest, and he frowns. Grabbing my finger, he curves his hand around mine, holding it to his beating chest.

"Let's get to the shower," is all he says before his familiar strong hands scoop me up, and I loop my arm around his shoulders, feeling the solid muscle and briefly wondering what he looks like underneath his clothes. I huff, not liking relying on him for this as he walks me to the bathroom, then sets me on my feet. The act genuinely takes me by surprise, with the amount of care and attention I am getting.

"Next time, you should wear boots and not be so clumsy," he says under his breath, and my hackles rise immediately.

"I tripped over something in the backyard," I push back at him as I flick my dirty hair out of my face. *God, what a nightmare.*

"It was a surveyor stick."

My brow crumbles as I look at him.

"How did you..." Realization dawns, and I scowl at him as my fingers grip on to the bathroom door. "You put it there, didn't you?" I feel my face redden as the pent-up anger I have been feeling toward this man rises within me.

"I did." He nods, not even lying about it.

"Unbelievable!" I say, slapping my hand on the door-frame, his concern for me now making sense. He wasn't doing it out of kindness, but rather guilt. "What? How?" Is this a deliberate ploy of his to get my property?

"Over a month ago. Before I knew about you, I

planned out what I wanted to do with the land. I forgot to remove them when you turned up," he explains, his expression stern. At least he is being honest.

"I should sue you. I should have you charged with trespassing!" I will never do it, but I'm sulking just the same.

"As I said... that was over a month ago. I forgot about them. They were not placed to harm you on purpose." He really has the nerve to look grumpier than me right now.

"Well, you can leave. You did your good deed. I am in the bathroom, I am fine," I say, steeling my spine. I look a hot mess and I need to get cleaned up.

"You are not fine. You can barely walk, you smell like shit, you have boxes outside, and the animals need locking up. Or did you forget the amount of work required to run a farm already?"

My shoulders pull up around my ears, but I don't say anything because he is right. Instead, I swallow my pride and take a big breath.

Tanner steps back from me and leans against the far wall, his arms crossed over his chest again, watching me like a hawk as I slowly close the bathroom door on him. I take a big breath and bite my tongue to push past any pain. I am so angry. This is all his fault. None of this would have happened if it wasn't for him.

15

TANNER

She looks cute when she sulks. Her lips purse and she gets these little lines around her mouth that make me want to kiss them away. When her eyes squint, they get this fire in them that is sexy as fuck. I shake my head, trying to dislodge the thoughts.

Leaving her to shower, I make my way down the stairs. I can't look at her anymore because I am so pissed off at this entire situation. I rub my chest, because for the first time in a very long time, my heart feels like it is about to lurch out. Either that or I am having a fucking heart attack. I need to move, to expel energy.

The stress and worry about her hurting herself, along with the realization that my plan to own this property is not progressing like it should, has completely pushed me to the edge. But not as much as the new feeling swirling in my stomach, the one that feels like I am about to take flight just thinking about the fact that she is staying. *Staying.*

I spend the next twenty minutes outside, pulling out

those stupid stakes, and getting her goat *Garry* and the cow into the barn, as it is almost dusk, and locking up the shed. Then I bring in all the boxes and pile them up against the wall in the dining room where I spot some others. By the looks of things, she has single-handedly supported the entire US economy with her spending.

Walking back outside, I collect her basket of eggs, and as I do, I pick up her cell. It lights up with missed calls, many from a contact named *Josh*, and I balk. *Is that her fiancé?* That thought sits heavy in my gut because it is in direct conflict with the image I have of the slither of her black lace underwear that my eyes snagged on to earlier.

As I get back inside, I place everything on the kitchen counter and look at the time, surprised to see it is already late. The sun is lowering, and I have missed the entire afternoon at the distillery—yet another thing that frustrates me. Lacy will be fuming since I told her I would only be gone for five minutes.

"Tanner!" I hear her yelp out for me. She sounds like she's in pain, and I run, panicked, up the stairs, moving at the speed of light. I'm not even thinking until I push open the bathroom door and see her gripping on to the vanity for dear life, her body half on the floor. *In just a towel.* I swear to God, she's teasing me on purpose.

"Shit. What happened?" I jump into action, swallowing harshly as I try and get my shit together. I help her up so she can stand on her good leg.

"I was turning off the taps. One got a little jammed, and I slipped as I tried to tighten it," she says quietly, almost resigned. I look at the taps, noticing one still dripping slightly, and I lean in to tighten it off, the act taking some strength that I know she wouldn't have in her right now.

"You might need a plumber to look at that. Here," I say, passing her a different robe I find hanging on the back of the door. It is thicker and longer than the other one, and I give her my back as she puts it on. Once she is clothed, I walk over to her and gather her under her arms, lifting her off the floor. She smells amazing. Fresh, floral, and it dawns on me that she is completely naked under this robe.

"I can walk," she mumbles, the anger we both had having dissipated. Her hands wrap around my shoulders, the fight all but left her.

"I know," I tell her, not wanting her to think she can't handle anything, because she can. Shit, just moving here on her own is enough to show me she is fiercely independent and capable. I put her back into her room on her feet near the bed. She sucks in a breath as her hands slowly run down my neck from where she was holding me, and we stand facing each other, and she looks up at me like she is trying to figure me out.

The air around us is thick. I try to ignore the feel of her soft body and the way her wet hair falls in waves down her back, making her look like a *Sports Illustrated* model who is walking out of the ocean.

"Thank you. I think I've got it now," she says, her voice low and breathy, and I immediately step away, nodding.

"I'll be downstairs," I confirm before walking out of her bedroom, closing the door behind me, and taking a big breath.

I head straight to the kitchen, seeing her laptop, files,

and rough sketches on the counter. I pick one up. It is a sketch design of a kitchen, and it looks amazing. She has the whole room opened up in an open-plan style, her eye for detail and her spatial awareness not something that can be easily replicated. There is another sketch of an outdoor love seat. Looks like she has plans to place it on the porch. The design is a little different than what you would normally see. More of an oval with soft edges, and I stare at it, appreciating her design skills. I know just by looking at it that it will blend in well with the outdoor area and also complement the house.

My cell vibrates in my pocket again, calling me back to reality.

It's Connor.

"Hey," I say quietly as I walk around the old kitchen, thinking I will start something for dinner since she will find it difficult to do it herself tonight. She is exhausted.

"Where are you?" he asks, sounding concerned.

"The neighbor's house," I murmur, not really concentrating on his question as I have tunnel vision to get food for Victoria. I look inside the cupboards, pulling out some dried pasta that I can cook up quickly for her.

"The neighbor? Lacy has been trying to call you all day. No one knew where you were..." His concern changes to relief, but I can hear his curiosity.

"She hurt herself," I say, boiling the water and diving back into the cupboard for some sauce that I can use. I spot some ready made in a jar, and deciding not to poke around in her cupboard further, I pull that out, a basic pasta meal now in the works.

"Is she okay?" Connor asks.

"She hurt her foot and can't really walk. I'm just locking up the animals."

"Yeah, yeah, just doing the neighborly thing, I am sure," Connor teases, and I sigh.

"Son. I need to ask a favor." The heaviness I thought I would feel in my shoulders at changing business strategy doesn't present like expected.

"What's up?"

"Tell Sawyer to rip up the adverse possession." I know that is the right thing to do. She has plans here, plans to make this house and home and to maybe even stay here. I rub my eyes, the feeling of not going after the thing I want nipping at me. But the image of her sexy-as-sin body wrapped in that towel imprints on the back of my eyelids, so it is all I see whenever I close my eyes, reminding me that there is now something else I am interested in.

"Are you sure? I mean, we have planned on having that land for months now." He is pushing me to look at all angles. It is the smart, sensible thing to do. But I know what is right, and I need to leave Marie's place alone and go with expanding my business on another parcel of land.

"I'm sure. Make the call," I confirm.

"Fine. Our plan B is just as good anyway. I'll call Sawyer now. I'm coming home tomorrow. I managed to get everything sorted this afternoon while you were playing nurse," Connor says, and I smile as I stir the pasta.

"See you then." We end the call just as I hear her.

"Make yourself at home, why don't you." I look up,

seeing her in her sweats, her hair piled high on her head, her face makeup-free and gorgeous. She's like all my dreams rolled into one.

Breathe, Tanner. Just breathe. Fuck, I can't remember the last time I cooked for a woman. As a teenager, I never cooked for Connor's mom. I was too shell-shocked that we were pregnant, and we were still kids ourselves, our own parents managing those type of chores. When Connor arrived, she ran out of town so quickly, there was no time to play domesticated family together. I have dated, sure, but I go out for dinners, never cooking for anyone.

"You've got to eat," I say, wondering if I sound as bad as I think I do.

"Thank you. Kitchen has seen better days, hasn't it?" she says, hobbling a little easier now as she pulls a stool at the counter to sit and watch me.

"I saw your design. It's pretty good," I tell her, and she smiles, and if that doesn't make me want to tell her jokes every damn minute I'm with her, I don't know what will. We have been too busy arguing, and I never really saw her smile up close. Not at me, anyway. Her whole face lights up.

"Thanks. I love interiors and designing new spaces."

I can see the passion in her eyes with just that simple comment. It is then that I realize I haven't really asked her anything about herself.

"So did you work in design back in the city?"

She snorts. "No, I sold advertising space for magazines. But I have always wanted to do a project like this."

She looks around the house before picking up her drawing of the kitchen design.

"Do you have a kitchen manufacturer yet?" I ask as I stir the sauce and find the bowls.

"No. I've been trying to find a builder that will take on my design and build it for me, but I haven't had any luck."

Guilt. That must be the only reason the words fall from my lips.

"I have a guy. I will ask if he is available," I say, knowing that Griffin's team can do it. He is excellent at this kind of thing.

"Really?" she asks, her smile one that looks as if I just gave her the world.

"I'll call him tomorrow." I nod in confirmation. Her eyes narrow on me as her smile fades.

"It's still a no on selling you my land, just so you know," she says, watching me skeptically.

"Just eat your pasta." Sliding a bowl of pasta over to her across the kitchen counter, we both start to dig in, happy to have come to our truce.

16

VICTORIA

I thought for sure I would stumble down my stairs to find him gone. He just saw me outside in my robe, then barely wrapped up in a towel. I couldn't scare him away more, if I tried. But while I am completely mortified, the way his eyes not only looked at me hungrily, but the fact that he was also gentlemanly enough to pass me my robe quickly, turn around until I was decent, and then help me to my room afterward, had me swooning so hard that I was almost lightheaded.

Truth be told, I haven't felt attractive since I found Josh with Natalie. I mean, if I can't keep my new fiancé interested in me, then clearly I have some work to do. But the way Tanner was just looking at me instilled a boost of confidence. When I managed to pull my embarrassed self together and get dressed, I looked in the mirror, wet hair, fresh skin, but happier than I have been in a long time. My eyes are actually sparkling. I think it is the fresh country air or something.

It has been a while since someone has cooked for me,

and even though it is a simple meal of pasta, it tastes heavenly. After the day I have had, I half thought about locking myself in my room until he left.

He is a total contradiction. One minute, demanding I sell him my property, and the other, falling over himself to look after me. A man like Tanner must have women lining up. Probably has a different girl each week. I swallow down the bitter taste of jealousy that prickles my tongue and relax.

"I packed up outside for you," he says as he takes another bite. I look out the window and see everything is tidy. "I also called Kevin's mother, Annabelle. She said she will send Kevin up early. He can let out the goat, check the eggs, and milk the cow and so you don't have to worry about it. She just asked if they could have some eggs."

As much as his thoughtfulness makes me want to swoon, I wonder if he is genuine or just trying to sweeten me up so he can pull the wool over my eyes and grab my land.

"Of course. I will tell Kevin to help himself," I say, nodding. "What is their situation?"

"Kevin's dad passed away a little over a year ago. It has been a bit tough on them. She has a two-year-old as well but has just started back at work as a teacher at the local elementary school. The town supports them, but they have struggled at times."

My heart breaks at hearing that, and I swallow as I take in the information. Then I remember what he told me when we were fighting, and I want to know more about it.

"So you have a son?" I ask, then shovel in more pasta. I am starving, having not eaten for most of the day.

"I do." He only nods.

"What's his name?" I ask, and he looks at me surprised. "What?"

"You know nothing about me at all, do you?" he asks inquisitively, head tilting as he looks at me.

"No. Should I?" I snort. Is he being arrogant or serious?

"No. Just most people around here know everything about everybody, and, well, Connor and I are well known for the distillery and such."

"I don't really drink whiskey. I have heard of the Whiteman brand and did a little research on the town when I moved, but I can't say that I dug too deep into the distillery to know much," I tell him honestly with a shrug. He obviously does well for himself. Hell, he just flew to his property in a helicopter; his truck looks like it costs more than this house, and his collection of watches is impressive. I'd assume the whiskey business is soaring. But money has never been a huge motivating factor for me.

"Connor is thirty-five," he says, and my fork stops midway between my mouth and the bowl in shock.

"Thirty-five?" I clarify. *That is older than me.* "And your wife?" I ask tentatively, because he doesn't wear a wedding ring. There isn't even a tan line. He also acts like he is single, but you never know these days, and before I get too close to him, I should actually find out that small fact.

"I got Connor's mom pregnant in high school when

we were both teens. We decided to keep the baby. A few weeks after he was born, she skipped town, and I haven't seen her since."

While he shares his history, I can see his body tighten. He isn't overly comfortable or happy about the topic. My heart hurts for him because I can't imagine what that would have been like.

"Her loss," I toss out to him as I continue to eat, and the question about his age pulses in my brain. I've never dated an older man. Never really spent any time with someone who was decades older than me. I am not sure how many men my age would actually assist me as much as Tanner has today. It could be the small-town way, or it could be the Tanner Whiteman way. Who knows. All I know is that it feels nice being around him. Not forced, not fake, not mindless small talk. As I take another bite of pasta, I can feel him looking at me.

"What about you?" he asks tentatively, and I look up, meeting his deep-brown eyes.

"No kids," I say, smiling, trying to lighten the mood, and his lips quirk.

"Married?" he asks, and I swear I see him holding his breath.

"Nearly. Caught my fiancé Josh sleeping with his colleague. Then I lost my job, and to top it all off, I received a letter that my long-lost auntie had died. It's been a hell of a year so far," I tell him honestly. We are both sharing our dirty laundry and getting it out in the open. It is refreshing. When I used to meet men in the city, I found that everyone would cover up their little red flags in order to meet someone nice. Dating in New York is a dog-eat-dog world at times.

"His loss," he mumbles, throwing my own words back at me. We smile at each other just as my cell rings, and I grab it from nearby.

"Speak of the devil…" I reject his call, frowning as I notice another five from today alone.

"Is he harassing you?" Tanner asks, sitting up taller, clearly not happy about something. His chest is broad, his muscles defined, and I lick my lips. *God, this man is good-looking.*

"Just another man who doesn't take the word no very well," I say, clearly teasing him, and his brow only deepens, so I clarify. "It is fine. He will stop eventually."

Tanner grabs my bowl and continues to surprise me as he cleans up the kitchen, washes the dishes, and wipes the counters. I start to assist, but my cut pulls a little and I wince, which earns me a growl and another scowl from him, making me stay put.

"Put my number in your cell, in case you need help again, and yours in mine." He hands me his phone, and I look at it, then back at him, my eyes wide. One, I am pissed off that he thinks I can't handle myself. But two, it is a move that surprises me. Josh never let me near his phone, always said it was an invasion of privacy. I guess now I know why. He probably had so many girls' phone numbers in it that he didn't want me to see.

"I will be completely fine on my own, but in case *you* need *my help,* I will add it." I take his phone and add my details, sending myself a text so I have his details too. He smirks, seemingly finding me humorous.

"Call me for anything. I will be here quicker than anyone else," he reiterates, and I swallow past a lump in my throat. Where the hell did this man come from? So full of concern. I watch him in awe before a yawn breaks out just as he finishes cleaning up.

"You need to sleep," he says, again telling me what to do, but I don't have the energy to argue anymore.

"Yeah, it's been a big day," I agree, starting to feel my eyelids become heavy.

"I'll help you upstairs and then lock up the house behind me. Kevin will be here before school, at around eight."

"Okay. That would be great. Thank you." I'm a little bamboozled by it all. He is doing so much. I have never had this level of support before. I mean, Fiona was great with wine nights, and I miss my mother dearly, but this is on an entirely new level.

We remain quiet as he picks me up and takes me up the stairs. His hands are warm, firm, and comforting. Sighing, I relax in his arms. I am not sure if it is my imagination, but I think I feel his thumb rub my upper back a little, and I look up at his face, seeing him already looking at me. We stare at each other for a moment, our eyes searching each other's as he comes to a stop.

"We're here," he says quietly, but my breathing has all but stopped as I look at his lips, then flick my eyes back to his. He hasn't lowered me, and I haven't made a move either, my hands still wrapped around his shoulders. My tongue darts out to moisten my dry lips, and I see his jaw pop as his eyes follow the movement. But then he's straightening and lowering my feet to the floor. Heart racing, I turn to say something to him, but he is already out the door. I stand, waiting as I hear him downstairs, and then his footsteps come back up and he walks back into my room with my cell phone and charger, a glass of water, painkillers, and my sketchbook.

"Need anything else?" he asks, and wide-eyed at his action, I shake my head.

"Thank you, Tanner. Really," I tell him, feeling breathless. He nods once, his eyes on mine for another moment.

"Good night, Victoria," he says, and I watch him swallow roughly.

"Good night," I whisper to him, and he turns, walking out the door. I slowly lower myself to sit on the edge of the bed, listening to him closing and locking the door as he said before his truck starts up outside.

It is only then that I release the breath I didn't know I was holding, and I fall back onto the bed. Closing my eyes, I instantly dream of a tall, dark-haired grumpy man.

17

TANNER

I'm trying to work, my paperwork pile now sky-high and my emails coming in thick and fast, but every time I blink, all I see is her perfect body. Her peaches-and-cream skin, her pink cheeks, her curves, the tease of her black panties under that short robe. I couldn't sleep all last night, checking my phone every hour in case she needed me. I didn't even want to leave her. I had to force myself to walk out of her bedroom last night, because the way she was looking at me, coupled with the way I feel about her, I didn't trust myself, and I don't want to take advantage of her. But I struggled with that decision all night.

I know Kevin went to her place this morning to collect the milk because I have already spoken to his mom. As a token of appreciation, I had Lacy take up a few bags of groceries to help her and the kids out for the next few weeks. The local church assists her out with these things, but I try to support where I can.

Now walking around the warehouse at the distillery, I

am waiting for Connor who came back this morning to go over our stock for the month. I scroll through Victoria's social media, looking at image after image, seeing her ideas come to life. She is talented, there is no doubt. Why she hasn't been working in this area of interior design, I have no idea.

I spot a new photo on her social media from this morning of her foot elevated, resting on the arm of the sofa. I feel the stress leave my shoulders a little, knowing that she at least got downstairs safely this morning. When I double-click the image, a heart pops up on the screen, then I follow her page. *Isn't that what kids do these days?*

"Why are you on social media?" Connor asks from over my shoulder, and I jump so high my cell almost flies from my hand.

"Dammit, Connor," I growl at him, although not upset, just surprised.

"What are you doing?" he presses, eyebrow quirked as he tries to peek at what's on my phone.

"Nothing," I say quickly, then close the screen and pocket my cell.

"Who are you following? You hate social media." His eyes thin in question.

"No one." I wasn't about to text her... see if she needed anything.

"Bullshit," Connor says, walking in front of me with a shit-eating grin on his face.

"Don't speak to your father like that," a new voice says jovially, and we look to the side to see Huxley, Hudson's brother and our longtime family friend, strolling into the warehouse. He spends a lot of his time in Baltimore these days, but we are happy to have him back in town.

"Like he said," I tell Connor, smiling. I love my son, but now that we are both older, we are even better friends.

"Are you texting a woman?" Huxley pins me with his gaze as he walks over to where we are standing. Shaking hands, he backslaps Connor, the two of them friends since they could walk.

"No!" I huff as I shake his hand in greeting and hug him just the same. Since he married the love of his life, Lucy Bloomer, here in Whispers, he and Lucy have become a regular local couple and spend as much time in Whispers as they can at his ranch on the outskirts of town. The luxurious ranches of the many wealthy people who come here are spread all around Whispers. I have a vacant plot ready for building, on what locals call Billionaire Boulevard, but I prefer to live here, close to town, in my home at the back of the distillery, right where I need to be. Connor has built his own place, also on distillery land near mine. This is our home, always will be.

"He is just looking at her social media," Connor teases.

"Holy shit. Who is she?" Huxley asks, pulling back and looking at me in shock.

"No one," I tell them both as Connor smirks my way and Huxley looks dumbfounded.

"From Whispers? Who is it? I know everyone in Whispers." Huxley continues trying to get it out of me. He doesn't know *everyone*.

"None of your business," I say, just as Connor says, "Our new neighbor." That earns him scowl.

"You know you can have a girlfriend, Dad. I have been waiting for the day that you actually commit to someone." Connor's smile doesn't waver.

"I don't have a girlfriend," I reiterate, but they don't care. By the looks on their faces, they are having a fucking field day.

"Who's the new neighbor?" Huxley asks, his interest now fully piqued.

"Hudson didn't tell you?" Connor says, and the two of them start talking all about Victoria like I am not even here.

"My brother hasn't mentioned her..."

I am surprised by that, because Huxley and Hudson are joined at the hip, the two of them always meeting here as one lives on the East Coast and one on the West Coast.

"She is from the city, lives in Marie's old place. Her niece," Connor says. "I think Dad likes her..."

"She is half my fucking age." Although the visions of Victoria practically naked at my feet last night are still very vivid, regardless of our age difference.

"So?" Huxley asks, and I'm already shaking my head.

"That's what I said. Age is just a number." Connor gives me an *I told you so* look.

"I mean... you will need someone to wheel around your wheelchair soon," Huxley jokes, and I roll my eyes.

"Alright, that's quite enough, asshole," I growl, running a hand through my hair. If they keep this up, I will head home for the day.

"Maybe you should go for her then, Connor?" Huxley offers, and I almost buckle at the thought.

"Not his type," I say too quickly, and they both look at me before they double over in laughter.

"What is this? Are you two really ganging up on me? You know what? She might be more suited to you, Connor," I relent, even though it kills me. They are much closer in age... It would make more sense.

"Ahhh, not for me, Dad. I'm not looking at the moment. Besides, I think this one has you all up in knots already."

I feel tension instantly ease from my body. I would never stand in the way of my son finding love, but I am relieved that I saw her first.

"It's about time you dated properly, Dad, don't you think?" Connor says to me, his face now serious. *Here we go again.*

"Tanner, if I have learned anything, it is to not let the past affect my future," Huxley says, slapping my shoulder, and I roll my eyes again.

"She is just the neighbor. Nothing more." I try to drill that statement into my own brain. A very sexy neighbor, but my neighbor just the same.

"So you won't care if we go over there, then. You know, introduce ourselves," Connor says, rolling up the sleeves of his shirt and grabbing his keys. I grind my teeth.

"She doesn't need new people around."

Connor raises an eyebrow at me.

"Bullshit. Now I really want to meet the woman who has you all tied up."

"I parked out front, we can take my truck," Huxley says, already walking away.

"Knock it off," I reiterate, but they're not listening.

"I'll take over a bottle of whiskey as a gift. I hear she is a bit quirky and always wears pink. I think we have something pink in the gift shop we could take as well. You know, get on her good side," Connor says, stepping over to grab a bottle from the shelf.

"She doesn't like whiskey," I tell him, and he stops mid-stride.

"Really? What else doesn't she like?" Huxley asks as they look at me, both of their smiles threatening. I can tell they are holding in their laughter. Assholes.

"Drop it. Both of you." Releasing a heavy breath, I think they can finally see how serious I am.

"Fine. We will meet her some other time," Connor says, laughing.

"You do the stock." I point at Connor. "You go back to your wife." I point at Huxley. "I've got to call Griffin," I tell them both, walking away from them toward the door. I need to organize Griffin to come and look at Victoria's kitchen. Preferably this week, because I know she can't do a lot and having this ball rolling will help.

"What's Griffin doing for us now?" Connor asks, and it's a very valid question. I do need Griffin for my other project, but that can wait.

"Just helping out a friend," I say as I quicken my pace to walk out of the warehouse.

"Must be a pretty good friend to get a builder like Griffin involved," Huxley says to Connor, loud enough for me to hear.

"Hmm, the only friend whom I know needs a builder would be our new neighbor?" Connor yells out to me as I step outside, and I hear the two of them cackling. Once I slam the door behind me with a huff, I call one of the country's best builders to get him sorted for renovating my new neighbor's kitchen.

Because that is just the neighborly thing to do. *Keep telling yourself that, Tanner.*

18

VICTORIA

The cut on my ankle stings as I stretch up on my toes, getting the last bit of painting done near the roof cavity before I can finally call the outside complete.

It hurts more than I thought it would, although I haven't really kept off it like I should have. Now I am worried it might start bleeding again if I pull it too much.

I try not to look down as I am pretty high off the ground and am doing my best not to rock this ladder. I grabbed it from the shed, and it has seen better days. The last thing I need is to fall from this height, but I need to get this done. Everyone told me it was too high and that I needed to hire a lift or get some scaffolding. Even Bob wouldn't do it. But I am not hiring a lift or spending all that money on scaffolding when I know I can do it myself.

I took on this job, and I need to complete it, and while I prefer to be on solid ground, I also don't want this small patch of unpainted boards to be the thing that makes me fail. I lost my job, I suck at relationships, I need to get this right.

My grip is white-knuckled as I swipe the paintbrush across the boards, just as I hear a truck pull into my driveway. I look down over my shoulder, spotting the familiar black and gold truck, and my breath catches. *Tanner.*

"What the hell are you doing?" I hope his bark is worse than his bite as Tanner jumps out of his truck with something in his hand before slamming the door, looking up at me like I am crazy.

"Just knitting a tea cozy from the golden thread of my hair. What the hell does it look like I am doing?" I shout down to him. His strides are quick to the base of my ladder, which he is now holding on to tight. He might want my land, but at least he doesn't want me to die for it.

"You are ten feet in the air. On an old timber ladder that looks like it is about to snap in half!" he yells, and I roll my eyes at his clear disbelief in my abilities.

"Oh, don't be so dramatic. I just had to paint this little section that I didn't get to last week," I tell him as I take one last look at my quick paint job and deem it a success.

"Will you get down? You are likely to fall and break a bone or something." His growl is low and deep, and it shouldn't make my skin break out in goosebumps, but it does.

"Trespassing again, I see..." I yell down to him as I start my descent. I go slow, because as demanding as he is, he is right, this ladder is a bit unsteady, and if he wasn't holding on to it, I may have had an issue coming down it.

"I came to check up on you," he says, and I almost

misstep at his words. "Take it easy," he warns as I find my footing again and keep stepping down. *Check on me?*

"Still feeling guilty about the surveyor stake in the ground?" I ask with some sass as I am almost to the bottom.

"Maybe my intuition knew you would be crazy enough to climb a ten-foot ladder with an injured foot." He is sarcastic today too. *What a joy.*

"Well, if your intuition is so good, then what is it telling you now?" I hit the lower rungs and turn, not realizing just how close we are. The breath leaves my lungs as we are now face-to-face. Mere inches between us as my breasts barely graze his chest. He doesn't step back, and I don't attempt to move either as he looks at me sternly.

My mouth dries immediately as the memory of him seeing me yesterday in nothing but my robe flies forward in my mind. The way he looked at me like he wanted to eat me whole has been on a constant thought rotation all night and day. And now as we stare at each other in furious heat, my heart starts beating harder and my stomach is doing flips. I am still not sure if he is genuinely caring and interested in helping me or just doing it for his own business benefit. I am at war with myself over each thought.

A strand of my hair is loose, and the breeze pushes it across my face. Before I can move to get it, his hand shoots out and brushes it away, his fingers skirting across my cheek slightly. All words leave me as I suck in a sharp breath at the light touch, our eyes never leaving each other's.

"It's telling me that these boots I got you will fit better

than whatever the hell you have on your feet right now," he grumbles, and my gaze flicks down to the bright-pink slides I am wearing. I agree, it's probably not my best shoe choice, and I should have known better than to wear something like this on a ladder, but I did, and I am fine.

"You got me boots?" I ask him, tilting my head. Is he trying to butter me up? Maybe he thought I was serious about suing him.

"Hell knows you need them. Can't be running around this place in bare feet again, or whatever the hell those are." He nods to my feet, and I am wondering if this man has ever laughed before.

"Unless the boots are pink with rhinestones, I don't think they will match my wardrobe," I say with a smirk, just trying to push his buttons.

"You have enough sparkle in you, baby girl. I don't think you don't need anymore. Besides..." he says as he pushes away from me and starts walking out the back. "You need boots to be at one with nature, not scare the poor animals away."

I watch him walk toward the shed, my mouth open in surprise, my body reeling. *Baby girl.* That alone has my pussy clenching.

Seeing the bag that now sits at my feet, I pick it up, pulling out a boot. I don't know a lot about work boots, but I know this label, and they are pure leather and expensive. I look at the size and am even more surprised that he got it right.

Brushing down my clothes, I run my hands through my hair, watching him sort out the animals and put them away for the night. There must be an ulterior motive. I have never received a gift just because from a man. There has always been a reason. As I watch Garry follow him willingly, I frown. I swear that goat hates me.

"Now what do you think you are doing?" I ask, stepping toward him.

"I called Kevin's mom and told her not to worry about sending him up to help tonight," Tanner says as he walks closer. His words make my heart pound.

"Why is that?" I ask, eyes thinning as I take in his expression for any sign of deception.

"I brought dinner," he says gruffly, and I tilt my head to the side as a tingling erupts in my stomach.

"Dinner?" I ask, not able to hide my shock.

"Rochelle from the diner makes a good chicken pie," he says by way of explanation before walking past me back to where he parked.

"Front door's open!" I shout to him as I barely contain my smile before shuffling inside and turning on the oven. He comes in through the front door, putting bags on the counter, and looks at me in the kitchen where I am cleaning up a little.

"Sit and rest your ankle," he says, pulling out a chair from my dining table and waiting for me to move.

"I can help cook." My hand finds my hip, feeling defiant.

"Why do you always have to be so argumentative?" he asks with a sigh.

"Argumentative? Why do you always have to be so demanding?" I ask, my voice rising. He walks up to where I am standing with the look of warning in his eyes.

"Just remember, I did ask nicely."

"Wha—" I don't get out the rest of the word because he picks me up bridal style, and I rush to grab his neck.

"Tanner!" I yell as I am swooped up in his arms.

"Well, I did ask nicely." He smirks, and it almost makes me laugh.

"You're incorrigible," I murmur, but my hands relax around his neck. I feel it then. His thumb rubbing my back, like he did last night. It has me melting into his hold a little more.

"Maybe so, but you should rest your ankle. I don't need to spend more time bandaging you up just because you won't take it easy and decide climbing ladders is the smartest thing to do." Leaning down, he places me on the chair. His hands run around my body, resting on my waist, and I lower my hands to cup his neck, but I don't let go.

"Are you going to keep arguing with me every time I see you?" he asks, our lips a hair's width apart. I can feel his hot breath on my skin. His eyes search mine, his face relaxed, yet his jaw still strong. All we need to do is lean into each other a little and we would kiss. I have no idea what is happening or how I feel about it. One minute, we are bickering, and the next, he's caring for me and coming here with a new pair of boots and cooking me dinner.

"Probably..." I tell him with a small smirk as my eyes flick from his eyes to his lips and back again. *Why do I want him to kiss me so much?*

He grabs my leg, and sparks shoot up my thigh as his hands run down to my ankle and he ever so gently moves it onto the other chair, ensuring that it is elevated.

"That alright?" he asks as his eyes search mine once more, and I momentarily forget how to speak. "Does it hurt?"

"It's fine. Swelling has gone," I tell him breathily. He looks at my ankle and runs his thumb over it, his large warm hand still cupping it softly.

"It's still a little bruised," he murmurs with concern.

"It looks worse than it feels," I assure him. This touching and close proximity is leaving me hot all over. I take in a breath and move my shirt a little to flap some air on my face because I feel beetroot red.

"Let me get dinner." He steps away, and I blink a few times, wondering if that actually happened or was just my very vivid imagination.

"I called a builder friend of mine to come and look at your kitchen plans," he says as he puts the pie into the oven to heat while my eyebrows shoot to my hairline.

"Really?" I ask, sitting up. "Could they help?" I don't have a lot of options. Whispers and the nearby towns have a few people, but many of them are already booked with jobs for the next few months, and those that were available just didn't get my vision.

"He will be here in a few days. He said he will take a look." Tanner nods, moving around my kitchen with ease, pulling out plates and cutlery, napkins, and glasses. I can't continue keeping my thoughts to myself.

"Why are you being so nice?" I ask him outright, and he stops what he is doing and looks at me, confused.

"How so?" he asks.

"You got me boots, you called your builder, and now

you're cooking me dinner. *Again.* I can't remember the last time someone cooked for me aside from you last night."

He pauses, looking at me with a furrowed brow.

"What about that idiot ex of yours?" he asks, and I sigh.

"No, he never cooked. Never did anything, actually." Now that I really think about it, our relationship was so one-sided; I have no idea why it lasted as long as it did.

"Asshole," he murmurs, plating up the salad and pouring the wine.

"Total asshole," I agree as he walks the glasses of wine to the table.

"Call it being neighborly," he says, answering my question.

"I thought you wanted me gone?" I test him a little and watch his face tense.

"Maybe you are growing on me." With a soft look that might as well be searing, he turns back to the kitchen to finish prepping, and I take a sip of wine, watching him over the rim of my glass.

Tanner Whiteman is growing on me too.

19

VICTORIA

It has been a few days since I fell in the yard and my leg is almost completely healed. The new boots I now own are definitely helping. They are comfortable and not overly ugly, and they go well with my jeans.

Tanner has been in contact via text every day, which is nice, but I am still on guard. I haven't seen him since the other night when he cooked me dinner. Instead, Jasmine and Lacy have been coming by, helping me where I need it. But really, we have just been enjoying wine nights and lots of giggles and too much online shopping for the house.

The other thing that has been consistent, though, is Josh. His calls are excessive. I continue to ignore them, which seems to have the opposite effect, because his calls have increased to almost hourly. I don't want to talk to him; I don't even want to acknowledge his existence, but his daily barrage makes me think I need to address this issue. Otherwise, I'm not sure if it will stop.

"I can't believe you broke your leg." Fiona huffs a

laugh as I hold my phone between my shoulder and chin, cleaning up a bit.

"I just sliced it a little. It is perfectly fine," I tell her, laughing at her exaggeration.

"So your sexy neighbor came in handy, then?" she teases.

"He cooked me dinner... helped me with the animals." I ignore her remark about him being sexy, even though he most certainly is. I look out the back window at Garry. He is doing a fantastic job of chewing the grass down, but I am increasingly worried about his weight.

"Hey, do you think I need to be monitoring Garry's grass intake?" I ask Fiona out of the blue.

"The goat?" she asks, confused.

"Yeah. He has a full pot belly. I wonder if goats can get bloated from eating too much grass. Is it a calories in versus calories out situation, like us humans? I wonder what his metabolism is like..." I bite my lip, watching my four-legged friend. "Do I need to be monitoring his protein and carbs? Does he need a diet of pellets or something?" I sigh at myself as Fiona laughs at me.

"I have no idea. But why don't you ask your neighbor? I bet he knows exactly what to do."

"Maybe..." I slump on the arm of the sofa, now back to thinking about the man who consumes my thoughts these days. Tanner is right; I have no idea what I am doing here, and I need to call the local vet and get a health status on the animals. Although the cow, which I have since named Marmalade, and the chickens seem happy enough.

"The images you put up of your new curtains got a lot of likes," she mentions.

"I love them. My new shower screen and vanity have been installed too. Bob kindly came over and finished off the floor sanding that I had left, and between the two of us, we also managed to seal the floorboards with some gloss. The place smelled for a good two days, but now it is amazing."

With the painting done and the floors complete, I now need to get new carpet arranged for upstairs, fix the fireplace, and get it into working order, plus order the new light fittings, furniture, and décor, and the two biggest items, the new kitchen and laundry.

"Ugh. Sounds exhausting," she moans, and I laugh just as I hear someone shout.

"Hello!" Tanner's voice bellows from outside, and I jump a little in surprise. Walking swiftly to the front door, I open it quickly, surprised because I didn't hear him drive up. Clearly, I was in my mind too much.

"I have to go. Tanner is here," I whisper to Fiona.

"Ohhh, I want an update," she whispers back, giggling.

"Later," I tell her and end the call.

"Hey," I greet, as he and another man who looks like every girl's wet dream walk toward me from his truck. My breath catches in my throat at the sight, and I make a mental note to call Fiona back as soon as they leave and tell her to move to Whispers immediately. The status of men in this town is phenomenal. As my eyes flick back to Tanner, who's looking relaxed in his standard uniform of black shirt and jeans, I suddenly feel parched. His sleeves rolled up to his elbows show off his thick forearms, and his shirt is open at the neck, giving the slightest hint at his chest.

"How's your ankle?" he asks, frowning as he looks at me. Straight into overprotective mode. I have come to realize that he does actually care about me. Because if he was just being nice to get my land, then he could just leave me here to fail. He isn't doing that.

"I'm fine, just like I told you yesterday and the day before," I tell him with a smirk, looking up at him as he doesn't hesitate and walks straight up the porch steps to where I am standing. His furrowed brow doesn't soothe as he looks down at my leg and back to my face again, and my breath hitches as I feel his hand curve around my waist.

"You shouldn't be on it too much," he says quietly, our heads close as the other man watches us. Tanner is immediately back into concerned mode, and if I could breathe, I would speak. But his thumb rubs up and down my torso slowly, and I feel the heat of flames flick across my skin that have left me speechless. This man. My God, he makes me weak at the knees. I shake my head, getting myself together.

"I'm not. Just because you haven't been here to see it doesn't mean it didn't happen," I bite back, and his frown turns into narrowed eyes.

"I don't believe you," he says, and I huff. We stare at each other, the fire in us both reigniting, and I only look away from him when the man standing nearby clears his throat.

"This is Griffin, my builder. I thought he could look at your kitchen for you."

My eyes widen in surprise before I smile at our visitor. This is yet another thing Tanner doesn't need to do, and in doing so, totally contradicts him wanting my property. I think Tanner might just like having me around.

"Nice to meet you. Come on in," I say, shaking his hand. Tanner drops his hand from my waist and opens the door for us, and I lead them both inside.

"This looks great! Much better than it was!" Griffin says, looking around, surprised. I smile, because although there is still a lot to do, it is really amazing. Better than I could have imagined.

"You said you have been resting," Tanner growls, aiming his scowl at me.

"I did," I tell him with a shrug, only fibbing a little bit. There is no way I can rest. I have to get this house renovated and styled. I need to remain focused.

"Not by looking at this, you didn't." He waves his hand around my living area, where I have a new rug on the new floorboards, new furnishings, and my new sofa and armchair.

"Bob helped, Jasmine and Lacy too. Besides, I stayed indoors. I didn't want another surveyor stake to trip me up again," I snip, annoyed at his overbearing attitude.

"This the kitchen, then?" Griffin says, walking that way, pretending he isn't hearing us bicker.

"She has plans," Tanner says to him, and I fetch my sketches and pass them to Griffin. His eyebrows shoot up.

"This is..." He flicks through the pages, where I have drafted different viewpoints of the kitchen, my 3D sketches outlying exactly what I want. The last page contains all the appliances and the materials for the cupboards, including the color scheme as well as the marble for the countertops.

"Is it doable?" I ask, holding my breath. I look at Tanner, and he's already watching me closely.

"I mean, it won't be cheap to do," Griffin says, and my heart sinks for a beat. I don't have much money left. I knew the kitchen would be expensive, and it would probably take all that I have.

"We can make it work," Tanner says quickly, his eyes boring into Griffin.

"We can make it work." Griffin nods to Tanner. "When do you need it completed?" Griffin asks, looking back at me.

"Oh, well, I really need it as soon as possible, but of course, I am aware you have other projects," I say, trying to be understanding of his schedule since he seems to be the only builder capable of building the kitchen how I visualize it.

"When do you want your project started?" Griffin asks Tanner. I didn't realize Tanner has a project in the works.

"This one can take priority," Tanner confirms with a nod, and Griffin smiles, biting his lip, looking like he is trying hard not to laugh. I frown in confusion. Why is Tanner helping me so much if he is just going to swoop in and take my land? Maybe Jasmine was wrong about the legal takeover, or maybe he has had a change of heart...

"Are you local?" I ask Griffin, realizing I know nothing about him and should look at his quality of work.

"I work countrywide. I own a company called

Patterson Constructions," he says, and my eyes widen a little.

"As in, luxury builder, Patterson Constructions?" I ask hesitantly. Everyone who works in interior design knows them. They are literally the best builder in the entire country.

"Yep. That's the one," he confirms with a proud smile.

"Oh, so you reside in Whispers?" I try to sound cool and not like I am fangirling over here. How did I not know this man lived here?

"I don't really reside anywhere; I move around all the time... Let me get this quoted up, but I think we can probably get this made and installed within the month. Tanner said that you might also need a laundry fit out?" Griffin asks, and I stand rooted to the ground in shock. A week ago, I couldn't find one builder to make the kitchen as per my design, and now Tanner walks in with his friend, who happens to be the builder to billionaires and celebrities, and suddenly I have it exactly how I want it and within the month.

I bite my lip, thinking about my budget. I know it isn't going to be cheap, and if I include the laundry, I will have no reserves. Tanner clears his throat, and I look at him as he continues to eyeball Griffin.

"Tanner tells me you have a solid social media profile. If you want to do a collaboration, that could work well for me. I usually build large-scale ranches and homes, but I am starting a new division which will concentrate mainly on renovations rather than new builds. This could tie in really well for both of us. If you want to do a before and after that we can use in our portfolio, I will knock the price down," Griffin suggests, looking back at Tanner, who nods at him. I feel like I am missing something here, but I go with it.

"I would love that. I have about fifty thousand website visits a week at the moment, and it is growing fast," I say, both proud and surprised by the sudden and rapid rise in people now interested in my Woman of Whispers platform.

"Shit." Tanner's eyebrows rise.

"Whew. That's a lot," Griffin says. "Especially in such a short amount of time."

"I guess it just resonates with a lot of people," I tell them, shrugging.

We spend the next thirty minutes going through the entire house. Griffin can take care of not only the kitchen and laundry, but will also assist with joinery for a mini mudroom, wardrobes, and cabinets for the bedrooms. He's also suggested I look at a small expansion, where I could put a master bedroom downstairs. It makes sense, I have the room, and he has offered to draw up the plans to show me what he is thinking. I don't have the budget, but there is no harm talking about the possibilities.

"Give me a couple weeks to put it together and source the product. The stone countertop will be the issue, but I have a guy, so hopefully he can help," Griffin says as we walk back to the main living area.

"Let's take a photo. I can put it up on my socials today," I say, and Griffin nods with a smile. "Make yourself useful," I tell Tanner, thrusting my cell toward him as Griffin and I stand together in front of the amazing open fireplace that came up so well after a bit of scrubbing this week. Besides a small grumble, Tanner does as I ask, and I realize he has been mostly quiet for the entire time, letting me lead the discussions with Griffin and only offering an opinion when asked. In complete contrast to Josh, who always talked over me at every opportunity and used to like being the center of attention wherever we went. His scowl deepens as he takes some images. I have no idea why he is extra grumpy today.

"I need to take a call. I will wait for you outside, Tanner. Good to finally meet you, Victoria. Looking forward to our project." Shaking my hand, he grabs his cell as he walks out the door.

I sigh, looking back at Tanner. "What's your problem?" My hand finds my hip, knowing something is up.

His jaw pops and his face hardens. "You need a security system," he states, and I stand up straighter.

"What? Why?" I ask, totally bamboozled.

"Number one, your asshole ex is still calling you," he grits out, clearly upset. Now the frown he had when taking our photo makes sense, as Josh probably called while Tanner had my phone. "Number two, you have fifty thousand website visitors; your socials are well into the hundreds of thousands. Your video of the new blinds yesterday went viral and had almost a million views." He stalks toward me, stopping mere inches in front of my chest. I swallow at his closeness, feeling my heart thud louder.

"I am not worried about any of that," I say, waving off his concern.

"What is this ex capable of?" Tanner pushes, not looking happy.

"He is harmless," I counter quickly.

"He has called you at least five times since I have been here." Tanner's voice rises.

"It's just calls," I tell him, although even I can admit it's excessive.

"You need some cameras."

My shoulders tense. We are at it again. After the other night, I thought we had a breakthrough. A ceasefire. But he is back to his bossy, dominate self, telling me what to do. I don't even reply before he's continuing.

"Victoria. You are a single, beautiful young woman living here alone. You have already said your ex is a persistent asshole. You have just told me you have thousands of people now extremely interested in your renovation, not to mention that they know exactly where you are located."

Shit, he is right. I promoted Whispers and this place because of what I want to do with it when it is finished. Open it up for others who are struggling, who need a new direction like I did. Given my thoughts on that, I need to be a little more anonymous with locations moving forward. But...

"I don't need security," I tell him forcefully, because even if I did, my budget is not going to stretch that far yet.

"Let me get it for you," he offers, and I look at him, wide-eyed.

"Tanner..." I start to say, shaking my head, because that is not happening.

"It would make me feel better knowing you are safe."

My eyes thin even as my stomach flutters.

"Why? You want me gone anyway," I state, and his face flickers with confusion.

"What are you talking about?" He steps even closer.

"I know what you are up to. I didn't want to believe it actually. But now I know, you have been so nice and perfect and gentlemanly to me, when in reality, you are just trying to sweeten me up because you are trying to take my house straight out from under me!" My voice gradually rises until I'm yelling. I feel stupid for even thinking Tanner was anything more than a businessman wanting my property. He is silent, watching me carefully, his eyes never once moving from mine.

"What are you—" is all he gets out before I but in.

"I know all about your legal pitch to grab this property by adverse possession. I know you put in paperwork to get this house straight out from under me," I grit out, my breaths coming quicker. His jaw clenches, and now he looks pissed.

"If you would stop talking for a minute, I could tell you that I already ripped up the paperwork and canceled the request."

I am so angry that his words don't register.

"So were you just lying to me for the first week we met, or have you been lying to me right up until this moment?" I throw my hands up, huffing.

"I never lied. I ripped the paperwork up! Stop arguing with me just this once!"

"You stop arguing with me!" I yell back, and before I know it, his hands are on my face and his lips are against mine. My heart stalls, his lips warm and my cheeks hot in his palms.

My breath is stuck in my chest as he walks me backward a step until my back hits the wall. Our lips fight for the others, our tongues tangling, and my hands grip on to his arms, needing to hold myself up so I don't fall. I hear a small growl in his chest, and my pulse thunders in my ears as his hand drops from my face to my ass, where he picks me up, my legs immediately hooking around his waist.

"Tanner..." I whisper against his lips, my hands almost shaking in a mix of shock, desire, relief, and a mounting pressure of wanting more. More of him. More of this. Pinning me against the wall, my arms lock around his neck, his kiss so brutal, I almost feel branded. His large hands grab my ass, squeezing, as I pull his head to my own, ensuring our lips stay together as he swallows my moan.

All the fighting, all the tension, all the desires I have had overflow into this kiss, and I never want it to stop. Garry bleats from outside, pulling me from my thoughts and back to reality, and Tanner slowly pulls back a little. My eyes search his as we both pant, breathless.

"Fuck, I have wanted to do that since the moment I laid eyes on you." His voice is gravel, and my thighs tighten around him.

"I don't think anyone has ever kissed me like that before," I say, my fingers coming to my lips. They are throbbing, tingling to the touch. I've been completely and thoroughly kissed.

"You deserve to be kissed like that every damn day," he says, pressing a light kiss to my lips, and I feel my body shudder. His grip on me is still tight, his thumb rubbing my thighs as they stay firmly around him, our bodies close.

"Are you offering?" I tease as I move my hips a little, wanting more friction, and I feel him hard against me.

"You keep moving on me like that, baby girl, and I swear Griffin will get a show that he wasn't prepared for today." Tanner's voice is rough and low and pulsates right to my core. Right now, I don't care about Griffin, my pussy is throbbing. It has been months since a man held me, kissed me, and touched me in this way, and my body is on fire.

"Best you get back to your friend, then?" I whisper, my mouth dry. We have bickered ever since I arrived, but it is now very clear exactly what we think of each other, and like a volcano, we are both very close to fully erupting.

Tanner looks at me closely, pulling in his lower lip, and I literally feel my world tilt a little at the way he is looking at me. "I need to take him back to my jet."

"Jet?" I question, not understanding.

"I flew him in today to look at your place. He is currently working on a new project in Aspen," he explains, and my shock is evident.

"You flew him here? For me?" I ask in disbelief.

"I did," Tanner confirms with a nod.

"Why?" That couldn't have been easy or cheap.

"Because you have a vision, and it needs to come to life."

I am glad he is still holding me because I would fall over otherwise. I don't tell him that my main motivating factor is not to fail. I can't go back to the city with my tail between my legs. I need to make this work. He moves, carrying me to the sofa and placing me down gently.

"I'll see you tomorrow," he promises, but I don't get a chance to ask any more questions before his lips meet mine in another soft kiss. This time it is slower, and we take our time. He cups my jaw with one hand, and I am complete putty for him before he stands up, growling, and walks toward the door.

"You are getting security." He opens the front door, not taking no for an answer as per usual, and I huff.

"I'll think about it," I call out, and I hear him chuckle as he closes my door. I lie back on my soft new sofa, listening for his truck as it drives away, and then my house is quiet again. Bringing my finger to my lips, I feel them hot and throbbing.

My body is like mush, my legs weak, and while I have a million things I should be doing, I stay on my sofa for a while, thinking of my dark, grumpy neighbor. How he's given up on fighting for the house. How he's helping me see through my dream.

And how much more I want to do than just kiss him.

20

———

TANNER

I kissed her yesterday. It was fucking amazing, and it's all I have been thinking about. So much so, I hardly slept last night. Her knowing about the legal takeover I was planning took me by surprise, but I should have known that people talk in a small town, and it was only a matter of time before she heard whispers of it. But I am glad to have it out in the open, and after our kiss, I am even more glad that it was already canceled. Now, as I put my plan for today together, I text her so she knows that I am coming and what to expect.

> Be there in five. Put on your swimsuit.

I watch the screen and see the dots dancing.

> Oh, hello, neighbor. Back to telling me what to do again? Swimsuit? Where are we going?

I ignore her sass and text back immediately.

It's a surprise. See you soon.

I pocket my cell, grab my things, and load up my truck. It isn't often I play hooky from work, but the sun is shining, and I want to see her again. Jumping in my truck, I call Griffin as I drive.

"Hey, Tanner," he answers immediately.

"Hey, can't talk long," I say as I start to pull out of my driveway.

"In a hurry?" Griffin asks.

"Just heading to the neighbor's place," I tell him honestly.

"Connor tells me you fancy her?" Griffin asks, and I bite my back molars.

"Don't believe everything my kid tells you," I grumble, although he isn't wrong. Shit, the way her body was responding to me yesterday has had me harder than wood in my pants all day.

"She has a lot of talent. That sketch was amazing, and the way she has made so many simple changes to the property already that have had a major impact is pretty impressive," Griffin says as I turn the truck into her driveway.

"I thought so too. Glad you agree. It is a hobby of hers, I think, but I can see her potential," I say, a small amount of pride filling me as I talk about her.

"So what about your other project?" Griffin asks me, and I know I need to focus on that.

"We will need to get started on the plans for the accommodations. We can put them on the east side, grow some trees for privacy..." I say, thinking out loud. Marie's property was always my number one choice, but like any smart businessman, I always had a backup. While the east side is not as pretty and doesn't have the mineral springs, it will still bring in people and be a success. The fact that my new neighbor is renovating and planning to stay fills me with something new. Kind of feels like hope. Now that I know she is staying, I don't want the fact that I wanted her place to be front of my mind so I am letting it go. With that out of the way, I can progress my accommodations elsewhere on the property and get to know her better. On equal footing. Because every time we are together, whether we are arguing or kissing, it is the best damn time I have had in a long time.

"I think it will be fine there. That was always plan B."

"Sounds great. I'll be back next week to go over plan B and to pick up that limited edition whiskey that is now mine after giving you my day yesterday." I can tell he's smirking just from his tone.

"Thank, Griff. I appreciate it," I tell him honestly.

"Good to see you interested in something other than the distillery. It looks good on you," he says sincerely.

"She would look good on anyone."

He laughs before I end the call and pull up in front of Victoria's house.

I sit in my truck for a moment, spotting her in the yard. She hasn't seen me yet, so I watch her working in the garden, her knees in the soil. I admire her work ethic. It is something that runs strong in me as well. Her hair is down and around her shoulders, her hands in gloves. They are bright pink with frills, and I wonder where the hell she got them from. But just like the bright-pink footwear she had on the other day, I am starting to see she has these little out-of-place wardrobe choices that, in the city, no one would bat an eyelash at, but here, she pops brighter than the sun. I like it, a lot. I have never known anyone to move to the country and settle in as quickly as she has. And that brings my thoughts back to how good it felt to kiss her yesterday. How our banter and bickering has softened us both. That kiss is burned into my brain and was one of the best kisses I have had in all my years on earth. Now that I have had a taste, there is no doubt I need more.

"Planning on coming in or just watching me like a stalker?" she yells out, and I smile. I should have known she knew I was here. Jumping out of the truck, I walk over.

"Ready to go?" I ask, though I know she isn't.

"Where are you taking me?" She stands from the ground, brushing off her gloved hands to get rid of the dirt.

"I have somewhere special to show you," I tell her, not giving anything away.

"And I need my swimsuit?" She sounds intrigued as she narrows her eyes at me playfully. My eyes canvass her body in the cute sundress she has on, and I nearly groan. She looks good in fucking anything.

"Do you have any swimwear?" I suddenly realize she might not have packed any. She looks at me for a minute before a smile appears on her face.

"The mineral springs?" she asks with a little pep, her eyes wide, having just figured it out.

"'Bout time you saw exactly what your property

offers, isn't it?" I'm itching to have my hands on her. Stepping closer, her smile widens as my hand wraps around her waist.

"Give me five minutes," she says, almost jumping with excitement in my arms, and I smirk as I squeeze her waist.

"What, no arguing today?" I ask her, and she laughs.

"Well, I only argue when my grumpy neighbor tries to tell me what to do with my land. Since you are being nice, I can be nice too." Her voice has a ring of tease to it, and I hum in contentment as I watch her run up the porch and inside. By the time I grab the blanket and picnic I organized from the back of the truck, she is back down to me.

"Okay, ready," she says, locking her front door, and I grab her hand, walking her around the side of her place and through a gate at the fence line.

"Oh, this is so exciting. Is it far?" Her hands are small, soft, delicate as they entwine with mine, and I can't take my eyes off her looking around the green fields, trying to take it all in from her perspective. I have looked at these rolling hills all my life, but I now get to see them through her eyes, and with the sun shining, it is a beautiful day for it.

"So the distillery land starts over there." I point it out. "Your property line starts here, and then you have all the way over to that point over there." She takes it all in as we continue to walk farther into the field.

"It's a lot. I mean, I obviously saw the plans, but it is so different seeing everything like this," she says, her expression relaxed. I look at her, noticing her hair blowing a little around her face and the shadows on her cheeks from her long lashes.

"The mineral springs are down this small path," I tell her as I lead her down into a small valley, the hills creating a private setting, and I can already hear the small flow of water from the nearby stream that puts me more at ease.

"It is so beautiful and quiet," she says in awe. We walk together, my hand never leaving hers. The peacefulness lowering my shoulders, her hand in mine feels all too perfect. I got Rochelle at the diner to put together a picnic lunch for us today. My chefs at the distillery restaurant were too busy, and I wanted something more casual anyway.

"So you grew up here, on this land?" she asks, looking up at me.

"All my life. The distillery land was where our family home was. Once my parents died, I turned it into the distillery it is today. I live at the back of the distillery, as does my son Connor," I tell her, and she smiles.

"I grew up in a high-rise apartment. Central Park was the closest nature walk for me, and even then, it is always bumper to bumper with people. This just feels so..." she trails off, taking a big breath in. "...perfect," she says, and I rub her hand with my thumb as we continue walking through the track.

"So you, Lucy, and Jasmine are becoming good friends?" I know they have been spending time together and I'm curious if she is making friends here.

"The girls have been amazing. So helpful with the house and also just great to have girly catch-ups," she says just as we reach the bottom of the trail, the large spring on show for her.

"Wow." Wide-eyed, she comes to a stop. "This is amazing," she says, taking a tentative step forward. The water glistens, and on a day like today with the sun high, the warmth down here is like a hit of serotonin.

"The spring is a natural mineral spring, so the temperature is a bit warm but very soothing," I tell her, and she bends down to feel the water.

"This looks like heaven," she says, her smile wide with pure delight. "What are we waiting for?"

"Let's go." Pulling her along, I find us a spot on the grass nearby. I lay out the large blanket and towels and put the picnic basket down. As I get our things sorted, she disrobes, kicks off her shoes, and lifts her dress from her frame, and as I look at her, I almost stumble. She is in a bright-pink bikini, and I am starting to understand that it might be her favorite color. It fits her all too perfectly, pushing her breasts up a little, the curve of them teasing me. Her skin is smooth, her body curvy, and as I take in her perfect ass, the swoop of her waist, then the perfect curve of her ample breasts, I forget that I am staring.

"Something wrong?" she asks coyly, knowing exactly what is happening. I decide to fight fire with fire, and I grab my t-shirt from the back of my shoulders and pull it over my head.

"You like pink?" I ask as I throw my top next to her dress, watching her eyes roam, a light tint coming to her cheeks.

"It's my favorite color." She smiles as she tentatively steps into the water. My eyes continue to roam her body, and I think pink is now my favorite color too. Having lived a life of just Connor and me for years, I never had the heavy influence of a female in our life. So pink, lace, cute sundresses, and anything else that is feminine has been completely absent.

"Careful, it can be a bit slippery," I tell her, grabbing her hand again, not wanting her to slip and take a fall. She has already been too injured for my liking.

"Ah-mazing," she groans as she submerges, her eyes closing, the warm water immediately soothing her. I follow suit, the water hitting my tired muscles, and I feel the relaxation taking over on contact.

"Amazing is right."

We both swim a little and get used to the water. It is so warm, a small amount of steam rises from the surface, our skin now shiny with moisture.

"No wonder the kids come here. This really is heaven." Floating on her back, her breasts push up out of the water, and I swallow harshly at the sight. I am itching to pull the pink cup down and put her nipple in my mouth.

"I am not sure the kids relax like this. They probably get up to mischief every time they are here," I tell her as I stand, brushing the water from my hair. It is deep but only comes to my chest. Victoria won't be able to touch the bottom, though.

"How often do you come here?" she asks me as she slowly swims around me.

"Well, Marie never used it so she didn't care who came here. Maybe once a week, if I could manage it. It's a nice quiet spot to think. De-stress."

"So the distillery keeps you pretty busy, then?" She swims closer to where I am, floating right in front of me.

"There is a lot going on, that is for sure," I say as she swims right past me, and I lean forward to grab her hand. "Come here." Pulling her toward me, her body glides through the water, and she giggles, the sound making me jut my chest out even more.

I smooth my hand around her waist and pull her body against mine. Her soft skin feels amazing, and my hand splays over her lower back, my other hand running up her side.

"Does everyone always do as you ask?" she asks me teasingly. Her hands slowly run up my arms, the water dripping down my bicep tickling me as she cups my neck.

"You tell me," I say gruffly. "Give me those lips..." Not able to hold back a moment longer, I move my hand and tilt her chin up. Her lips lift a little at the sides in a small smile before she proves my point and leans forward, giving me exactly what I asked for.

I hug her tightly as her lips meet mine, and I kiss her softly, taking my time. My hand moves from her chin to cup her jaw as I deepen the kiss. The water keeps her buoyant in my arms, but I keep our bodies sealed together, liking the way we fit. Our kiss yesterday was passionate, desperate, and needy. This one is all those things but slowed down enough to feel everything fully. Deliberately.

"You are so good at that," she murmurs on my lips, her body curving into mine. I feel her legs shift before they hook around my waist, and I drop my hands immediately to cup her ass, my fingers digging under her swimwear as I squeeze her cheeks in my hands.

"You are... so fucking sexy," I growl on her lips in between our kisses. Her body moves on mine, her fingers threading into my hair, her breasts pushing against my naked chest. The only thing between us is her flimsy bikini and my swim shorts, both doing very little to shield our desires from one another.

"Now if you had started with that instead of demanding I give you my property the first time we met, then we could have had a swim like this that much sooner," she says cheekily, and I smile wide against her lips and let out a chuckle. She is right.

She pulls back to look at me. "With kisses like that, it kinda makes a girl feel wanted," she says softly with a smile that almost makes her look dazed.

"With lips like yours, it's hard not to want more," I tell her straight as I take her lips with mine again, this time with more vigor. Holding her body to my wet chest, my hands cup her ass, one trailing up her back, touching her as much as I can.

"Tanner," she moans as her hips grind into mine. I'm hard as stone at the sound of my name on her lips like that.

"Hey, what are you doing here, old man!" I hear someone yell, and I pull back sharply. Victoria gasps as her head swivels around, quickly looking in the direction over her shoulder where the voice came from.

"Shouldn't you be in school?" I growl at the local boys who have turned up. All in their shorts and stripping off.

They are generally good kids, but I know that they are currently playing hooky. Victoria's grip on me tightens.

"We have a free afternoon, came for a swim. Good thing we found you; we don't want an old guy like you having a heart attack down here. Looks like you were already getting mouth to mouth," a kid I know as Joey says, and his friends all laugh.

"He's a bit cheeky?" Victoria says, looking at me, her eyes sparkling in delight.

"Too cheeky for his own good," I tell her as I look back at the boys, who are now running off the sides and jumping in the mineral springs, using the water as their own party pool. They are all teenagers, fit, tall, the zest of youth running through their bodies, and I have never felt older than I do now as I watch them all splash and play around. That was me once upon a time. Now my hair is gray, my face more wrinkled, yet I'm with this beautiful woman in my arms, who is now chuckling at the craziness of it all.

"There goes our serenity," she says, smiling at me like I gave her the world. But she doesn't move. Her legs remain wrapped around my waist under the water, her hands still looped around my neck. I run my hand up and down her bare back, enjoying the fact that she didn't leap out of my arms in embarrassment when the kids arrived.

"You want to stay?" I ask, because I have no idea how long these kids will be here.

"Sure. I mean, if you do have a heart attack, I think we both know that I am very good at giving mouth to mouth," she teases, and I growl, eliciting a loud cackle from her as she throws her head back, laughing out loud.

I take the opportunity to kiss her glistening skin at her collarbone, making my way up her neck and back to her lips.

Never in a million years did I ever think I would be here doing this. Whispers has been like a sanctuary for me. Somewhere that people knew my history. I never even thought about bringing a woman whom I met from the city here. I kept the two lives very separate, because having a woman here in my town makes it real. Makes it serious. I can't have a fling in Whispers, and now with Victoria in my arms and kissing her in front of the local teenagers, I am treading on thin ice because I am not sure she will even stick around.

But for the first time ever, I am willing to give it a try.

21

TANNER

"Victoria?" I holler from her front porch.

The door is wide open, the screen still closed. After spending the entire day together at the spring yesterday, laughing, playing, touching, and kissing, I have been eager to see her again. I had so much work to catch up on overnight, which took twice as long as normal because all I could think about was how good she felt in my arms and how I want to get back to her to finish what we had started before the kids turned up. I was expecting her to jump from my arms and maybe run to cover herself, but she didn't care that people saw us together. I know the small-town gossip is probably going into overdrive, but she laughed and stayed in my arms, not put off by any of it. I am a little nervous with her being so much younger, but she had no hesitations with it yesterday, so I hope she feels the same way I do.

"In here," she calls out, seeming a little preoccupied. When I walk in, I see why.

"What's all this?" I ask, spotting her sitting on the floor with a few boxes around her, paperwork and photos everywhere.

"Marie's things." She looks up at me, smiling, and just like that, I feel the stress in my shoulders soften and my dick harden. Today, she is wearing her signature bright-pink lipstick, making the blue of her eyes even brighter. I have no idea where the hell she has been all my life, but fuck, I am glad I met her now. *She was in kindergarten, asshole,* the devil on my shoulder reminds me.

"Anything interesting?" I ask her, taking a seat on her soft sofa, wondering if I could find something like this for my place. It feels like I am sitting on a damn cloud.

"Some old papers and things. I found this, which was interesting..." she trails off.

"What is it?" I ask as she hands me the paper.

"It is a letter from my father to Aunt Marie. Looks like they had a dispute over this property a few decades ago. It was around the time that he brought Mom and me here for a visit," she says, frowning as she thinks. My eyes skim through the letter. It isn't nice. Her father is basically threatening Marie with legal action and a whole range of other things in order to get this property.

"Marie mentioned that it was her parents' place, but we never got into the details," I murmur as I try to think back. Marie was always pretty private about her family life. I am sure my parents knew her parents, but they weren't close.

"From this letter, and a few others I found like it, it seemed my father thought he was more entitled to the property than Marie. Although she was the older sibling and lived here already. My father skipped out of the family home when he was much younger, and I don't think he ever returned until he brought me and Mom here years later."

"Family disputes when a parent passes are common."

"I know. But they sound nasty," she says with a frown.

"As you said, it was decades ago. Your father has clearly moved on, given that I have never seen him around and Marie never said anything." I try to calm her concerns, although mine are also heightened. I remember what Connor found on him, and now I really want to get some security cameras installed here.

"Anyway, enough about that. Look what else I found." She lifts an old photo album, and I sit forward, looking down over her shoulder.

"Who is it?" I ask her, and she giggles, the noise making my heart thud. *Fuck. Get a grip, Tanner.*

"It is me," she says, smiling, and I look closer, seeing a young Marie with a young girl on her lap. She's blond with two cute pigtails, digging in the dirt. If I didn't already know it was her, the pink bows might give me a hint. "I told you I was here before."

"Marie looks young. Who is that in the background?" I ask, seeing a man.

"That's my father. I barely recognize him. He left Mom and me when I was a kid. I haven't seen him since." I get the feeling that is not something she regrets or misses. I take a hard look at the man to see if I recognize him, but I come up blank, so I move the conversation in a different direction.

"This photo was taken a few years ago," I murmur,

looking at the landscape behind them, seeing the main distillery being built.

"I think I was about five or six," she says, and I mentally do the math and realize she is even younger than Connor. I swallow harshly.

"Cute then and cute now," I say, my gaze moving from the pictures and back to her.

"I bet you say that to all the girls," she teases, looking up at me. She has a carefree expression on her face, and her long hair flows down her neck and over her shoulders.

"Only the special ones," I tell her in jest with a wink. I can't actually remember being this flirty with anyone else. Not in the bright light of day without a few whiskeys under my belt and certainly not in Whispers.

"Special as in good, or are you being sarcastic?" Putting the album down, she sits up on her knees. With me leaning forward on the edge of the sofa, we are now almost eye to eye.

"As in very fucking good," I growl at her, and the temperature in the room lifts about two hundred degrees. Her hands run my up legs, and she positions her body between them.

"That swim yesterday was better than good before we got interrupted," she whispers, her cheeks turning pink as her chest moves up and down a little quicker. My mind whirls at how good she felt, her bare skin, her moaning and grinding her hips against mine. We have bickered since we met, but there was always this under-lying tension, and I want to rip these clothes off her and have her scream my name in ecstasy rather than frustration. I tried to go slow at the mineral spring yesterday, tried to be a gentleman, but now I am barely keeping it together.

"That swim was fucking phenomenal..." I reach out and cup her cheek, my thumb brushing against her jaw slightly as our eyes meet, knowing exactly how this is going to end.

"I vote we do that again." Her breathy voice is my undoing.

"I second that motion," I say, having been waiting for this moment all day. I move quickly and scoop her up off the floor and into my lap as a small squeal of surprise flees from her lips. Her legs fall on either side of mine and her hands run up my arms.

"That's better... right here with me..." Pulling her face to meet me, I take her lips with mine. I'm greedy. It has been a long time since I felt like this, and I never want this feeling to end. When I sweep my tongue across her bottom lip, she opens for me, and I don't hesitate to kiss her deeply. She tastes sweet, warm, and welcoming, her lips soft, and I bite the bottom one a little. She rewards me with a moan, the sound running from her mouth to mine and all the way down to my cock, which is now throbbing in my pants.

"At least we won't get interrupted here," she whispers against my mouth as she grinds down on me, her hands running up my neck and diving into the hair at my nape. She is right. No one is coming. It is just me and her and our desire for each other. I hold her tight, but with her on top, I let her lead. I know what I want, and now I need her to show me if she wants the same thing. But with the way she is moving and moaning and pulling my hair, I think I have my answer.

"It has been hard staying away from you today, baby girl." The endearment feels so natural, and she whimpers in response, kissing me even more hungrily. My hands slip around her waist and grip her full, round ass cheeks, molding them in my hands.

"Tanner," she pants as my lips leave hers and trail down her jaw, her head falling back, baring her neck to me.

"You are so fucking beautiful," I murmur, captivated by the feel of her in my arms, the scent of her perfect skin, and the movement of her hips as they rub against mine. My hands lift from her ass, and I caress them up her back, cupping her waist and moving them around her front, my thumbs brushing against the sides of her breasts and back down again. Her body is incredible.

"Your hands feel like they are everywhere," she says as I find her ass again and start moving her hips in rhythm with her little jolts. Fuck, it feels good. To have her in my arms, but to feel her grinding into me. My cock is burning for release, pressing so hard against my zipper from feeling her warmth.

"I want to touch you," I tell her, and her breath hitches before she speaks.

"God, yes." Her tongue delves into my mouth, tangling with mine, as my hands find the front of her sweats and glide underneath the waistband. When I hit lace with my fingers, I can't hold back my groan.

"Pretty lace is my kryptonite," I tell her in between our kissing, her hands cupping behind my head and pulling my mouth to hers. Women in lace is a favorite of mine. The hints of skin that show through the lace, the soft feel of it. Damn, just feeling it on my fingers, knowing it is the only thing covering her pussy is a turn-on.

"I'm starting to think that maybe you are mine," she admits, then seals it with another searing kiss, and my breath lodges in my chest. She wants me. I want her. It's game on.

I lean into the sofa as she sits back slightly and whips her t-shirt over her head, throwing it to the floor. Her hair falls around her bare shoulders, showcasing her see-through matching lace bra, her pink nipples peeking through. My eyes canvass over her beauty and the fact that she is opening up just for me.

"Jesus," I moan, not hesitating as I run one hand up her naked torso to cup her breast, molding it in my hand, squeezing it and rolling her nipple. I hear her breathing quicken, and I grab her at the nape of the neck and pull her back to me, slamming my lips to her. In the same moment, I slide my hand under the lace underwear and feel her wet pussy.

"Oh God... yes...." she moans, our kiss becoming more frantic as I glide my finger around her wetness and over and over her clit repeatedly. Her body shakes with each touch and her hips move faster against my hand.

"You are so wet, baby girl. Is this all for me?" Slipping a finger inside her, my palm presses against her clit. Fuck, she is gorgeous.

"Yessss. Oh... my... God... yes... That feels so good," she whimpers, holding on to my shoulders, leaning back from me a little as she grinds down harder. In this position, I get to watch her, eyes closed, head back, face toward the ceiling. Her long hair cascades down her back and sways back and forth with the movement. I have one hand cupping her ass, still pushing and pulling her hips in motion, my other hand finger-fucking her, and I feel like I am the luckiest fucking asshole on the planet.

"That's it... Have you been thinking about yesterday? About how much you were grinding on me, how hard you made me? You haven't left my mind," I say, slipping in a second finger. Mewling, she nods and bites her bottom lip. "Good girl... Fuck my fingers... that's it..." My praise for her has the desired effect as her movements become hastier. As I rub my thumb over her clit with tighter circles, her body quivers.

"I'm going to come... Oh God, Tanner, I am going to come!" Her voice rises an octave before her mouth opens in a silent scream, curves shaking through her release as she grinds down on my hand. She looks fucking magnificent. Panting, she slows her movements, and I do the same, relishing the arousal now coating my fingers. When she looks back at me, cheeks flushed, her blue eyes glisten, and then she fucking smiles. It lights me up inside.

I'm not sure how it can get better than this.

22

———

VICTORIA

Oh. My. God.

I can't remember the last time I orgasmed like that. I don't remember ever having an orgasm in this position, grinding on a man's hand, having him call me his *good girl*. Those words alone make me almost combust again. My body is quivering as I watch him. I can barely get my thoughts together as Tanner moves his hand from my underwear, brings his fingers to his lips, and sucks.

"Shit," I whisper, wide-eyed, still panting on his lap, my body on fire. I have never had a man do that before. Lick me from his hand, and wow, it is hot. Leaning in quickly, I put my lips to his, kissing him feverishly and tasting myself. He is right. Yesterday at the springs is all I have been thinking about. It is almost like my body yearns for him. It is a feeling I haven't had for a long time. Even with Josh, I never felt like I needed him. But with Tanner, I ache for his touch.

He growls in my mouth as his tongue fights with

mine. Cupping my face, he pulls me closer, like he can't get enough. I grip on to his shirt against his strong chest, ensuring he is real and that this is really happening. As his hips jut up a little, I feel him underneath me. *All of him.* I let my hands fall from his chest down his torso, taking my time, feeling his hard body underneath until my palms hit his belt. With my heart thumping, I sit back slowly, my lips throbbing from our kiss as I catch my breath and grab the leather at his waist.

"What are you doing?" His voice is gravel, his eyes on me so intense I feel it to my core as I undo his belt. The leather is firm yet soft, not unlike the man himself.

"What does it look like I'm doing?" I tease, licking my lips. I pop open the button on his jeans and lower his zipper, all the while he watches me closely.

"It looks like you are a woman who knows exactly what she wants," he says, and I smile. Because for the first time in my life, I resonate with what he is saying. Not just here and now with him. But this house, this town. This life.

"I am. And I plan on taking it." With his pants now open, I slide down from his lap and gently kneel on the floor at his feet. My breathing quickens in anticipation.

"Shit," he murmurs as he shifts a little, helping me push his jeans lower. Gliding my hands up his legs, I pull down his underwear, noticing a trail of salt-and-pepper hair leading beneath his boxer shorts, the tight ones. Full designer brand. As his length pops out, I almost cough in surprise. My eyes are glued to him. His cock is as big as every other part of him and has me swallowing roughly.

You're not in Kansas anymore, Victoria. My eyes flick to his and see him watching me.

"Wrap those lips around me, baby girl, and let me feel that throat of yours." He nostrils flare and my pussy clenches. No one has ever talked to me the way Tanner has and it turns me on. *A lot.* In front of others, he is such a good neighbor, the man about town, friendly to everyone. But here, right now, his dirty talk is my undoing, and I feel my feminism wane because all I want to do is please him just so he can call me his good girl.

"Since you asked so nicely," I say sweetly, and his eyes alight with mine locked on his. Lowering, I take the tip of him in my mouth and moan. He hisses a little at the initial contact, which only makes me want to hear more of the sound. Wrapping my hand around the base of his cock, I taste, lick, and tease him.

"Mmmmmm, that's it..." I hear his chest rumble, so I suck on him fully, hollowing my cheeks as I start bobbing up and down. His cock strengthens even more, feeling thicker and longer, and he fists his hand into my hair.

"God, I knew that mouth was going to be good. It's fucking perfect, like every other inch of you..." He groans as I take him deeper. Pulling my hair up high, he holds it tight on my head, the sting in my scalp welcome as he watches me take him deeper.

I bob quicker, as his other hand grips the back of my head. My mouth is wide, and as I feel him hit the back of my throat, I moan.

"Fuck, you are so good, baby girl, so fucking good."

My pussy throbs at his words. I think I could come

from his voice alone. Squirming, I try to get some friction, my lace underwear doing little to help the situation.

"Jesus, like that. You look so pretty with my cock in your mouth," he grits out, and I watch his torso muscles flex and tighten. "I'm close, baby, and I don't want the first time I come to be in your mouth. Get up here. I want you to ride my cock." *Yes, please.*

I pop off him and stand up, removing my sweats and underwear.

"Just as bossy in the bedroom," I murmur as I stand in nothing but my bra and watch as he grabs a condom from his wallet and sheathes himself. My heart trips over in palpitations.

"Come here," he says, grabbing my hands, and I step toward him and saddle his lap again. "This alright for you?" His eyes search mine.

"This is perfect," I say as I sit up a little and guide him to my entrance. My breath catches as he starts to slide inside, already feeling the stretch.

"Mmmm, fuck." His voice vibrates from his chest and feels like it travels throughout my entire body as I he slides deeper to fill me completely. "Look at how you take me."

"So good," I whisper, biting my bottom lip.

"Move those hips, baby girl. Ride me."

And I do. I grip on to his shoulders, taking him over and over, bouncing and grinding like my life depends on it.

"Tanner, oh..." I moan his name, barely thinking straight. He is so thick, I feel him somewhere different inside me with every motion.

"That's it, baby… You're squeezing me so fucking hard… Your pussy is begging for me." His head pushes back into the sofa, watching me with a groan as I work him over.

"You feel so good," I whimper, just as one of his hands moves from my hip to my breast, pinching my nipple through the lace.

"Give me your mouth." Sitting forward, him now on the edge of his seat, he pulls me close, his arms wrapping around my back, his mouth fighting with mine. Our lips now sealed, he grabs my ass in his hands and starts pulling me up and down, tightly gripping on to my flesh.

"So good… So good, Tanner. I need this. I need you…" I begin to pant against his lips as my hips thrust on top of his, my clit brushing his pelvis over and over again.

"Fuck me, baby girl. Take what you need. Your pretty pussy feels so fucking good on my cock," he says gruffly, before his thumb is on my clit and rubbing in circles.

"Oh God, Tanner…" I whimper at his touch. I am highly sensitive from my last orgasm, his words and the way he touches me making me even more heightened.

"Look at your beautiful breasts in this lace…" His lips move from mine and kiss lower, burying his head in my chest, his thumb still rubbing me, his movements faster.

"I'm going to come," I warn him, body trembling as my core tingles.

"Together." He sits back on the sofa again, watching me. One hand on my waist, he guides me over his lap faster, his thumb still treasuring my clit, chasing the high.

"You like to watch me," I pant out, smiling.

"You are a fucking vision." Gritting his teeth, I know he is close as well.

"I like your eyes on me," I tell him honestly. I like the way he looks at me like I am his and he can't get enough. Just that thought has me clenching around him.

"Come for me, baby girl. Let me watch you unravel on my cock." His words ignite me, and I combust with a high-pitched scream I don't even recognize.

"Oh shit," I pant as flames continue licking my skin. "Shit, I'm still coming... Right there. Oh my God!" I grind into him at a feverish pace, my release pulsing through me until I can't see straight. His smile is wicked as I bite my bottom lip, then he pinches my clit, and I just about convulse with another scream. This time, it's his name. And that seems to set him off.

"Fuck. Me," he roars, thrusting up into me with abandon, coming straight after me with his arms holding me close. I'm still feeling tremors of pleasure as we both pant, our bodies hot, him still inside me. My cheeks are probably bright red, but I don't care because I feel all tension leave my body in his embrace.

"I think I died," I murmur, my forehead now resting against his shoulder, moving in time with his breaths as his chest rises and falls rapidly.

"...and went to heaven," he finishes the sentence as his hands move, coming to my waist before running up my bare back and down again.

"That was so good," I say, almost in disbelief.

"That was better than good."

I feel heavy in his arms as he wraps me up and hugs me, pressing soft kisses on my head.

"Did you know coming here today that your visit would result in an orgasm?" I ask him, and he chuckles.

"You're full of surprises, that's for sure." His lips brush down my jaw, his hands now caressing up and down my sides, making me moan. The two of us are slowly coming back to earth, but I don't want this to stop. Everything about him feels so good.

"So are you," I say honestly.

"This isn't how I usually spend my weekdays," he says with a smirk.

"Who knew all it took was a little lace," I tease, smiling at him.

"There's more to you than lace, baby girl, a whole lot more."

And just like that, I see myself falling for Tanner Whiteman a little more.

It is then I hear a ringtone, and I sit up, frowning. "What's that?"

"My phone. Ignore it," he says, looking lust-drunk, and I smile before I lull back against him and resume my previous position. Before I can say anything, I hear it again.

"You sure you don't want to get that?" I ask him, turning my head to look at him.

"I'm pretty comfortable," he murmurs, before leaning down and taking my lips. He kisses me softly and slowly. In complete contrast to how he kissed me earlier.

We are lost in the moment, but the distinct ring breaks through again.

"You should get it," I tell him, sitting up, our moment broken.

With a sigh, he runs a hand through his hair. I lift off him and put my clothes back on and he zips up his jeans, grabbing his cell.

"This better be good," he growls into the phone, and I laugh, him softening immediately as he looks at me.

I don't hear the other end of the conversation, but I can tell by the way his face contorts that something isn't good.

"Jesus. I'll be right there." He ends the call and stands immediately.

"I need to go. There has been an incident at the distillery," he says, and my smile instantly morphs into concern.

"Everything alright?" I ask as he grabs his things.

"They were a hell of a lot better about ten minutes ago," he drawls in his deep tone before cupping my jaw and pulling my lips back to his. Our height difference is noticeable, and I lean up to reach him, his warm lips now so used to mine.

"I'll call you," he murmurs, going back in for another quick kiss.

"I'll be here," I tell him, and I see his eyes light up in what looks like appreciation before he steps away and runs out the door, back to his truck, and speeds away.

23

TANNER

I wanted to stay with Victoria all afternoon yesterday. Who wouldn't after she gave me the best blow job of my entire life and came on my cock, leaving me breathless and instantly wanting to do it all again.

But I got a call from Connor, and the day went downhill from there. Now I rub my eyes because I have had little sleep. It took us all last night to clean up, all morning to fix what was broken, and now a full day later, we are all feeling defeated. I stand in one of my aging rooms, surveying the team who have all been called in. My jaw is tight and my head is already throbbing, the memory of my beautiful neighbor now pushed to the back of my mind while I work out how to fix this mess.

"Tell me again how this happened?" I ask, looking around at the team, who're all full of remorse and sadness.

"It was an accident," Lacy says. It isn't her fault, but I know she takes everything to heart.

"I'm sorry, sir. It was my fault. There were flowers on the side, and I have allergies. I sneezed, and my hand must have slipped when I was steering the forklift," one of my workers says, and I breathe out, nodding. I look at him, taking in his red eyes and his running nose. He isn't lying, if the amount he is wiping it is any indication. It was an accident; these things happen. But as I glance at the spot in my aging room, where only twenty-four hours before it was covered in broken oak barrels and fermented whiskey, the stench is still strong, and this has set us back a little bit.

"What the hell are flowers doing in my barrel room?" I ask, confused, looking right at Connor and Lacy.

Connor shrugs and shakes his head so I look at Lacy.

"Jasmine came by. I was busy with the shipment out the back, so I left her to it. She knows not to put any flowers in here, though, so I don't know why she did," Lacy says, frowning. I take a breath and try to calm my anger. I have a good team of people here. All locals and all who have been working at Whiteman's for years. We'll figure this out. "Maybe we can make what's left of this batch a limited edition?" she suggests.

"How so?" Connor barks, as pissed off as I am. Lacy stiffens, and I look between them. They don't know each other very well. I hired Lacy a few months ago and Connor has been in the city for most of that time.

"Well, maybe we can design a special label, potentially design a new look bottle. Market it a little different-ly?" Lacy explains, and I am now seeing her Marketing and Communications degree coming in handy. I nod at her to continue.

"We could cut the aging process, and then offer it as a special edition for the holidays?" Connor chips in, and I like that idea.

"What would we call it?" I ask, looking around the group of staff, who, although deflated from losing so many barrels, are starting to look more hopeful. It isn't every day the forklift pierces a barrel, which has a domino effect on the others, leaving us with less than half the aging barrels we had in this particular room. It is one of the reasons I put in multiple aging rooms. All with fire walls between them. The distillery is huge, with five different aging rooms, the main restaurant and tasting area, as well as the manufacturing and bottling space and our warehouse.

"We could make it a gold label?" Lacy suggests, and I like it, but it isn't different enough.

"This will be stupidly exclusive. I estimate what, maybe a couple of thousand bottles at best. The name needs to be more. Meaning more. It has to be different," I prompt them, and they all look deep in thought.

"What about creating our own sub brand. Whiteman's Next Door?" Connor says seriously.

"Next door?" My brow furrows, wondering what he is thinking.

"We could market it as the exclusive whiskey you share with your friends. Your *neighbors*." He gives me a look, and I raise an eyebrow. He is a smart-ass sometimes, and I know he is teasing me, but in front of all our staff, I can't berate him.

"We market it like the beverage of choice to celebrate

the holidays, keeping you and your neighbor warm from the inside out," Lacy says, her smile small but starting to build.

"Next Door?" I ask the group of staff, and I get a few nods with positive comments.

"Instead of a black label, we can make this one navy blue. We could then replace the golden WW logo of our regular batch with a golden door. *Next Door by Whiteman's. Meant to be shared,*" Lacy says.

"I like it," I say, nodding. It really is a great idea, and there's definitely meaning behind it. Exactly what I was hoping for. "Alright, let's get back to work," I tell the rest of the staff. The whole place still smells like pure alcohol, and after a spill like this, it can become a fire hazard. My team now needs to do some serious deep cleaning before they go home for the day, so they all start to get busy as Lacy, Connor, and I regroup.

"I can get the design team to mock something up?" she asks, looking excited.

"Do it. You can manage this project, Lacy," I tell her and she looks at me, wide-eyed.

"Really?" she asks with bated breath.

"Treat it like your baby. You've been here a few months now, so I'm promoting you to marketing manager. You and Connor can work together on this release." If I had a feather, I think it would knock her over.

"Thank you, Tanner," she says with an eager nod. "I won't let you down."

"I know." Lacy has proven herself. Time and time

again, she has gone above and beyond. Things are not great at home for her, but a young woman like her really needs to start her career, and if Whiteman's can help her, then I feel like that is what I should do. She smiles wide and jumps on the spot before turning and leaving the warehouse on cloud nine.

"You want me to babysit her?" Connor asks me, seemingly less than impressed.

"Don't underestimate her. She finished top of her class. She is only back in Whispers because of her mother," I tell him as we walk to the boardroom.

"I don't have time to babysit her, Dad. I have our tax position to get sorted; I need to dot the i's and cross the t's on Van Cleef. Not to mention, I need to get back to the city for a meeting with the overseas distributors about finalizing the contracts," he says, and I pause to look at him.

"Just do your best. I will be here with her most days, but I think it would be good for you to get to know her," I tell him, and he sighs.

"Fine," he grumbles like he is ten and I am asking him to do his chores, and I smile at that memory as we close the door to talk privately. Walking to my chair, I see a floral arrangement on the sideboard. We have no external meetings this week, so I am surprised.

"Connor, what the hell are flowers doing in my aging rooms?" I am still totally baffled by that.

"No idea. I think Jasmine probably thought that since we take our tour groups through those rooms, that maybe we wanted to brighten up the place." He sits and sighs, the weight of this issue now firmly on our shoulders.

"I am starting to think hiring her to add floral arrangements wasn't a smart idea," I murmur as I run my hands through my hair.

"They are good in the restaurant and at reception," he offers, and I nod. "How's Victoria doing?" Connor asks, changing the subject, knowing I was with her yesterday when he called me.

"Fine. Her ankle is all healed. But..." I try to get my thoughts together. It feels like it has been weeks since I saw her, not just twenty-four hours. "When you did that finance search on her, you mentioned her father?"

"Yeah, there wasn't a lot on him. He has a small criminal record, plus bankruptcy. Why?" he asks, and I lean back in my chair.

"Victoria found some old paperwork from Marie's. Some letters from her father to Marie that were pretty nasty. Talking about the ownership of the property."

"You think now that Marie is gone, he might show back up?" Connor asks, coming to the same conclusion I am.

"Maybe. Maybe not. I am going to put a team on him. Find him. Watch him." I sit for a moment and think.

"Well, his financial situation didn't look good..." Connor says.

"Desperate men do desperate things." I tap out a text to the security team I use to tee up a meeting to talk about it tomorrow.

"Well, right now, we need to talk about our expansion plans. After what happened yesterday, I need to go through the quarterly numbers with you," Connor says, pulling out his laptop. And just like that, my ache to see

Victoria deepens. So I text her quickly before we get into it.

> I'll be working all night. Sorry again for rushing out yesterday.

> It's okay. I have found another album of photos so I am busy looking through family history.

> Any more cute pigtails?

> No, but will this do?

I look at the text as an image comes through. It is of her bare shoulders and part of her chest. She has nothing on but her white lace bra. It is not at all revealing, but my cock stirs already.

> You're killing me.

> Death by orgasm?

> Sign me up. I'll see you tomorrow.

> Don't work too hard.

Huffing, I look up and see Connor grinning at me. I roll my eyes and pocket my cell, still thinking about her. It feels nice to be wanted. And her independence is something that appeals to me. Her smile, her smarts. The way her body curves and the way her face transforms when she comes. I am starting to catch serious feelings

for this woman. And I don't know what the hell to do
about it.

VICTORIA

My body feels tight as I readjust myself on the floor. I have been here all day. After Tanner had to run out for an emergency at the distillery yesterday, I found another few boxes and have been spending my time going through them all.

Finding that letter from my father took me a little by surprise. Then finding more of them, along with legal letters, made it all a reality. I knew my father wasn't the best father or husband in the world, but these letters to his own sister are threatening, borderline harassment, and most certainly not something you would ever want to receive from a family member. It is clear he wanted this property, but not to live in like Marie. Maybe to sell, try and make money from, and I can see the dates of these letters and the details involved. Some of them are dated well after he had already left Mom and me, so it wasn't for him to provide his family a better life. I have no idea what to think of them, other than they continue to paint him in the same dark light my mother has all these years.

Mom mentioned we only came here a few times when I was younger, but there are a lot of photos of us. It is clear that Marie loved having us here. There are photos with her and me mostly, but also ones of her and Mom laughing outside. The ones of my father are few and far between, though, and I can tell that they never got along, even back then. I make a mental note to chat with Mom about it again. Maybe she will have some more information.

I pull out another large envelope, this one looking professional and with Jerry's legal firm stamp on it, the same one he used with my letter. It is the formal outcome of a court case between Marie and my father. One that is dated about ten years ago. Dad sued her for the property, citing family ownership, but as I read, I can see that Marie won that battle, my father getting nothing but legal bills by the looks of things. I throw the paperwork back in the box. This whole family history is becoming very negative. I set aside an old recipe book to look through later before my eyes fall on a photo.

"Oh my…" I say in awe as I lift it from the box and stare. It is Marie and Tanner. He is much younger, but there is no doubt it is him. The two of them are standing together outside. He must be in his early twenties, and it is a great shot of the two of them. They look happy but very stoic and reserved, and I smile as I take it all in. It warms my heart to know that they knew each other and helped each other out over the years. I put the photo in a small pile of others that I have, keen to make a large photo wall that runs up the length of the stairs.

My cell rings, and I grab it, needing a distraction from

my family drama, but Josh's name lights up the screen. This is call number ten today, and I have been ignoring him, but with a sigh, I bite the bullet and finally answer.

"What do you want?" I ask, preferring to skip the niceties. He doesn't deserve it. He doesn't deserve anything. I can't even believe I was with this guy.

"Victoria? Oh shit, you answered," he says, sounding surprised. I hear background noise, like he is in a car and I am on speakerphone. I roll my eyes even though he can't see me. I have no idea why I even accepted his stupid proposal and why I ever thought being with him was a good idea. Sure, he swept me off my feet at the start, but I ignored all the red flags and warning bells. In hindsight, I think it was because dating in New York was such a competitive sport, I was relieved to not do it a moment longer. Now after meeting Tanner and experiencing the butterflies and natural chemistry and developing feelings I have with him, I can't believe what I almost missed out on.

"Stop calling me, Josh," I tell him in the coldest voice I can muster.

"Victoria. No. We need to talk," he rushes out, almost desperately.

"We don't. We have nothing to talk about."

"But I miss you. I love you," he says, and I frown. Love? I swallow down the realization that I never loved him. I can't believe I almost married a man I didn't even love. The thought of what my life would have been like makes my stomach sink.

"You don't, Josh. Now please stop calling," I tell him again, losing my patience.

"I found you on social media. I am going to come to see you. I will book a plane ticket. We need to talk face-to-face."

That has me sitting up straight, and Tanner's voice rings in my head, talking to me about security. Not that I fear Josh, but if he found me so easily, then I really do need to be mindful.

"Josh. Seriously. We are over. There is nothing that will change my mind."

"You are my fiancée. We are getting married," he states slowly, like he is trying to drum it in and I am just being a silly toddler throwing a tantrum. *He is such an asshole.*

"No, Josh. I am not your *fiancée*. We broke up when I caught you having sex with your colleague, in my bed, in my apartment while I was looking for a wedding dress!" My voice gets higher pitched and angrier with every word, but I try to control myself because he is simply not worth it.

"It was one time. The last time with any woman aside from my beautiful wife for the rest of my life. A final fling."

I have heard it all before and I don't want to hear it anymore.

"A fling too many. Look, I just don't love you. I'm not sure I ever did. It is over. I am not coming back. Good luck to you, Josh. Goodbye." I end the call, wondering why he can't just get over it. I know it isn't love. He doesn't love anyone but himself.

I have been on cloud nine since seeing Tanner yesterday, but now after the letters from my father and the call from Josh, I feel jittery. I don't want to sit around here all day, and I feel uptight with nervous pent-up energy. I am not sure if I should drive, though. My ankle is healed, but I haven't driven in a while. Shaking that silly fear away, I get up and grab my things and head out to the truck. The door squeals open, and I jump in, starting it a few times before it finally seems to connect, and I head straight to the diner to grab dinner.

"Hey, Victoria. Welcome. I'm Rochelle," an older woman says from behind the counter as I take a seat on a stool.

"Nice to meet you," I say with a smile, not worried that she knows exactly who I am even though we have never met before. It is the small-town way. "I wanted to come by and pick up something easy for dinner. Tanner brought a chicken pie the other night and it was delicious."

She smiles immediately, giving me grandma vibes, and I adore her instantly.

"That Tanner is a man after my own heart. If only I was a few years younger," she says, giving me a wink and a smile. I huff out a laugh. She is adorable. "We have another wonderful chicken pie we can wrap up for you."

"Sounds great. Thank you." I smile, noticing her telling a young waitress to gather the pie for me. I get the feeling she is new and Rochelle is showing her the ropes.

"How is that ankle of yours? Tanner said you took quite the tumble," Rochelle asks, and we fall into a comfortable conversation about Marie's place and how the two of them were friends. It feels nice to meet more people in the community and makes me feel more connected to both Aunt Marie and the town in general.

"Your pie," the young waitress says, sliding it onto the counter. She looks a little nervous, and I look at her name tag.

"Thank you, Nikki."

She gives me a small smile but doesn't say much else.

"You enjoy that, dear," Rochelle says. "And let me know if you need anything, although it looks like you are back up and about already?" A look of slight concern takes over her face.

"Thanks, Rochelle. Just don't tell Tanner I was here. I don't think he wanted me driving until my ankle was one hundred percent," I whisper to her like I am telling her a secret, knowing full well she will tell him immediately. Her smile widens as I slip from the stool with the pie in hand.

"Your secret is safe with me. But darling, half the town saw you today. Tanner will already know that you have been driving around," Rochelle offers, and I huff. *Of course he will.* I smile at her and Nikki as I walk out the door and back to my truck. Getting out for a bit this afternoon was exactly what I needed, and I enjoy the fresh air with my window rolled down. As I pull up to the driveway, I park closer to the house, gather my things, and go through the front door rather than the back for a change.

But something catches my eye before I head inside. Stopping short, I look at my front garden bed, and there are tire marks like someone has run over it. I frown, as whoever it was also ran over one of the rose plants and damaged them. It must have been Tanner. He drove out of here pretty quickly yesterday afternoon when he got the frantic call from the distillery.

"That man..." I growl out loud to myself as I huff inside and put the oven on to warm up the pie. Glancing out the back window, I see the animals in the shed, so Kevin must have come and gone already. Garry is bleating louder than usual, but I will check on him a bit later.

As I step into the living area to pack up the photos and boxes I have out, I stop short and balk. Because there, right where I left it on the top of a box, is a photo of me and Marie, the one from when I was six and sitting on her knee. Except now, there is a big red rose lying on top that I didn't put there. It is one from the front garden bed. My breathing quickens and my palms start to sweat as I look around the house from where I stand, seeing nothing else amiss. I walk to the front door and inspect the lock because I am positive I locked the door when I left. But there is nothing to indicate any damage.

"I am such an idiot," I mumble, understanding washing over me that I probably forgot to lock it in my haste to get into town. Maybe Tanner came back, and as a peace offering for running over the garden, he put the rose inside. I sigh, rolling my shoulders. That has to be what happened.

Picking it up, I bring it to my nose, smelling my favorite scent and smiling. Tanner Whiteman may be grumpy, but he is also a charmer.

25

TANNER

I usually love working long days and nights with Connor here at the distillery. It is the way we have worked for years. But with the issue in the aging rooms, then us going through numbers all night last night, then online legal meetings today with Sawyer, it has been days since I last saw Victoria.

I look at my watch again, seeing it is now early in the evening. I told her I would come back over today, and I hate not being a man of my word. I have sustained on some text messages, and while she didn't mention it, I already know she has been into town because Rochelle told me when she came out today to deliver lunch to all the staff.

"So our financial projections are solid for the next eighteen months. We have had year-on-year growth since you started Whiteman's, Dad, and it is only getting better," Connor says with a wide but tired smile on his face.

"We work hard. We deserve it. Whispers deserves it," I

tell him, sitting back, exhausted. Numbers fly through my mind, legal contracts that I need to sign, the new Van Cleef deal that needs distributing dates finalized. My team has also started farming the barley so I can get started on making the next batch. But none of that has the same amount of brain space as Victoria.

"Want to go to the bar for dinner?" Connor asks, looking at me. We need to eat and relax and stop talking about business.

"We should, it is Lacy's last week there. Come next week, she will have her own office here and be working on the marketing plans for the next twelve months," I mention, watching him for his reaction.

"Her mom is pretty sick, right?" Connor asks with a frown, and I nod.

"Cancer," I tell him, and he sighs. It is a shit disease; I've lost too many people to it already. "I'm going to start building the ranch," I tell my son, changing the subject, and he looks at me with surprise.

"Why? You have had that piece of land for decades. You love living here on-site at the distillery." A mix of concern and confusion takes over his face.

"It's time. I will still live here, but I want to start thinking of the future, and having some space away from it all will be good. Griffin already made the plans and I have approved them. He has started on the block already." It is down the back roads, not far from Huxley and Hudson's family estate, just outside of town. Secluded, but not too far away.

Billionaire Boulevard is what the locals call it. The land sizes are huge, the trees tall, thick, and old, offering complete privacy. People who own ranches or land in that area spent millions sealing the roads, erecting privacy fencing, and putting in all the necessities, such as satellites and cables to run their corporations from there if they wish. Connor himself purchased a piece of land there a few years ago as well.

"From what I hear, you know a good interior designer. Maybe she can help you." Connor has the very same thought I have had on my mind as well. I need to talk to Griffin and get the plan fully in action before anything else, though. Just as I'm about to respond, my cell phone vibrates on the table and Victoria's name appears.

"Hey, baby girl," I croon to her automatically, the warmth spreading across my chest at seeing her calling me. I watch Connor smirk, and I ignore his stare.

"Tanner!" she screams, and I stand up so fast my chair hits the wall behind me.

"What's wrong?" I ask, Connor already jumping up and out the door, and I run to follow him. "Are you okay? Are you hurt? Is it your foot?" We run outside, straight into the truck, my heart lurching.

"Victoria?" I yell through the phone as Connor takes off down the road, because she hasn't answered me. Deep despair crawls up my neck like I haven't felt in decades. She is breathing heavily, panicked.

"It's Garry!" she wails, just as we pull up at her place and I jump out. I have never moved so fast in my life.

"It's the damn goat," I say to Connor, who visibly relaxes, but I'm still on high alert. I spot a large smile coming to Connor's face as he follows me out of the truck, the two of us running to the backyard where I see all the lights on in the shed.

"I'm here," I tell Victoria on the phone before I pocket my cell and Connor and I run toward the shed. He looks at me, the two of us a little less stressed as we jog around to the back of her house. I spot the rosebushes flattened at the front, and I frown. She obviously ran them over when she went to town yesterday, probably didn't hit the brake properly or something.

"What the hell is she doing out here at night on her own? Fucking coyotes. I haven't seen any bears around Whispers for years, but that is a possibility as well. Bobcats too," I growl to Connor.

"Calm down. You literally just spoke to her. She is alive." Connor chuckles, finding my panic over her hilarious.

"Tanner!" Victoria yells for me from the front of the shed, her eyes wide, her hands shaking. The nights here are cool and she is wearing a bright-pink beanie on her head. In all the darkness, she at least stands out.

"I'm here. What's going on?" I ask her, scooping her into my arms and against my chest. She is trembling a little, and I pull back, running my eyes up and down her to make sure she is okay and all intact.

"Garry... something is wrong," she says, worry written all over her face, and I follow Connor inside the shed and hear him laughing. Walking up to where he stands, I spot the goat lying on the ground in its pen and pull up short.

"Did you know it was pregnant?" Connor asks me as he tries not to laugh some more. I had a pretty good idea, but with everything going on, I had forgotten to talk to Victoria about it.

"Pregnant!" Victoria shrills from beside us, and we both look at her. She is pale, full-blown shock taking over.

"I thought it was a possibility," I murmur, moving slowly into the pen to check on the goat.

"Wait? What?" Victoria asks, looking between the two of us. Her expression of horror is almost laughable since it's spring and new babies are born every minute around here. I try to breathe through the immense fear I just felt. My heart rate lowers, my shoulders relaxing at the sight of her. Even though she is stressed, she looks amazing. Her hair is down, her skin is glowing, and she is wearing a cute pair of Daisy Dukes and the boots I got her. The farming lifestyle suits her.

"Hi, I'm Connor. I've heard a lot about you." My son's smart-ass smirk is on full display as Victoria looks at him, not understanding what in the world is going on.

"How can a male goat have babies? What kind of town have I moved to?" she says in disbelief, her head shaking.

"The goat is a female. *She* is currently in labor." I squat down next to the goat and run my hand over its belly, feeling the contractions. She still has a while to go. Hell, she will probably be in labor most of the night.

"Oh my God!" Victoria says, her hand slapping her forehead.

"Why did you think it was male?" Connor asks, looking at her like she is crazy. *My kind of crazy.*

"His name is Garry!" Victoria says, exasperated, waving her hands around.

"Not anymore." Connor snorts with a laugh, and I smile, liking that they are getting along.

"Oh my God. This cannot be happening." She starts pacing the shed. "Oh, Garry, no wonder you hated me; I thought you were a boy!"

It bleats at her like she understands.

"Need anything?" Connor asks me, and I shake my head.

"I got it," I tell him, as I know he is tired. He's seen many animals being born and probably has no desire to wait up all night to watch another one.

"You're leaving? You can't leave! Do we need a vet? Do we need a doctor? Do I need to boil water and get towels?" Victoria rambles.

"Now I know why my dad likes you so much. Have a good night, you two," Connor says with another laugh, and I shake my head as Victoria's mouth is agape, looking between me and Connor's retreating form.

"Just don't run over my roses like your dad did yesterday!" she yells out to him, and he waves as he gets into the truck and drives away.

"Take a breath, baby girl. It is all good." Coming up behind her, I put my hands on her shoulders. As I rub her arms up and down, I feel her take a deep breath, her body relaxing at my touch. The shock of seeing the goat like this was a lot for her.

"But Garry. Is he in pain? I mean, is she in pain? Oh my God, what do I call her now?" she says, spinning to face me, looking confused and crestfallen.

"Relax. I think she will be in labor for a little while. Let's go inside, grab some coffee and blankets, and make ourselves comfortable."

"Okay... if you're sure," she says, looking between me and the goat and back again.

"I'm sure. Come on." Grabbing her hand, her fingers immediately entwine with mine as we walk back to the house. The night is still, there are no clouds, the stars on full display. We make it a few steps before she stops, and I turn to face her.

"Thank you for coming so quickly, Tanner," she says, smiling softly as she looks up to meet my eyes.

"Anytime. You need me, I will be here." And I mean it.

She lifts up on her tiptoes and places a small kiss on the corner of my mouth. It feels nice. Her. Here. The silent night, the stars, her gratitude. Her honesty. I am starting to realize that I would do almost anything for her already. Including sitting up all night to deliver a baby goat.

"Come on. I'll make us some coffee," she says, then leads me inside, and I follow her immediately, not letting her out of my sight.

26

VICTORIA

"Why did you tell Connor I ran over your roses?" Tanner asks me as we walk back to the shed with a flashlight, him with a pile of blankets and me with two hot coffees. It is now late. After we got everything organized and I cleaned up my boxes in the living room, we decided to sit with Garry for the night and ensure she is okay.

"Because you did." I scoff at him as we set up our picnic place in the shed, sitting in a clear area, some straw underneath us to soften the floor. I am so relieved that he is here. I wasn't sure if I should call him or not, but I am so glad I did. He dropped everything for me and was here the moment I needed him. That feeling is like a balm to my skin, enveloping me in warmth that this man cares about me.

"No, I didn't," he says with a frown. We both take a seat, and I sigh. We are back to bickering already.

"Yes, you did. I think it happened the other day when you tore out of here to fix the problem at the distillery," I tell him, waving my hand around. I see him deep in thought.

"Who else came past here the last few days?" he asks, and my eyes narrow on him.

"No one. That's why I went to town because I was so bored. I noticed the roses when I got home," I tell him, wondering why he is not admitting it.

"So you did go to town?" Smirking, he quirks an eyebrow. I think he's enjoying calling me out. *Shit.*

"Fine. Yes, alright," I say with a huff, knowing full well he thinks I should have been resting and elevating my ankle to ensure I don't overuse it, but we both know I am fine.

"Rochelle told me," he says with a chuckle.

"I thought she was on my side!" I gasp. What happened to women sticking up for women?

"Baby girl, everyone in this town is on Whiteman's side."

I swoon where I sit when he calls me baby girl. It is like a tonic, immediately softening me and wrapping me up in a soft Tanner cocoon.

"Back to the roses. I know it was you because you left one in the living room for me," I say with a smile. He's not the only one being called out today.

I feel him tense next to me and snap my head up to look at him. His face is stern, deep concern etched into his brow. "I promise you, it wasn't me, Victoria," he assures me, and my body seizes a little. "Someone must have come here when you were gone." He is serious, and I believe him. But that doesn't have me feeling any less uneasy.

"But if it wasn't you, who was it?" I ask, confused and a little scared. Thinking about who it could be, I shiver.

"You need security around here," he says adamantly, taking my hand and softly squeezing it.

I sigh, my lips thinning as I think. I don't really want this place locked up with cameras everywhere. That alone would make me unsettled. Josh did mention coming here when I answered his call... Maybe he left the rose. All the signs point to him, and he sounded desperate enough. I look at Tanner, wondering if I should tell him.

"You might be right," I say, quietly nodding to him. "I'll do some research on what cameras to get." I tell him, already adding it to my mental to-do list, having no idea where to even start with all that. I don't like the idea, but safety needs to come first.

"Will you let me help you? I have a team. They can get the cameras and install them. It's your home, so you just tell them where to put them, but I can get them here for you," he asks, his eyes searching mine.

I am so used to doing everything on my own, I feel almost odd accepting his offer. But he isn't being bossy. He isn't telling me what to do. He is asking me and respecting my independence, and as I take a deep breath, I find myself smiling. I am not annoyed by him wanting to take control. Instead, I like how he is being protective. It's kinda sexy and makes me feel cared for. I'm not sure I can use my words right now, so I nod.

"Good," he says with a matching smile, and as if he senses my fear, Tanner changes the subject and lets me calm my remaining nerves.

"I thought maybe you ran over the roses yourself with your injured ankle. How is it feeling anyway?" he asks, lifting my leg and placing it on his lap, where he inspects the small purple scar that now runs across my ankle before he starts to massage it.

"You massaging it is making it all so much better now," I murmur, smiling, as his large hands run up and down my shin, his thumbs kneading my muscles. I'm putting the rose issue behind me. I am sure it was just someone who came by for a visit. A friendly neighborly gesture or something, and although I thought I had, I mentally scold myself for not locking the door.

Tanner chuckles, but his hands don't leave my skin. He looks relaxed himself, his shoulders lowered, his normal scowl faded into a content smile.

Garry bleats, and we both look at my goat who is doing a great job, moving around a little before settling again. I don't know how I know, but I feel like it is getting close.

"What's your plan for this place once you're done with renovations?" Tanner asks, and we sit back against the wall, getting more comfortable.

"I was thinking I would make it a farm stay for women who need a place," I tell him, smiling.

"Why's that?" He looks at me curiously.

"Well, I needed a place. It came just at the right time in my life when I needed a change. I feel like others might need one too. Somewhere to help them get through a tough season in their life. I just think about the women who experience heartbreak or trouble from their husbands like my mom did or their boyfriends, who may not be as lucky as me. Maybe I can give them a place to get over their heartbreak or bad situations in life," I say, trying to formulate it, the idea still brewing in my mind as I talk.

"So, are you planning on staying long term, or just here for your season of change?" He's not looking at me now, his jaw set as he stares straight ahead at Garry.

"The more time I spend here, the more I love it. It is starting to feel more like home than the city ever did. I am not exactly sure what I will do for work from here, though. Whispers doesn't have a lot of options in that regard." I take a sip of the hot coffee, letting out a little moan as he rubs my calf.

Small towns are great in many aspects, but employment can be scarce, especially for someone from the city. I haven't thought too much about my long-term plans. When I took on Marie's place, I did it to get myself out of the bad situation I was in. I was running away from something, not running to something. But now things are better, and my life feels like it is aligning and more settled, like I was always meant to be here. But I have no idea what I would do for work, and while renting out Marie's Place will be able to pay some bills, I don't think it is something I could rely on.

"I think Whispers looks good on you," Tanner says, and I catch him watching me.

"I think it does too," I say softly, smiling, and I get one in return, before Garry bleats out loudly and Tanner moves my legs to jump up.

"It's time," he says, and my panic flares.

"I AM NEVER HAVING CHILDREN," I say adamantly as I try to recover from what I just saw. A baby goat lies next to Garry.

"Hold up, there is a second one," Tanner says from where he is positioned next to the goat.

"A second one? What do you mean, a second one? How many do they have?" I shriek. They did not teach this at my school in the city, that is for sure.

"I think just the two," Tanner says, grabbing an old towel just as the second kid is pushed out, and I need to hang on to the fence of the pen to get a handle on the situation. Garry has been birthing for hours and now we have two baby kids. Both white, looking almost identical, except for a black patch that looks like a collar around one.

"Another girl," Tanner says, standing to come closer to me. Garry is still panting.

"Is Garry alright?" I ask him, and he looks at me funny.

"You know you need a new name for your goat." He chuckles.

"Gertrude. Maybe Gertie for short," I tell him, having already thought about it.

"Well, Gertie is fine. She just needs to finish the birthing process and she should be right as rain," he says, looking down at her. I step forward tentatively.

"Good girl, Gertie. You did a good job, momma." I stroke her head. She gives me a little bleat and a soft nudge, and I now know we will become friends after this.

"I can't believe we had babies!" Standing up and smiling at Tanner, my eyes water.

"Babies are a lot of work, you know."

"Speaking from experience, I assume? Had baby goats before?" I tease, as we look back down and see Gertie feeding her babies, the whole thing completely happens naturally.

"I had a baby human, and he was hard enough work." Tanner scoffs, leaning against the wall and taking me with him. His hands settle on my waist as mine rest on his chest. "But it was all worth it."

"I can imagine," I say, feeling admiration for him.

"Do you want kids? Baby humans, I mean?" Tanner asks, and his question takes me by surprise.

"I think so. It isn't something I think a lot about, but I would like to be a mother." I wait to see if he makes an excuse and leaves. But he doesn't, so I test the waters a little. "What about you? Ever thought about having another child?" I ask tentatively.

"I have never really thought about it, but I guess if the right woman came along..." he says, our eyes catching intensely as a moment of truth runs between us that has my heart racing. "Besides, if I did it again, it would be a hell of a lot different than thirty-five years ago, that is for sure." He smiles, which is contagious.

"Tell me about that time." Tilting my head, my fingers play with the collar of his shirt. He lets out a breath, like the weight of the world rests on his shoulders.

"Some of the hardest years of my life. I had this little person, and I had no idea what the hell I was doing. I was distraught because his mom had up and left. Thank God for my parents, because they did so much for Connor and me, especially in those early years," he says, and my heart feels heavy.

"Was he an easy baby?" I ask, smiling, and Tanner smirks.

"No. Not at all. Never slept. Hardly ate. In the end, I finished high school with him strapped to my body in a carrier because he wouldn't settle unless he was with me. Once school was done, I stayed home with him, helped out my parents, helped out others around Whispers, and made money that way. I spent time with my father making whiskey because it was a hobby he had for a lot of years. When I took a keen interest, he taught me everything he knew. I ended up doing local college at night, and when Connor went to school, I made whiskey during the day. Batches and batches of whiskey," he says, chuckling.

"Sounds like you worked pretty hard." I have no idea how I would cope in a similar situation. His resilience and work ethic make him even more attractive.

"The days were long, but the years were short. Our whiskey became popular around Whispers and the surrounding towns. It grew slowly but strategically and purposefully, and by the time Connor got a bit older, Whiteman's Whiskey was a fully-fledged company turning a good profit. I had made enough money to send him to the best college, where he made some great contacts there, and they have helped us along the way. The rest is history."

I smile, loving his story. He has achieved so much. His life already so full, while I feel mine is only just beginning. Our age difference is sizeable, and most of the time, I don't feel it, but hearing about what he has accomplished, it is noticeable.

"You have done an amazing job, Tanner. With everything. The whiskey. Connor. He looks a lot like you, you know," I say, leaning closer.

"He has been a good son. But obviously an adult who doesn't need his old man much these days." Shaking his head, his hands meet behind my back to embrace me.

"Well, maybe you can now help me with these baby goats. Because we both know I have no idea what I am doing," I say to him, grinning, before I turn in his hold to look back at them, his hands lowering to my hips. "How did I not know she was a female?" Moaning, I rub my face, and he chuckles. "I am such a bad farmer."

"You are coming around. Nice to see you in the boots I got you," he says, as I lean my back against his chest, resting my head on his shoulder, looking up at him.

"They are surprisingly comfortable," I admit, kicking my leg up and wiggling my foot.

"Speaking of comfortable. We need to shower," Tanner says, and I look us over. He is right, we are a mess.

"A shower for two?" I smile, raising my eyebrows in question.

"You read my mind, baby girl," he growls as he cups my cheek and kisses me, leaving me breathless.

27

———

TANNER

"*A shower for two,*" she says, and I do the only thing I have been wanting to do since I saw her last.

I growl, kissing her. My need for her is growing, the intensity in which I desire her almost consuming me. But I go slow, teasingly so, and pull her near as my mouth takes hers completely. I feel her open for me, her lips taking mine just as needily and her body softens, leaning against mine. Her hands grab on to my shirt, pulling me closer, and I lower my hands, running them down her neck, her torso, and then cupping her ass, removing any remaining space between us.

"Tanner," she breathes against my lips like I am her antidote to everything, and I lift her up by her thighs, her legs wrapping around my waist. Sealing her body to my own, our kiss turns more heated, and my hands slide up the bare skin of her upper thighs and straight under her Daisy Dukes.

"God, I have missed you, baby girl," I say into her

mouth as my hands caress her soft skin. It has only been a few days, but it feels like a lifetime. Her hands smooth up my neck, the tension I felt last night with the numbers and the legal contracts, the anger I felt the other day when my whiskey was ruined, now all dissipating. Her hands massage my scalp, and I moan in contentment as I pull her hips against mine so she can feel exactly what she does to me.

"We should go inside." Her warm breath hits my lips as her body starts to grind into mine, and her hips moving a little is almost my undoing. I squeeze her ass as her breasts rub against my chest, and I fail to see how any man could deny this woman anything, so with her in my hold, I walk us toward the house. My lips still haven't left her, as I nip and peck her jaw, her neck, her cheeks, and her hands continue to delve into my hair, massaging my scalp and nape so well that I want to fucking purr like a cat.

My strides are long and purposeful as I walk us up to the back porch, push open the back door, and march us straight past the kitchen. The lights are on, the house warm and inviting, just like the woman in my arms. I crave to trace every inch of her, and I hold her tight and race up the stairs.

"Tanner!" she squeals at the sudden movement, gripping on to me, but I would never let her fall and she knows it. I have barely slept in days. I should be exhausted, but right now, as I push us through her bathroom door, I have only one thing on my mind.

"Get your clothes off," she says to me as she slides

down my frame and throws her own t-shirt onto the floor, her boots and shorts quickly following.

I smirk at her, teasing, "Now who is bossy," as I grab my top and pull it over my head, just as she turns on the shower and jumps in.

"Oh, this feels good," she moans as she ducks under the spray of hot water, and I take off my jeans. I watch her closely, the way the water cascades over her curves, dripping from her breasts and over the swoop of her ass and down her thighs. She runs her hands through her hair, which is now wet and long down her back, her face fresh and flushed.

The vision of her already makes me hard.

"Coming in?" She looks at me, water dripping from her lashes and lips.

"Oh, I am coming," I say before I walk in and join her, closing the shower door behind me. She isn't wrong, the water feels amazing. Hot, the bathroom now steamy, I close my eyes and let the water hit my head and run down my face, then I feel her hands on me. One smoothing down my bare torso, her lips following the movement, while the other is wrapping around my shaft, giving me a few pumps, and I suck in a breath.

"What are you doing, baby girl?" I ask her, my torso muscles tight as I duck out of the water and look down.

"I just want to say thank you for coming to my rescue." Her lips trace my lower abs, smiling, her tongue darting out and tasting my damp skin before she kneels on the shower floor.

My hips thrust out, pushing myself in her hand as she leans forward, her lips now level with my cock. "You going to say it, or are you going to show me?" I ask, pushing her a little, and she smirks.

"Tell me what you like, Tanner," she mewls as she takes my tip in her mouth and suckles on me, my eyes just about rolling back in my head from how good it feels. Fuck, this woman is too much. What I like? Tell her what I like? That I like her. That I want her. That I want to feed her my cock, make her come while also coming to her rescue, cooking her dinner. Massaging her feet, helping her renovate, and making a home here in Whispers. With me.

"I like it all, baby," I growl as she continues to tease me with her mouth. She looks fucking amazing on her knees before me. The water is hitting my back, but beads of water still run down her body, dripping from her breasts. My mouth waters, wanting to suck them.

"So greedy," she murmurs, and I like this side of her. This naughty, sexy side that is starting to come out. Her confidence with me is building.

"Only with you. Fuck, Victoria," I groan as she sucks me hard, still just my tip, and I am on the edge for her to take all of me.

"You have a beautiful cock, Tanner," she says, her hand pumping me slow. I feel myself thicken even more in her touch.

"You have a beautiful mouth. Now, how about you stop teasing me and open wide and let me in." As the words leave my mouth, she slides her lips down farther, her tongue lashing out and swirling around my tip, and she moans around me.

"Fuck... baby..." I cough, as my hand slaps on the tiles in front of me.

"Mmmmmmm," is all she says as she takes me deeper, so slowly, it is making me tremble, her hum vibrating through to my balls.

"Jesus, Victoria," I say, gobsmacked at the way she shows her appreciation.

Her other hand runs up my legs and rests on my ass, pulling me toward her, and I touch the back of her throat before she pulls back and then does it again, her movements now rhythmic, taking me deep each and every time.

"Look at your pretty mouth taking me. Goddamn perfection." I look down at where we are joined, her mouth wide, my cock filling her. Resting my hand in her hair, I gather it up in my fist, ensuring the hair is out of her face as my hips begin to thrust in time with her rhythm.

"Is your pussy throbbing, baby girl?" I ask, and she moans in response as I see her squirm on her knees.

"I can't wait to get my mouth on you and return this favor," I warn her as my movements increase in speed. Her hand leaves my cock, dropping down her body, her fingers now playing with her clit.

"That's it, baby girl. Play with yourself. Are you going to come while I fuck your face? Is that what you want?" I grit out, and she nods as her nails dig into my ass cheek, pulling me forward some more.

With one hand, I lean against the shower wall, and with the other, I hold her head and thrust into her mouth over and over, all the while looking at where her fingers play, her movements frantic. I will never forget this visual.

"I'm going to come... I am going to come down your pretty little throat... Are you gonna scream around my cock, baby?" I growl, and she closes her eyes and takes me even deeper, moaning around my length as her eyes meet mine.

"Good girl, good fucking girl."

My talking must do the trick because her muffled moan becomes harsher, sounding like a scream. Her eyes never leave mine as her body trembles, which tips me over the edge, my thrusts shortening before I come hard down her throat with a groan.

The water continues to cascade over us, and she pulls off me slowly before sagging against the floor of the shower, taking deep breaths with a wicked smile on her face. Leaning both hands on the wall, I look down at her, breathing out a laugh at how incredible that was.

"Now it's my turn." I help her stand, her eyes alight.

I run a hand up her body, loving touching her, exploring her, until I reach her chest, and I cup each breast, feeling them warm and heavy in my hand.

"I love you in lace, but these are exquisite," I murmur to her as I mold them in my hands, bending to take a nipple in my mouth.

"Hmm, you have such a way with words..." She moans as I suck on her nipple, her back immediately arching, and I trace the curve of her with my hands.

"Spread those legs for me, baby." I lower myself to my knees in front of her. The water still streaming, I kiss down her front, taking my time to pepper kisses to her skin, wanting to mark every inch with my lips.

It has been a while since I knelt in front of a woman like this. And right now, all I can think about is having her come on my face, and I am not waiting any longer to taste her.

"Can you give as good as you get?" she asks coyly, and I smirk against her skin, reaching her pubic bone and moving my hands to her upper thighs.

"You tell me." My mouth hits her center, and she gasps, jolting against me.

"Tanner..."

I don't hesitate. I have been dreaming of her for days, of kissing her, of tasting her, and now I have my chance. Looking up briefly, I see her head pushed back against the tiles and her eyes closed, her mouth agape. When I lick her clit, she releases a little moan that is barely audible but sexy as hell.

With a moan of my own, I close my eyes and refocus, tasting her, sucking on her clit, and my hands run up and down her bare thighs before I grab her knee and throw it over my shoulder, opening her wider for me.

"Oh my God," she whimpers, her hand coming to my head, fingers digging into my scalp. My hands smooth up the backs of her thighs to her ass, and I push her into my face even more.

"Yes, like that. Oh shit, just like that." She is gasping already, grinding for more, and I can't get enough. There is seriously nowhere in the world I would rather be than buried right here in her pussy, taking her to orgasm.

"Tanner, please. Yessss."

I look up at her, seeing her biting her bottom lip. Growling, I devour her wholly, and her hips move faster against me.

"Oh God, oh God..." she pants. "Don't stop. Please don't stop," she chants over and over, and there is no way in hell I am stopping. I suck on her clit harder, flicking my tongue around and around, and then she screams, panting my name like a prayer and she comes. Her body shudders, her hips stopping their movements, so I kiss her softly before I remove her leg from my shoulder and kiss up her thighs.

"I feel lightheaded," she murmurs, and I huff a laugh as I stand, my body also feeling like Jell-O.

"Let's get out and dry off. I want you in bed with me," I tell her, and she opens her eyes and gives me a small smile.

"That sounds like a great idea," she says as I turn off the taps and grab the towels. The goats will be fine until morning, which gives me a good few hours with her until then.

28

VICTORIA

As I walk around the yard, tidying up from my gardening and talking to Fiona on a video call, I yawn. My mind is tired, and my body is still sore in places it hasn't been for some time. I then smile, thinking about the reason that is the case.

"That is like the fifth time you've yawned already today," she says, looking at me suspiciously.

"I'm tired. The new goats kept me up all night," I say, but it must be the look on my face that gives me away.

"You said they were born before midnight. So what else went on last night? What time did Tanner leave?" she asks like an FBI interrogator. Not much gets past her.

"Oh, ahhh... about nine," I say, before biting my lip, "a.m." I wait for the penny to drop.

"Holy hell, you had sex with the hot neighbor!" she almost screams through the phone, and I laugh at her.

"Well, it kinda wasn't the first time..." I tease her. It has been a little while since we last spoke and so much has happened.

"Wait. *What!*" she yells, and I hear her colleagues all shush her at her office before she moves into a meeting room for privacy.

"Should I be offended that you seem so shocked?" I ask her as I put away my gardening tools and sit on my back porch steps to chat.

"I want all those details, but I am at work and I don't want to get fired. So how was it? I mean, anything would be an improvement from Josh, right."

I smile, the wide, lip-splitting grin hasn't left my face all day. After our rendezvous in the shower, we went to my bed and stayed there all night, enjoying each other some more before he had to leave this morning right after breakfast.

"So much better, and Fi..." I say, thinking about my words. "He is, like... so good at like everything. He came straight over last night when I called. Dropped everything for me and my panic over Gertie. He cooks for me, he looked after me when I hurt my ankle. I mean, I don't think anyone has ever done anything like that for me before. Certainly not a man."

"You really like him, don't you?" she asks, and I look at her with a deep breath. I do, but I don't want to admit it out loud yet. It already feels too good to be true.

"He has a body like a Greek god, and if it wasn't a crime, I would demand he walk around naked all the time just so I can look at him," I tell her, laughing.

"So did Tyler," Fiona says with a sigh.

"Did he ever call?" I ask her, knowing that she had a great time with him the night before my life imploded, but it seems it was a one-night thing.

"No. I guess you just can't win them all," she says glumly, then snaps herself out of it. "Anyway, back to your man. When are you seeing him again?" she asks, just as I hear a truck in my driveway and look up to see his familiar black and gold branding.

"He actually just arrived." He told me this morning he would come back after work tonight, and now as the sun sets on the horizon, he proves yet again that he is a man of his word.

"Argh. Alright, go. Have sweaty, amazing sex with your hot billionaire neighbor. Tonight is hair washing night for me, and just for fun, I might even shave my legs too. Don't worry about me," she says sarcastically, and I giggle at her as I watch Tanner step out of his truck, his eyes already glued to me as he starts striding over.

"Wait, let me show you something." I laugh as I press a button and flick the camera around so she can see the vision I am seeing. Tanner, tall, dark, and brooding, his sleeves rolled up to showcase his muscular forearms, his shirt fitting him extremely well over his broad shoulders.

"Oh God. I hate you," she says, and I can't stop laughing.

"I love you too," I singsong sweetly. "Gotta go. Talk later," I tell her before I hang up.

"Who you loving, baby girl?" Tanner asks as he steps closer.

"My friend, Fiona. She is working late."

"Do you miss it? The city? Your friends?" he asks as he steps toward me, his hand immediately circling around my waist and pulling me to him. His lips meet mine in a quick greeting.

"Yes and no. I grew up there so I miss some things. Fiona and my mom, mostly. I miss going to my local florist and grabbing my favorite pink peonies when they are in season. But also, Benny's," I say, sighing, really missing Benny's.

"What's Benny's?" Tanner asks with a little crease between his eyebrows.

"It's this old school diner in Soho. They make the best burgers," I tell him with a mock frown.

"Maybe you can take me there sometime?" His thumb rubs my lower back, and my frown turns into a smile that he is already thinking of me in his future.

"I would like that. But only if we can go to Maison Pickle afterward." I tap his chest.

"Maison Pickle?"

"They make a twenty-four-layer chocolate cake that is ah-mazing." My mouth already salivates.

"Now you are just making me hungry." He chuckles, kissing me on the lips again. This one is slow and sweet, like he is committing it to memory, and at his touch, my body goes liquid in his arms until my stomach grumbles so loudly it is mortifying.

"I think I am making myself hungry," I murmur against his lips.

"Let me lock up these animals for you, and then we can go." Pulling back, he starts to walk out the back to get the place locked up for the night.

"Go? Go where?" I ask him, never tiring of seeing his profile or his ass in his jeans.

"I'm taking you out for dinner. To the bar. Burgers

might not be as good as Benny's, but right now, we need to eat."

Marmalade saunters into the shed, and he locks the door.

I look down at myself in my t-shirt and jeans. "I need to change."

"You look fine," he says, walking back to me.

"I look a mess!" I tell him, waving that off. He is being absurd if he can't see it.

"Baby girl, you look beautiful. Besides, I want to undress you myself, and if I do that now, we won't be leaving for dinner..." he says as he stands in front of me, his hand once again gliding around my waist.

"Fine. Let me grab my things," I say in a mock grumble before I push off him and run inside, taking exactly two minutes to put my hair up in a top knot, spray on some perfume, and swipe some pink gloss on my lips before I grab my bag and run back out to him. He is standing waiting for me, with the passenger door open, and I swoon so hard I misstep on the porch steps and almost face-plant into the gravel.

"Need me to carry you?" he calls out with a wicked smile on his face, knowing exactly why I stumbled.

"No. I am a strong, independent woman. I can take care of myself," I say, giving him a little sass as I walk around him and jump in.

"Don't I know it," I hear him mumble before he closes my door, and he takes me on our first dinner date.

29

TANNER

As I predicted, everyone is here tonight, and they all swivel in their seats to look at me walking into the bar holding Victoria's hand.

"Why is everyone staring at us?" Victoria whispers to me out of the side of her mouth.

"Because they can't understand why a beautiful young woman like you would be holding the hand of an old guy like me," I tell her, only half joking. It is probably what they are thinking, but I would like to think that I have more respect in this town for them to have that as their first assumption. In reality, it is just that we are publicly announcing we are together. Which I know will fuel the town gossip grapevine for weeks.

"Ohhh, well, hello, you two," Lacy says as Victoria and I slide into my booth at the back. We have a little more privacy back here, but not much.

"Hey, Lacy. Tanner here thinks the burgers could rival Benny's in the city, so I am keen to try one." Victoria's face lights up at seeing her friend.

"Make it two, Lacy, and I'll take a whiskey. My usual," I tell her, nodding, and Lacy's smile stays firmly in place as she glances between us.

"I'll have a cola, please," Victoria says, and I watch them as they look at each other like they are having a silent conversation, and I raise my eyebrow.

"Girl code," Victoria murmurs before Lacy runs off to put in our order.

"So you like burgers and chocolate cake, but you don't like whiskey?" I ask her, just before Lacy is already back with our drinks. That is one bonus to owning the bar; I always get served first.

"Hmm, it's like drinking gasoline," she says, taking her straw in her mouth and sucking on her drink. I pause as my eyes take her in, her neck as she swallows and the small hum of approval she makes. I have to clear my throat before I can talk.

"It is precision chemistry. Mine is a luxury to be enjoyed," I tell her mockingly. I don't expect her to like whiskey, but if we are going to continue spending time together, she will need to get used to the smell, at least.

"It's a bit like coffee." Sitting back against the booth, she watches me.

"Coffee?" I ask because I am not following her train of thought. It is one of the things I like about her, all these almost quirky things she does. She moves to a small town on her own. Wears a little pink on her every day of the week, regardless of the outfit. Walks up ladders in bright-pink slides and runs around barefoot in nothing but a pink robe. Thinks a pregnant goat is a male, and now puts whiskey and coffee in the same category. It makes no sense to me, but I know it all makes perfect sense to her.

"Well, I don't drink coffee. It makes me too jittery. But I do like the smell of it and the initial taste."

I take a sip of my whiskey and let her finish.

"Same as your whiskey. I don't like to drink it, it burns my throat, but I like the smell of it on your breath and the taste of it on your lips," she says sweetly, and I am glad I am sitting down because those words from her almost have me choking on my latest release.

"Here're your burgers," Lacy interrupts, sliding our plates in front of us, and Victoria smiles wide as Lacy retreats, like she didn't just tease me with her words.

"Okay, moment of truth..." Victoria says as she picks up her burger and takes a big bite and nods to me in approval. She moans as she chews, and I grab my whiskey glass so hard I am surprised it doesn't shatter in my hand, and then I down the entire thing immediately.

This woman makes me feel completely smitten in every way imaginable.

I HAVE BEEN in the city for most of the week, and as I sit in our high-rise office, I can't wait to get back to Whispers and back to Victoria.

"Okay, gents, well, I think that is everything," Valerie Van Cleef says, smiling. One of the richest women in the country has just done a business deal with Whiteman's Whiskey, placing us in all her hotel establishments countrywide. It is a good deal, one that I was hesitant about at the beginning. Whiteman's is exclusive. I don't produce our whiskey for the masses. The value of our brand is in its limited editions and unique high-quality development. Our clientele are wealthy families, millionaires and billionaires. That's why our friend, President Harrison Rothschild, named it the only whiskey he drinks when he indulges. When he made that statement, our sales went nuclear.

"Great to see you again, Val. Looking forward to seeing Whiteman's in your VIP lounges," I say as I stand, shaking her hand.

"Don't forget, we have that fundraiser for the Bloomer Books Literacy Program in Baltimore next week," she reminds me, and I nod. I don't go to many galas these days, but I do support the Rothschilds, and I know Valerie is close with Huxley and Lucy, just as we are.

"We will be there," Connor says, and she smiles as she shakes his hand. He walks her and her small team out as I sit again.

My time in the city, even though it is only every month or so, is time I prefer to be home, yet I know business doesn't work like that. Connor doesn't love being here that much either. Our deals are always done with the top end of town, and while Whispers is becoming extremely popular with the wealthy and celebrities, the city is still where many deals are done. On previous trips, we spent the week working, eating out at fancy restaurants, and meeting ladies. Usually, with Sawyer or one of our other friends in tow. But this time, it is different.

"That's all done. Shipment dates have been organized, and Lacy is getting our marketing and our PR agency onto the strategy. A few more weeks and it should be all easy sailing," Connor says, stepping back into the boardroom. I nod, thinking about the special batches of whiskey I have made, aged a little less than I prefer, but this line will be more accessible for those who frequent Van Cleef establishments.

"It's all going to plan, then," I say mindlessly.

"It is. On track." He pauses, looking at me. "Soooo, are you bringing Victoria to the gala?" Connor asks me, and I take a breath.

"I haven't asked her yet, but I will." I nod to him.

"So going public in the city already. I heard you took her to the bar the other night, so it must be going well?" Connor says as a question, and I smile. I haven't stopped thinking about her. It is going well. Really fucking well.

But I also can't stop thinking about who ran over her rosebush and put a fucking rose inside her home when she wasn't there.

"She was certainly unexpected," I say honestly.

"I like her. She is good for you."

"Is that your way of giving me your approval?" I ask him. Because it matters. What Connor thinks matters a lot.

"You don't need it, but you have it. Does that mean she is someone you plan to have in your life for a while?" He looks at me seriously.

"I'm working on it." I'm not able to stop my smile as my mouth curves up of its own accord. Just thinking about her makes me happy.

"If you're happy, Dad, I'm happy," Connor says, and I swallow hard. I don't like not being able to see her when I want. When I am home at the distillery, I know she is only a minute away. Since Gertie had her babies, I had been with Victoria every day until I had to fly out for this trip. I did what I needed to at the distillery, and then every night, I went over to help her lock up the animals and we had dinner together. I spent the night with her, making her moan my name over and over, and then struggled to leave her in the morning. Now being miles away is harder than I thought it would be.

As if the universe feels sorry for me, my cell chimes, and I see a notification from her. Clicking into her socials, I see she has posted a photo.

"Cute," Connor says, and I look up at him quickly, seeing him looking at his phone as well. "I can't believe she called the kids Gabriella and Gemma. Is it a 'G' theme or something? And what is up with the name Gertie?" He huffs a laugh, and I smile wider. Like my son mentioned, she is a little crazy.

"Don't say you are following her too?" It is becoming clear that my son has latched on to her social media, and we are looking at the same image of my girl, who's looking beautiful carrying two baby goats, one under each arm.

"Everyone is, Dad. Her social channels are extremely popular. Look at how many likes she is getting. She has hit a gold mine," Connor says, and I frown as I look back at the image of her. All I see is her beauty, her grace, and her smile. The way her face lights up, her eyes glistening with pure happiness. The breeze pushes her hair to the side of her face, framing her cheeks and flowing over her shoulder. I see the way she is holding those baby goats so tight, as if they were her own children and she doesn't want to let them fall. What I don't look at is the amount of likes and shares and comments, and when I do focus on that, I feel unsettled because there are literally thousands and they are increasing by the minute.

"I think someone was in her house the other day..." I murmur to Connor. "The rosebushes, the ones she mentioned I ran over. That wasn't me, and it wasn't her, but whoever it was, they also left her a rose inside." The anxiety of familiar panic runs up my spine. The same feeling I got when I searched for Connor's mom for months and months and in the end couldn't find her. When I found out she was okay, the relief was there, but the pain didn't subside.

"Maybe it was Jasmine or Lacy?" he says, already knowing what I am thinking.

"I think someone was there who shouldn't have been," I tell him, my nostrils flaring as I look at him. I have given my security team all the information I have on Marie and Victoria's father, which, to be fair, isn't much. But something in my gut tells me that he isn't a good guy.

"It was probably her and she just didn't want to tell you. Knowing how grumpy you would be," Connor mentions, and I take a deep breath. Maybe he is right. Maybe I am being too protective.

"Maybe..." I say, thinking about it.

"We just have this paperwork to finish, and then you should grab the car back to the jet," Connor says, and I frown in confusion.

"Jet?" I have a few more nights here to go through

some other paperwork and meetings Connor has arranged.

"You have been here for a few days, and I have never seen you so disconnected. I thought maybe you should go back early, see Victoria. See your new babies. I can handle everything here for the rest of the week."

I look at my son, my emotions mixed. It has always been the two of us. My sole focus in my entire adult life has been him and Whiteman's. I worked hard to make something of myself, to be a father he could be proud of. I worked hard to get him into the best college, get him everything he needed. I was there for every homework assignment, every bump and scratch. I tried to fill the role of both parents, rarely having any time to myself. The tides are now changing a little, the two of us can feel it.

"Who knows what I will find when I get back there. The bloody cow is probably in calf, and then we will have a whole barnyard of animals," I tell him, scoffing a laugh.

"I always wanted a sibling. I just preferred it to be of the human variety," he says as we bring up the next item of business and get down to work, but me with an extra spring in my step, knowing I will be home soon.

30

VICTORIA

After being outside most of the day, then taking a photo with the goats, which immediately went viral, I am now at my computer with my favorite music blaring.

I look at the flowers that Jasmine brought over today when she stopped by on her way home from the flower markets this morning. It was a surprise visit, and I was happy to see her.

Smiling, I look at the posey she brought me because I love flowers, even though red roses now give me the creeps. This week, I have removed any location-identifying imagery and information from my website and social media channels. I still mention Whispers, but I now will keep my specific location anonymous. Regardless, Josh's calls are still incessant, and I haven't answered again. I have no idea when he will stop, but he needs to.

With a sigh, I shake off the heavy feeling and look around my abode. The house is amazing. It is looking better than I could have ever imagined. It smells like cookies because I made one of Marie's recipes. I felt bad because I left Jasmine to babysit the goats in the shed earlier when I came in to get them out of the oven and onto the rack, trying to cool them down for a while before I took one out for her to taste. But she took an instant love to them, like we all have.

Now with the house in order and smelling like cookies, it is like my thoughts and Pinterest boards literally came to life, and in the flesh, the house just looks so much better. The new carpet is installed upstairs, and I have selected new light fixtures. I purchased a new bed and side tables, the main bedroom now going to be extremely luxurious. I still need to organize a chimney sweep, but the biggest thing to tackle is the kitchen. Seeing an email from Griffin waiting for me in my inbox, my stomach does a flip in anticipation as I click on it.

I still can't believe that the country's best and most sought-after luxury builder is doing *my* kitchen. Tanner is obviously friends with him, and I am starting to understand that Tanner is friends with a lot of high-profile people.

Opening the email, I start to read, taking a quick breath. The quote is much lower than I ever thought possible. I frown, wondering how that can be. But I see he has offered a heavy discount for social media partnership opportunities, and even though I know my little place on the internet is popular, this discount is significant. Grabbing my cell, I look at my socials. My audience increases daily, and while I don't know a lot about social media strategy, I can tell that my channels and blog seem to resonate well, and I have even had a few brands reach out wanting to collaborate already, something I have yet to navigate.

I am happy with Griffin's offer, but hesitant. I am not used to people being so nice or offering so much when my return offer seems so little in comparison. My bank balance is nearly zeros, and with no job prospects, I am running out of time and ideas. My eyes scan further and full-blown shock rolls over me. He talks about working on a new project in Whispers, a luxury ranch that is being built just out of town. The owner wants nothing to do with the design, and given my flair for interior decorating, Griffin offered me up to work on the project.

"Holy shit," I whisper to myself as I stare at the screen, astounded. This is like my dream job. Working with the top builder in the country on a new build. I read further, seeing that I have a multimillion-dollar budget and the project also takes into account a high project fee to pay me in advance if I need it. Apparently, the owner of the ranch has seen my socials, likes my aesthetics, likes that I am a Whispers local, and wants me to do this for him. I sit back in my chair, dumbfounded. Ever since I left the city, my world has realigned. I am doing what I love with my interiors. I am living in a community that is welcoming and beautiful. I have a grumpy neighbor who gives me the best orgasms of my life and makes me feel special every day. I wonder if Tanner knows about this. He probably knows who the owner of the land is, at least.

Jumping up from my chair, I start to dance around, so happy and excited. I want to share the news with someone. I go to call Tanner, but balk because he is in the city this week on business, and I shouldn't interrupt him.

Then I go to call Mom, but it goes to voicemail. No doubt she is out for dinner with friends. I am too nervous to sit still and want to shout it from the rooftops, so I grab my keys, deciding to head into town. I have a feeling that Jasmine and Lacy are probably at the bar, and I will call them from the road. They'll be excited, and then maybe the diner will still be open, and I can treat myself to a piece of cake to bring home later.

I quickly grab my things and head outside to the shed, looking at the truck. I am not sure how long it will keep going, but I can't afford a new car right now, so it will just have to do. Ignoring the creaking door, I jump in. Nothing can dampen my excitement. My smile is wide as I reverse out of the driveway and hit the road. I haven't driven in the dark a lot yet, but the truck doesn't go fast, so it is okay. As I get onto the main road, I dial Lacy and put my cell on speakerphone.

"Hey, Victoria!" Lacy says, and I can hear the music in the background so I know she is at the bar.

"Hey! I have good news, and I need to celebrate!" I tell her, not able to hide my enthusiasm as I dance in my seat.

"Ohhhh, do tell!" she says, and I laugh.

"I want to tell you in person. I am so excited I can barely stand it!" I say, almost squealing. Turning the corner, I realize I am going a bit fast, so I take my foot off the accelerator and touch the brake lightly.

"I'm at the bar. Jasmine is here too. Come down."

"No, no, no, no..." My whole body tenses, heart in my throat, as my foot pushes the brake pedal harder and nothing happens.

"Victoria?" Lacy asks, sounding concerned.

"The brakes don't work! The brakes don't work!" I scream at her as I panic. The roads are dark and quiet, but my hands sweat as I grip on to the wheel, my foot pushing down on the brake, to no avail.

"Shit. Where are you?" Lacy asks in a rush.

"Oh my God. Lacy!" I scream, fright taking over because I don't know what to do. I have hardly driven in the city, and I certainly never was taught how to stop a car if the brakes fail. I look up out of the windshield as I hit the brakes over and over, but nothing happens. The road is dark out here, nothing but my headlights leading the way.

"Victoria. We are coming!" I hear Lacy say, and it sounds like she is running.

"The corner! The corner! *Lacy!*" I scream as a sharp corner approaches, and the road starts to slope downhill, the truck picking up speed.

"Oh no! No, no, no!" I yell as I continue to slam my foot on the brake pedal. My body is shaking, and I sit up straight in my seat. I don't know if I should take off my seat belt and try to jump out of a moving vehicle or if that will be worse because of the speed I am traveling.

Then it is almost like it happens in slow motion. My hands grip the wheel, and I brace myself as I turn the truck around the corner, going way too fast, but I need to try. But the old truck can't take it. The rolling happens instantaneously, and there is nothing I can do.

"*Lacy!*" I scream as the truck plows off the road and through a fence into the field. I can't see anything as my headlights flicker on and off and the truck rolls. My body's thrown around as I roll for a second time, the truck creaking, windows breaking, but as old as it is, the seat belt holds me tight. It pulls against my body, and I feel like I am in a washing machine just tumbling out of control before the truck comes to a stop on its side and the pain in my chest intensifies. My head thuds, the quietness now deafening as I look up and out the broken windshield. The full moon above shines bright, and I am looking straight at a small herd of cows.

"Lacy..." I say quietly, my eyes moving around the truck, seeing nothing but mangled and dented metal and broken glass. I have no idea where my cell phone is or my bag. I wiggle my toes and my fingers, and everything moves as it should. Then I roll my ankles and wrists before bending my knees and elbows. My body aches, but nothing is feeling severe, and even though there is broken glass, I don't see any blood.

I take a deep breath in and feel pain in my chest from where the seat belt held me. As the shock starts to wear off, so does any bravado, and my eyes water as my hands shake. I turn my head, and the pain in my temple intensifies, so I remain still. I don't have the strength to move. Knowing that Lacy will find me, I close my eyes and try to breathe out my panic and wonder how life can go from fantastic one moment to almost fatal the next.

31

TANNER

After a late lunch with Connor, and one more meeting that I committed to while in the city, which went over the allotted time, I am now in the jet, Whispers coming into view as we descend.

Feeling a little tension leave, I'm eager to get to Victoria's, even though it is late. She might be asleep, but I will take great joy in waking her up. At that thought, I look over to the horizon where our homes are and frown. It is dark, nothing amiss, but something feels off. I tug at my collar and roll my shoulders before I pull out my cell and send her a message, telling her I'm home early and will come by tonight. Her persistent ex, her lost father, none of it adds up, and along with the rose in her house, it all puts me on edge. Glancing at my cell, I see nothing back from her, which is unusual, but she is probably sleeping or engrossed in work or something.

As I get off the jet, I crack my neck, feeling jittery, unsettled. Not usually how I feel when I land back at home.

Just as I'm speeding out of the airport in my truck that my team left for me this afternoon, my phone rings. It's Lacy.

"Tanner!" she says before I've even fully said hello, and I immediately know from her tone something is wrong.

"Talk to me, Lacy." Pressing the accelerator down a little more, I move quicker than I should, but the roads are quiet and I know this place like the back of my hand. If I have lost more barrels due to a forklift accident today, I won't be happy.

"It's Victoria!" she says, out of breath, hiccupping and clearly distressed. "There's been an accident. Hudson is here. The sheriff. She's... she's..." My heart feels like it has fallen out of my chest and been stabbed into a million pieces as I head through Whisper's main street, only a few minutes out from Distillery Drive.

"She's what, Lacy?" I bark at her, needing to hear the words.

"She's hurt, Tanner. She crashed Marie's truck, and now we are at the hospital."

I take a deep breath in, the urge to get to her over-whelming. Slamming on my brakes, I turn my truck around and drive back in the direction of the hospital. It's mere minutes away, so I get there quickly, as Lacy explains to me that she was on the phone with Victoria who was unable to stop the truck. It flew through the fields not far from home, and Lacy immediately went looking for her.

"I'm here," I say, hanging up the call as I skid to a stop in front of the hospital. I see Hudson's car here and feel relief that he is still in Whispers. I also spot Lacy's and the sheriff's, his red and blue lights still flashing. As I run to the entrance, my adrenaline's at an all-time high.

"Tanner!" Lacy calls out, waving to me from the front, and I run up to her.

"Where is she?" I demand. Lacy pushes inside, and I follow her as we make our way through the hospital. The familiar smell of antiseptic and the stark white walls and floor almost have me squinting.

"In here!" Hudson's stern words hit me from down the hall, obviously hearing us, given no one else is in here tonight. I have known Hudson for many years, and I know by his tone he is in professional mode. That has me even more panicked as I stride toward the room. I come to a sudden stop as I see her.

Victoria is lying in the bed, hooked up to a few monitors, a nurse tending to her, with Jasmine right by her side. Her clothes are dirty and ripped like she was dragged down a gravel driveway. Dirt covers her legs, face, and body. Blood and shredded skin on her legs, her eyes are red, her cheek swollen and starting to turn purple. My mouth feels dry as I look her over, ensuring she is in one piece.

"I'm okay," she croaks out before coughing, and I stride toward her with my stomach in knots.

"What happened, baby girl?" I ask her, my hands coming to her face. I touch her so softly I can barely feel her cheek as my eyes roam over her face and body, my teeth gritting tightly together, and my heart is lurching out of my chest, hating seeing her like this. I feel Hudson grab and squeeze my shoulder, a silent request to keep myself in check because he knows I am about to lose my shit.

"She had an accident. Appears the truck was taking the corner at speed." I glance up and see the sheriff standing there looking at us. When I look back to Victoria, her eyes are glassy. A lone tear falls down her cheek, and I catch it, wiping it away.

"It's okay. I'm here. I'll take care of everything," I tell her, also needing the reassurance myself because I feel like I am going to have a fucking heart attack. I smell the faint aroma of gasoline and engine oil, and I wonder what kind of shape the truck is in.

"The brakes didn't work," she whispers to me, her hands shaking a little, so I grab them and give her a squeeze of support.

"It's alright. Everything will be alright. Don't even worry about any of that. Just rest. Hudson will take care of you," I tell her, kissing her gently before I pull back and give Hudson a death stare.

"A small concussion, but the rest is superficial grazes and bruising. She can go home tonight. She is one lucky woman. It could have been a hell of a lot worse," he tells me. "I've got her." With a nod, he confirms she is truly okay, and I squeeze her hand again before I stand up and step toward the door, the sheriff following me into the hallway.

"What happened?" I ask him quietly, feeling something is amiss.

"Speed. She took the corner too quickly. The truck is a total loss," he explains.

"She wasn't speeding," I tell him straight up, and he

just raises his eyebrows like he doesn't believe me, which pisses me off even more.

"Speed is the only factor. She took the corner too fast. It was dark. She is a newcomer and doesn't know the roads." My anger only rises when he shrugs like it is an open and shut case.

"Sounds to me like you are making assumptions rather than doing any type of investigation." I tell him what I really think, and his eyes thin as he looks at me.

"It may not have only been speed. We have taken blood to run a tox screen as well," the sheriff says, proving that I can, in fact, be more pissed about this.

"There is no way she was drinking and driving," I spit at him. *Why is Victoria getting this small-town cop bullshit?*

"Standard procedure. I need to do it."

I grit my teeth together and give him a silent nod. I have known him and his wife, Rochelle, for years. They own the diner, and Rochelle cooks lunch for my team every week. We have spent holidays together. Worked together on community projects. He knows that I am not happy about any of this.

"I think you and I both know there are no drugs or alcohol in her system."

"Then speed is the only factor," he says, and my shoulders stiffen.

"She wouldn't be speeding." I sound like a broken record as I run my hands through my hair, trying to think. "She said the brakes didn't work, but that truck was serviced just before Marie died. I took it there myself. There is no way the brakes were faulty."

"What are you implying, Tanner?" He watches closely, and I seethe next to him.

"Do you already have the truck?" I ask him, wondering if I should take a look at it.

"My boys pulled it from Bob's farm. Fence will need fixing, but she didn't hit any animals or buildings, so there was minimal damage to his land," he says. I don't give a shit about Bob's farm, and in this situation, I know Bob wouldn't either.

"She wouldn't have been speeding. Especially not at night. Not in that truck. It could barely drive as it was."

"Tanner," he warns, and I turn my body to step toward him.

"That is my fucking woman in there," I bite out, pissed off that this happened, angry that we have no idea what exactly caused it, and upset that I wasn't here when she needed me. The familiarity of not being able to find someone, for not being here and with her, reminds me of when Connor's mom left. The red and blue lights in the darkness of the hospital parking lot look the same as they did that night when me and the whole town of Whispers spent days and nights looking for her, thinking she was lying hurt or dead somewhere. It wasn't until a week later her parents got a note, telling them she was in fact okay and had run away to start a better life. Then the whole town looked at me with nothing but pity. Pity for the kid left holding a baby.

The sheriff looks at me with a little more empathy and nods, now understanding exactly who she is to me.

"I'll get it looked over. I'll let you know if we find anything."

I leave him standing in the hallway as I step back into the room. Victoria needs me now, and I am not leaving her side.

32

VICTORIA

The house is quiet. I have no idea of the time, but it is pitch-black outside, and the way I am feeling, I would guess it is past midnight. Sitting on the sofa, I think about the night over and over. The sheriff didn't believe me when I said the brakes failed. I know he thought I was speeding or drunk.

"Girls, you better get going home. It's late," Tanner says to Lacy and Jasmine, who followed us home to ensure I was okay. I give them a small smile and wince, the pain in my cheek constant. I have never been in a car accident before, and now as my cheek throbs, I would never like to experience one again.

"We will be back in the morning," Lacy says to me as Jasmine squeezes my hand.

"Thanks, girls," I tell them, trying to smile.

"I've left the painkillers with Tanner. Hudson said to take two before bed tonight. They will help you sleep," Jasmine says, giving me a small smile.

"Thank you." My words sound useless because I have

no idea how to repay them. They were the first to arrive at the accident after hearing it on the phone. They called Hudson and the sheriff and the paramedics to get me to the hospital. The whole night is a blur and, to be honest, one I would rather forget.

With a sigh, I lean back into the soft sofa as I watch Tanner follow them both out the door, watching them get into their car and drive off safely before he comes back inside, locking the door behind him. He is laser focused as he strides to the kitchen, then to the back of the house, locking the back door, making sure everything is secure.

"Let's go, baby girl," he says, swooping me up in his arms, and I fall back into his hold completely. "You need a bath." As he walks us up the stairs and into the bathroom, I close my eyes and soak in his warmth, remaining quiet and letting the memories of the night sweep over me now that we are alone. I feel safe and snug in his arms, almost drowsy. The smell of gasoline lingers, but I am not sure if it is stuck to my throat and nostrils or in my hair. Thank God, the vehicle didn't catch fire, but the gas tank was obviously punctured because that is all I can smell. Tanner sits me down on a chair in the large bathroom before turning on the bath.

"Can you lift your arms?" he asks as he grabs the bottom of my t-shirt. I obey his request and put my arms up, only wincing slightly with the action. I am taking that for a win given what I have just been through. Tanner peels the top from my body, going so slowly and tentatively it is almost making me cry again. I swallow and try to stand, to do it myself. I hate feeling so dependent.

"Sit," he growls, and my body obeys again, my butt

hitting the chair swiftly as he leans down, his actions deliberate as he takes off my socks, rubbing my cold feet in his large, warm hands in the process.

"That feels nice," I say quietly as his hands run up my legs and he looks over the grazes on my shins and thighs. I see his jaw clench, but he doesn't say anything, opening my shorts and lifting me up so I am standing.

"Hold on to my shoulders."

I do, and he pulls my shorts and underwear down my legs gently. I grimace as the clothes scrape against my bare legs, stinging my body, and I lean my forehead onto his shoulder, feeling lightheaded.

"I got you," he says softly, his hand sweeping around my bare middle, the other opening my bra at the back and then pulling it from my shoulders. He kisses my bare shoulders purposefully, like he is cementing his feelings into my skin. His lips pepper my shoulders and neck, and then he pulls back a little and quickly whips off his shirt, standing in front of me naked from the waist up. I am one hundred percent bare, and I take in a breath, looking at this rugged man who is currently treating me like one of the world's most rare and expensive artworks.

"This is going to hurt, isn't it?" I whisper tentatively, knowing that the water will bite my grazed skin as he wraps me in his arms and lifts me back up bridal style.

"It's warm, not too hot. We need to get the mud and dirt off you," he says as he lowers me into the claw-foot tub. I haven't had a chance to experience this exquisite bath yet, so I guess this is one bonus to a horrific evening. My body submerges, and I close my eyes tight and breathe through the sting.

"I got you," Tanner whispers, his hands firm on me, not letting me go for a moment. The water feels amazing, but it does sting as I predicted. Slowly, the warm water becomes comforting, and I relax. Tanner's face is right in front of mine as I open my eyes, looking at me with concern.

"I'm okay," I say, breathless, wanting to ease his fears. He doesn't say anything as he looks at me, his hands running up my bare back as he helps me to lie back, his torso now damp as well.

"I put some oil in the bath to help your grazes," he says, grabbing a washcloth and dunking it in the water. I am about to grab it from him when he continues. "Lie back and relax." He reaches the end of the bath and picks up my foot. Bringing it out of the water, one foot at a time, he wipes it with the washcloth and a little soap. His hold on me is soft, deliberate, and not leaving an inch of skin untouched. My breath gets caught in my chest as I watch him, concentrating on my skin and body like he is trying hard to make sure everything is intact. It isn't until he moves to the other foot that my eyes close. I feel his hands cup my ankle, then my calf, his movements tender across my grazes on my shins. His hands then run up to my thighs, and still, his strokes continue, washing every inch of me. I have never been bathed before. Sure, I have had a few massages from time to time when I felt like treating myself, but that has nothing on this.

I feel like I almost doze off as Tanner takes his time with me. His hands moving slowly across my skin, every inch of me caressed, his eyes running over every bump, curve, scratch, and bruise. He gets to my neck and chest, and I open my eyes to watch him again, extreme concentration on his face.

"Thank you," I say quietly, because I needed this. A tender hand. Someone to just take care of me, just for tonight. Tomorrow, I can go back to looking after myself.

"No thanks needed. Lie back and let me wash your hair," he says, and my eyebrows rise a little. But his hand cups under my head, cradling the weight, and I sink down into the water a little farther as he saturates my hair. Sitting back up, he starts massaging my scalp softly with the shampoo, digging in with just the right amount of pressure. He runs his thumbs down my neck and back up again, releasing the stress in my muscles he somehow knows I hold, before rinsing my hair, letting the water flow through, and then repeating the action again with the conditioner. As his large hands hold my head, he looks down at me, looking right into my soul, and the throbbing I felt in my head before now dissipates.

If someone had told me that Tanner Whiteman was capable of this when I first arrived in Whispers, I would have laughed in their face. But the way he is handling my body has my chest burning, along with my eyes as they threaten to water just from his tender touch. With the job of bathing me now done, he sits on the small seat next to the bath and watches me.

"Tell me what happened..." He swallows roughly.

"I was working at the computer," I start telling him, closing my eyes and visualizing it. "I had some good news from Griffin about the renovation and I was happy. Wanted to celebrate. So I got in the truck and called Lacy because I knew they would be at the bar." Opening my eyes, I look at him and his hand comes into the bath to hold mine, our fingers entwining as his thumb rubs back and forth.

He remains silent so I continue. "Everything was fine. I was driving the limit, no other cars. But I pressed the brakes to start to slow down for the corner, and it didn't slow. I started hitting them really hard, but nothing happened. The corner was coming up, and instead of slowing, the truck felt like it was going faster and..." My heart stutters a bit as I try hard to remember all the details.

"You swerved, took the corner at speed, and flipped into the field?" he asks, his voice hoarse.

"Something like that," I tell him, and he nods.

"When was the last time you drove the truck before tonight?" he asks, and I take a deep breath.

"Um, I think a few days ago. I went into town to see the girls and pick up some groceries."

"Was it working okay then?"

My body stills as I look at him. He is holding his anger well, but I can tell his shoulders are tight.

"It seemed fine. I didn't notice anything different about it, but I have only driven it a few times. I don't know how long it sat in the shed before I started using it," I say honestly.

"Okay. Time to rest," Tanner says, leaning into the bath and pulling the plug, then helping me out. My legs aren't strong enough to hold me up entirely now that my body has turned to mush at his touch. He wraps me up in a robe and again lifts me bridal style, walking me to my bedroom. Then he places me on my bed, drying my hair as best he can with the towel.

"You don't have to do all this," I say wearily.

"I want to." He is firm, and I am too tired to argue tonight. Instead, I close my eyes and take a breath.

"I want my mom," I say to myself quietly. I miss her. I have been here for a while now, and even before I moved, I hadn't seen her in months. It is times like this that I feel like I need her more than ever.

"Okay," he says, and I shake my head, not meaning to say that out loud. "Here." Bringing over my comfy pajamas, he once again handles me tenderly as he dresses me, his touch soft, his hold warm. Then he pulls back the blanket, guiding me into bed, and as my body hits the mattress, I close my eyes and sigh, the new bed enveloping me completely.

"Weren't you meant to be away until the end of the week?" I ask.

"I missed you," he says matter-of-factly, and I smile.

"Have you seen Gertie and the babies?" I'm just now realizing I hadn't put them in the shed for the night.

"They are fine. Don't worry about any of that. Take your pain meds and get some sleep. You need your rest." Handing me the water and tablets, I do as he says and down them before I snuggle in my new linen, my body feeling heavy, my mind thudding in a dull beat but exhausted.

"Tanner?" I say to him as he crawls in to lie down next to me.

"Yeah, baby girl?" he says, his hand coming to my face and brushing my hair away.

"Thank you for taking care of me." My eyes close, and I don't hear his reply before sleep takes me under, but I feel his warm hand as it scoops around my middle and he pulls me to him, tucking me under his arm and cradling me to sleep.

33

VICTORIA

I am a little sore, my head still throbbing, but the painkillers Hudson gave me last night were amazing. I fell right to sleep in Tanner's arms and felt like I slept like the dead. *Dead.* Like I nearly was last night... My thoughts swirl, and I sit up and shake the morbid feeling away. I don't need drama, negativity, or anything like that. But I can't help the panic that flew through my body for those seconds when the car wouldn't slow down and I hit the corner.

I close my eyes and shake my head again as I stretch a little, looking at the empty mattress beside me. Tanner was here when I fell asleep, but the spot is vacant now. Glancing at my legs, my skin is still sore and red, but also soft from where he bathed me last night.

I smile, thinking of the gruff burly man and how gentle he was. Tentatively, I slide out of bed, going slowly. I wait for any dizziness, but it doesn't come, and I sigh in relief. I feel stronger and not as fragile as last night. Seems that not only the bath and painkillers worked well, but as I look at the clock, I see it is just before midday. I must have slept like twelve hours. I obviously needed it.

I gingerly make my way to the bathroom. The house is quiet, so maybe Tanner left already. I am sure he has lots of work to do since he is back from the city early. I know he will have a lot more questions, but aside from the grazes on my leg and the lump on my head, I actually don't remember anything else of importance. Looking at myself in the bathroom mirror, I gasp at my reflection. My cheek is red, my hair is everywhere, and my body has a large bruise down my stomach. Sighing, I decide to get in the shower and clean up before calling my mother.

The hot water stings initially, but it feels good on my aching muscles. My stomach growls, so I am quick in the shower, before slipping on my jeans and a light sweater, hiding the grazes and bruising. I pin up my hair and apply a little makeup, diminishing the redness in my cheek, and I already feel a hundred times better than I did when I first woke up.

I think I hear voices downstairs and my nerves spike before understanding washes over me that it must be Tanner. Walking down, I hear multiple people, and I pause at the bottom, looking into my kitchen, which is now sparkling clean. And that's when I spot Lacy, Jasmine, and "Mom!" I shout, and all three women look at me as I stand in shock, seeing my mom for the first time in months.

"Oh, sweetie, how are you feeling?" she says with relief, walking toward me with her arms wide. I don't know if it is the shock of seeing her, my emotions just getting the best of me, or the fact that I haven't fully dealt with what happened last night, or maybe even all three. But I break down, tears fall, and a howl leaves my throat as I basically collapse into her open embrace.

"It's okay, sweetie," she coos, her arms wrapping around me and rubbing my back. I cling to her, not believing that she is here, when the back door slams open, and I jump.

"What happened?" Tanner stands tall in the doorway, looking at the girls in the kitchen before he spots me and immediately walks over.

"You're awake," he says softly, his frown deep as his eyes search over me. "How do you feel?" he asks as I step back from mom and wipe my eyes.

"My mom is here!"

"I know. I flew her in early this morning." He nods simply, and my heart skips a beat.

"You did?" I ask with disbelief.

"You said last night you wanted to see her, so I flew her in," he says, like flying a person halfway around the country is a simple task, such as picking up some milk or bread from the store.

"It was a very nice jet too," my mom whispers to me, and I look between them both, wide-eyed.

"Rochelle dropped off some lunch and also some pastries," Lacy says from the kitchen, and I see the sheriff standing just behind her.

"How are you? You slept well?" Jasmine asks, coming over and standing next to my mom.

My mind is a whirl of information as my eyes remain wide, looking at everyone.

"Breathe, baby. Just breathe." Tanner steps toward me, his hand circling my waist and pulling me to him. I do as he says and take a big breath and look at my mom, who winks at me as she looks from me to Tanner and back again.

"I need a tea," I murmur as he lets go of me and smiles.

"That's my girl," he says, and I grip on to him so I don't swoon at his feet. *My girl.* No one has ever called me that before, but I like the idea of being his.

"Come, we have a pot on," Mom says. "This place looks amazing, darling. You have done so well and so much already."

Tanner walks me to the dining table, helping me sit as Lacy brings over some tea.

"I will leave you girls to it," he says, kissing the top of my head before walking back outside with the sheriff.

"Well, I think that one is a keeper," my mom murmurs as her lips hit her coffee cup. "These flowers you have here are beautiful, Victoria."

I turn to look at my dining table, noticing what she's talking about, and balk. Right in the middle is the largest bunch of pink peonies I have ever seen. My eyes widen in shock. They are beautiful.

"How...? I mean, where..." I stumble over my words.

"It seems like I wasn't the only thing that man flew in for you. These are out of season. He must have arranged for them to be overnighted." My mom squeezes my hand.

"Tanner will get you anything you need," Lacy murmurs, and Jasmine sits silently, watching everyone. My heart thuds. I only mentioned my favorite flowers to him the other night. My eyes are glassy again already as I look at my mom.

"I still can't believe you are here," I tell her as we all sit around the table, and I take a sip of my tea, feeling it warm me from the inside out.

"I can't believe that happened last night." My mom shakes her head and looks at me with concern. "How are you feeling?"

"I'm okay. I feel much better today."

"Well, the whole town is talking about it," Jasmine says with a small smile on her face.

"Of course they are. Probably think I was speeding or had too much to drink," I say, rolling my eyes as I take another sip of my tea, instantly feeling better.

"I don't think so. The sheriff found something," Jasmine says, looking at me seriously, her eyes flicking out the back door.

"My tox screen?" I ask, confused, staring at her, and I hear the back screen door open again as both Tanner and the sheriff walk back in.

"What's going on?" I ask, looking at everyone, knowing that I am missing something.

My mom grabs my hand, giving it a stronger squeeze.

"We had a team look at the truck this morning," the sheriff says, and my eyes flick from his to Tanner's and the deep scowl he now has.

"And?" I ask. I have a feeling that whatever he is going to say will be big.

"You were right. The brakes did fail," he says, and I take in a big breath and release it. I wasn't sure if they would believe me or not, but I am glad to now have proof. My shoulders relax immediately, feeling vindicated.

"So you believe me now?" I ask him, just to be sure.

"That's not all, baby girl," Tanner says cautiously, coming to stand next to me, and I look at him, confused.

"What else is there?"

"The brake cables weren't torn from damage. They were cut. Cleanly," he says, and my eyebrows rise.

"Cut?" I ask, wondering if I am understanding this correctly.

"Looks like someone tampered with your brakes on the truck. It was deliberate," Tanner grits out, and I see his jaw pop, not happy. Nerves ripple through me.

"How? When? What?" I can't find words. I am in shock.

"We don't know yet. The sheriff is working on it. Aren't you, Sheriff?" Tanner says bitterly.

"I have a forensic team that will come to town tomorrow to look at the truck and see what they can find out. But, Victoria, I need to ask you if there is anyone you can think of who would be doing something like this. Anyone been around or visiting this week?" the sheriff asks, and I shake my head.

"I mean, Josh calls, but he wouldn't know his way around truck brake cables. I can't imagine him doing something like this," I say, looking at my mom. "Mom?" I ask for her opinion. *He wouldn't, would he?*

"I don't think so, but I think every avenue needs to be investigated," she says, nodding at the sheriff, and I feel Tanner squeeze my shoulder gently.

"Anyone else?" the sheriff asks, and I shake my head,

coming up blank. I have no idea why I would be a target for anyone.

"All the people who visit me are in this room. I didn't have any deliveries these past few days or anyone else here," I tell him honestly.

"Let me walk you out, Tony," Tanner says to the sheriff, who says his goodbyes, and I sit dumbfounded with the girls.

"What is happening?" I ask, tears stinging my eyes. "Why would someone do that?" I ask again, but the girls are quiet. No one seems to know what to say.

"I have a feeling that Tanner and the sheriff will find whoever is responsible for this. Don't worry, sweetie, you will be fine," my mom whispers to me, and I swallow. Her soft smile of reassurance is doing very little to make me feel better, so I cradle my cup of tea in my hands and listen to them make small talk, all the while wondering who wants to see me dead.

34

TANNER

I t's been a week, and we have no leads. And I am angry. The ex is elusive and on leave, not that I have told Victoria that. She seems convinced that while his calls are excessive and disruptive, she doesn't believe he is capable of such a physical threat to her safety. But the issue is, no one can locate him, just like her father, as he's apparently nowhere to be found either.

She has just lived like normal, digging around in the garden, making sure Gertie, the babies, and Marmalade are happy. But I am still livid. I have been at her place every day, looking after the animals with Kevin as she heals from her wounds, and her mom stayed for the week, taking care of her. The two of them have been shopping up a storm in Whispers and getting the inside of Marie's place ready for the kitchen replacement that is happening soon. I loved seeing her face light up while spending time with her mom, but I haven't been in her bed since the crash, and I am eager to see her today. I thought meeting her mother might be weird. Hell, we are closer in age, both parents, but the common thread we have is the care we have for Victoria. Meeting and chatting with her mom was effortless, and she didn't seem to have a problem with me or my age. Her only issue was that I was to take care of her daughter, and I swore to her before she flew out this morning that I would. Now, as I end the online meeting with Sawyer, I lean back in my chair, sighing in frustration.

"Hey, Tanner," Jasmine says, popping her head in the door. I frown because it's the weekend and the office is empty. I am not sure who let her in, but she probably came via the restaurant.

"Hey, Jasmine. How can I help you?" I ask, standing, wondering if she is here about Victoria.

"Oh, just stopping by, dropping off the new floral arrangements to the restaurant for the week," she says, smiling. I hired her to fill the distillery with local flowers when she opened the florist. Something I did to support her, trying to encourage small business in the town. "I got your favorites this week."

"Have you seen Victoria today?" I ask, keen to get her friend's feedback on the situation. I know Jasmine as well as anyone in this town can. But I wouldn't say we are close or anything.

"Oh no, I haven't, but I wanted to talk to you about something, actually," she says, stepping farther into the boardroom and closing the door behind her. My body stiffens immediately.

"What?" I ask, stepping to the side, eager to hear what she has to say.

"Well, I am just a bit worried about her. With Marie's

place and the social media, I mean, someone tampered with her brakes, Tanner. It is too much, and what happens when she just leaves and goes back to the city? It's bringing a lot of attention to town that might not be the good kind…"

"Leaves?" I ask, tilting my head, my heart stopping. Last I spoke to Victoria, she was staying. A fact that I am very supportive of.

"She obviously can't handle the small farm she has, and once the house is done, it will be a money pit to keep going. She misses her mother greatly, and now her safety is compromised," Jasmine says, worry etched on her face. None of what she is saying makes a lot of sense. Victoria already has a plan for the property that will bring in some income. I know she misses her mom, but her mom isn't in the city anymore, and in terms of handling the farm, she is doing better than anyone expected.

"Well, Jasmine, I don't think she is going anywhere. Was there anything else?" I ask, wanting to get out of here and over to see the woman I can't stop thinking about.

"No. No. I just worry about her, that's all," she says with a small smile, one I match. It is nice that Victoria has local friends, and both Jasmine and Lacy have been there for her from the start. I know she appreciates them.

"We all do," I confirm as I step toward the door and open it, offering Jasmine to walk out first.

"Okay, well, have a great afternoon and let me know if you need anything. I am always happy to help."

"No worries. Thanks, Jasmine," I say, closing the door and walking to my office in the other direction. I dump my laptop and paperwork and walk straight back out to the front of the office building and push out the front door. I need some fresh air and warm sunshine, so I stand in the driveway for a moment, letting the sun hit my face, thinking about things.

The sheriff has nothing. He and his team continue to patrol the town, and they have been doing drive-bys up and down Distillery Drive all week in case they see anyone or anything. All the locals are on edge and eagle-eyed for anyone who doesn't look like they belong. I called my security team that I use periodically, and they have already assessed and measured Marie's place and they will be installing cameras within the next few days.

I take in a breath, looking around outside at the front of the distillery office. The weekends are always popular here, and the restaurant is full, the parking lot over-flowing with tourists, all who drive here to sample my whiskey in the tasting room, have a tour of our facility, and then indulge in a meal in my restaurant before driving off later today. But here near the office, the garden is quiet and in the parking lot sits my truck, along with a few of the workers' cars, and the new truck I ordered a mere week ago. My standard black polish shines bright against the sun. I hope she likes the logo. Lacy helped design it. Marie's Place in a blue that matches the tiles on the fireplace she likes so much.

Looking up the driveway, I see a vision walking toward me. Her hair loose and blowing in the breeze, a summer dress that floats on her body, looking like God answered all my prayers. I step toward her, meeting her halfway, surprised to see her here.

"So this is your lair?" she asks with a smile. She must

have walked here. It isn't far, and with the truck now ruined, she has no way of getting around. The girls or I have been her chauffeur most of the week.

"What have you got there?" I ask her, my hands immediately going around her waist and pulling her closer to me. I can smell fresh cookies. My downfall.

"Well, I don't have much to really give to people to say thanks for all the help over the last week, so I found another old cookie recipe in Marie's things and thought I would try it this morning. You are my guinea pig. If you like them, then I will make a big batch and deliver it to everyone who has been over to see me or send me well wishes," she says, my hand absentmindedly rubbing up and down her back.

"No one expects anything," I tell her.

"Yeah, but it is a lot. Rochelle with the food, the girls for visiting and driving me around..." she says, sighing, obviously feeling overwhelmed with all the support she has received. I decide to take her mind off it for a while.

"Well, now that I have trapped you in my lair, come in, let me show you around," I say, swallowing. I have never brought a woman here before. She calls it my lair, but it is certainly my space. My whole life is poured into this place. The bricks and stone I helped to lay, the design of the building I drew when I was young and just dreaming of having a business like this. I am proud of what I have built, but it showcases all of me, like opening up myself and giving her everything of me, leaving me raw. I hope she likes what she sees.

"You seem worried." She looks up at me, concern furrowing her brow.

"I just haven't ever brought anyone here. People come to the restaurant and for meetings obviously, but... I have never brought anyone here who really means something to me," I tell her honestly, and my chest burns as I wait for her response.

She looks from me to my distillery and back again. "You know I like you for you, right? Not all this. Just for the man you are," she asks me, and I balk. I never knew I needed to hear her say it. People associate me with my whiskey so much, it is almost like we have become one. But for her to point out that the Whiteman's brand is not what she is with me for, it settles something within me, and I smile.

"Just don't sniff too much; I don't want the tourists to be put off," I tease her, knowing she will probably never sample my liquor.

"Can't promise anything," she says, smiling, and I walk with her inside the admin building, taking the cookies from her and putting them in my office.

"So this is where all your deals are done?" she asks, glancing around. I lean against my desk and watch her take it all in. Taking a quick look at the bookcase, the photos of Connor and I that I have around the room, then she looks over the bar, the crystal decanters and glassware, along with a few shelves of bottled whiskey, the limited editions I have made over the years.

"Some of them," I say, liking her in my space. In my world.

"I love this table." Her hands run up and down the recycled timber of my desk, feeling the bumps and ridges.

"I made it a few years ago," I tell her, and she looks at me, wide-eyed.

"Made it?" she asks, head tilting my way.

"Out of old whiskey barrels."

"It is amazing. You could sell this type of thing," she says in awe, and my chest warms with pride.

"Nah, it's just a hobby. The whiskey keeps me busy enough." Taking her hand, I pull her to me. She smiles, standing between my legs where I sit on the edge of my desk, my hands curving around her waist. I feel like I can finally breathe when her hands glide up my arms and circle my neck.

"Hey, baby girl," I whisper, leaning down and kissing her slowly. It is an *I have missed you* kiss. Because even though I saw her every day, I still missed kissing her, touching her, and having alone time together. Now in my office in the peace of the afternoon, I'm relieved.

"Hey..." she breathes out, melting into me as I rub my nose with hers.

"Come, let me show you around," I say, grabbing her hand, and we walk out, slowly looking around my space as I show her the office and one of the barrel rooms.

"This is how we store the whiskey during the aging process," I tell her, spotting a tour going on down at the other end of the space, all getting the same information. "I have another seven rooms like this, the whiskey all at different aging stages and a variety of single malt or grain, depending on what I am trying."

"I still don't really have any idea of the difference between all the whiskeys, but I can appreciate it."

I kiss her forehead and bury my nose in her hair,

taking a breath before I pull her along again, and lead her into the main distillery.

"This is where the magic happens."

Her eyes widen as she looks over the large shiny vats and tubes where fermentation and the distillation of the product takes place.

"Looks like a mad scientist lab," she says with a laugh.

"It can feel a bit like it some days too."

"So I am guessing you were a science major?" She looks up at me, curiosity sparkling in her eyes.

"Sure was. Turns out, I am pretty good at it," I say with a smirk, then I wrap a hand around her waist and pull her body back into mine. We stand toe to toe, our heads close, and I take a moment to really look at her.

"How are you feeling, baby girl?" I ask her as I rub up and down her back. The tour group followed us in, and while I see them gawking at us, I couldn't care less.

"Better. Physically, much better," she says, her eyes on mine.

"And mentally?" I ask, eager to see where her head is at.

"Mentally, I don't want to think about it anymore. I think about who it was and why every minute of every day and I am tired. I have no idea, nothing," she says, her tone soft but frustrated, and I nod. I know she has been because I have been doing the same.

"Another thing that's been on my mind, though…" She pauses, and it makes me a bit nervous, but then her smile takes over her whole face. "I can't believe you flew my mom in and got me those incredible flowers." She is looking at me like I hung the moon for her. "Thank you so much, Tanner. For everything." Running her hands up my arms, they settle around my neck as she leans in.

"Anytime," I tell her, kissing her on the lips and almost getting lost in the way she feels, but then I hear the tour group's chatter. Pulling back, I press one more quick kiss on her cheek, then walk us past the group. I don't want to get negative reviews for passionately kissing and offering them a show.

The tasting room is packed full of people, and then the restaurant is also full to the brim, everyone sampling, eating, and buying. Heads turn to look at us as we walk through. I am well known for the whiskey, but I don't jump into the spotlight too much. A few people come to introduce themselves, and one family even asks for a photo. I don't make a habit of being here, so my presence is a novelty to our restaurant staff, who are all smirking at me. All the while, Victoria smiles wide, taking it all in.

I try to see it all from her eyes. The footprint of the property is massive, the warehouse and bottling facility not anywhere I have even taken her yet, and I appreciate that the business I have built is not like anything she has ever seen before. I watch as her gaze sweeps over everything, the smile never leaving her face, and I notice the admiration and pride within that expression. It makes me feel like a king.

I am proud of two things in my life. My son and my whiskey, and getting to share that with her makes me the luckiest guy in the world.

35

VICTORIA

I have been on edge all week. I jump at every noise. I have barely slept. I am scared to get into a vehicle. Thank God my mom was here; otherwise, I wouldn't have left the house. The fact that she forced me to go outside and to get into cars has been what has helped. I didn't disclose my uneasiness to her, but she just knew. Mother's instinct, I guess. Pushing me to face the fears so they don't consume me was overwhelming, but I am glad she did.

Plus, I got to spend the week with her, all thanks to Tanner. But I missed him. Missed his protectiveness, the way he just seems to know what I need and when. Even though I saw him every day, ensuring that Mom and I had everything we needed, including taking us to town and driving us around, I didn't have him in my bed at night, and he was respectful in front of my mother, stealing little kisses but otherwise being the perfect gentleman. My mother swooned hard and approved of him, something she never really did with Josh, I now realize. Although who wouldn't approve of the man who had his private jet collect her and bring her promptly to me, pay for everything while she was here, as well take such good care of her daughter? I have never seen my mom smile so wide, her stresses seemingly disappearing more and more as the week went on.

I watch him like a king in his kingdom here at the distillery, smiling as his customers ask for a photo, people shaking his hand and whispering as he walks past them. He stands tall, obviously proud, the leader he is, and I want to jump his bones. I am so turned on by his passion, his abilities, his smarts, tenacity, and discipline. Not to mention, he dropped all of this at a moment's notice to help me. The week of having him near, but not near enough, has my body on edge. I may bake cookies for the townspeople for their help, but I plan on returning the favor to Tanner in a completely different way.

"You're staring," he murmurs to me with a sexy-as-sin smirk, like he knows exactly what I am thinking. I blink a few times as I gaze up at him, coming back out of my thoughts.

"There is a lot of you to look at," I say cheekily, and he chuckles, taking my hand in his again. The smell in the restaurant is amazing, and when he drags me outside to the courtyard, the tables out here are full as well. It is clearly popular, and I see a few locals, but most people are unfamiliar.

"It is busy like this most days of the week. Tourists book us out months in advance." He leads me through to a small cottage garden. The flowers are breathtaking, the aroma instantly hitting me, and I inhale deeply.

"This is beautiful," I tell him, looking around at manicured boxed hedges, roses, daisies, lavender, and wildflowers. You name it, it is here.

"Connor and I planted this for my mom. When she was alive, this was her favorite spot. She used to sit here and read or knit. Like her own little private space away from the craziness of life." *This man.*

We stick to the path that takes us through a thick, high hedge, privacy signs erected near the walkway as we move through a gate. It is clear that this is now his private land, not for the tourists or anyone else. I look around everywhere, not wanting to miss a thing, and I see nothing but expansive manicured lawn, the grass a vibrant green, and sitting right on it is a luxury log cabin.

"This is my place. Connor has one too, just over there." He points to the left, and I see one that is almost identical a few hundred yards away. The grass between the two is vast, green, and pristine. Whoever does their landscaping is an expert, that is for sure. I take another deep breath in and feel my shoulders relax. It is quiet, the place surrounded by tall, thick hedges, which also hide what I think is a fence. It is like his own garden oasis; you can't even hear the activity of the distillery from here anymore.

"This is amazing..." I say in awe. I turn to look around, spotting the top of my house in the distance. "Look! There I am!"

"I can see you from my porch," he says, opening the front door and leading me inside. It is darker here and my eyes adjust. It is exactly how I imagined Tanner's place to be. Very rugged, large, and masculine. He has very high ceilings and oversized windows, the place made from dark timber that's brightened by the clear blue sky shining in. I spot his kitchen over to the side, clean, polished, with every amenity you would expect. It is luxe. Just like the man who owns it.

"Is this the kind of decor most ranches around here have?" I ask him, thinking about the project I am undertaking with Griffin. After I recovered for a few days, I got back to Griffin by email to let him know that I would take on the job. I have started a Pinterest board, but seeing Tanner's place now, it makes me think a little harder.

"I guess a ranch is just like any other home. It needs to take into consideration the people who will live in it, but I think a place like Whispers has a certain style. You need to bring the outside in a little," he offers, and it makes sense. It is a nice vibe, most definitely welcoming, warm, but also secure and strong. I look at Tanner, who is watching me closely. The two feelings should be a little contradicting, but they aren't. They work perfectly.

"I have taken a job with Griffin," I blurt out, having not told him anything about it yet. The whole car accident derailed my news.

"You have?" he asks, surprised.

"He needs help doing the interior of a new ranch build here in Whispers. I started working on it this week."

"You did, huh?" He smiles as I basically bounce on my toes with excitement.

"It's a big project," I tell him, looking around again, getting ideas.

"After last weekend, you should be resting," he tells

me, concern suddenly etching his features, but I am so sick of resting. Especially as my eyes meet his. Everything else fades away.

"I don't want to rest," I tell him teasingly as I take a small step toward him. My voice is full of innuendo.

"But you are still recovering." He swallows roughly, his Adam's apple bobbing as I trail my hands up the front of his shirt.

"I slowed down because of my ankle, and now I slowed down because some asshole cut my brakes. I don't want to go slow anymore..." My heart picks up pace in my chest as I step away, my fingers moving to the buttons on the front of my dress, itching to get it off.

"You had a big scare," he says, still not reaching for me, even with how close I am. I need to feel him, I need his hands on my body. It's like he's holding himself back.

"I'm fine. I feel better just being here with you, Tanner." Opening the first button and then the second, I bite my lip as my eyes flick to his. I don't want him to be scared to touch me. I need his touch, I crave it. My body heats just thinking about it, and I open my dress, exposing my chest.

"You aren't healed, baby," he says gruffly, his teeth gritting, and I know I am getting to him.

"Maybe not. But I am burning for you," I say, my voice breathy, as his eyes drop to my chest. "Touch me, Tanner." I drop my sundress from my shoulders, the fabric gliding down my body to the floor, and I stand in front of him in nothing but my matching white lace underwear.

"Goddamn. Look at you."

In two large strides, he's smashing his lips to mine as

his hands wrap around my middle. Melting into him, I breathe out the stress I was holding all week and give myself over to him.

"You want me to touch you? You burn for me?" he whispers over my lips as he cups my face, looking into my eyes. The intensity makes me shiver as I nod eagerly.

With a growl, he picks me up, my legs circling his waist immediately, and then he drops to his knees.

"Tanner," I breathe out his name as our bodies meet the floor. My hands grab at his shirt, and I find his buttons, frantically opening them, needing to feel his skin on mine. He lowers me to my back, and I lie under him, his knees between my legs on a soft rug he has right next to an open fireplace. Images of what this would be like when snowing outside infiltrate my mind, a new desire now unlocked, before his lips on me pull me back to the moment I'm so desperate for.

"Oh, baby girl, I missed hearing you say my name like that," he says, his shirt now off, and leaning back up, he makes quick work of his boots and jeans, his eyes traveling down my body and back up again. I squirm under his attention, but only for a breath before he's pulling the lace from my hips, lowering between my legs, and pressing his lips to my core.

"And I missed this," I hiss the words, my breath escaping me as he laps at my wetness like a man starved. I'm panting within a minute, euphoria already overwhelming my senses as he lifts my hips up from the rug, his hands curving around the back of my thighs, his head completely buried against me.

"Oh God... Oh God... Oh God..." I whimper continuously at the contact as he doesn't come up for air. His tongue is warm and delves into me, over and over, making me gasp; his lips suck my clit, his whiskers scratch just right, his moans give me butterflies, and all of it together has me seeing stars.

"More, Tanner. More, please," I beg of him, and before I know it, he's kissing his way up my body, eyes level with mine.

"Tell me what you want," he grits out, his eyes on fire, his chest heaving and red. The two of us are famished and just about feral for each other. After the week I had, I need it, I need him.

"Fuck me, Tanner," I tell him, and he listens immediately. Lifting my leg, he places it at his hip and I curve it around his waist to bring him closer.

"Anything you want, baby girl. I can't deny you a thing," he growls as he lines himself up and pushes inside me, giving me exactly what I want.

36

———

TANNER

Like a red flag to a bull, I am raging, my cock hard and throbbing, my hunger for her insatiable. Her body arches, gasping as we melt together, and it feels like I am finally home after a long absence. The relief in my bones is instant, the feel of her around me incomparable, and as I gaze down into her eyes, I swear on everything that is holy this woman needs to be mine. Permanently.

I try to go slow. After the week she had, I wasn't sure if she wanted me to touch her. I tried to be there for her, but I didn't know what she needed or when. The vision of her bloody and dirty, lying in that hospital bed is a memory of mine that won't be erased anytime soon, and the pain and anger I have felt about it still simmers under my skin.

I want to give her everything she asks for, including fucking her right here on my living room floor.

As her request fell from her lips, understanding washed over me that I would not deny this woman anything. So I thrust into her fast, hard, and hungry.

When she dropped her dress and presented herself to me in her pretty white lace like a fucking angel, she knew what she was doing. I peeled off her underwear like I was unwrapping a fucking present. A gift from God directly to me is exactly what she is.

"Yes... yes... yes..." she chants as I piston into her, all tenderness forgotten, my dire need to have her, consume her, make her come over and over the only thing on my mind. I lose control around her every single time and today is no exception.

"Fuck, baby girl, you are so fucking good... too fucking good," I grit out, my jaw tight as I watch her underneath me, her breasts bouncing in her lace bra, her mouth open, her hair splayed on my rug. My hand wraps around her lower back, tilting her hips a little so I hit that spot inside of her that I know makes her crazy.

"Oooooh... My... God!" she cries out, her eyes widening a little.

"That's it... Wrap your other leg around me," I tell her, and she does so immediately. I lower my hand, both now on the floor on either side of her as I thrust into her with powerful, purposeful strokes, hitting that spot every time. Her legs remain wrapped around me, clenching as I suck on her neck, tasting her and breathing her in.

"Tanner, yes. Tanner..." She says my name on each panted breath as sweat builds on our skin. I feel mine prickle, my orgasm close, and I see her biting her bottom lip, knowing she is as well. Then I remember—

"Fuck, condom," I tell her, slowing a little. Going bare is not something that I have felt in a very long time. I should have known with her it would be perfect.

"Don't stop. Please don't stop... I'm on the pill..." she says almost desperately, and that combined with the pink hue of her cheeks and the lust shining in her eyes, has my length twitching inside her to keep going.

"You sure?" I ask again, not exactly sure myself. Connor's mom told me she was on the pill and look how that turned out. But I can trust Victoria. I know that. And as strong as I am, pulling out of her right now is something that would take all my strength and then some.

"Tanner... Oh God, don't you dare stop." Her hips grind up into me, taking me fully inside her, and I groan as I speed up again.

She is not my ex. I am different now too. I trust her. Explicitly.

"I can't stop anything when it comes to you. You are so fucking perfect," I growl as my thrusts continue, bringing my hand to her clit and watching her nipples pebble under her lace.

"I'm going to come." Gripping on to me tight as her core pulses, I smirk as I change tack. I smash our bodies together, my lips sealing hers, and I roll over, putting her on top.

"Bounce for me, baby..." My hands smooth up her back, unclipping her bra. Throwing the white lace down and off her arms, her hands connect with my chest, and she starts to ride me with abandon.

"Fuck," I murmur at the visual coupled with the feeling. It feels different, her hunger for me just as apparent as mine is for her. Naked, perfect, all mine. I have dreamed of having her like this, getting to enjoy seeing her take what she wants so badly. Her breasts are phenomenal, and so is her ass as I grip it tight.

"You're... so... big..." she pants out as I hit her deep, her hair falling around her shoulders as her hands grip on to my chest.

"You take me so well... like the perfect fucking woman you are..." I tell her, and she gives me a little smile as my hands squeeze her ass harder, helping to pull her up and down my cock.

"Tanner... Right there," she warns, using my name like I know she does when she is just about to explode.

"Fuck me, beautiful," I tell her softly, leaning up to take her nipple into my mouth, and her hips speed up as she moans long and loud.

"Ahhh... ahhh! Tanner!" Her orgasm ripples through her as she looks to the ceiling and lets out a scream, her body shaking. I grind her onto me and she keeps coming, whimpering as her nails dig into my chest, leaving half-moons in their wake. My eyes run over her nakedness, enjoying every moment of her pleasure. I am still rock-hard, but I let her catch her breath for a moment, hips still rocking as she looks down at me. Her eyes sparkle when they meet mine, her hair cascading around her pretty, flushed face.

"Turn around and get on all fours," I command, and her eyes widen before it turns into pure lust. She lifts off me, turns, and gets on her hands and knees. Lifting up, I get on my knees behind her and sink back into her warm, dripping center.

"You have such a fucking fantastic ass..." My hands encase her waist and I hold her tight, thrusting hard into her from behind. Her ass jiggles like her breasts and now I can't decide which part of her body is my favorite. I grit my teeth as I feel my own orgasm close, and I know it isn't her breasts or her ass that I like, it is all of her. Inside and out.

"Oh my God! You are so deep," she moans. and the sounds make me bite my own lip as I feel my balls tighten. It feels so fucking good. Everything about her feels so right.

"I want you to come again," I tell her, needing to get another orgasm from her, loving the fact that she comes so fully with me.

"I can't," she says, but I hear her already panting, her pussy clenching around me again.

"This perfect pussy is telling my cock a totally different story, baby girl." My words have the desired effect as I feel her tightening around my length. I am not sure how much longer I can hold out, but I grit my teeth harder and keep going.

"Ah! Oh God, Tanner." Her gasp turns to a whimper, almost in shock that she is about to orgasm again so soon.

"Fuck, you make me so hard, beautiful. You're made just for me. I feel you gripping on to me, wanting more, you greedy girl. My perfect, greedy girl," I grit out, and she explodes with another scream of my name, gripping the rug beneath her as she throws her head back. Curving her hips slightly, I hit her G-spot with my thrusts, and as her pussy flutters, I let go.

"Fuuuuuccccckkkkkk!" I roar so loud, my orgasm one for the record books, making me dizzy.

"Holy shit," she breathes out, her body quivering with

mine, my grip on her waist hard as I continue to grind into her, shooting my release deep. Pulling her back to me, we fall together onto the rug and catch our breath.

"White lace is a go, then," she pants with a chuckle.

"It's not the lace, baby girl. It is all you," I tell her, kissing the top of her head and curling her into my side. Exactly where she belongs.

37

VICTORIA

As the morning light peeks through his blinds, I look around Tanner's bedroom. This big, dark, wooden sleigh bed is luxuriously comfortable. I am warm, snuggled, and feel entirely content. He has photographs of Whispers around his room, the landscape, some of the distillery that I recognize. All in black and white. A large bathroom is off to the side, and his walk-in closet rivals the size of my shed. I spot an equal mix of suits and jeans through the opening; the contradiction of the man continues even in his wardrobe choices.

After our rumble in the living room and showering, we talked all night over dinner, before we fell into bed and made love again, our stamina for each other like nothing I have experienced before.

I am falling for him. Hard. What started as a fury of passion has turned into something more. Much more. I have no idea what it means. I can't get a handle on it. I have never felt this way. He consumes me. Every waking moment, my first thought is him. That didn't even happen with Josh and I was engaged to that asshole. Looking at the ceiling, I say my thanks to the Lord above for helping me dodge that bullet.

"Penny for your thoughts?" Tanner asks from where he is lying next to me in his crumpled bedsheets. His hand darts over and runs across my naked stomach, tenderly caressing my skin before he cups my breast.

"Hmm, just thinking about things," I tell him as I turn over, the two of us lying face-to-face. "What about you?"

He looks down at my body and back to my eyes. "I'm just thinking about how perfect your naked body is and how perfect it looks in my bed. I am remembering the first time I saw it in your bathroom when you hurt your leg."

"I thought you said you didn't see anything!" I smack his chest playfully, shocked, because that little memory was one that filled me with embarrassment.

"Oh, I saw enough. It's been ingrained in my brain ever since," he says, huffing a laugh.

"Hmm, well, I like looking at you naked too," I admit, and he winks at me.

"I really like having you in my bed," he says, pulling me to him, and my body slides across the sheets and into his arms. "Or your bed. Just you and me in bed is what I want."

"I could get used to this as well." Pressing a soft kiss to his lips, his hands trail up and down my back.

"So next week, I have an event in the city... I would like you to come with me. Be my date?" he asks, and I hold my breath.

"Really?" I ask, smiling. "What is it?" I'm keen to know more about his city life.

"Fundraising dinner for a literacy program in Baltimore. We will go, then get the jet back to New York that night and stay in my penthouse for a few days. It might do us both good to get out of here for a while." He says it all so casually while I reel at the information.

"I'm not sure I have anything to wear to a fundraising dinner," I say with a frown.

"I will get something for you. I'll organize it all, you just say yes." He searches my eyes, and I smile even brighter.

"Then yes," I say without any more hesitation, leaning in to kiss him again. He pulls back a little and looks at me, his fingers lightly brushing down my arm and leaving goosebumps in his wake.

"Last week when the accident happened..." Pausing, he shakes his head. "I just..." He stops himself again, trying to find the words. "Wasn't sure if you would pack up... go back home..."

I'm shaking my head before he's even finished.

"I'm not going back to the city, Tanner. I like Whispers. I like Marmalade and Gertie. I like you," I admit, feeling vulnerable. I hold my breath as I wait for his response.

"I think I fell for you the moment I laid eyes on you." His smile reappears at hearing my confession, his hand coming to caress my cheek, and I lean into his palm.

"Sounds like we are on the same page, then," I say carefully, seeing nothing but extreme adoration in his eyes.

"Sounds like it," he says before he seals our words with another mind-melting kiss.

"THE WEATHER IS SO beautiful this time of year," I say, looking around the landscaping as we walk together back to the distillery. It is early, guests still have not arrived, but the workers are getting things ready for what no doubt will be another busy day. Once we get to the driveway near his office, the walk for me to get home is only about five minutes from here.

"Here," he says, throwing me a set of keys.

"You want me to drive your truck?" My heart pounds a little in fear but also excitement. His truck is luxe.

"No, you can drive your own." He points to a truck in the driveway. I look at it, shiny and new, black like his, but the logo is different. It is blue with a picture of a house, Marie's Place written underneath it.

"What?" I ask, as I look at him, confused.

"It's yours."

I think my heart actually stops.

"What? I can't accept this. Tanner, you have done too much already." I am never going to be able to repay him.

"You can," he says, nodding like it is a done deal.

"I can't," I say back, shaking my head, even as my stomach flips. It is too much.

"Baby girl, it is all yours." Cupping my face, he tilts my head up to look at him. He's actually serious about this... but I need to stand firm.

"Tanner," I say in a stern warning, but the warmth in my chest wants me to accept it.

"You need a vehicle to get around in. I can't take you all the time."

I balk because I do need a vehicle, and I don't want to be a burden to him or the girls who have been chauffeuring me all week. He knows my weak spot.

"But I can't afford this. It's too much," I tell him honestly. My eyes flick to the truck and then back to him.

"Yeah, but I can, so it's yours." He's smirking now.

"Tanner!"

"Baby girl. Get in, let's go for a drive, and go take a look at this property you are designing," he says smoothly, and that's enough to spark my interest and distract me for a moment.

"You know where it is?" I ask him, surprised, though I thought he might.

"I know everything about this town. It's down on Billionaire Boulevard," he confirms as he walks past me, slapping my butt to move me along.

"Do you know who owns it?" I ask as I run after him, the large gift he just bestowed a distant memory now that we are talking about interiors. Rushing to unlock the truck, I pull myself up. It is a fair ways off the ground, but I like being this high. I take a moment, pulling in some deep breaths, but the overwhelming panic doesn't come.

"Breathe, baby girl. It's alright. I promise," Tanner says, looking at me from the passenger side, and I swallow before nodding to him.

"So, do you know who owns it?" I ask him again as I push away the negativity and fear and buckle up.

"Maybe," he says coyly as he puts on his seat belt.

"Want to tell me?" I quirk an eyebrow his way as I get a feel for the steering.

"Nope. From what Griffin tells me, you are in charge of the design and to tell you the owner may skew your ideas," he says, and I frown. He makes a good point.

"You're no fun." I huff as I turn the key and hear the truck come to life. Looking at him, my smile's wide at the rumble. This truck is much newer than Marie's, and I already feel safer. My stomach flutters once more at his thoughtfulness. He knew how much I needed this.

"You got it?" he asks me to ensure I am comfortable.

"I got it," I say, nodding as I reverse and start to drive.

Within fifteen minutes, I am driving right up the driveway of the property.

"Wow, this is so beautiful." I'm in awe, trying to watch where I am driving but also take in the surroundings. I park at the end of the driveway, and we get out.

"Good view, isn't it?"

We meet at the front of the truck and look out. A large green lawn spreads out before us, but then farther out is what could be miles of rolling green hills. You can just make out the distillery too. It is almost like this property oversees the entire town.

"It is far enough away to be private and high enough to not have the view interrupted. It is almost like one of the photos in your bedroom," I comment, remembering the photographic art on his walls.

"The frame is up..." he says, turning, looking at the start of what will be the house.

"It is much bigger in real life. I have seen the plans,

already started with my ideas, but seeing it now makes it all so much more real," I say to him as we walk up to the frame and step inside, going through each room.

"Griffin's team works fast; that is what he is known for. He has multiple teams and runs multiple projects at once," Tanner says, looking over everything with a critical eye as my mind is whirling with so many design ideas.

"Oh, the living space is much bigger than I realized..." I murmur as I walk into that space. Even though there are no walls or ceiling, I imagine them and frown.

"What are you thinking?" Tanner asks, observing my reaction.

"Well, this is the living space. The plans have this walled up. I was thinking of an open fireplace and mantle, but..." I say, moving around, trying to look at it all.

"But what?"

"Well... what if it was a wall of windows instead?" I suggest, and his eyebrows rise.

"Windows?"

"Hear me out. They would need to be thick and have some structural support, but this view, it is too beautiful to just have a normal large window and then block it all off. What if instead it was kept open, with large sliding doors that you can open right up, bring the inside out and outside in. It would be amazing in spring and summer, and then in the cooler months, you close it up but still get the view. The fireplace could go to the side instead." As I'm visualizing it all, I see him deep in thought.

"Floor-to-ceiling windows... I think that is an

amazing idea and probably why the owner wanted you to design it. You should tell Griffin," he says, and I smile at his support.

"Come and tell me what else you are thinking."

Taking my hand, we spend the next thirty minutes going through each room, and every time I do, a new visual comes into my brain. I can't wait to get home to start sketching and pulling imagery from online.

"Oh, there needs to be a helipad over there," Tanner says, pointing to the side.

"What?" I ask, having never thought about that.

"Oh, baby, this place needs a helipad. It is too far away from the airstrip to drive. Especially at night," he tells me, watching me closely. That makes sense, considering the type of wealthy person who probably owns this place.

I nod silently, thinking about how magnificent this is going to be. He comes to stand behind me as we look out over the vista. Taking a big breath in, I feel his hands wrap around my waist before he leans over me, kissing my cheek.

"It's perfect out here," I tell him whimsically. This would be my dream house.

"It sure is," he agrees, pulling me to him, the two of us feeling contented surrounded by large trees, a soon-to-be luxury ranch, and just the sounds of the birds and wildlife. It's perfect.

38

VICTORIA

We arrive to the jet, and I swallow harshly.

"I have never been on a plane like this before," I say, looking out at the plane before us and wondering what this experience is going to be like.

"Nervous flyer?" Tanner asks me as he helps me from the truck. A scurry of people takes our bags and loads them, and one of Tanner's team members jumps in his truck and drives it off to park it for him. I don't fly a lot, but it isn't the flight I am nervous about.

"No, it's just so new and shiny."

He lets me walk up the stairs first, and I go slowly, wanting to take it all in.

"Wow," I breathe out as I reach the main cabin and step inside. It is exactly what you would expect. The lights are on, the finishes shiny. The leather seats look like butter. It is browns and creams and almost a soft yet masculine kind of tone.

"This paneling is really beautiful. You made this,

didn't you?" I ask Tanner, already knowing he did. It has his signature design all over it. Running my hand along the wall, I feel the whiskey barrel recycled paneling and its smooth bumps underneath it. The very faint smell of whiskey lingers in the space, and I like it.

"It took a while, but I got it how I wanted," he admits, and I smile. I like the way he brings a little of himself into each of his spaces. It makes me think of the ranch I am designing and how I wish I knew the owner so I could do exactly that for them.

"And these seats..." I sigh as I brush my hand over the top of the leather seat, before I sit down and the softness encases me.

"Lambskin. Softest leather you can find." He likes me appreciating his things, but there is a lot to appreciate.

"Of course you would have a bar in here." I laugh as my eyes rest on the lit-up display of crystal glasses and decanters, all full with different whiskeys.

"Of course," Tanner says smugly. "Wherever I go, my whiskey is not far away."

"Oh, and a candy jar!" I jump up and head to the small bar, bypassing all the whiskey and grab a handful of candy before sitting again. When I look up at Tanner, I see him smirking at me.

"I like your little idiosyncrasies," he says, taking the seat next to me. "Are you ready?" Grabbing my seat belt and putting it around me, he ensures I am secure before doing his own.

"As ready as I will ever be," I tell him with a wide smile, trying to tamp down the nerves I feel.

I am not scared or worried, but this is a big step. Traveling together, going to an event with his friends and business associates. I have no idea what it is about or who will be there, but I know this is the kind of thing he gets invited to regularly. *Who does he normally take as his date? What is expected of me?*

I take a deep breath and close my eyes, trying to calm my racing thoughts.

Like he knows exactly what I am thinking, I feel him lean in and I smell his whiskey breath as he takes my lips with his softly before murmuring, "I can't wait to have you on my arm tonight."

As the plane lifts from the ground, I open my eyes and see him right in front of me. There is nowhere else I would rather be.

WE MADE IT TO BALTIMORE. Tanner booked the penthouse at the Four Seasons for a few hours just for us to rest and then get ready, and as I walk in, my nerves are sky-high. The jet here was amazing, the town car and driver who picked us up all felt extremely luxurious, and now as I walk around a full-size living room, I am gobs-macked at this type of lifestyle.

"Are you alright?" Tanner asks tentatively as he watches me from where he stands. He is dressed differently today. His shirt and jeans obviously reserved for Whispers, now he is in dress slacks and a crisp button-up shirt, looking every inch the billionaire he obviously is.

"This is so pretty," I comment as I look out the

windows over the harbor, seeing the sunlight dancing on the water.

"Baltimore is nice. Connor and I come here a bit because we have friends here. The Rothschilds and Huxley Hamilton, a local kid Connor grew up with," he explains, and I feel my throat close up.

"Rothschild? As in the president?" I ask, looking at him wide-eyed. It is a charity gala in Baltimore; what does he mean, the Rothschilds?

"Yes. As in the president." He leaves no room for question. *Holy shit. My boyfriend is friends with the first family.*

"Is the president going to be at this event tonight?" I am almost too scared to hear the answer. Not because I don't like him. I mean, he is a nice president from all accounts, but me swanning around at an event where the president is in attendance. Fiona is going to wet her pants when I tell her.

"Yes. Him and all his family. It is their foundation we are raising money for. A literacy program," Tanner explains as he walks toward me slowly, like he is approaching an injured animal. Maybe it is because my breathing has quickened, my palms also feeling sweaty.

"Oh..." is all I can say, trying to get my nerves under control.

"Oh?" he asks, looking unsure.

"It's just, the president and his family... Phfft." My cheeks heat, and I flap my hand in front of my face because I feel like I am overheating.

"Come here," Tanner says in his low voice that makes my legs move to him almost automatically. He reaches for me and pulls me into his arms, securing me to his chest, and I immediately relax.

"What if I say the wrong thing or, like, trip over my heels or something? I have been wearing nothing but those boots you got me for weeks. What if I forgot how to wear heels? Or worse, do I have to drink your whiskey and pretend that I like it?" I ask him, smiling, and he growls against me.

"You don't have to pretend anything. You are perfect exactly how you are." His words are comforting, and I take a deep breath and exhale slowly as he continues.

"One, you will look perfect. You always do. But I have a team coming who will dress you and do your hair."

"What? Seriously?" I ask, dumbfounded. He said he would take care of it, but I thought he just meant a dress. I practically packed an entire hair salon and makeup counter in my bag because I had no idea what I needed.

"Two. The president is just a normal guy. One of my good friends. He won't care if you fall over or say the wrong thing. In fact, I think you and his wife will actually get along very well."

While I obviously don't know her, I have seen the first lady in the media, and she is someone whom I would love to meet.

"And what's three?" I ask him, and he looks at me, confused.

"Three?"

"Yeah, you had one and two, but what is three. These things usually come in threes, so what is your three?" I ask, and he chuckles.

"And three... we have a few hours to kill before

anyone gets here, so I think we should go and rest. Maybe take a nap?"

My body relaxes even more with that idea now planted.

"Just a nap... I can't meet the president all flushed and with a post-sex glow," I warn him, even though I can guarantee that the two of us will not be very well behaved once we hit that bedroom.

"Fine, nap only. But naked," he says seriously, like he is negotiating a work deal.

"Deal," I say, holding out my hand to shake.

"Nap time starts now." Before I can even blink, he's throwing me over his shoulder.

"Tanner!" I squeal at the unexpectedness, laughing as he slaps my ass and struts straight to the bedroom, kicking the door closed.

We both know the deal is off.

I TAKE a nervous breath in as I look at myself. I am sparkling. There is no other word for it, and I know when Tanner sees me, he is going to love it.

"The dress is perfect on you," the stylist says as she pulls the last zipper, and her team takes all the bags away.

"Thank you so much, I really appreciate all your help. I can't believe he picked this one," I say to her, smiling, wondering how he is going to get through the formal dinner tonight with me dressed like this.

"Oh, he didn't. This is a new one that just came into our showroom today, and I brought it with me on a whim. But I think he will like it," she says, giving me a wink before walking away out the door, leaving me with my own reflection.

I swallow, looking at myself again. I used to wear heels and makeup every day for work, but never like this. I am glammed up.

If the nerves about being on Tanner's arm in front of everyone would dissipate, that would be good. If I am honest, I am looking forward to it. It has given me something else to think about other than what I've been through lately. I close my eyes and take another breath, pushing those thoughts aside before I grab my clutch and walk out to the living room.

I spot Tanner in the kitchen, pouring himself a whiskey, and I pause to watch him while he is oblivious. He is in a tuxedo, and I thought I would be ready for it, but I am not. He is without a doubt one of the best-looking men I have ever seen. He's dapper, mysterious, distinguished, and butterflies start to swirl at seeing us both dressed up like this.

He glances at his Rolex, and I break out of my stare. I don't want to make us late.

As I walk toward him, he looks up, his eyes widening as he almost chokes on the liquor in his mouth.

My lips are glossy and red, the focus point of my face with the rest of my makeup minimal. My hair is in soft waves floating down my back. But it is this dress that has his jaw dropping.

"Are you speechless?" I tease, enjoying this reaction from him.

"Just about." His eyes remain glued as I get closer. "You look delectable, baby girl."

I hum as I give a little twirl, then stand before him and watch as his gaze falls down my body and back up again. This dress is long, grazing the floor, but fitted to my curves. The top is strapless, showcasing my shoulders, and forms perfectly around my breasts. But it is the material that has him growling. Black lace, thick enough to cover the important areas, but see-through at my legs.

"This dress is amazing. It almost looks like you don't have any underwear on underneath it." He groans, jaw clenching as his hands finds my hips. I look up into his eyes and smile.

"That is because I am not wearing any." I hold up the pair of black lace panties and put them in his palm.

"Fuck." He looks like he is about to faint as his grip on me tightens, and I laugh seeing him like this. It's endearing and also the biggest turn-on.

"We need to go. If we wait a moment longer, then we won't be leaving at all," he grumbles, throwing back the rest of his whiskey before he kisses me, the taste of him and his signature batch now tainting my lips.

"Are you ready?" he asks, looking deep into my eyes.

"I'm ready," I say with a nod as we walk out the door.

39

TANNER

I watch her from where I stand at the bar across the room. She is talking animatedly with Huxley's wife, Lucy, Valerie Van Cleef, and Beth, The First Lady. All four women have broad smiles, acting like they have known each other for years and are hatching a plan.

"So you hard-launched your relationship with the neighbor, then?" Huxley asks me, passing me a glass of whiskey, which better be my own; otherwise, he will wear it.

"Hard-launched?" I ask, taking a sip, tasting last year's whiskey release. Smiling, I feel the smoothness of my hard work glide down my throat.

"You bring her out, on your arm, to an event where there are media, a red carpet, the who's who of this town. They have never seen a woman on your arm before. It will be all over the gossip pages tomorrow. I can see the headline now. *America's most sought-after billionaire bachelor finally meets his match*," Huxley mocks, watching me carefully over the rim of his glass.

"Is that what you call it these days?" I murmur, ignoring his statement, my eyes still glued to the woman across the room. *My woman.* He is right. It will be all over the news, both gossip and business. I am sure my PR agency will be fielding a few calls throughout the next few days. It is unusual for me to be seen with a woman. I keep my private life low-key, usually just coming to these things on my own or with Connor.

"She is nice. Beautiful. Smart. What the hell does she see in you?" President Rothschild says, grabbing my attention as he butts into our conversation. Best friends with my son, Harrison is newly president and doing a damn good job of it too.

"Mr. President." I give his hand a shake. It is nice to see him, even if it is always fleeting.

"Nice to see you looking so happy for a change, Tanner." He looks at me with the same smirk both Connor and Huxley do. *Assholes.*

"I'm always happy," I say sarcastically with a grin.

"Don't tease my father. It is about time he found someone, and Victoria is a perfect match for his grumpy ass." Connor comes over, slapping the president on the back, which has his secret service stepping forward. Harrison waves them off.

"I met her earlier, a smart woman. Fits in with the girls already. I am sure Beth will want to catch up with her again soon," Harrison says before someone whispers in his ear, and he nods. "Might come out to Whispers soon. I will call you." Then he's shaking my hand again. As soon as he comes, he goes, many more hands to shake tonight, as we are here to raise money for his sister's literacy foundation.

"He is like Batman; I only ever see him at night these days," Connor says, taking a sip of whiskey.

"Did you just call the president Batman?" Victoria asks, smiling as she slides into my side and my arm wraps around her on instinct. Connor watches us closely, and his grin widens.

"Yeah. You should hear what I used to call him in college," my son says, and she laughs.

"Oh, I am sure I don't want to know."

My smile is wide as I watch my son and my girl chatting like old friends. She has done that all night. Talked to everyone, been present in all conversations, networked, smiled for every camera, made new connections. She fits right in like she's been to a hundred of these events.

"Saw you talking with the girls earlier?" I ask her quietly as Connor and Huxley chat among themselves.

"I was telling them all about my plans for Marie's Place. They were really interested to learn about it. Apparently, they know a lot of single, struggling moms from the literacy program, and they think that maybe the Rothschild Foundation could look at funding families to have a vacation break a few times a year at Marie's," she says excitedly, and my chest swells with pride.

"Sounds like you have had a great night." Pulling her close, I kiss her on her forehead, then hear a camera click nearby.

"So there are a lot of cameras on us tonight?" she whispers, looking up at me.

"Hmm. I guess it is an oddity," I tell her and watch her brow furrow.

"Oddity? What is?" she asks.

"That I am here with a woman." I take a sip of my whiskey as I let that sink in.

"Who do you normally bring to these things?"

"Connor."

"Really? Why not dates?" she asks, still looking surprised.

"Because I never found anyone I desired having on my arm until now. Someone I don't want to be without." The honesty of my words hits us both as we look at each other, her eyes sparkling as they stay locked on mine.

"Excuse me, Mr. Whiteman." A young woman with a clipboard appears, breaking our moment.

"Yes?" I look at her while I squeeze Victoria's waist, keeping her close.

"I don't mean to interrupt, but I am part of the event crew, and I am here to tell you that the item you donated for auction has been won. The sum of seventy-five thousand dollars was reached by the president himself," she says with a grin, and I smile and nod. I knew Harrison would bid on my whiskey. He has started a collection.

"Oh, you donated something? I didn't know that." Victoria looks at me with a large smile, and I hear more cameras click.

"Mr. Whiteman always does; we are so grateful for all his support," the young woman, who is obviously working for the Rothschilds, says.

"Well, what did you donate?" Victoria asks me.

"The first bottle of our next release. It's a limited

edition. Only a few thousand bottles will be made, so it will be exclusive."

Her eyes widen, and I can tell she has more questions.

"I will email you the details tomorrow. I just wanted to let you know," the young woman says before she leaves us to it.

"Seventy-five thousand for a bottle of whiskey? What makes it so special?" Victoria asks me once we are alone again.

"It's a new brand, one that Connor and Lacy came up with. We are not releasing it to the public, only keeping it for exclusive order only," I murmur, taking another sip of whiskey, not believing I let them talk me into it.

"That's exciting. What did you call it?"

I can't help but smile and shake my head.

"Next Door. A whiskey to be enjoyed with your neighbor," I tell her, and her face stills before her smile gets even wider and she laughs. It is contagious, and I start to laugh as well, so much so, the people around us start looking over. I spot Connor eyeing us from nearby, clearly wanting to know what is going on too.

"Are you telling me that I have been an inspiration to your brand, Tanner?" Victoria teases, her eyes glistening.

"Oh, you inspire me every day, baby girl." Holding her close, I press a light kiss to her painted lips.

"I might have to try this release. Since I am what inspired it and all," she hums, looking up at me, and I like that idea. I like it a lot.

"I have a test bottle at my penthouse in New York. We can try it tonight."

"Sounds like a plan," she says, her fingers smoothing

my suit lapel as the look in her eyes turns blazing. I know we have the same thing in mind, and with that, I check the time, seeing a few people starting to leave.

"We should go," I say to her, and she nods eagerly.

"Are you two trying to get on the front page of *Society News* here or something?" Connor asks, looking at us like we are fascinating and insane all rolled into one.

"Better my smile than my resting bitch face that I am most likely to have," Victoria quips. "I need to go and grab my bag. Give me a moment." Stepping away, she moves through the crowd, many people stopping and talking with her. Her presence is magnetic, and in that dress, I am surprised I was able to last this long before getting her out of here.

"I have never seen you laugh like that, Dad. Not out in public, anyway." Connor looks at me, surprised. I have never thought about it before, but he is right. I generally don't enjoy these events. I prefer to be at the distillery than in the city. But tonight, I have had fun. I enjoy being in the company of my friends, and that will never change, but having Victoria with me just made it all the better.

"She brings out the best in me," I tell him honestly, still watching her.

"She certainly does," Connor confirms with a smile, taking me in like he is seeing me for the first time.

It is all her. She does this to me.

40

VICTORIA

"My feet are killing me," I say to Tanner as we take the elevator up to his penthouse. Our bags are already here, the car bringing us straight from the jet. I could get used to this private travel. Everything is so much quicker, easier, and less stressful.

"Let me help you," he says as we reach his floor, swooping down and picking me up, walking me across the threshold of his door and into what can only be described as interior porn.

"Holy hell," I gasp, wriggling out of his hold until he puts me down.

"Look at this view!" I almost squeal, walking toward the large floor-to-ceiling windows. "Look at your ceilings! They must be at least twenty-five feet high?" I have never seen anything like it.

He chuckles behind me, and I turn to face him with complete shock. Taking off his jacket, he unbuttons the collar of his white shirt before sitting on the arm of the sofa, watching me.

"I wondered if you would like it," he says, and now I look at him like he has gone mad.

"Like it? This is crazy. Oh my God, you have a grand piano in your living room. You can see all of Central Park from your sofa!" I am almost yelling now with excitement. I am in interior design paradise.

"You can see the Hudson from the bath," he quips, and I whip my head around to look at him again. *I think I might faint.*

"Tanner. This is insane." I find something different to obsess over everywhere I glance. "I am blown away. I need a full tour. That hallway looks so long, I could play a game of tennis in it," I tell him as I peek around the corner, spotting artwork on the walls I am pretty sure should be in the MET.

"We are here for a few days, so you can spend as much time poking around as you want." Standing, he walks toward me. I watch him, his shirt unbuttoned, his cuffs rolled, and my heart now races for an entirely different reason.

"I am starting to understand how this all happens when you sell whiskey for seventy-five thousand dollars a bottle." I mean, I knew he was a billionaire. His watches, his trucks, his distillery, his jet. But seeing the city life he leads, the people he networks with, this penthouse which stands taller than any other building in this city, it is all a little overwhelming.

"Speaking of which..." he says, making a small detour to what looks like a very well-stocked bar. There are bottles on the wall, all backlit like a restaurant or lounge, his brand front and center, along with bottles of wine and champagne. "Want to try it?" Grabbing a bottle that looks a little different than his usual ones, he passes it to me.

"Next Door," I say, looking at the golden doors on the navy label, and I huff another laugh at Lacy and Connor for naming it such.

"Did I already tell you how beautiful you look tonight?" Tanner asks quietly as he moves to my back and places small kisses on my bare shoulders.

"You did. But there's no limit," I tease breathily. His lips warm my body all over, and my head falls back to rest on his chest as he kisses up my neck, making my breath leave my lungs and my body relax on his.

"Let me take that," he says, grabbing the bottle from me.

"Mmmm... you smell like whiskey," I hum, so used to the smell now and loving it on him.

"Smell this." Opening the expensive bottle, he holds it to my nose. I take a small sniff and the aroma hits my senses. It is strong, but not obnoxiously so.

"I can pick up hints of butter," I say, having no real idea if that is a scent I should be smelling, but it is what comes to mind.

"Good girl," Tanner purrs, and my pussy clenches.

"What else?" he asks, and I take another sniff.

"Hmm. Maybe a little honey?" I'm even less sure about that guess, but he smiles.

"Very good, baby," he says before he puts the bottle to his lips and takes a sip. But he doesn't swallow. He places the bottle on the dining table and cups my face with both his hands, pressing his lips to mine.

I part my lips as he kisses me, whiskey filling my mouth and his. Moaning, I swallow a little, the burn instant, but his mouth doesn't waver as his tongue dives in. I feel drips of whiskey running down my lips, and he moves my head in his hold to lick up my neck, taking every spilled drop into his mouth.

"I like it," I whisper, my body temperature reaching volcanic levels.

"It tastes even better on your skin."

"My turn," I say as he pulls back and looks at me. Watching his chest rise and fall, I take a deep breath as I run my hands up his body and start to open his shirt buttons. He waits, enjoying my touch until the last button opens, and he pushes it off his shoulders, throwing it from his arms.

"That's better," I murmur, picking up the bottle beside us and spilling a little across his bare chest, relishing how it runs down his muscles. I lean forward, my eyes on his as I lick my way from his stomach to his chest, gathering it in my mouth. His growl is low and deep as his nostrils flare.

His torso's now completely naked and damp. Tanned skin, the tattoo on his arm on full display, broadly defined muscles in his shoulders, chest, and torso. The sweeping of salt-and-pepper hair across his chest follows a path into his pants, almost begging me to touch. He is by far the most masculine man I have ever seen.

"I love lace, but I need this off," he murmurs, pulling me from the table and turning me around, grabbing the zipper on my back and sliding it down, the lace dress falling from my bare skin and puddling at our feet. Even though my back is toward him, I see him in a large mirror that is opposite me at the other end of the dining table, and I watch him as he drops his fingers to my bare shoulder and traces them all the way down my spine. His eyes are laser focused, like he is admiring a one-of-a-kind piece of artwork, taking my breath away. My skin immediately pebbles where he touches, goosebumps running across my flesh, and my breathing becomes more rapid.

"I want you, Tanner," I whisper, and his gaze meets mine in the mirror. I don't wait for him to talk before I turn around, me entirely naked, him still with his suit pants on. My hands glide down his torso until I hit his belt, and I undo it quickly, followed by his trousers, before they fall to the floor to meet my outfit and he kicks off his shoes.

Tugging his boxers down, I pull back, and he swallows roughly as he silently looks at me. Admiring my body, his eyes move from mine to my lips to my chest and back again. My belly flutters every time I have his attention like this.

"You're quiet..."

"I'm just taking you in," he says before lifting me up and settling me onto the dining table. His hands cup my face again, taking me in a kiss so scorching, I feel like I will combust. My body tingles as he grabs my ass and pulls me right to the edge. "Lean back," he commands, and I bite my bottom lip, because I like this version of Tanner. The one that talks dirty, that is full alpha male. The one that is so focused on me, yet still seems like he can't get enough.

Lying back on the cool timber dining table, I do exactly what he tells me to do. I arch my back seductively, and my heart thuds as he continues admiring me like I am his most prized possession before he grabs the bottle of whiskey.

"Are you ready?" he asks, and I nod just as he starts to pour.

41

TANNER

My whiskey hits her bare body across her chest, and I immediately bend down and lick it up, my tongue tracing her nipples. They pebble at the sensation, and I take one in my mouth, sucking her and my whiskey together and moaning against her skin.

"Tanner." She pants my name, the pour a little unexpected, and arches her back even more.

"Oh, baby girl, you look so pretty covered in my whiskey," I murmur as I pour again, more this time, the liquid trailing across both breasts, running down her sides to the table and a little moving lower into her belly button. My tongue darts across her skin, following the little rivers of honey-colored whiskey, and I lap up every drop. I feel almost like I am having an out-of-body experience.

"Kiss me, let me taste," she begs, wanting more, and I growl at her request, loving her tasting my hard work. Years of blood, sweat, and tears have gone into making my brand, my business, my whiskey, and to see her wanting it, wanting me, I feel like I finally made it all worthwhile. I sip a little more from the bottle and lean over her, putting my mouth on hers and letting the liquid fall to her tongue, before I kiss her wholly, the two of us swallowing the liquor together.

Removing my mouth from hers with a growl, my tongue glides straight down her naked body again, lapping her breast, sucking her nipple, and she moans at the contact. Her skin is sticky, the whiskey remnants and the heat of her skin building the aroma, and I can smell the butter and the honey she spoke of earlier. As I stand between her legs, I feel them widen, and as I hold the bottle in one hand, my other brushes down her body and grabs her thigh, pulling it up to hook around my waist.

"You're so perfect like this, so open for me. But mmmmm, baby girl, you covered in lace tonight... Fuck, it was a sight." I groan from where I am sucking on her breast before I move to the other one, giving it the same lustful treatment.

"Did you like it?" she asks teasingly, knowing damn well how much I did. Her hand skirts down her body, and she runs her fingers across my hair. I love when she does that.

"You looked so fucking sexy." My voice is low, almost guttural, and I feel her squirm a little underneath me. Lifting from her breasts, I look into her desire-filled eyes before I pour a little more whiskey. I rub it into her chest and then slowly down her body, between her breasts, down her stomach, and all the way to her hips, spreading the liquid all over her until her curves are shining.

A small mewl leaves her lips as I move my hand even lower and cup her bare pussy, then spread the liquor over her sensitive skin.

"I love your pussy," I murmur as my fingers softly run up and down her center, feeling her delicate skin, teasing her a little. She's glistening wet, waiting for me.

"Tannerrrr," she purrs, writhing as I touch her seductively slow, her breathing becoming more rapid as her hips grind for more.

"Yes, baby girl?"

"Stop teasing me," she moans, and I pour a little more whiskey onto her pussy, her skin now covered in my claim.

"Open more for me. Let me look at you," I growl as I grab her knees and open them a little wider, causing any pooled liquid to run down her center again. I can barely contain myself as I kiss the inside of her thigh, my lips dragging over her skin.

"Tanner..." She moans my name again, her head falling to the side as she lies on the table in front of me. Eyes closed, she bites her lip.

"Let me taste you." My voice is a mere rumble as my cock throbs to feel her.

"Yes, please. Yesssss." She's whimpering, panting already, the anticipation building as my hands continue to trace and smooth over her body, and then I lower my mouth, hitting her pussy and my whiskey. My eyes close as I moan in pure ecstasy.

Her body jolts a little at the contact, and I suck on her clit as her hands grab each side of the table underneath her. She cries out as I swirl my tongue and grip on to her thighs, burying myself deeper. My heart thuds as I take in this moment. I have never done this before. Never poured liquor on anyone, never mind a seventy-five-thousand-dollar bottle. If someone suggested it, I would call them crazy. But this woman, in my penthouse with the glittering lights of the New York City skyline flickering around us, her perfect naked body under mine... Nothing is ever going to beat this. Moving my hands up her soft body, I cup her breasts and tweak her nipples.

"Oh God! Tanner," she gasps as I mold her breasts in my hands, my tongue consuming her essence like it's my life source. I feel like I am in an alternate universe. It is like my dream fantasy coming to life. Victoria spread out on a table, opening herself up entirely for pleasure, and me lapping at her juices, my whiskey, tasting everything all at once. I never want to stop.

"Uh-huh... yes..." I feel her hips starting to move against my mouth, but I don't slow down, I'm too far gone. My cock is rock solid, but all I can think about is her. Her legs start to shake as I suck on her clit again, before my tongue delves inside of her, repeating that motion over and over. Body rocking and writhing, her hand grips my hair, the other holding on to the table's edge.

"Mmm. You're gonna come for me, aren't you, baby girl?" My words are spoken against her clit, and she jolts into me.

She's moaning and whimpering incoherently as her hips rock against my face, fingers now digging into my hair. She massages my scalp, and I feel my eyes roll back into my head, the pleasure I am currently experiencing unmatched and I'm not even inside her.

I hum in contentment, in wanting, my mouth not leaving her for a moment, making her gasp a second time as her whole body trembles.

"Tanner... Oh God..." she pants, breathless. Sitting up, her hand still on my head, her hips rock against my face, taking what she needs from me.

"Tanner... Tanner... Tanner..." she says over and over as I grip on to her hips, keeping my mouth on her, my tongue sweeping across her center, then sucking on her clit. Convulsing, she grinds against my face, but I hold her tight, my tongue not letting up, ready to make her come. Unable to hang on anymore, she falls back with a choked moan, her body completely at my mercy. And I show none as I slip two fingers inside her, rubbing right against the spot to set her off.

"Tanner!" she screams as I feel her come, the sound almost deafening and the sexist thing I've ever heard. I suck on her hard once more, then lap up her release nice and slow as she settles down from the high. Her thighs grip my face tightly, and I groan as she withers in my hold. "Oh shit... Oh my... God..." she pants, her body completely liquifying against the table. I slowly pull away, pressing a few more lingering kisses to her core that make her twitch and whimper, licking her softly, before I kiss her inner thighs and stand. She is quiet, her breathing labored, her eyes closed, and I smile when I see the dazed smile curling her plump lips.

"Good girl. Let's see if I can make you scream my name a few more times before the night is over," I tell her, watching her lust-drunk eyes flutter open to look up at me.

She already knows I'm going to fulfill that promise as I lift her up and her arms and legs wrap around me.

"Make love to me, Tanner," she whispers against my neck, and my brain stutters a little, that word not something I've associated with sex in a long time.

Kissing her hungrily, I stride toward the bedroom, slowly lowering her to the plush bedding. When our lips part, she takes my face in her hands, my body settling on top of hers.

"You mean a lot to me, Tanner." Her eyes search mine, waiting for my response as my chest warms.

I run my hand down her arm, entwining our hands and lifting them above her head as my other grabs her waist, tilting her hips as my cock slides along her warm, wet center. She gasps as I push in the slightest bit, feeling the stretch.

"You mean the world to me, Victoria."

And with that, I slide into her fully, her body welcoming me as her free hand grasps my shoulder and she moans my name.

"You feel so good every time, baby. You are so beautiful," I grit out, watching where we're connected. Seeing my length delve into her over and over again, hearing her pant and whimper, my cock throbs with need. I'm a big guy, and I'm trying to go slow and easy, take my time, but it's difficult right now with my feelings for her becoming over-whelming.

"We fit so good together. Tell me you feel it too," I say

to her, letting myself be vulnerable like she has been with me.

"Yessss, I feel it." She nods, lifting to kiss me so passionately, and my movements pause entirely. My tongue tangles with hers, and her hips grind up into me, sliding herself over my length in slow, seductive strokes. "I want you. I want this all the time."

Goddamn, she's a dream.

My teeth grind, jaw tight as I pick back up with abandon. Thrusting faster, she clenches around me, her nails digging into my nape. I watch her breasts bounce, back arch, and the visual only brings me closer to the edge.

"You are so fucking perfect. Are you all mine, baby? Are you my good. Fucking. Girl?" I'm growling as I pound into her now, our threaded fingers parting to hold on to each other. My arms slip beneath her body as hers wrap around my waist, our chests glued together, the only space between us enough to thrust as deep as I can go.

"Yes! Yours, yesssssss," she's cries out, her pussy pulsing around me.

My lips gather hers in another kiss as I slide my hands below her ass, holding her up to grind against my pelvis as I slow my strokes to massage where she needs me.

"I'll give you anything you want, always. I will give you the world, Victoria. Come for me, baby," I rumble across her lips, and she reacts as if the words caressed her.

With another scream that could rattle the windows, her body shakes, legs tightening around my waist to keep me in place as she works her hips to keep coming. And that's all I need to let go. Groaning into her neck, I thrust into her one, two, three more times, collapsing on top of her. The two of us now spent.

Pressed together, I kiss her neck, feeling her heart beating against me, pounding just like mine. It feels new, like something's shifted into place. I take a breath and pull back a little, our foreheads meeting. A sheen of sweat and whiskey covers us both as I hold her in my arms, the two of us panting like we just ran a marathon.

"Tanner, that was..." she trails off, her hand moving up and down my back, leaving tingles that could put me to sleep.

It was everything.

"I know, baby girl. I know." Rolling off her, I pull her against me to look out the window at the city view below. She hums in contentment and snuggles back into me, getting as close as she can as my arm wraps around her waist.

The night has been perfect, and I feel those three little words burning my chest. But I keep them close. Just for now.

42

VICTORIA

I watch Tanner grabbing his things from where I sit on his sofa overlooking Central Park. I love this view. I love this city, and I miss it. But I miss Whispers and the peacefulness it brings even more. We spent all night wrapped up in each other, then I spent all morning walking around his penthouse. It's incredible. Whoever he had do the interiors certainly knew what they were doing.

"Are you ready?" he asks, coming to stand beside me.

"Well, am I dressed okay?" I ask as I stand, his hand coming to my hip like a magnet.

He is taking me out for lunch but won't tell me where. I look down at myself. It's a casual outfit, just a light sweater and jeans, with my thin scarf as my hint of pink.

"You're always dressed okay," he says with a smile, looking down at me like I am his everything. My stomach flutters.

"A few months ago, you would scold me for not having proper boots," I tease as I narrow eyes playfully.

"A few months ago, you were my annoying new neighbor."

"Mm-hmm. And now?" Lifting up on my toes, I press a kiss to his cheek.

"And now you are still my neighbor and still annoying," he says with a smirk, tapping my ass and making me laugh. "You look beautiful. Let's go."

Taking my hand in his, we head down to a waiting town car and start our journey.

"Soooo, where are you taking me?" I ask, intrigued, as my body melts into the leather seats of the town car. Tanner reaches out and takes my hand in his, his palm warm against my skin, and I am not sure I have ever felt so content with a man.

"You'll see." Looking out the car window at the city landscape, he doesn't give anything away.

"Is it more whiskey tasting?" I ask cheekily, and his head swivels to look at me, his eyes a molten brown.

To say last night took us to a whole other level is an understatement. I am not sure if it was the whiskey, the big night at the gala, the luxurious penthouse, or maybe just being away from Whispers, but we were explosive. I have never felt as connected to another person in my life, and I find myself falling even harder with every day that passes.

"No whiskey. Not yet. Did you like it?" he asks, watching me carefully.

"The whiskey or the tasting?" I clarify, my voice teasing. His thumb strums my hand as his other comes to his face, and he brushes them across his lips like he is remembering the taste of last night.

"Both," he says, his eyes not wavering from mine.

"I am not a whiskey connoisseur, but I really liked the liquor last night. I haven't had a tasting like it before, and I would like to do that again. It seemed easier to drink..." I say, and a small growl emits from his chest.

"Me too," he agrees, and his smile is almost deadly as I feel the car pull up to the curb.

"We're here." Bringing my hand to his lips, he kisses it before jumping out and keeping the door open for me. I slide along the seat and take his hand again to step out, looking around and seeing the familiar street.

"Benny's!" I shout so loud the people walking past turn to look at me.

"We need to eat, and you said they had the best burgers," he says simply, and I look at him, wide-eyed. I mentioned it once, and he remembered.

"Oh my God, I am so happy!" My smile's wide as I grip on to his hand and step toward him, giving him a kiss to show my gratitude. His other hand wraps around my waist, pulling me close. It isn't just the burgers, although they are delicious. It is the fact that he remembers my little comments, the things I like, and wants to experience them with me. He listens.

"Come on, let's go eat," he says, pulling me along, and I follow him quickly, my stomach now rumbling.

We walk in and the place is busy, but they greet Tanner like they know exactly who he is, and we are taken to a table farther down the back. A few people look at us, and I know it isn't because of me, but rather the tall, brooding man leading me to the back. It isn't a posh place. Even though he is in jeans and a sweater, he looks more distinguished than anyone else here. Tanner probably won't even like the burgers after the absolute smorgasbord of divine food we ate at the gala last night.

"About time you got here. I was about to eat my left arm!" a female voice says, and my breath catches.

"Fiona!" I scream and run the remaining few steps to her. She jumps up from her seat, and we hug for probably a full minute. It feels so good to see her.

"What are you doing here?" I ask. I told her we were coming, and I had plans to call her tomorrow to arrange to catch up.

"Oh, lover boy neighbor here wanted to make sure we got to see each other. He suggested Benny's, and then I told him that I would marry him if you didn't," she says, smiling and I laugh, missing her.

"So you have already met?" I ask, looking between her and Tanner.

"Not officially. I'm lover boy neighbor, Tanner Whiteman," Tanner says with a chuckle, holding out his hand.

"Fiona. Best friend, hurt her and you die. Pleased to meet you," Fiona says, and as they shake, I smile. It feels good seeing my two favorite people together.

"She is more likely to hurt herself the way she climbs ladders and drives cars, but I will always be there to save her."

Fiona laughs, and he winks my way, even as I roll my eyes.

"Let's eat. I have heard all about these famous burgers, so they better live up to the hype," Tanner says, pulling out my chair, and I catch Fiona looking at me with approval on her face.

"We should totally go to Maison Pickle for cake afterward. Give Tanner the cake experience too while you're at it," Fiona suggests, and my eyes widen in excitement.

"Already organized. They are expecting us," Tanner says, and I sit in shock. He catches my surprised gaze and smiles, making my chest spread with warmth. Grabbing my hand under the table, he gives it a squeeze. "You're staring and drooling..." he murmurs jokingly, and I huff a small laugh.

"Oh my, you two are so cute." Her smile is giddy as she picks up the menu, looking at it like she has no idea what to order, when in reality, we always order the same thing every time.

My shoulders lower, and I feel so much gratitude sweep through me as I sit here taking in this moment. Tanner is amazing. Making such an effort to meet my friend and take me to the places he knows I miss the most. He hasn't let go of my hand under the table, his thumb running over my skin, and I swallow roughly. The feelings I have for this man are coming in thick and fast. He couldn't be more perfect if he tried.

"So, how is the house coming along?" Fiona asks as she sets the menu down.

"It's looking great. I only have the kitchen and laundry to do, really. I'm just waiting on the builder to come," I tell her, not able to contain my broad smile.

"I knew you would do it. You're stubborn like that," Fiona quips.

"Tell me about it," Tanner murmurs, and I turn my head to look at him.

"What? Are you two ganging up on me already?" I say in jest, smiling as they both share a look of amusement.

"I just mean that you always push yourself. When you set your mind to something, you do it. I knew that house would be the perfect project for you, and I knew that no matter what it took, you would make it into something really beautiful," she says, and it fills me with pride. It was a big job, and now it is almost complete. But the fear of failing, the fear of setting out to do this mammoth project and not succeeding, that was a scenario I didn't want to deal with.

"Push herself is right. You have a strong work ethic, Victoria. The property has never looked as good as it does now, and that is all due to your commitment and hard work," Tanner says, squeezing my hand, and I feel my cheeks heat at his compliment.

"It just needed a bit of love, that is all," I say to them both, playing down my achievements a little.

"So, have you been to your apartment yet?" Fiona asks, just as the waitress comes to take our order.

"Apartment?" Tanner asks, looking at me with a frown, his soft eyes now wrinkled in confusion.

"Yeah, I still have my apartment here," I say sheepishly. We haven't really talked too much about logistics, but I know Whispers is now home.

"I didn't know," he says, quietly watching me. I feel like I have done something wrong, but I push the feeling down.

"I kept it just in case Whispers didn't work out. You know, a safety net," I try to explain with a small shrug, because it really isn't that big of a deal. Tanner's face is deep set before he nods, and then his cell rings. Pulling it out, he looks at the screen.

"It's Connor. I need to take this. Excuse me," he says, standing and pressing a kiss to my head. I watch the back of him as he walks outside before Fiona kicks me under the table.

"Oh my God, he is sooooo into you. He has been staring at you in awe from the moment you arrived," she says, and I smile, feeling giddy. "Plus, wow, he's a good-looking man."

"I know. He really is perfect," I say as those familiar flutters return to my belly.

"Perfect is right. He flew you here, brings you to your favorite burger place, then is also taking us to grab cake. From everything you've told me already, too, I mean, seriously, he is a keeper." She takes a sip of her cola, smiling around her straw as she looks at me.

"I think I am really falling for him, Fi," I tell her honestly, and her face turns serious.

"Are you in love with him?" she asks me point-blank. I am quiet for a moment, thinking about her question. I moved to Whispers only a few months ago, and the whole thing has been such a blur. But I'm nodding before I even get the words out.

"Yes. I am in love with him," I say, breathing out, my chest feeling hot and heart beating faster at the realization.

I am in love with my billionaire neighbor.

～

TANNER and I have been in New York for a few days. He agreed that Benny's did, indeed, have the best burgers. So much so, we also went back the next day. After we enjoyed some delicious cake, Fiona and I took him to our favorite little bar, the one where she met Tyler. But he was nowhere to be seen.

Although the city was home for me for so long, it does feel strange coming back. It has been months since I was here last, and even though I grew up in this city, there is nothing familiar about his lifestyle. A penthouse in the sky, looking like it is straight out of a magazine, does nothing but spark creativity in my design thoughts, the city luxury now ingrained in my brain.

"Well, here it is," I say, stopping at the door of my apartment while I fish out the keys. It was a nice morning, so we walked here through Central Park, holding hands and people watching like old lovers. Now I watch Tanner looking around the hallway. It is nothing like his, but it is neat, safe, and in New York, that is luxury to me.

"I finally get to see your before," he murmurs, smiling at me. His hand stays firmly around my waist, always keeping me close. We haven't talked any more about me keeping this apartment. But as a single girl moving to a small town, I knew I needed a safety net and had to look after myself.

"Hmm, well, it's not as luxurious as your place, so keep your expectations low," I laugh, opening the door and stepping inside, then turning on the lights to brighten up the place. "Home sweet home," I say, but the words feel foreign. Picking up the mail from the floor, I place it on the kitchen counter as Tanner walks in slowly behind me, taking it all in, a small smile on his face.

"It's cute and has personality. Like you," he says, looking way too big in this small apartment.

I sigh, almost shuddering as I take it in myself. It truly doesn't feel like home anymore. There is a slight stale smell, it feels cold and claustrophobic, and memories of Josh fill the space, making me feel like I am stepping back in time.

"I'll just go and grab some things." I'm already itching to leave and thinking I will pack up everything permanently at some point soon. A few days here is not long enough, and this trip was about the two of us having some time away from the craziness of Whispers.

"Sure, take your time," Tanner says, walking into the living room and looking at the photos on the wall. I watch him for a moment, taking his time like he is memorizing each photo. My heart warms having him here with me. Watching him take in my former life and not balk at it. I see him smirk as he picks up a photo of my mom and me, an old one from Halloween.

I have one more month left on my current lease until I need to renew, but with paying money on this apartment, plus the money I need to live and renovate in Whispers, my bank balance is taking a beating, and it isn't sustainable. But I can't move permanently without long-term job prospects. The work I am doing with Griffin is great, but it could be a one-time thing. It may not lead to anything.

Like everything else in my life, though, I will figure it out. When I want something enough, I always do. With that thought lodging in my brain and in my heart, I head to my bedroom and pack two bags with as much as I can fit, knowing that my time living in this apartment is most likely coming to an end.

Because in Whispers and with Tanner is where I want to be.

43

TANNER

I pick up a framed photo and smirk. It is of her and her mother, taken a few decades ago, I would bet. Obviously, Halloween or a party because they are both dressed up. Her mom is a witch and Victoria is in a round pumpkin suit, with an orange face. My eyes canvass the entire shelf of photos. They are all of her and her mom, a few of her and Fiona, but no men. None of Josh or her father.

Putting it down, I walk around some more. It is small, quaint. Decorated extremely well. I can even see some of her uniqueness for finding quality decor, as the fabric of the cushions on her sofa look like nothing I have seen before yet match the rug almost perfectly. Both eye-catching and subtle.

When she mentioned at lunch the other day that she still had her apartment, I was dumbfounded. Shocked, really, because I thought she was all in on Whispers. On me. I have felt a little off since then, wondering if she isn't feeling the same connection to me as I am to her. It feels good together. I have never felt like this with anyone before, not like I do with her. She said that she kept it as a backup, which does make sense the more I thought about it. A young woman coming to a small town on her own, you always need a backup plan. But I hope now we can gather her things and she can be a permanent Whispers resident.

I can't help it that the fear of another woman leaving still haunts me.

A knock at the door pulls me from my thoughts.

"Can you answer that?" she calls out, and I turn and open the door.

"Oh, you're not Victoria," an older man says with a frown.

"Tanner Whiteman. Victoria is just busy at the moment," I tell him, sizing him up.

"Well, this is her lease renewal," he says, holding up some paperwork. My heart feels like it stops.

"Lease renewal?" I understand she kept this apartment for a backup, but why does she need to renew again? She is staying in Whispers, isn't she?

"Twelve months, as is required. She just needs to sign and then send them back." He pushes the papers into my hand, and I swallow roughly as I nod to him. Grinding my jaw, my fear mixes with frustration and confusion.

"Have a good day," he says, turning and walking away like he didn't just drop a bomb on my life. My gut feels heavy as I look at the paperwork, my eyes running over what it entails.

"Who was it?" she asks from behind me as she places two bags near the sofa.

I close the door and turn to face her.

"You're renewing your lease?" I ask her, but my words come out with bite. My body is thrumming, and she looks a little taken aback, so I take a deep breath and try to get a handle on my feelings.

"Oh. It is building policy. I have one more month on the current lease, and then... I mean, I have no idea how I will do with the job Griffin gave me. If it doesn't work out, then—"

"It will work out, baby girl," I cut her off, my shoulders lowering a little. I understand her concern.

"But Tanner..."

"No buts. Tear it up." I hold the papers out to her. I feel tense, like she is slipping from me, and I don't like it. The papers in my hand crumple at the corners due to how tightly I am gripping them.

"Tanner," she says my name in warning, and my frown is back.

"Tear it up," I grit out, needing to see her commit to staying in Whispers. With me. She can't leave me. I don't think I could take it.

"You're not letting me finish. I need to look after myself. Once I know how things are panning out, I can make a more permanent decision." I can tell she's becoming upset as her eyes narrow and her hand finds her hip, and it brings me back to how we started. All that bickering and fire, only this time, it's more sad than it is exciting. She's not getting it. That I'd do anything for her.

"I can look after you," I tell her simply, hoping to ease her fears, but her frown deepens.

"I don't want you to look after me. I can look after myself."

I should have known she would be stubborn.

"I don't want you to be stubborn." While I love her independence, I need her to know that I've got her, no matter what.

"You are so frustrating," she says, rubbing her head like I give her a headache. When I step closer, she takes a step back, and it only increases my worry.

"If you are going to leave Whispers..."

"I'm not leaving Whispers!" she shouts, her hands flying out to her sides.

"Then why are you signing a lease?" I demand, then take another step closer. She doesn't move away this time, only huffing as she shakes her head at me.

"Because, like I said, I needed a backup and building protocol says I need to sign for twelve months. If I could only sign for a few months instead, I would. What are you not understanding?"

"What are you not understanding? *I'm* your backup," I tell her again. The look on her face could sear me to the spot, but even so, I step forward a little more.

I am not sure how much clearer I can make it. I will pay for everything she needs. I will get her anything she wants. This woman came into my life like a whirlwind, and I want her in it forever.

"I almost married a man I stupidly thought was my support in life and look how that turned out!" she yells, her gaze on mine as she now looks up at me.

"Don't be putting me in the same sentence as that

asshole," I grit out. I swear to God, I am going to pick her up and not let her go.

"You can't pay for me to live, Tanner. I need a job," she says, taking a deep breath as her tone eases.

"I can, and while I want you to be fulfilled in your career, I want you to know that I've got you. You can do whatever you want in life to make yourself happy. Money doesn't need to be a concern. I'll catch you, baby girl." Bringing myself one last step away, we're now toe to toe. I need to touch her, be close to her.

"I need to catch myself," she says softly, but now she won't look at me. My frustration settles in my chest, and I rub the ache.

"You are so damn stubborn," I say, shaking my head, exasperated.

"You are so demanding," she counters, and any softness I may have brought to the surface completely dissolves.

"Hell yes, I am. Now rip it up." My voice rises, and I see her shoulders tighten. My heart is thumping. I have never wanted anything more in my life than this woman, and I am aching to secure our future together. But she won't let me.

She doesn't respond for a moment, and the silence has me on pins and needles. Instead, she bends down and picks up her bags, walking past me, snatching the paperwork from my hands as she heads for the door.

"I'm done talking about this, Tanner. Let's go."

Neither of us won this one, and I know neither of us feels good about it either. I watch the empty doorway she steps through, feeling sick to my stomach. Her independence and stubbornness are the things I admire most about her, and now they are working against me.

Swallowing the lump in my throat, I walk after her, locking the apartment up, and hoping like hell I didn't just fuck this all up already.

44

TANNER

It's been a week since New York and we have become professionals at not addressing the elephant in the room. Once we landed back in Whispers, we shared a long kiss and a look of understanding, and that was that. Life has gone on as normal, and while that settles me, I still feel slight unease that she has a backup plan that isn't me. And I still don't like that we haven't spoken more about it. That I haven't given her the apology she deserves.

I step back from the love seat I have made her and admire my work. I have been spending late nights at the distillery under the cloak of working, but really, I have been making this for Victoria.

"Tanner?" Her voice is unsure as she opens the back door to her deck. I tried to be quiet. I knew she was on the phone with her mom, but I drove over and placed this on her deck, wanting it to be a surprise, and just finished wiping it down.

"Hey, baby girl," I say sheepishly as she walks out the door and stops short, her pretty eyes widening.

"What is that?" she whispers, taking another tentative step toward me and the new timber love seat that now adorns her deck.

"I made it," I tell her, and she looks at me sharply before looking back at the seat. "For you."

"It's just like my sketch..." she says in awe, running her fingers across the finish.

"I know. I saw it on your kitchen counter a while ago."

"Tanner, this is..." Her eyes meet mine as they well up a little.

"I was an ass, and I'm sorry. We had such a great time in New York, then I was surprised that you still had your apartment. I thought you were happy here, and it scared me that you might not stay." Nerves take over as I wait for her response, but her sweet smile calms them instantly.

"I am happy here. I am happy with you." Her hand reaches out and grabs mine. "I have no plans to leave, but I just needed to—"

"I know. You need a fallback plan. I get it, I do. And I should have respected that," I say, understanding that a woman like Victoria needs to look after herself. Even if I plan to ensure that she knows I am here. Always.

"Tanner, this is... No one has ever given me something like this... *made me something.* It's so beautiful. So perfect." Stepping up to me, her hands wrap around my neck and her lips meet mine.

"Want to take a seat?" I ask, smiling against her mouth. With a little squeal, she sits back against the wood, humming as she taps the seat beside her.

Sitting on her new love seat, watching the sunset, her head resting on my shoulder, everything feels like it's back on track.

"Okay, so what are we doing about the expansion into accommodation?" Connor asks me as we sit around the boardroom table with Sawyer. My mind isn't on the business, my whiskey, my son, or this conversation. It is firmly on Victoria.

"Well, Marie's place is off the table," I confirm to everyone, needing that cemented in both their brains. Just the mention of that property has me back to thinking about Victoria. I know she loves it here. We haven't said the words to each other yet, but I feel it. Deep within.

"She has it looking nice," Connor says, nodding. He appreciates her design skills, and when I told him about her ideas for my ranch, he was blown away. He now wants to build his too, which will be next door to mine, his land size similar but with a slightly different outlook.

"You must really love her," Sawyer says with a frustrated sigh, and I send him a look that says to kindly shut up.

"In terms of the business, you are changing the strategy and now building something entirely different. Not to mention, she is doing the interior design of your new ranch—something you have had for decades and never made a move on till now. I would say Sawyer has made a fair assumption," Connor says with a small, knowing smile, and my eyes thin.

"We need to pivot. Marie's place was never a done deal. That is why we had flagged the eastern side of the distillery as a plan B. As for my ranch, it is about time I moved out there. I am getting old. I need some space."

It all makes sense, but if Victoria hadn't come along, I wouldn't be moving.

"The Tanner I know would not have given up so easily. The Tanner I know would have offered her millions to get that piece of prime land," Sawyer says, leaning back in his chair and assessing me.

Sawyer is successful in his own right, but most of his business comes from us. We are, by far, his largest and best client, due to all the deals we do. He is spending more and more time here in Whispers, and a thought occurs to me that Jerry, Whispers' only town lawyer, will be retiring soon, and so the town will need someone new. If only he didn't hate the country so much.

"I am allowed to change my mind," I tell them with a shrug, the two of them now watching me.

"I think you love her. Especially if that new wood-working project is anything to go by," Connor says. I look at him but remain quiet, but he can see it in my eyes.

"Shit, I am right," he whispers in awe before his small grin turns wide and he sits forward with renewed enthusiasm. "I mean, I knew when you brought her to the fundraising dinner, then stayed in New York for a few days, that you were making a public statement. But shit, love is pretty serious, Dad."

"Oh, hi, boys. Sorry, I didn't know anyone was in here," Jasmine says, pushing through the door, interrupting our conversation. I frown. This is the second time she has done this now, and while she has a large floral arrangement in hand, I don't normally bother with flowers in our boardroom unless we have special guests. Of which Sawyer isn't.

"We are just in the middle of something," Connor says, looking at her, confused.

"Sorry I just had a spare arrangement this week and thought I could pop it in here. I will just put this down and be on my way." She gives me a wide smile as Sawyer looks at her intensely. I nod to her, and she takes a few steps inside and places the arrangement on the table before retreating quickly with a wave.

"She is odd," Sawyer says the minute the door closes.

"She's fine," I grumble, not wanting to think about her and needing to get the meeting back on track.

"She is just keeping the distillery looking good, plus trying to gain more business, I think," Connor says, and I agree.

"How many people need a florist in a small town like Whispers? I mean, wildflowers grow all around here. Your garden alone could probably serve as a florist, given the size of it," Sawyer says, looking at me.

"I am pretty sure the florist is one of the busiest businesses in town. Especially now that more people are moving here, having events, weddings like Huxley's and things," Connor explains, and Sawyer nods in understanding.

"Well, with the new accommodations, we can probably put a package together. Something with the local community of businesses, which would be nice?" I offer, looking at Connor.

"A romance package with flowers, maybe a food hamper from Rochelle too, and it would be good if we could use the natural springs?" Connor suggests.

"They are Victoria's now, but we could talk to her about it. Let's get it all built first and then look at packages, but I think something like that could work well. Open up a new revenue stream that is not just about the whiskey."

I know not everyone likes whiskey, and if we can offer something else that is just as enticing, then people will come and maybe enjoy one or both, expanding our product offering.

"You should open a spa," Sawyer says sarcastically, but my eyes meet Connor's immediately.

"That is a very good idea..." Connor murmurs as we stare at each other. The silent conversation we are having gets both our minds working overtime.

"We could have whiskey-themed treatments..." I say, tapering off, thinking about my night in the city with Victoria and the way the whiskey ran over her body. I know nothing about day spas or treatments, but I also know Victoria doesn't drink whiskey or have the appreciation for it yet, and she's my motivation here, keeping in mind everyone else who might feel the same as she does. If I took her to a distillery, she would be bored. Unless they offered something for her that she could do that would entice her to visit too.

"Definitely something we should think about. Especially with all the rich clientele that are starting to move out here. Whispers doesn't have anything like that, and coupled with the mineral springs, I think it has a lot of potential," Connor says, and I agree. The expansion into accommodation and now potential spa sounds like an exciting prospect.

"Let's get a consultant in as well and see what might work."

Connor's already tapping out some notes on his laptop, eager to try something new.

"Sorry to interrupt..." Lacy says, walking into the boardroom, and my shoulders tighten in frustration at being interrupted once more until I see the sheriff right behind her.

"Tony?" I ask, standing, immediately on guard.

"Hi, boys. Tanner, I wanted to come and talk to you as soon as I heard."

I nod for him to continue, my heart pounding.

"Talk is around town of a strange man popping up these last few days. I couldn't get ahold of him, but Rochelle saw him this morning. He was asking about Marie's Place." He nods to me, and my body hums.

"What did he look like?"

"She was busy, so didn't get a good chance to check him out, but he had dark hair, looked like he was from the city. Could it be this Josh guy we are looking for?" Tony asks, and my gaze meets Connor's. *It has to be Josh.*

"I'll go over to Victoria's to make sure she is alright and let her know." I nod to the room full of people who look at me.

"Need us to take a look around town?" Connor stands, ready to do whatever needs to be done.

"My boys will handle it. I am just doing a courtesy by telling you. We can't go arresting or roughing up an innocent man. Could be a tourist. Could be no one. But the minute anyone sees or hears anything, call me," Tony says, and my nostrils flare.

"It also could be the asshole who left her for dead by tampering with her truck," I state, letting him know that I will not be calling him until I am ready for him to clean up my mess. Grabbing my cell and keys, I'm out the door, rushing to get to Victoria.

45

VICTORIA

I click through the presentation on my screen, butterflies of excitement swirling in my stomach.

"So if we open this up here, then I think it would be really beautiful," I say to Griffin, the two of us on a video call, talking through my ideas for the ranch. My sketches are looking good. I have a few more tweaks to make, but my vision is finally coming together.

"I love it. It makes total sense. It is unique, and we should be able to get the materials needed reasonably easy. You have a really good eye for this kind of thing. Ever thought about making it a permanent gig?" Griffin asks, and I smile, my heart racing at what this could mean for me.

"It would be a dream of mine, really. I have loved pulling this together," I tell him, now knowing that if I can pull off my ideas for this ranch, my portfolio will be kick-started and maybe I can start a new career in the world of interior design.

"Well, I know the owner will approve, and let me tell

you, when this project is done, I am sure I will have another one waiting for you. Whispers has a lot of billionaires ready to move there. They already have the land; they are just waiting to build. The work Tanner and Connor have done to that town is astounding. I have even got a plot there," he says, smiling, and it is contagious. When I first moved here, anytime anyone said Tanner's name, I tensed. But now I have nothing but pride and joy for the man who makes me smile even when he isn't here.

"Lock it in, then, because I am ready!" I say excitedly. This is the opportunity I have been waiting for, and hearing Griffin say it cements everything here for me. I won't be signing those lease forms back in NYC, and I can't wait to tell Tanner. We were a little distant when we got back. But when he turned up with the love seat on my back porch, I completely melted. Him and Whispers are now my home.

"So the team is on track with the build so far. But as I am sure you know, sometimes there are hiccups, which can derail things. I estimate that we will be ready for interiors in a month or two, so start preparing and shopping. I will need the final paint colors and then the light fittings first. You have the funds now and access to the account. Plus, you can ship everything to the block. I have lockable shipping containers there to hold goods until we are ready for them," he explains, and I continue to take notes.

"Any further feedback from the owner on the color palette?" I ask, thinking about it. I am going natural, with timber features.

"He said for you to design it how you would like to live in it," Griffin says, and I snort.

"Yeah, in my dreams," I say through a laugh, but it's filled with longing. I can't imagine living somewhere like that. "If I won the lottery, this ranch would be exactly how I would want to live."

"Yeah, it is one of the biggest and most expensive builds I have done. The quality of it is amazing. Okay, I've got to run. Are you all good with everything else?"

"All good. Thanks, Griffin," I say before we end the call, and I grab my pen and continue taking notes like a madwoman so I don't forget anything from our conversation. I then spend the next hour sourcing products online that I know will take a long time to get here, like the soft rugs from Switzerland that I plan to have on the floor in front of the open fireplace and the chandeliers from Austria that I know will sparkle at nighttime, giving both an elegance and a feminine touch to balance out the large spaces.

Hearing a car pull up outside, I lift my arms, stretching out the kinks in my back from sitting for far too long before I get up and go to the front door. I am already smiling as I step out, assuming it is Tanner, but my smile drops and my mouth gapes as soon as I see who it is.

"Josh?" I ask, dumbfounded as he hops out of a black sedan in his suit, holding a large bouquet of red roses. The bunch is large, ostentatious, and months ago, it would have had me breathless at their beauty, but now they just make my skin crawl and I swallow bile.

"Hey, Victoria," he says with a wide smirk, puffing out his chest.

"What are you doing here?" I ask incredulously. He's here. In my space. Uninvited.

"I told you the other week I wanted to come and see you." He looks confused, like he wasn't expecting a frosty reception.

"But how did you know where my place even was?" I removed all locations from my social media, and I know Fiona wouldn't have told him.

"I asked around. Pretty easy to find, actually. I just had to ask for Marie's place," he says, and I internally curse.

"But what are you doing here? We are over. Have I not made that clear enough?" I state, my shock now giving way to anger.

"I came to beg for you to come back. I miss you. We were good together. I want you back in the city with me."

I frown as I look at him.

"Why? What happened to Natalie?" I ask, crossing my arms over my chest, as I have absolutely no intentions of going back to him or the city. He takes a step closer to me, and instinctively, I take a step back.

"I love you, Vic. It's always been you. You are the one for me." He says the right words, yet the way they fall from his mouth sounds deceiving.

"Not when you fuck someone else, I'm not," I tell him straight, not falling for his bullshit.

"I'm sorry. It was one time, a stupid mistake. Everyone is asking when you are coming home."

I tilt my head in confusion.

"Everyone?" Fiona is the only person I am still in contact with back in the city and she hasn't said anything.

"George, Trevor. The guys." *His bosses.*

"Oh yeah, what are they saying?" I ask, trying to understand what is happening here because I know there is an ulterior motive. He doesn't love me. He doesn't take care of me. He has never put my needs first, never looked after me when I was sick, never supported my dreams of design. He never took an interest in me at all.

"They just want to see you again, that's all." *Weird*. I met them a few times, but we are not friends.

"I'm not coming back, Josh," I tell him calmly. After Griffin saying there could be other jobs, I am excited to have Whispers as my home now.

"Fuck it, Victoria!" he yells, jolting me as he throws the flowers down on the ground, his pleasant façade now all gone. This is a new side to him I haven't seen before. "You need to come home. Now," he grits out to me, and my eyes thin.

"Why?" I push him, knowing something is not right. I want to know his motive.

"I might miss that promotion," he says, seething.

"Promotion?" The penny drops. "Ah, so your bosses want to see me before you get your promotion?"

He remains silent, his teeth grinding together almost comically.

"I'm right, aren't I? They won't give you a promotion unless you showcase that you are on your way to happily married bliss. Shit, why didn't I see this earlier," I say, chuckling to myself. I am such an idiot. "That is why you proposed New Year's Eve, isn't it? In front of all your bosses. Not because you loved me, but because you need to portray a happily married life in order to get your VP status at work."

He may work on Wall Street, but the company he works for is very family oriented and they have a clean public image that I suspect they want to keep.

"I'll pay you," he says, and I huff another laugh before extreme anger overtakes me. The nerve of this man.

"You need to leave." My hands settle on my hips as I straighten my back, my tone not one that leaves any confusion.

"I am not leaving without—" he starts, but I don't let him finish. We. Are. Done.

"Get off my property before I call the sheriff." I threaten the words that never in a million years did I ever think I would say. But I will. I will have him arrested for trespassing and email his bosses directly.

"Stop being so stubborn and get in the goddamn car." Walking toward me swiftly, he snatches my wrist.

"Let go of me!" I yell as I try to pull away. He is such an asshole.

Then I hear it. Tanner's truck screeches into my property, coming to a skid, stopping abruptly where we stand. Gravel and dust flies out from his sharp braking, and the truck looks even bigger this close, the black gloss now menacing. Tanner jumps out and is on us quicker than I can take a breath.

"Get your fucking hand off my fucking woman!" he roars, and I rip my hand free of Josh's hard grip as Tanner paces toward us.

"Now you are in trouble," I murmur to Josh under my breath, rubbing my wrist that is throbbing from his grip. He looks at me, having no idea what is about to happen. *Idiot.*

Tanner's eyes flick over me quickly to ensure I'm okay before he focuses on Josh. He is livid, and if I didn't know him like I do, I would be fearful.

"Oh shit," Josh whispers, just before Tanner's fist connects with his face.

"Tanner!" I scream, grabbing his arm. "Stop!"

Josh has no hope against a man like Tanner, and I don't want him getting himself in trouble over me like this. Josh's body slams against the ground, blood already dripping from his nose. Tanner ignores me and grabs Josh by the collar, lifting him entirely off the ground one-handed, so high his feet are dangling.

"Call the sheriff, baby girl," he says in his sweet voice that I know is reserved just for me, and I calm down a little.

Josh looks between Tanner and me. "Baby girl?" he questions, blood continuing to drip from his nose that is now red and swollen as he tries to stand, but Tanner has him tightly by the scruff of his neck.

"Yeah, *my* girl. Now let's see what the sheriff has to say about you. Maybe you have the same tools in the trunk that you used on her truck?"

46

TANNER

My eyes haven't left his. Blood pulsing through my veins, my ears ring with the adrenaline rushing around my body. My anger's right on the edge as I look at this absolute moron who has a death wish, turning up here and touching my girl. His nose is broken, I made sure of that.

"I have no idea what you are talking about. Let me go," he says, throwing his arm back across my forearm to release the hold I have of him at his collar. It is useless. I am not letting him go. A freight train couldn't release my hold. I itch to hit him again, but I know Victoria probably wouldn't like it, so I refrain.

"Is this your car?" Tony, the sheriff, asks him, and my eyes thin. He arrived as soon as Victoria called, given he and his team were nearby.

"It wasn't him." I hear her voice from behind me, and my head turns quickly to look at her. Her arms are wrapped around her body, looking frightened. "Tanner, it wasn't him," Victoria says, looking me right in the eye. Her shoulders slump, and I know she is disappointed it isn't him who cut her brakes. If it was, it means this would all come to an end, and she could finally fully relax.

"Look, I have no idea what you all are talking about, but if you don't let me go, I will have you charged with—"

"With what? Trespassing? Harassment? Assault? Because so far, those are the things you will be charged with," I tell him straight. Regardless of whether he cut her brakes or not, he still came here, touched her, and continues to call her every hour of every fucking day.

"If you have nothing to hide, then you will have no problem answering a few questions," the sheriff says, and Josh nods.

"Tanner?" Tony says, and I let go of his shirt, Josh stumbling now that he isn't in my hold. I step back so the police can do what they need to as they start questioning him, and I feel Victoria's small hands circle around my bicep. Lifting my arm, I immediately bring her into my side as we both stand and listen.

"That night, I was at a work dinner. I have a hundred witnesses. I even have photos on my phone and social media," Josh says when asked about his whereabouts the day of the car accident.

"Asshole," I murmur to Victoria as my skin burns, wanting to end him.

"I don't disagree, but it wasn't him. I know it wasn't." I feel a small shiver go through her. Understanding washes over me that she is still very fearful.

"I think you should probably stay with me for a while," I offer, because I don't want to let her out of my sight.

She sighs. "I love spending time with you, but I don't want whoever it is to run me out of my own home. That means they win," she says defiantly, and while I admire her bravado, it does little to settle me.

"Fine. I will stay here with you, then," I tell her adamantly, and she smiles.

"We will need to look into your alibi, and in the meantime, you need to come to the station," I hear Tony say before Josh yells.

"This is bullshit! You are not worth this shit!"

"You're priceless," I grit out quietly so only she can hear. This guy is a moron, but I agree with Victoria; he doesn't look like the kind of man who would know anything about a truck in order to cut cables. He could be the one to run over her rosebushes, but I doubt it. Which leaves only one man now on my radar. Her father. If only I could find him.

"Alright. In the car. You will be charged with trespassing, assault, and harassment," Tony says as his men grab Josh and put him in the back of a cop car, and within minutes, they leave. Another officer drives Josh's car away for a search.

"We will charge him, but he will be free to go, with an escort, back out of town, and not to return until his court date. But I don't think it was him who cut your brakes," Tony confirms with us. "His alibi seems solid. He fits the description of the man around town. I believe he is a scorned ex-lover, maybe, but I don't think a guy like that knows his way around the hood of a truck to know where the brake cables even are."

I feel Victoria stiffen in my arms.

"Man around town?" she asks, looking at me.

"That's what I came over to tell you," I confess to her.

"There were sightings of a strange man around town. Rochelle said he was in the diner asking about this place. A guy in a suit, darker hair," Tony says, and I feel her take a big breath.

"That matches Josh's description. He also told me he found me by asking for Marie's place around town. But if he didn't cut my brakes, who did?" she asks, and Tony looks remorseful.

"We don't know. We thought we had our guy. I would suggest that you have someone with you at all times for a little while. Just until we see if we can get a handle on the situation." Tony looks at me seriously. I know that look. It is the same look he gave me when we couldn't find Connor's mom.

"I won't leave her side," I tell him, and he nods before stepping back and getting into his car, following his team to deal with Josh.

"I mean it," I say, looking down at her. "I am not leaving your side."

"Tanner, you can't stay here twenty-four seven. You have a business to run." She shakes her head, not accepting it.

"I will get a security team here. Whenever I am not here, they will be," I reiterate, and she sighs, not happy but at least she's relenting. I need to keep her safe.

"You mean a lot to me, you know that?" Kissing the words into her hair, I rest my lips on her head. My arms circle her waist and pull her in tight, her body melting into mine.

"You mean a lot to me too," she says on a breath, and my heart thuds.

"Never in my life did I ever think someone would make me feel again," I tell her quietly, and I hear her swallow. Looking down at her, tears prick her eyes.

"Tanner..." She whispers my name, but I cut her off, pulling away a little. I hold her hips, looking her right in the eye. I need her to see the truth in them. Need her to know how serious I am.

"You are it for me, baby girl. I have never been more grateful for Marie than I am right now. She knew. This was all part of her plan. I think I fell in love with you the first time I saw you, and every day since, you have completely consumed my thoughts. I want you with me all the time, until the end of time. I love you, baby girl." My breath leaves my lungs as I search her eyes.

"Tanner Whiteman. There is no doubt in my mind that moving to Whispers and meeting you was the best thing that I have ever done in my life. I have fallen completely and utterly in love with you, and—" I don't need to hear anymore. I cut her off mid-sentence as my lips hit hers, and I wrap her up tight, one hand cupping her face. I feel euphoric and I smile as I kiss her. She is obviously feeling just as excited because she starts giggling against my lips, even more when I pepper kisses all over her face and down her neck.

"Tanner!" she squeals, pure delight taking over her

expression, her worried eyes now sparkling. Picking her up, I twirl her around and I feel like my life is just beginning.

47

VICTORIA

"Gertie's Goat Milk," I say to Kevin as he looks at me like I am crazy. What is it with this town? Don't they understand that there are so many business possibilities? My mind runs a million miles an hour with them. I'm keen to share my business idea and excited by the prospect of building something new.

This has never really happened to me before. When I lived in the city, I got so used to the nine-to-five grind that, other than design, I didn't think too much about other opportunities. Having an entrepreneurial spirit was not something I would've said about myself. But out here in Whispers, my ideas are flowing.

"People will spend money on goat milk?" Kevin asks me as we sit in the shed, looking at the goats as they feed.

"Well, not the milk, per se, but maybe we can use it for soaps or creams or something? I have been reading about it," I tell him, thinking that this could be a great little hobby for him.

Griffin's team are here ripping out my kitchen and getting the new floorplan ready, so I've spent most of the day outside. With all the noise and mess, it is at least getting my mind off the fact that someone, somewhere, has a target on my head for some reason. I shiver. Not knowing who it is and why they are trying to hurt me is what scares me the most. This past week, my appetite has gone. I have barely slept. Even with Tanner by my side every night, I can hear him thinking, in the same situation as me, and the two of us are completely clueless when it comes to figuring out who might be out there and when they will strike again.

The security cameras I was so against are now fully installed, camouflaged and the same color as the house so they don't stand out as much as I was expecting. I also have a team of two men stationed at the front of the property. They can see exactly who is coming in and out, both day and night. Again, something Tanner organized. They do give me some peace, even though they are a little annoying. I look up and see one walk past the shed again, doing a perimeter walk, which they do on the hour, every hour.

"How much milk do you need?" Kevin asks, and I smile. I have at least got him thinking about it.

"Well, I am not really sure, but I think we could probably make a few bars of soap from each day's worth of milking," I tell him, needing to do more research on it.

"How soon will the baby girls be able to produce milk?" I ask, because with two young female goats, plus Gertie, then we already have three on the roster.

Kevin looks at me again, a little unsure, a little inquisitive.

"It could be a joint venture, Kevin. You and me. We will have our own business and split the profits fifty-fifty," I tell him, smiling. He is a tween, so he'd probably rather be playing sports or something, but a little hobby that makes some money never hurt anyone.

"My mom makes soap," he says, and my eyes widen. *Jackpot!*

"She does?"

"Yep, she uses the lavender from Tanner's distillery garden and some oils and things, but never goat milk. We don't know anyone with a goat," Kevin says with a shrug. Of course she does; Tanner would give the people around here the shirt off his back.

"Well, you do now." And just like that, our plan is hatched.

"A GIRLS' night?" Tanner looks at me like I just asked for a million dollars. It isn't a big ask under normal circumstances, but I need him to go back to his place for a night. He needs a decent sleep, some time with his son and business, and needs to relax and not worry about me. I am doing enough of that for both of us.

"Yes. Face masks, wine, movies, talk about boys. A girls' night," I explain. I have been cooped up all week, and I need a bit of fun. When Jasmine suggested that she and Lacy come over for the night, I jumped at the chance.

"What boys?" he questions with a frown, and I chuckle as I throw some dirt at his face.

"The tall, dark, grumpy kind." I smile as I get back to planting the flowers I got from town. I am trying to make a floral paradise around my home, to give it a bit of color.

"I don't know..." he grumbles, the look on his face full of concern.

"Please. The guys will be out front. I know you have a million things to do at the distillery. So you can have the night off babysitting me, and both the girls can come over instead." I will miss him. I love having him in my bed every night. But I do know he is busy, and I feel guilty for taking up so much of his attention lately.

It has been a week since Josh was charged and released. The sheriff ensured he left town, and I was told he moved so quickly, he left a cloud of dust in his wake. Asshole.

"I don't feel good about it, baby girl," Tanner admits, sitting back on his heels.

"I know you are concerned. But really, we will be fine. You are only a minute away at the distillery. I will call you if I need you," I tell him, trying to give him a reassuring smile. I love how protective he is of me, and I know he is worried, but I will be fine.

I can see him thinking about it. Connor calls him regularly, and Lacy said that they are busy with new deals, so I know he needs to be there, spend some time with the team. His to-do list is probably a mile long by now.

"Promise to call me?" he asks.

"I promise," I say, my grin instant as he pulls me close.

I kiss him, pulling his head toward mine, his face now covered in soil, and he slaps my ass as we laugh at each other. I don't need his permission and he knows I am not asking for that reason. But he is as wound up by this threat as I am, and his protective nature runs deep. This is a nice compromise.

"Oh, I have a surprise to show you!" I say, almost completely forgetting as I jump up and dust myself off.

"What is it, baby?"

I remain tight-lipped as I grab his hand and pull him inside.

"Ta-da!" I say as I sweep my arm across the new photo wall I constructed this morning while he was at work.

"What's this?" he asks as he takes a step forward, looking at the photos.

"These are some of the photos I found in Marie's things. I got matching frames to display them. See, there is me as a kid, playing outside." I point it out, and his eyes move to where I am pointing.

"Cutie," he says, smiling.

"And that is Marie at Christmastime," I continue, and his eyes roam, following my arm.

"Looks good." He nods.

"And this is one I found of you and Marie," I say, holding my breath. I hadn't told Tanner I found this one, and as I watch him look at it, his eyes widen.

"Where did you get this?" He looks at the image intently, a small smile on his lips.

"In one of the boxes. I thought it was a nice one."

"I'm just a kid. But I can remember this moment. It was just after I helped her build out some garden beds with leftover barrel wood." Leaning closer, he kisses my cheek. "I like that you already have a picture of me in your place."

"I wanted you on my wall. You were a big part of my aunt's life and now you are a big part of mine. Now we have to take some new pictures to add the wall. Make some memories together," I tell him, and he is quiet for a moment as he looks between me and the photo and back again.

"Oh, baby girl... I can't wait to make more memories with you..." he says roughly. I stare at him for a moment, barely blinking, then his hand comes up and brushes my cheek. "You need to promise to call me before you fall asleep tonight and call me the minute you wake up. Please," he confirms, his tone softening, and I nod.

"I promise."

48

VICTORIA

Lacy looks at me with wide eyes, and Jasmine scoffs like I am being ridiculous.

"How many different businesses are you planning on doing?" Lacy asks, incredulous. I am grateful that she is here. With her mom sick, she can rarely get time away from her caring responsibilities. As it is, she needs to leave soon. Jasmine's the only one who will be spending the night with me.

"Well, Marie's Place won't be booked all the time, and even then, it may not be a huge moneymaker. Working with Griffin is really what I want to do, so I think that will be what keeps me busy the most. But Gertie's Goat Milk offers a great side hustle, an opportunity to give something back to Kevin and his family. His mom is a teacher, but she seemed excited to expand on her hobby of soap-making, and who knows? If it becomes a success, then I can expand it into my interiors work or something like that."

Excitement bubbles in my chest as I think about the possibilities.

Now that the house is almost complete, I am ready for what life in Whispers will look like for me. But the fear is what has been consuming me and I hate it. Ever since I moved here, I have had nothing but new opportunities present themselves, not only by way of a new job and new business, but also love. If I can just find out who is trying to harm me and get them behind bars, that would certainly make me sleep better at night.

"I can give you some rose petals. You could see if Kevin's mom can make rose-scented soaps or something? I could sell them in the shop," Jasmine offers, and my smile widens.

"That would be amazing!"

"We could put it in our gift shop at the distillery too. I am sure Tanner won't mind..." Lacy says, wiggling her eyebrows.

"Oh, I think Tanner would do anything for our Victoria," Jasmine says.

"What are you implying?" I ask coyly.

"Tanner has been this town's most eligible bachelor for years. I have never known him to even date a woman around here. Then you show up, and *bang*! You are literally together twenty-four seven," Jasmine says accusingly, and I giggle.

"So, are you two serious?" Lacy asks, a little more reservedly, and Jasmine takes a large sip of her wine, watching me.

I take a moment to look at them and swallow. "Yeah. We are. He told me he loved me, and I said it too. He is it for me," I admit, and Lacy breaks out in a wide smile. Before I can get too deep with my feelings, I jump up.

"I'm going to go take off this face mask," I say, smiling. "Then we can chat some more and put on a movie."

"I will get some more wine," Lacy says, standing to go to the nonexistent kitchen that currently holds a few bottles of red and the pizza boxes from earlier on a foldout table, since Griffin's team have gutted it. The new joinery will be installed tomorrow, and I can't wait to get this house completed.

"I am going to go outside and see if those good-looking men want a coffee or something," Jasmine says with a laugh, jumping up too.

"They must be starving. I never see them eat," I mention as I scrunch my face. This mask Jasmine made me put on to relax me is now very dry and tight on my face.

"Leave them to me!" she hollers, then grabs her coat and walks out the front door, and I run up the stairs, needing to move.

I hit the bathroom and close the door, filling the sink with hot water and grabbing a washcloth. I start to scrub my skin, but it isn't really working.

"This is stuck on my face!" I yell out to them as I scrub so hard it almost hurts and my skin turns red. I grab some face oil and refill the sink with renewed hot water and massage the oil on my face. Luckily, it already works much better, and I sigh in relief.

Hearing a large bang from downstairs, I pause, my heart racing immediately. I poke my head out the bathroom door, about to call out, but Jasmine beats me to it.

"Sorry! I just dropped that large coffee table book!" Jasmine yells, and I take a deep breath. It is more a decor item than an actual book, but the photography is nice.

"No worries!" I shout my reply, knowing that book weighs a ton.

Closing the door again, I lean over the sink, splashing the hot water on my face, then I grab a new washcloth to wipe my face again. The process is taking much longer than it should, and I just want to get back down to the girls. Looking up into the mirror to see my reflection, the air leaves my lungs. The hot water created so much steam, the mirror fogged up. But that isn't the issue. It is what is written on it that makes my breathing stop.

This property is mine, baby girl.

I suddenly can't breathe. *Is it Tanner?* Is he the one who is trying to scare me away? He had access to my truck to tamper with the brakes, to my house to leave the rose. He was upset that the sheriff didn't find anything to hold Josh... He wanted my property, and now his nickname for me is on the mirror along with what seems like a threat.

I try to breathe through the panic, but I can't. *It can't be him...*

Another loud thud from downstairs pulls me from my shock, and I jump before I open the bathroom door.

"Lacy?" I shout as I slowly open the bathroom door, my heart thundering, my body now on high alert. She doesn't respond, so I slowly walk down the stairs.

"Lacy?" I yell again, feeling a cool breeze and seeing the front door open. Maybe she and Jasmine went back outside, talking to the security guys. I swallow roughly, the overwhelming feeling something isn't right nipping at me. Spotting my cell on the coffee table where we were sitting, I quickly step down the last remaining stairs to grab it.

"Jasmine! Lacy!" I yell even louder, panic now evident in my tone as my hands shake and legs tremble. But it is all quiet as I turn into the living room.

I'm almost to the coffee table when I see movement to my left and look up mere seconds before an object is slammed into my head, the force hard enough to knock me from my feet, and I hit the ground on my hands and knees, hard. My head thumps, but I am still conscious as I moan at the pain.

"I don't think so, *baby girl*." The nickname is no longer a term of endearment and said with a hiss as I hear a familiar voice from behind me, and I turn swiftly.

"What..." I try to turn my head and look up. "Oh my God!" I gasp just before Jasmine's hand connects with my head, slapping my face, and I fall again, hitting the ground, my head smashing into the coffee table, my vision now blurry as I become instantly disoriented.

"You're coming with me," she says, grabbing my ankles and dragging me out the back door. I try to kick, confused, scared, unsure of exactly what is happening. But my body feels like Jell-O, my head fuzzy.

"What... Why..." I croak out as I do my best to get out of her hold. But it's impossible. She is dragging me across the floor toward the back door so swiftly, I don't have a chance to grip on to anything. If it was a fair fight, I would have a good chance of winning, but now, as I look at Jasmine, I don't even recognize her anymore. Her eyes are wild and hold none of the kindness I have come to know. Her movements are jerky, her smile long gone.

"Because you came into town acting like Little Miss Fucking Princess," she grits out, pulling me outside to the porch, making absolutely no sense. The cool air hits me but does nothing to wake me from my confusion. Jasmine stops suddenly and lifts her arm, then hits me across the head on the other side. It's so violent and unexpected that my head slams back against the porch decking, and I moan, my hands coming to my head just before she yanks my body down the back steps, my head banging on each and every one of them as my vision starts to fade.

"No... No... Jasmine... I don't understand," I murmur, barely lucid as she continues to drag my body outside into the night sky and across the yard to the shed. Straight past the two bodies of the security team as they lay lifeless on the porch steps. I try to get to them, but I see one with blood dripping from his ear, and the other's lips are blue, almost like he has been suffocated or poisoned. My stomach tightens like I may be sick. *How could she do this?*

I hear a commotion before I spot the outline of Marmalade as she bolts from her sleeping quarters, and then I hear Gertie and her kids bleating before they all run from the shed.

"I moved here a year ago and never got his attention. He barely even notices me." She continues talking to herself, not looking at me, only walking with tunnel vision to the shed.

"Who? What?" I ask, not understanding. She is

clearly out of her mind, and I wonder if she is on something.

"I thought the brakes would work. If it didn't kill you, I was at least hoping that you would be charged with dangerous driving and speeding. Both things I know he hates. But noooooooo, Little Miss Princess got out of that one too!" she screams, and my body shudders. The woman whom I considered a friend is totally unhinged, and if I survive tonight, I know that between her and Josh, I need to do better at selecting friends.

"Tanner?" I ask, my mind slowly connecting the dots.

"Yes, *Tanner!*" she screams at me, and I flinch. "One of the richest men in this country, single for years, does everything for everyone. I moved here just to meet him. I moved here to shoot my shot, and he never even gave me the time of day. But I persevered. I tried to see him every day, driving out to the distillery, making fucking floral arrangements for him. Making myself known and present. But *you!*" She pauses after terrifying me to the core with her scream filled with disdain, and I don't register what she is doing until I spot Lacy. Fear consumes me at the sight.

Lacy looks at me with wide eyes from where she is hanging from the roof. Rope is wrapped around her wrists, and they are pulled above her head, her feet dangling, her mouth taped with black duct tape. She starts yelling, which is muffled from the tape, and thrashing about on the ropes, but Jasmine ignores her as I feel tight rope burning around my bare ankles.

I struggle to kick out of her grip, my body panic-striken, doing anything to not be tied up by my ankles.

But I'm seeing double, and my head feels like it is full of cement. I can barely breathe, let alone fight.

"Jasmine, don't do this..." I pant out. "Please, Jasmine." Tears come to my eyes. I have no idea what she has planned, but seeing Lacy hanging from the rafters gives me a pretty good indication.

"Do you know how angry I was to hear that he loves you. *You*! A stupid city girl who doesn't even know how to run a *farm*!" she yells as she walks the other end of the rope over to the pulley and starts yanking on it.

"Jasmine, let's talk about it. I am sure this can all be worked out. Tanner is a nice guy, but you're right, I am just a stupid city girl. I can move back there, away from here," I tell her shakily, meaning none of it. I need to tell her what she wants to hear.

I manage to roll onto my stomach, but the rope tenses, and I know I have only mere minutes before I will be unable to do anything. The pain in my head intensifies, the sting on my skin harsh from gravel rash, but I close my eyes, trying to push through it and stay conscious. Vomit crawls up my throat from my efforts. My head feels like I am underwater, but I can still hear the animals calling, running everywhere all over the yard.

"There is nothing to work out. This is the end. You and your friend Lacy here are done, and I am going to skip town. Whispers is a shit town, and Tanner is an asshole for choosing you over me. Over *me*!" she screams as she pulls, and my ankles lift from the ground momentarily before dropping again.

"No, Jasmine. Stop. It doesn't have to be this way," I say, pleading with her as I wiggle like a worm, doing anything to make it more difficult for her and buy us some time. But she uses all her strength and pulls again. My heart feels like it's about to beat out of my chest, and I sob before I try again.

I kick from the ropes, and I think I succeed as the rope relaxes, but when I see her standing above me, looking down at me like I am nothing, I know the end is near. She grabs a gas can from the side that I have never seen before and splashes it around the shed. The fumes of gasoline immediately hit my nostrils, and I cough as the strong smell slides down my throat. Lacy screams and thrashes as I stare at Jasmine, my shock and approaching hopelessness giving way to overwhelming rage.

This setup is obviously well planned. She knows exactly what she is doing, and I wonder how long she has had this organized. I think through everything. The roses, the cut brakes, she had full access to my place, my property. The way she would look every time Tanner and I were together. At the time, I paid little attention, but in hindsight, there were signs.

I have no idea what I am doing, but just like when I hurt my ankle, I roll straight over to her as fast as I can and hit her right behind the shins with every ounce of power I have left in me. She falls onto her knees, gasoline coating her and me completely.

"You stupid bitch!" she screams, her hand lifting into the air, the can now raised, and she slams it down on my head.

The last thought I have is of Tanner.

49

TANNER

I throw another chip on the table. I am down almost a hundred thousand now. My mind is not on the game of poker with my friends and son, but on the woman next door.

"Why don't you just call her. You are obviously worried," Connor says, and I want to. I want to drive over there. But I know she needed a bit of space, and the girls were eager to get together. When I quizzed Lacy about it earlier, she mentioned Jasmine had been the one to arrange it. Lacy was not too keen to leave her mom for the night but had made arrangements for someone to be with her so she could be there with Victoria.

"What do they do on girls' nights anyway?" Hudson asks, and I frown at him, wondering why he wants to know.

"Face masks, wine. Talk about boys," I grumble, repeating the words Victoria told me this afternoon.

"I have never known you to lose a night of poker as

badly as you are tonight," Connor comments with a smirk, him being the current beneficiary of my bad bets.

"He has good reason to," Hudson murmurs, looking at me. At any other time, tonight would be a great night. All the boys here, talking shit, having a few beers. But I am on edge.

"Has the sheriff found anything? Anything at all?" Huxley asks, then throws down his cards.

"Not a thing," I tell him, just as my cell vibrates. It is my security team from the city, so I answer quickly.

I listen to their update and frown, not happy about any of it, then I hang up, the boys all looking at me.

"Security team. They found her father," I say, and Connor sits forward.

"And? Was it him?" he asks quickly.

"He died a week ago. Self-inflicted, apparently."

Victoria obviously doesn't know, which means her mother doesn't know either. I am not looking forward to telling her that news.

"So it could have been him, then?" Huxley puts it out there, and I lean back in my chair and sigh. "I don't know. I am trying to think who would be after her. Who would want to see her hurt? Nothing is making any sense." Following Huxley, I throw my hand down as well, joining him in defeat.

"Nothing odd has happened since she arrived?" Hudson asks.

"Besides her brakes being cut, someone ran over her rosebushes and left a rose inside her house for her," I say, huffing at how ridiculous that sounds.

"Who could it be, really?" Huxley asks, shaking his head.

"No idea. The only people to ever go to her place are me, Lacy, and Jasmine," I tell them, taking a sip of whiskey.

"So does Lacy or Jasmine have any motive?" Huxley plays devil's advocate.

"It isn't Lacy," Hudson says so quickly that I look at him sharply and raise an eyebrow. He matches my stare, and if I didn't have so much on my mind, I would question him. He and Lacy don't know each other well, but I have seen him watching her whenever we are at the bar, and I assume he knows her a little from the medical support he gives her mom.

"What about Jasmine?" Connor asks, then glances at me with a furrowed brow.

"They are friends." I sigh, rubbing my chin as I think about it.

"She is a bit annoying," Connor remarks. "She is always hanging out at the distillery."

"I hardly see her," I tell him.

"Not sure how you miss her. She is there almost every day," he says with a scoff.

"She didn't grow up here, did she?" Huxley asks, not knowing her very well.

"Moved here a year ago. Started the florist. She is from a few towns over," I tell them.

"Williamstown?" Hudson asks.

"That's right," I say, looking at him curiously. "Why?"

"Well, she came in to see me about a cut on her hand

a few weeks ago, so I started a file on her at the hospital. Her last name is Bletcher," Hudson says.

"Like Boris?" Huxley snorts. The two of them are obviously on the same wavelength, but I have no idea what they are talking about. "As in, the car mechanic?"

"How many people do you know from that town with the same surname as him? It caught my eye, because as kids, we always used to sing the jingle of his TV commercial," Hudson says.

"Car mechanic?" Connor says, sitting forward, the air around us changing. "She would know all about brake cables, then?"

Heart stuttering, I am already up off my seat.

"When did she come in with the cut on her hand?" I ask Hudson, and he thinks about it for a moment before his eyes widen completely.

"Same day of Victoria's accident," he says, and I move so fast I must be a blur. I grab my cell and call Victoria while snatching my keys from the table. "Pick up, baby girl. Pick up."

With a growl, I'm sprinting out of the house as Connor, Hudson, and Huxley all run after me, the four of us hurrying out of my place and to our trucks.

"No answer. Fuck!" I yell as I jump into my truck.

"I'll call the sheriff," I hear Huxley yell as Connor jumps in beside me, and the two of us are already moving. The Hamilton brothers are right behind us.

"Fuck. Why didn't I see it? What the hell is her motive?" I spit out as I speed down Distillery Drive.

"She hangs around the distillery like a bad smell. I see

her watching you a bit..." Connor admits, and I look at him like he is crazy.

"I have never paid her any attention. I have never dated her, taken her for a meal, nothing."

Pulling up to Marie's place, I see the lights on out in the back shed.

"The shed," I say, jumping out of the truck, seeing none of my security guys I left here earlier and wondering where the hell they are.

"Victoria!" I yell but hear no one. Connor and I are halfway to the shed as Huxley and Hudson pull in.

"Shit," Connor says, stopping, and I follow his gaze. The two security men I had here both lie on their backs on the grass. Dead. Fuck, fuck, fuck.

"Victoria!" I scream, the panic and anger swirling in my body, taking over my senses. I put myself in front of Connor, prepared to take a bullet for him if needed.

"Do you smell that?" Connor asks, grabbing on to my shirt to stop my steps.

"Gasoline," I grit out. Spotting the cow and goats in the yard and not in the shed where I left them, locked up a few hours ago, only confirms where they are. My stomach tenses with unease, heart now racing with urgency.

"I'll check inside," Huxley says, and I spot Hudson down on one knee, checking for a pulse on the two security guys before he looks at me and shakes his head, standing back up. Connor darts off to follow Huxley in the back door, and I continue running to the shed with Hudson. Turning the corner, we both stop short.

Lacy and Victoria are hanging from the rafters of the

shed. Victoria is hanging by her ankles, blood coating one side of her face. She isn't moving, her eyes are closed, and I have no idea if she is even alive. My heart lurches, reaching out to her, my feet moving before my thoughts. Lacy hangs by her wrists and starts screaming the minute she sees us, her screams muffled by duct tape as she wriggles around on the rope, so much she starts swinging.

"Lacy!" Hudson yells at the same time I yell, "Victoria!"

But we're frozen in place as Jasmine steps out in front of them with a wicked smile. She is in a sports bra and leggings, looking like she is ready for a run, but I spot her clothes crumpled on the floor, covered in gasoline.

"What the hell is going on, Jasmine?" I question her as I take another small step toward Victoria.

"Oh, *now* you notice me? *Now* you look at me, actually *see* me?" She is almost screaming, her eyes wild, clearly a little unhinged.

"I'm noticing. I'm looking," I tell her carefully, not sure what the right words are to say. I spot Hudson out of the corner of my eye, stepping closer to Lacy. Jasmine's eyes stay fixed on me.

"I moved here for you, Tanner…" she says, sounding like she is now weeping, but no tears escape. "I moved to this town because you needed me."

I pull in a sharp breath. *This is all because of me?*

"You did?" I ask, trying to keep my voice calm as I watch everything and everyone.

"Yes. You and me, we are meant to be. I knew it the minute I saw you in the paper, talking about the distillery.

I moved here for us to be together." She's looking at me like a lost, sick puppy, making my skin crawl.

"Well, you never said anything?" I ask her, just as Hudson reaches Lacy, her tears constant.

"I was always at the distillery. Then this one showed up and got in the way. That's why we need to get rid of her, Tanner. So we can be together," she says, and then she actually fucking smiles at me. A chill runs through me, and I look from her to Victoria and swallow hard. I am not sure how injured she is, but I can see her chest still moving, so I take that as a good sign.

"Why don't you go sit outside, and I can finish this off," I say to her, hoping to get her out of here so I can get to Victoria. We need to get out of here.

"Really!" she shrieks so suddenly, I jolt, and I see Lacy and Hudson pause where they are now both standing, removing the ropes from her legs.

"You know what. I started it. I am going to end it. You can either come with me or burn in hell with her!" she spits out, lighting a match and tossing it to the floor. The flames and heat are instant. Jasmine runs out the back of the shed as I dart forward to Victoria, time now of the essence.

"Victoria!" As soon as I have her in my grasp, I get busy with the ropes on her ankles. The knot is basic, and I manage to pull it away quickly, her body falling to the floor.

"I got Lacy!" Hudson shouts.

"Run!" I scream at him, and he runs out the door with Lacy in his arms. I dip down to pick up Victoria. She is limp in my arms, her clothes coated in gasoline, and I look around, seeing nothing but flames now surrounding us. This isn't going to be good. There are no gaps, the gasoline poured in a circle around the ropes, barricading us in and preventing anyone from coming in to help.

"We gotta do it, baby girl. Hang on." Sealing her to me, I bury her head into my chest, and I sprint, following the same path Hudson did. The heat is unbearable, it singes my skin and my hair, but I close my eyes and run like I have never run before, hearing the shed start to buckle behind me.

I scream from the pain as I dash through the flames and right into the backyard. Dropping us to the damp grass, Hudson is on us in a second.

"Roll. Fucking roll," Huxley yells, and I pat down and roll Victoria, the heat in my back fierce.

"Dad, roll!" my son screams at me, and as soon as the flames on Victoria are out, I drop. Rolling and wriggling on the grass, I feel the temperature around me increase, and I grit my teeth. But as soon as I know I'm in the clear, I crawl over to Victoria. I push my pain to the back of my mind and hold her hand as Hudson works on her, Connor sitting with Lacy.

In the distance, I hear the sirens. I see the red and blue lights that fill my nightmares flashing against the dark country sky. The fire department pulls up and starts the flow of water, just as tears fill my eyes, staring down at an unmoving Victoria.

I pray on everything that is holy to keep my baby girl on earthside with me.

50

VICTORIA

My throat is sore. Almost burning, and I try to swallow, wondering if I have come down with the flu overnight. I roll over to my bedside table, hoping I put a glass of water there last night, but I can't really move. There is a pain in my shoulder, making me cringe.

"Victoria?" a male voice says, sounding far away. But it sounds familiar. "Victoria, can you open your eyes?"

The bright light is instant, and I blink a few times before I slowly come to. I am in a room that is not my own. With a very good-looking man gazing over me.

"There she is," Hudson says with a broad smile on his face, assessing me quickly.

"Hudson?" My voice is barely audible, raspy like I haven't used it in days.

"Good to have you back."

My eyes widen as I look around the room. I am in the hospital. The same room I was in on my last visit. I look to my side, but I don't see Jasmine. *Jasmine.* My memory floods back to me, and my heart thuds. *Where's Tanner?*

"Relax, you are safe. It is now morning. Things are all taken care of by that grumpy man on your other side," Hudson murmurs, obviously aware of the thoughts in my head. I swallow again and feel heaviness on my other side and look over. There he is.

"Tanner?" I whisper, as Hudson moves across the room, pouring me a glass of water.

"He hasn't moved from that spot all night, although he has barked a lot of orders at people," Hudson says with a small smile.

I look at my man at my side. His hand holds mine, his head resting on the bed beside me as the chair he is sitting on is pulled right up against the bed. He is naked from the waist up, and I see a large bandage across his back and arms. My stomach clenches.

"Is he okay?" I ask Hudson as I squeeze Tanner's hand, and his eyes open immediately.

"Baby girl?" he says groggily. "You're awake?" Sitting up, a small smile comes to his face as he takes me in.

"Here," Hudson says, passing the water over to Tanner. "I'll give you two some time." Walking out of the room, he closes the door behind him.

"Drink some water," Tanner says, standing, his demanding ways automatically soothing me. He holds my head as he puts the straw to my lips, and I take a few small sips, the water cooling and easing my throat. I smell smoke, I feel like I need a shower, and my shoulder is wrapped, so I obviously did something to it.

"Jasmine?" I ask him, and he nods, his face hard set,

his lips thin. He puts the glass down, holding my hand now with both of his. I see bandages on his hands as well. He looks almost worse than I do.

"When I got there, she had both you and Lacy hanging from the rafters of the shed," he says, his jaw popping as he swallows. I try to think.

"The last thing I remember is her tying my ankles, then she hit me." I lift my hand to my head, feeling a thick bandage, now understanding why I feel so heavy in the head.

"You have a concussion, a few stitches to your head. You also fell on your shoulder when I got you down from the rope," he says with a furrowed brow. "So that injury is on me. Dislocated your shoulder. You should be okay with that in a few weeks." He squeezes my hand, and I can see how guilty he feels, even though he saved my life.

"What about you?" I ask, looking him over.

"She started a fire. Her plan was to burn the shed down with you and Lacy in it." Releasing a heavy sigh, his nostrils flare.

"Oh my God. Where is she? How is Lacy?" I panic.

"Everyone is okay. Everyone is perfectly fine." His tone is an elixir, my heart slowing immediately. "Lacy is fine. A few bumps and bruises, but Hudson is taking good care of her in the next room."

I want to ask more about them, but now isn't the time.

"The shed is a total loss, but the animals are safe. Kevin is looking after them. Don't worry about the shed; we will rebuild. I already have Griffin at your place. He has one team cleaning up the shed and another putting in the kitchen and laundry." He nods, and I'm surprised but I don't know why. He's always making sure every-thing is taken care of. "I told him to proceed as you wanted, so by the time you get out of here, the house will be done."

He knows how much it means to me to get this project done, and he is helping me see it through.

"What about you?" I ask, my concern for him over-whelming.

"First-degree burns, nothing too bad. By the time I cut the rope from your ankles, the fire took hold, and I had to run us through the flames. You have a few burns to your legs, but nothing too deep," he says like it's nothing, and my chest tightens.

Wiggling my toes, I feel a slight sting in my calves. Then taking a breath, I ask the question I am dreading.

"Where is Jasmine?" I whisper the words, too scared to really know. I had that woman in my house, I had her in my life.

"The sheriff got her. Caught her trying to drive out of town. He already had his patrol out, and they managed to get her speeding down the road. She is locked up and being questioned."

I take another deep breath as I let that information sink in.

"Why did she do it?" I ask, and I see his face fall. I vaguely remember, but I know Tanner will have all the information.

"It was my fault. She was infatuated. Apparently. I had no idea. I never dated her, took her anywhere. Before you came along, I barely noticed her," he explains, looking guilt ridden once again.

"It isn't your fault. None of this is your fault. You saved me, Tanner. You came for me."

"I will spend the rest of my life making this better for you," he says, getting choked up, and I know by the look on his face he is taking the blame for Jasmine's infatuation.

"Tanner..." I say, my eyes watering.

"If you don't want to stay in Whispers, and you want to go back to the city after all this, I won't blame you." His shoulders sag, and my chest burns with the feelings I have for him.

"I want to be anywhere you are," I whisper, and his eyes shoot back to mine. "I want to be in your arms every night. I want to swim in the springs every week together. I want to take care of the animals, go to the bar on Friday nights, cook and cuddle and create a life together. Here in Whispers. I am not going to let someone who has a false grip on her reality try to take anything or anyone away from me," I tell him, and I watch the tension leave his body. I had already decided not to sign the lease papers for my old apartment. Tanner and Whispers are my home now. Nothing is changing that.

"I love you, baby girl, and I promise to make you happy every single day for the rest of our lives," he says, and as I smile, the tears finally fall down my cheeks.

"I love you, Tanner," I whisper, and he leans over, his lips treasuring mine before he kisses each and every tear away.

And in his arms, I'm home.

EPILOGUE - VICTORIA

I look up at the ranch, immense pride swelling my chest. We are about to hand it over, and I finally get to meet the owner and give him the one place that has every inch of my heart in it.

"I can't believe we did it," I say to Griffin as we admire the finished product. The project got derailed by a few months as I healed and then moved permanently to Whispers. For the past year, I have lived either in Marie's place or with Tanner at the distillery, but every night, we've been together.

"I have to say, it is one of my best projects. The photographer got a lot of great shots, and I am already fielding calls from people who have seen it on your socials," Griffin shares, and I smile. The two of us have become close over the months. We work well together.

"I had an email from a magazine this morning. They want to do a feature on the ranch and put it in their summer edition," I say, barely able to contain my giddiness. My portfolio has now grown. Between this and

Marie's place, my content creation has been immense. My social media has exploded, and I am now getting paid deals and sponsorships.

"So we will have a few weeks' break, and then start on the next one?" Griffin says, and my eyes light up.

"So it is really happening?" I say in disbelief, even though we have talked at length about me joining forces with Griffin full-time to become his interior designer and consultant. My dream job with my dream builder.

Life has really progressed since the incident. As Tanner promised, Marie's Place was completed while I was in hospital, and when I got home, I had just some finishing touches to complete. I have started hiring it out to help single moms and others who are struggling, my guests all coming from the Rothschild Foundation and the connections I made at the Baltimore gala all those months ago. Yet another thing I had Tanner to thank for.

"It is happening," he says as we both look back up at this mansion of a ranch.

"It's a bit sad, though, isn't it?"

"What is?" he asks, confused.

"Well, I put so much into this ranch. This is really how I would have my dream home. I even added all the personal touches I like, hoping the owner likes them too," I say, a little melancholy.

"Well, here comes the owner now," Griffin says, and I spot a big black truck driving up the driveway. I squint in the sun, not able to really see much in its bright rays, but as the truck pulls up, my mouth drops.

"What are you doing here?" I say as Tanner slides out

of the truck, and I almost swoon at how good-looking he is. I warm immediately, knowing how lucky I am.

"Hey, baby girl." He smiles, coming up to me, his hand sliding around my waist as he kisses me quickly.

"Tanner," I warn, not wanting to be seen as unprofessional. "The owner is going to be here any moment." I straighten my dress and turn to look at Griffin, but he isn't there anymore. Glancing around, I can't see him anywhere.

"We are the owners, baby," Tanner says, and my head whips up to look at him.

"What?" I just about balk. *What the hell is he talking about?*

"I purchased this land over a decade ago. I never thought I would develop it until I met you. This ranch you and Griffin have built and designed is ours. All yours and all mine."

My body is frozen in shock, but my belly flutters as I take in what this means. I can't talk, so he continues.

"We still have the distillery and Marie's place, but the ranch will be our home."

"Tanner..." I say, barely able to get the words out, my chest constricting, disbelief smothering me.

"Victoria," he says as his knee hits the ground, and I almost faint.

"When I met you, my whole world opened up. I was a shell of a man stuck in a cycle of working hard to raise Connor and build the business, never really thinking or wanting anyone by my side for any of it. But you walked in, all blond bombshell, bright pink, confident, and stubborn. You were like a breath of fresh air filling my lungs after being suffocated for too long," he says as he pulls a box from his pocket, and tears blur my eyes.

"So, baby girl, here at our new home, in our hometown of Whispers, will you do me the honor of being my wife?"

"Yes," I say without a second of hesitation before taking a big breath. A broad smile comes to his face, and he slips the ring on my finger. It is big, beautiful, and glistening in the sun.

"Yes, yes, yes!" I say over and over as he stands, picks me up, and swirls me around. Bringing my lips to his, I seal our deal. The moment is perfect, the view, the ranch I love so much, it all feels surreal. Until I hear a bleat and pull back sharply.

"What is that?" I ask, turning to face the noise, seeing a large buck walking in the field right in front of us.

"Oh, that's Garry," Tanner says, grinning as he puts me down on my feet. "I thought Gertie and the girls might need a man around here."

I smile, laughing heartily, and he kisses me again. Pulling back, we both look around at the vast amount of land we now have, no neighbors in sight, but a perfect view of Whispers, the distillery, and Marie's place, the new shed sitting tall and proud and bright red. I didn't know I could be happier, but he just proved me wrong.

"I love you, Tanner Whiteman," I say, cupping his face as his eyes lock on mine.

"I love you, Victoria Whiteman," he says with a smirk before picking me up and taking me inside to our new home, carrying me over the threshold. As I lean back in his embrace, I feel the familiar caress of his thumb on my back, and I realize something.

Everyone likes a good before and after, even me.

To FIND out where Tanner and Victoria are now, download this free bonus epilogue here;

ALSO BY SAMANTHA SKYE

HUDSON

I've never sought a savior, especially not a **billionaire**. But when a charming, **single dad** returns to my **small town**, memories stir of our shared past and our future feels increasingly intertwined.

As the town's new Doctor, Hudson Hamilton is hard to ignore. Not only is he now in charge of my moms medical needs, but he is also best friends with my boss.

His good looks and excellent bedside manner do little to tame the heat that swirls. But fantasizing never served me well and my life is chaotic, with one hurdle after another. No time to date, no time to daydream.

But he bonds with my mom, I bond with his son, and despite my hesitation, his caring ways start to break down my walls. But just like everything in my life, it doesn't come easy. Sinister things are at play.

Danger is lurking and it is coming from those closest to us.

Grab it today: https://books2read.com/hudson2

ALSO BY SAMANTHA SKYE

The Billionaires of Whispers

Tanner

Hudson

Connor - Coming 2025

Sawyer - Coming 2025

Sutton - Coming 2025

Griffin - Coming 2025

The Baltimore Boys

The Charming Billionaire

The Arrogant Billionaire

The Damaged Billionaire

The Secret Billionaire

The Bossy Billionaire

The Billionaire Babe

Men Of New York

My Legacy

My Destiny

My Fight

My Chance

Boston Billionaires

Coming Home

Finding Home

Leaving Home

Building Home

ABOUT THE AUTHOR

Samantha Skye is an international bestselling author. A country kid turned city slicker, she writes spicy and suspenseful contemporary romance novels that leave you hot under the collar and on the edge of your seat.

Samantha lives in Melbourne, Australia and when she's not plotting her next novel, she can be found travelling and chasing the sun.

To join in the conversation join Skye's The Limit Facebook group here;

https://www.facebook.com/groups/skyesthelimit books

ACKNOWLEDGMENTS

I am so excited that you read this book! I loved writing it and seriously didn't want to stop.

It is a big deal to write a book. To be creative, to put the words down, to bring the whole thing together and it takes an army.

I want to thank my family, for their constant support. Sharing me with spunky billionaires is not always fun, but you put up with it, give me space to grow and encourage me always. Thank you.

To my amazing cover designer Angela, I am sure you get sick of my emails, but you put up with all my constant nagging so well I don't know what I would do without you.

To my editor MacKenzie, seriously there would be no books without you. You give my words all those secret herbs and spices and I am forever grateful to you for everything you do.

To my proofreader Kimberly. You are truly amazing, giving my books that final drop of polish. I am so glad I found you and now you are stuck with me (sorry, not sorry).

To my author bestie Sharon. I am so grateful for our friendship, my world is so much brighter with you in it.

Special shout out to my amazing ARC Team - always

itching for the next book, I promise my fingers are typing as quickly as they can.

Thank you to all my readers. without you, none of this would be possible.

www.samanthaskyeuthor.com